## *The M*

"If you like your heroes c
walk, to buy THE MATCHMAKER. . . . Becnel gives us true insight into the human spirit and does not stint on creating the ideal atmosphere and recreating the era to near perfection. A powerful love story and a thinking reader's book."

—*Romantic Times*

"Once again, Rexanne Becnel delivers a special reading treat with THE MATCHMAKER . . . the supporting cast is fantastic, and the story . . . will richly entertain you and have you clamoring for more works by the talented Rexanne Becnel."

—*The Belles and Beaux of Romance*

## *The Mistress of Rosecliffe*

"A fitting and powerful end to the Rosecliffe Trilogy. The brilliant and golden threads of history, romance and magic are beautifully woven into a memorable tapestry. Ms. Becnel has brought the Middle Ages to life and breathes freshness and vitality into the genre."

—*Romantic Times*

## *The Knight of Rosecliffe*

"Becnel (THE BRIDE OF ROSECLIFFE) brings the Middle Ages to life with an elaborate plot, daring adventures and satisfyingly complex characters."

—*Publishers Weekly*

"Rexanne Becnel is a marvelous storyteller who breathes life into characters and captures the romanticism of medieval times. Sensual."

—*Romantic Times*

*More . . .*

"Becnel's latest work features thoroughly enjoyable characters and is strongly plotted and quickly paced. And her subtly formal prose style lends itself nicely to the medieval setting. This romance should appeal to fans of Penelope Williamson."
*—Booklist*

"An exciting, non-stop medieval romance . . . will leave readers anxiously awaiting the third tale from the magical Ms. Becnel."
*—The Painted Rock Review*

## *The Bride of Rosecliffe*

"Rexanne Becnel combines heartfelt emotions with a romance that touches readers with the magic and joy of falling in love!"
*—Romantic Times*

"Ms. Becnel creates the most intriguing characters and infuses them with fiery personalities and quick minds!"
*—The Literary Times*

"The pacing is quick, the passion is hot, the tone is intense, and the characters are larger-than-life. The plot contains enough twists, turns, and betrayals to keep the reader thoroughly engaged."
*—Booklist*

"[Becnel] paints a brilliant and romantic portrait of the medieval period."
*—The Writer's Write*

## *Dangerous to Love*

"Rexanne Becnel writes stories dripping with rich, passionate characters and a sensual wallop that will have you reeling!" —*The Belles & Beaux of Romance*

## *The Maiden Bride*

"A master medieval writer. Ms. Becnel writes emotional stories with a deft hand." —*The Time Machine*

## *Heart of the Storm*

"Great characters, a riveting plot and loads of sensuality . . . A fabulous book. I couldn't put it down!"
—Joan Johnston, author of MAVERICK HEART

"Rexanne Becnel combines heartfelt emotions with a romance that touches readers with the magic and joy of falling in love. Destined to be a best-seller from a star of the genre!" —*Romantic Times*

"Well-written and enjoyable." —*Publishers Weekly*

"Tempestuous and seductive, this winner from Rexanne Becnel will enthrall from the first page to the last."
—Deborah Martin, author of STORMSWEPT

## St. Martin's Paperbacks Titles by Rexanne Becnel

*The Matchmaker*
*The Mistress of Rosecliffe*
*The Knight of Rosecliffe*
*The Bride of Rosecliffe*
*Dangerous to Love*
*The Maiden Bride*
*Heart of the Storm*

# The Troublemaker

St. Martin's Paperbacks

THE TROUBLEMAKER



ISBN: 0-312-97755-7

Printed in the United States of America

St. Martin's Paperbacks edition / November 2001

St. Martin's Paperbacks are published by St. Martin's Press, 175 Fifth Avenue, New York, N.Y. 10010.

10 9 8 7 6 5 4 3 2 1

*This one is for*
*the good guys:*
*Phil, Harvey, Bobby,*
*Oscar, Glenn, René,*
*and Mo.*

# PROLOGUE

**BOSTON**
**APRIL 1827**

"HE isn't dead!"

Marshall Byrde stared at the letter in his hand, the brittle square of parchment gone yellow in the several decades since it had been sent to his mother. The date was clear enough, London 1798, and the signature, Cameron Byrde.

Most incriminating of all, the curt message left no doubt that Marshall's own life had been based upon a lie.

" 'I am wed now.' " He read the words out loud and they echoed across the years and miles as if the voice of the father he'd never known spoke them with his own lips. In his mother's silent parlor he read the cruel words Cameron Byrde had written to Maureen MacDougal Byrde twenty-nine years ago. " 'I am truly wed this time and so will not be joining you in America'—"

He couldn't read the rest, for the letter shook too violently in his hand. The man had not died. His father, whose name he had always carried with such pride, hadn't died on board the ship to America as his mother had always maintained. He'd been alive and well—

Marsh crushed the letter in his fist. Cameron Byrde had been alive and well a year after Marsh's own birth. Alive and well with his new wife in London, while his true wife and firstborn child had struggled alone in a strange country, half a world away.

He lurched to his feet, then abruptly sat down again, for the implications of the letter left him momentarily dazed. How could his mother have spoken so lovingly of the man all these years? So reverentially? How could she have continued to love him, a man who'd abandoned her and taken a second wife in her stead?

Then again, had his father ever truly married his mother?

He opened the crumpled pages and stared at the faded ink letters that slanted backward, just like his own. Was his mother really a Byrde? Was he?

The blood pounded in his ears, and he felt the dull headache he'd nursed all day rise throbbing once more. He'd buried his beloved mother yesterday, having arrived from Washington too late to bid her good-bye. Then last night he'd gotten quietly and desperately drunk. His mother. His only family. And he hadn't arrived until after she was gone.

Today he'd begun the heartbreaking task of sorting through her belongings. Her clothes. Her household goods. All his now, whether he wanted them or not.

He lifted his head and let his eyes sweep the neat parlor, with its papered walls and precisely arranged furnishings. He'd built her this house just four years ago with the profits from his last boxing match. She'd deserved it and more. But when he would have set her up in a grander abode in Washington, where his construction business was now based, she'd demurred.

"Boston is my home," she'd said. So she'd remained here, living for his visits.

A wave of guilt washed over him. She'd been waiting for his visit four days ago, a visit delayed by some problem with the new building he was constructing to house a commodities trading company. When he'd finally arrived in Boston, it was to find a black ribbon draped over the door knocker, and a burial notice tacked beneath it.

His sweet, fragile mother had died in her sleep.

"Gone to be with your father," her friend Mrs. Sternot had tearfully told him. "Together at last, God bless their souls."

Only Cameron Byrde had not died, at least not when his mother said he had. He could be living still.

Still reeling from the shock of his discovery, Marsh forced himself to search through the little embroidered box of letters and trinkets, the box that held the secrets of his mother's life. Were there any other secrets she'd hidden from him in there?

He found several newspaper clippings about his own achievements: the boxing matches of his earlier career, the ribbon cuttings and other events associated with his growing construction company. There was also a tiny likeness of him, drawn by one of his mother's employers as a gift when he was a little boy. But he found only two other letters from his father—and no marriage certificate.

It was enough to paint a clear picture of what had happened all those years ago. A sweet young woman in love with a cad. She must have found herself with child and Cameron Byrde had agreed to marry her. But it seemed the lout had soon regretted his offer and so had sent her away, on to America, with the promise that he'd soon follow.

Only he hadn't. A hundred pounds in an American bank, and he'd washed his hands clean of any responsibility for her or their child.

And so she'd been left alone, big with child and with neither family nor friends to turn to.

Marsh ran a shaking hand through his hair. No wonder she'd lied and claimed to be a widow. She'd had to lie to him, and to everyone else. Better to be a poor but respectable widow than branded a woman of no morals. She'd worked all his life to raise and educate him. She'd cleaned, cooked, and minded other people's children.

And she'd never remarried.

He stared at the thin stack of letters without really seeing them. She'd never remarried, though he suspected she'd been asked at least twice. Was it because she'd believed herself still married to Cameron Byrde?

It was that which raised Marsh's fury to a dangerous pitch. Yes, she had lied to him. Yes, she had hidden secrets she should have shared with him, her only son. But damn it all, that man had ruined her life! He'd stolen her youth, broken her heart, and condemned her to a life of drudgery and toil.

Worst of all, he'd kept her from ever finding happiness with some other man.

Marsh jerked up from his chair, shaking with impotent rage and the need to punch someone in the face—anyone! That selfish son of a bitch had destroyed the life of the gentlest, sweetest woman ever to walk God's green earth. For nearly thirty years now the bastard had gotten away with it.

But not anymore, Marsh vowed. Not anymore.

After burying his mother, he'd been at loose ends, lost and aimless, with no notion how to reorganize his life without her. But he knew now. His father had been alive twenty-nine years ago, and Marsh hoped to God he still was. For he had a score to settle with the man.

By the time he was through with Cameron Byrde, the gutless bastard would wish he had died all those years ago.

# CHAPTER

# I

**MAYFAIR, LONDON**
**MAY 1827**

SARAH Palmer wanted to die. She wanted to curl up in a knot beneath the bedcovers, to hide from the dawn and the scrutiny forced by the light of a new day. Most of all, she wanted to hide from the censure of her shocked and disappointed family.

Only she could not.

Her mother would never allow it, nor would her furious brother, James. He'd been the one to intercept Lord Penley's carriage and drag her out of it. He'd also been the one who'd challenged Lord Penley to a duel. To the death, he'd said.

To the death, for the honor of his youngest sister.

Sarah squeezed her eyes tight to remember last night's awful scene, yet still two hot, stinging tears leaked out. Once again James had saved her from the consequences of her impulsive behavior. But he'd never before gone so far as to put his life on the line for her.

Thank God their stepfather, Justin St. Clare, Earl Acton, had been there to restrain James from following through on his threat. She owed her mother's husband a great debt for that.

*And so you repay them both by hiding your head beneath the sheets like a child?*

Like a cautious fox gone to ground and now venturing back into the threatening and uncertain world, Sarah peered out from beneath the satin counterpane, then pushed it down and forced herself to sit up. She might as well face the music, dirge though it surely must be.

Sarah seldom rose before midmorning, so her brother's townhouse seemed somewhat foreign now as she made her way down the front stairwell. She hadn't summoned a maid to help her dress and as she reached the foyer she was glad. The two housemaids she encountered stared openly at her, though they ducked their heads when she frowned back at them.

Did everyone know what she'd done last night? Did they all know how close she'd come to utter, final ruin?

She tripped to a halt outside the breakfast room as a terrible thought struck her. Did they perhaps believe that she *had* been ruined?

She pressed her fingers to her temples in agitation. Wouldn't she believe it if she'd heard this very same tale about any other young woman of the ton? Wouldn't she whisper gossip behind her fan to all her bosom friends at the whirl of parties and routs and breakfasts? Her mother had often said that the suspicion of immorality condemned a young woman every bit as much as fact. Now she understood.

So it was that when she entered the breakfast room, Sarah carried a double load of guilt. Bad enough her own thoughtless behavior, but she also was ashamed for every bit of unflattering gossip she'd ever shared with her bevy of silly, fluttering friends.

James's stern expression did nothing to ease her mind. Neither did that of her normally mild-tempered stepfather. Her mother's presence at the table at such an early hour, however, sounded the direst note. Augusta Linden Byrde Palmer St. Clare never rose this early.

James's gaze flicked briefly over her, then away. "Sit down, Sarah. I suggest you eat a hearty breakfast, for you have a long day ahead of you."

Augusta cleared her throat, drawing his attention. "I will handle this, James. You and Justin did your part last night. Now it is my turn."

Sarah's heart stuck in her throat. But when her mother waved her toward the sideboard and its display of ham and biscuits and coddled eggs, she picked up a plate and dutifully filled it with food, none of which looked the least bit palatable. Whatever was to come, she deserved it. And she would accept her punishment with good grace, she vowed. What other choice did she have?

The three of them were arrayed along one side of the long table, so when Sarah sat on the other, she felt like a court petitioner, with the judges all frowning down on her. Her mother, clearly the chief justice, steepled her fingers beneath her chin.

"The way I see it, Sarah, we have two options."

We? Sarah took that for a good sign.

"You may either marry Lord Penley with a special license—"

"Marry him!"

"Will you please allow me to finish?"

Sarah swallowed hard and ducked her head. "Yes, Mother."

"Either marry the man or else leave at once for an extended visit with your sister in Scotland."

Sarah stared down at her plate, at the little blob of raspberry jam, deep red with tiny specks of a paler color throughout. It was lowering indeed to know that the man she'd been rabid to marry just yesterday had become so utterly repugnant to her today. At the first sign of adversity he'd dissolved like sugar put to the flame. His sweet, beguiling nature had melted, then scorched, revealing the craven coward at his core.

James's accusations about him were true. He was a fortune hunter—not that half of the ton was not. Almost everyone hoped to improve their situation through an advantageous marriage. But Lord Penley had apparently gambled his family into ruin. And if that weren't enough, it appeared he'd also dabbled in extortion with a married woman of some consequence, one with whom he'd carried on an illicit affair.

It was that which offended her the most, the fact that he'd actually extorted money from his married lover. She shuddered with revulsion at the thought, and at her own stupidity. Why had she not been able to see beyond his handsome face and charming manner? The truth was, he'd never cared a fig for her beyond the huge dowry that came with her hand. That's why he'd pressed her so ardently to elope with him. And she, fool that she was, had thought it all such a romantic adventure.

Thank goodness for her brother's timely intervention.

She sighed now and raised her gaze. "I'd rather go stay with Olivia in Scotland."

Her mother smiled. But James's scowl grew deeper. "How swiftly your opinion of that spineless son of a bitch—"

"James!" Augusta stiffened. "I'll not have such language in my presence!"

"Sorry, Mother. But like it or not, Penley is a spineless . . ." His jaw clenched and his nostrils flared with fury. "Penley is spineless," he managed, swallowing the curse with some difficulty.

"I admit it," Sarah put in.

"Yes. Now you admit it," he said, giving free rein to his temper. "But when I tried to warn you away from him, would you listen then? No. Of course not."

Sarah bowed her head and let his tirade pelt down upon her. Everything he said was true.

"And now you are ruined. If word of this aborted elopement ever gets out, no respectable man will ever offer for you."

"She is not ruined," Augusta protested. "Not entirely. Disgraced, perhaps. But I believe we can salvage her reputation. Come, James. Enough of this. Sarah knows she has done wrong."

Wielding his table knife like a weapon, James attacked the ham on his plate. "Yes. She knows she's wrong. But then, she knew she was wrong when she slipped out last month to go to Vauxhall with Mrs. Ingleside and the rest of that fast set, especially after she'd been told not to. She knew she was wrong when she attended that *bal masque* just last week with that sporting crowd from Mayfair. And she knew she was wrong when she sneaked out to that disastrous boxing match in Cheapside. She knew each and every time she was wrong—and those are only the escapades we *know* about! Yet, as always, she followed the impulse of the moment instead of considering the consequences of her actions."

Though Sarah knew he was right, she was unable to bear another moment of his sanctimonious tirade. "And I suppose you've never made a mistake!" she snapped.

"I've made my share of mistakes. I'll not deny that. But at least I've learned from mine," he shot right back. He turned to their mother. "God knows what sort of mischief she'll get up to in Scotland. You should have forced her to wed the first man who ever offered for her," he added under his breath.

But Augusta only smiled again and patted his arm. "If I could force my children to wed, I assure you, James, that you would be ten years married and with just as many children. Don't worry, Olivia will take good care of her. Between Byrde Manor and Woodford Court, Livvie will keep her little sister too busy to get into trouble. Plus, you forget how intimidating Neville can be when circumstances demand it. The two of them are certain to keep her in line." Then she turned her crystalline blue stare on Sarah, the one that always seemed to look right down into her soul. "You do know that this is the last straw, don't you?"

Sarah nodded. It was true. She could see that now. Her friends had all tittered at James's objections and tempted her to greater and greater self-indulgences. And she'd gone blithely along, refusing to see any danger in her behavior. But then, she'd always chafed at the strictures of proper society. So with each season in town she'd tested those strictures further, never considering the consequences she might someday be forced to reap. Even when Mrs. Ingleside had regaled everyone with poor Miss Tinsdale's fall from grace, Sarah had neither taken it as warning nor noticed the underlying maliciousness in the woman's manner. She had been too busy enjoying her new friends' amusing company.

But they were all like Lord Penley, she now saw. Selfish and grasping and mean-spirited. She was ashamed to admit how blind she'd been. And how selfish herself.

Why couldn't she have seen it yesterday?

Now she must take leave of London at the height of the season. No more receptions. No balls or evenings at the theater. And all those beautiful gowns she'd ordered but had yet to wear . . . She sighed.

At least she would be with her half-sister Olivia as well as her husband Neville and their growing brood of children.

She leaned forward earnestly. "You see before you a reformed woman, Mother." She ignored the rude noise James made. "I shall be as good as gold," she vowed. "Olivia and Neville shall have nothing to complain about. You'll see. Nothing at all."

Only two days by ship, yet when Sarah stepped off the *Gulls Wing* at the bustling port of Berwick-upon-Tweed, she felt worlds removed from London and, indeed, all of England. The air was crisp and salty, and colder. But that gave her reason to wear her new scarlet cloak, with its sweeping cape and sable collar and cuffs. She might be relegated to the Scottish hinterlands as punishment for her outrageous behavior, but that was no reason to wear sackcloth and ashes.

"The captain has sent for a carriage," her maid said as they stood along the rail. She was not Sarah's regular maid, dear Betsy. James had decided that Sarah needed someone older to accompany her on her journey, someone with a firmer hand.

As if she could get into any trouble on that ship or during the one-day carriage ride to Kelso. Sarah glanced at the stern-faced matron, only barely disguising her resentment. "Yes. I know. My dear brother has arranged everything and paid the captain well to do his bidding. And you also, I imagine." She arched her brows at the woman, even though she knew she was being unfair. But she couldn't help it. Two days in Agnes Miller's humorless company had her chafing at the bit. Thank goodness the woman would not be staying at Woodford Court, but rather was traveling on to Carlisle to visit her ailing mother.

The woman frowned, but otherwise ignored Sarah's ill temper. In a matter of minutes two men carted their luggage down the gangway and piled the numerous bags onto a sturdy but outdated carriage. Oh, well, there would be no one to see or comment about her mode of transportation, Sarah decided, once the captain saw her safely inside the vehicle.

She'd turned many a head as she'd descended from the ship and walked the short distance across the wharf, but none of them the sort she desired. Sailors, dockworkers, hack drivers. There were one or two gentlemen about, properly dressed in frock coats and tall beaver hats. But not another lady in sight. She might as well be wearing flannel, fustian, and clogs, for all anybody around here would care.

Then, recognizing the pettiness of that sort of thinking, Sarah subsided against the well-worn squabs, deflated. She was beginning to sound perilously similar to Caroline Barrett, who was widely regarded as the most frivolous goose in all of London. If the woman had one conversation beyond what she was wearing and who was jealous of her, no one had yet to report on it.

And *she* was acting just that silly and shallow!

Sarah leaned forward and peered through the carriage window. "Thank you, Captain Shenker," she called out with determined cheerfulness. "You have been very considerate of my comfort, and I appreciate your many kindnesses."

If he was surprised by the sudden sunniness of her attitude, the good captain covered it with a broad smile. " 'Twas my pleasure, miss. Indeed it was." He tipped his hat to her. "I hope your journey to Kelso is pleasant."

From behind the heavily laden traveling coach, Marshall

Byrde heard the exchange. Only he was Marshall MacDougal again, using his mother's maiden name, as he had on the boxing circuit.

He cocked his head. The lilting voice of the woman had drawn his interest first. But it was the reference to Kelso that made him tense to hear more. He too was heading for Kelso, for he'd heard his mother mention the place now and again.

After a fruitless search for his father in London, he was banking on the belief that if she had come from Kelso, his father might have lived there too. Perhaps the woman in this carriage might know something useful to him. Anything to speed up his frustratingly slow search for his bastard of a father.

He'd been a month at sea, ten days in London, and another several days en route to Scotland. All he'd learned for his trouble was that although his father's letters had been posted from London, the man had not been born, wed, or buried there. Nor did he live there now, according to the detectives he'd hired.

His mother's reticence on the subject of her life in her homeland had added nothing to his knowledge of the man. All he knew was that Maureen MacDougal had loved Cameron Byrde—and that he had not loved her in return.

So he'd decided to restart his search on his mother's side of the family. Only this time he meant to be smarter. This time he would infiltrate society by wearing the mantle of a gentleman and conspicuously flaunt his wealth. That's why he was in Berwick, purchasing a smart vehicle, with a showy team of horses, and a spirited saddle mount as well. He would infiltrate Kelso's society while his new batman fit in with the servant classes. For he was certain the answer to his question lay here, in Lowland Scotland.

And now, in the cumbersome coach near his own, he might have the first opportunity to see if he was right.

Except that with a snap of a whip, the coachman sent the heavily laden vehicle rumbling away from the dock and into town. Marsh muffled an oath of frustration. "How much longer?" he prodded Duff, his newly hired servant. "We need to be on our way."

The wiry fellow eyed him. "I've got to replace this broken leading strap. Take 'bout a quarter hour, guv'nor."

Marsh grimaced. Bloody hell. Then he spied a man staring after the carriage, and his eyes narrowed. Perhaps all was not lost.

"Excuse me," he said, strolling up to the fellow, who had the widespread stance of a sailor and wore a captain's hat. "Did I hear someone mention Kelso?"

The man gave him a quick look-over. "You're American, aren't you?"

Marsh responded with a friendly grin. "Guilty as charged. Would you like a smoke?" He held out a decorative case of neatly rolled cheroots.

When the captain's bushy brows arched in appreciation, Marsh went on. "I'm here on business. First time in Scotland. I'm heading for Kelso myself. That's why I asked."

The captain took one of the cheroots and sniffed it. "Virginia tobacco, or Cuban?"

Marsh smiled genially. He had him. "It's a special blend I have made to order."

A fifteen-minute conversation garnered him three bits of information. Though usually Highlanders, MacDougals could be found in the Lowlands too; the road to Kelso was best not driven after dark; and the young woman in the carriage was English, beautiful, and too spoiled for her own good.

"A right winsome bit a' fluff. But an expensive bit."

Marsh thought about that now as he urged the matched pair of bays into a steady, ground-eating pace. He hadn't had a woman since before his mother's death. Not on the ship, nor in London. But he found himself thinking of women now. Not that a haughty English miss was likely to provide him the sort of relief he needed.

He chirruped to the horses, preferring to handle them himself, rather than give them over to Duff. But his thoughts remained on the woman en route to Kelso. What was a young Englishwoman doing traveling in Scotland with only her maid anyway?

But he didn't really care. All he knew was that he had a hankering to have a pretty woman smile at him. If nothing else, it would remind him of his old life in Boston and Washington. Before his mother's death. Before her secret cache of letters had thrown his entire life on its ear.

He touched the lead horse lightly with the whip. Soon enough he would reach Kelso. And he would stay till he had his answers, and follow his father's trail until he had his revenge.

# CHAPTER 2

SARAH pushed up the collar of her cloak, cold despite the fire Agnes stoked in the fireplace of the private dining room they'd taken. They'd stopped for the midday meal at a cheerless-looking place. But the stew smelled delicious and her stomach rumbled hungrily.

"Tight-fisted Scotsmen," Agnes muttered when she found nothing but kindling in the log bin.

Sarah smiled, for her spirits had improved considerably over the course of the morning. "You'll have to watch that tongue, Agnes. For my sister is half Scots on her father's side, and my brother-in-law, Lord Hawke, is fully Scots, as are some of your mother's family, I am told."

Sarah took a secret pleasure in the dour woman's discomfort. Part of her good mood came from her anticipation of seeing Olivia and Neville. Life with them would certainly not be as exciting as London during the season, and there were no men of any merit to be flirted with in Kelso.

But there were other rewards. Neville kept one of the finest stables she'd ever had the privilege of riding from. That meant she would have access to the finest horseflesh and take real hell-for-leather gallops. Plus she would be free to ride astride, without her mother's constant scolding. And then there were also young Catherine and little Philip to enjoy.

So she ate a hearty luncheon, ignoring Agnes's muttered complaints. She would sleep away the afternoon, and by the time she awoke, they would have arrived.

When they returned to the coach, however, it was to find the coachman standing beside the team of rested horses, in conversation with a well-dressed gentleman. Sarah knew her role as a young woman of good breeding. Never acknowledge a gentleman to whom she had not been properly introduced—and coachmen were hardly considered suitable to provide that proper introduction.

She knew all that, and yet she slowed as she neared the coach, slowed and stared at the stranger longer than she ought. There was something intriguing about him. Not just his solid build and excessive height. Not just his wide shoulders and unfashionably long hair. There was something else, something she could not quite specify.

He was definitely not the sort of English gentleman she was accustomed to.

Then again, she was no longer in England.

She let her gaze meander over him, admiring the muscular legs beneath his breeches and the strong profile shaded somewhat by his beaver topper. A funny little tingle ran down her back and settled in the vicinity of her stomach. If this was an example of Scottish manhood, perhaps her sojourn to the hinterlands might not be so boring as she'd feared.

Then he looked up and caught her staring, and for a long, suspended moment she could not tear her gaze away. His eyes grew dark as jet, dark and yet glittering in the sunlight.

Agnes must have noticed their locked gazes, for with a none-too-subtle elbow to Sarah's side, the maid broke the mesmerizing pull of the stranger's eyes. In truth, it was a relief for Sarah to drag her gaze from his. Yet still, she resented the maid's interference. "You overstep your bounds," she hissed as she turned stiffly for the carriage door. But Agnes only folded her arms and stared unrepentantly at her.

Muffling a curse that would have done her brother proud, Sarah reached for the door to swing it open. But another hand was already there.

"May I assist you, miss?"

Sarah turned abruptly, startled by the low, masculine

voice. She was startled also by the impact of that dark, appreciative stare, so much nearer now. She shot a *so there* look at the disapproving Agnes, then refocused her attention on the man holding the coach door open with one hand while he extended his other to help her up the narrow steps.

Really, but he was a bold one. Hat on, gloves off. Any London gentleman would know better. But then, London gentlemen had proven to be a shady, unreliable lot. So she allowed the tiniest smile to curl the corners of her mouth, and considered him for a long, assessing moment. She folded her gloved hands neatly at her waist. "I don't believe we've been properly introduced, sir."

His grin increased. Then he removed his hat and made a short, neat bow. "I am Marshall MacDougal, at your service, Miss . . . Miss . . ."

Her smile increased also, just a fraction. "You are not British, are you, Mr. MacDougal?"

"I'm American," he conceded. "Is it my accent that gives me away?"

Primly she pursed her lips. "No. Your manners." She affected a scandalized expression, but one she knew he would not believe. "In our society a gentleman does not introduce himself to a lady."

"Oh?" He replaced his hat on his head. "Then how do women and men ever meet?"

Sarah could feel Agnes's disapproving stare, and the coachman's nervous one. But that only egged her on. "They meet through proper channels, of course. Family. Friends."

He shook his head. "That's too bad. I fear I am in for a lonely time of it, then, for I am newly arrived here after a short jaunt in London. And unfortunately I have neither friends nor family in Scotland to recommend me."

For a moment longer their gazes clung, and Sarah felt clearly the crackling tension between them. It was scary and exhilarating, and she knew one thing without a doubt. This was not a man who would ever want for company, especially female company. There was something in his eyes, some spark caused not solely by the spring sunshine.

She felt a little thrill shoot through her every time he looked at her.

No, not merely a little thrill. She'd felt a little thrill when Harlan Bramwell had looked at her. She'd felt a little thrill when Ralph Liverett had taken her hand. And Lord Penley, the cad.

What she felt now, however, was quite different from those little thrills of conquest. This was hot and tickling, trembling its way right through her body, making her heart race and her stomach clutch.

Fortunately, caution raised its head in the nick of time.

This impulsive surrender to her emotions was what had gotten her into trouble in the past, this reckless attraction to everything she ought to avoid. And one thing she knew instinctively: This man was someone she ought definitely to avoid.

So she schooled her face into a more serious expression and banished any flirtatious tone from her voice. "I suspect you will get the hang of things, Mr. MacDougal. Good day." And without further ado—or his assistance—she stepped lightly into the hired coach.

Agnes followed, slamming the door behind them, and in a moment they pulled out of the inn yard. As the coach rocked down the dusty roadway, Sarah congratulated herself that she'd behaved precisely as she ought: polite, but not friendly. Certainly she had not encouraged him, at least not toward the end.

But as she removed her hat and gloves and positioned a small pillow behind her back, she allowed herself the luxury of imagining just who this American was, and why he'd come all the way across the wide ocean to Scotland. Marshall MacDougal was his name, a Scottish name for an American man. Dark chestnut hair that glinted red in the sunlight. Black eyes that glinted blue.

Again she felt that traitorous little tremble in her belly, and she sighed at her own perversity. If the smooth and charming Lord Penley had been wrong for her, a forthright American like Mr. MacDougal would be disastrous. She had already learned, the hard way, that she was an exceedingly poor judge of men. She must work now to remember that fact.

But it was going to be hard, she acknowledged, closing her eyes. It was going to be so hard.

Marshall trailed a quarter mile behind the lumbering coach. The incident with the pretty young woman at the posting house had been instructive. If Boston's society was bound by intricate rules after less than two hundred years, English society was mired in them. He'd bought his way into Boston's elite. After all, in America, money was the primary arbiter of class. But British society was more complex, as Duff had swiftly apprised him.

"Fell flat, did you?" the outspoken fellow had said when the Englishwoman's coach had left Marsh standing in the yard, covered with dust.

Marsh had fixed him with a thunderous glare, but the man had continued on unperturbed. "The thing is, guvnor, this ain't America. There's women, an' then there's ladies. You've got to decide which ones it is you're interested in."

"And what of servants? Are they different here too, speaking up even when their opinions are not welcome?"

Unfazed by his new employer's ire, the man squinted at him. "You look the sort who kin handle hisself in a brawl, otherwise I wouldn't've took you on."

"You took me on?"

"That's the right of it. You're up to somethin', even if you ain't ready to tell me what. But I'm the adventurous sort, meself. I don't take you for the type as needs someone to fold his clothes and carry his bags. I'm thinkin' you have other reasons for hiring me than that. Don't know what, not yet. Meanwhile, best you understand that we Scots got our own ways. If you want to get along here, best that you learn 'em. An' I'm the one as can teach you."

Much as he'd resented the man's observant remarks, having lived by his wits all his life, Marsh had respect for others who survived the same way. Now, as he stared after the carriage ahead of him, he considered Duff's words. Maybe he could use a little assistance on that score. After all, that coachman hadn't been especially forthcoming, and even less so when the red-caped beauty had advanced so regally upon them.

Marsh rubbed one hand across the back of his neck. Damn, but she was a self-possessed little tart. Like a succulent red cherry, she looked delectable enough to eat. And well she knew it. Those bright blue eyes had sparkled with awareness when he'd approached her. She'd not been at all opposed to their flirtatious encounter—at first. But then he must have done something and she'd recognized his lack of social acumen. That's when her interest had cooled.

Was that what had cooled his father's interest in his mother? Had she overreached her bounds? Cameron Byrde must have been a man of some means if he'd settled a hundred pounds on her. But Maureen MacDougal, for all her gentle manner and quiet beauty, had been a simple lass from ordinary stock. She'd worked her whole life as a domestic in other people's homes. That's probably how she'd met the heartless Cameron Byrde.

Marsh's gaze narrowed on the luxurious coach up ahead. If his father was from anywhere around Kelso, then the pretty little snob in that behemoth carriage was sure to be acquainted with him. After all, like gathered with like.

By the same token, they excluded everyone they deemed not like themselves. He'd learned how to travel those circles in Boston and in Washington. He had the money to fit in when he worked at it, and the social skills as well. But here he was less certain. Though he now had the requisite servant, carriage, clothing, and horse flesh—and plenty of money—he could see already that it might not be enough. Perhaps Duffy Erskine was right. Perhaps the man could help him with the rest of it. All he needed was entrée into the right society. After that he could manage on his own. He'd done so in Boston, and he could do so here.

He was resolved on the matter several hours later as they crossed a narrow stone bridge to enter the town of Kelso.

It was a prosperous-looking place centered around a village green. He stared around him at close-set cottages, painted shop fronts, and busy village folk. Had his mother once walked these cobbled streets?

His palms began to sweat. Did his father walk them still?

He reined in at the sign of the Cock and Bow and handed his weary animal over to the ostler. "A room for me. And for my man," he said to the aproned innkeeper who came eagerly out to introduce himself.

"Yes, sir. And how long will you be staying, sir?"

*Long enough to wreak havoc on my father and whoever else contributed to my mother's grief and suffering.*

But to the shiny-pated fellow he only said, "A week. Maybe longer."

"Very good, sir. Very good." The man led the way to the register. "And what name shall I record here, sir?"

"Marsh . . . Marshall MacDougal."

"MacDougal." The man stared at him a moment. "MacDougal."

Marsh's gaze narrowed. Did the man know the name? Did he know the family?

"Is that spelled *ou* or *uo*?"

Marsh's even expression hid any sign of disappointment. "It's *ou,* and only one *l.*" He took the key the man handed him. "Tell me, Mr. Halbrecht, are there any sights hereabouts I should take in? Or perhaps particular social gatherings I ought to seek out?"

The man gave him a quick assessing look and glanced over at Duff, who was unloading the carriage. Apparently satisfied that this customer was a gentleman and kept a manservant, he said, "We have our own subscription hall with dances every Friday. It's not yet huntin' season, but there's prime fishin' in the Tweed. Course if you want to venture off the bridge, you'll have to apply to the stewards at the big houses. Mostly they make free with fishing along their shores. At Woodford Court they's only particular about the stretch right along the house."

"And the other estates?"

"They's only one other close around here. It's upstream a mile or so. Byrde Manor. Though it's not nearly so grand as Woodford . . ."

Byrde Manor! The words echoed in Marsh's head, drowning out the rest of the man's remarks. There was an estate called Byrde Manor. Had he this easily found the seat of his father's family? But what else could it be? Though his heart thudded with excitement, he somehow forced himself to remain calm.

"So you suggest I apply to the house for permission to fish their portion of the Tweed?"

The innkeeper shrugged. " 'Tis not strictly a necessity. Howsomever, I'm sure they would appreciate it."

No. Marsh didn't think they would appreciate it at all, not once his true identity was revealed. But for now he would court the Byrde family's approval and acceptance.

He thanked the man and turned for the stairs, patting the pocket of his riding coat that held the three letters Cameron Byrde had sent to Maureen MacDougal. His time in London had been a waste, but after only ten minutes in Kelso he might have located his father's lair, or at least have discovered a strong lead in that direction.

But was the man in residence at Byrde Manor?

He hesitated at the base of the stairs. Surely the innkeeper would know. But was it wise to reveal his hand so soon? In a town like this, gossip about a stranger was sure to spread quickly.

Fortunately, when he looked back, the innkeeper attached another meaning to his pause. "If you haven't any of your own, I've all the fishing tackle you need, Mr. MacDougal. You came to the right place, that's for certain." He smiled helpfully. "You just let me know if I can be of any assistance to you. Any assistance at all."

Marsh only nodded. No use to look too eager. Besides, he would know the truth soon enough. By this time tomorrow he might very well have come face-to-face with his father. Until then he needed to think on what he meant to say to the man, how he intended to behave.

Rage rose unbidden in his chest, as thick and choking as it had been when first he'd learned the truth of his parents' history. The confrontation was coming. He could sense it in every fiber of his being. But he had to be ready. He had to be in control.

Then God help Cameron Byrde, for his unwanted son meant to crucify him.

Sarah did not know whether to weep in frustration or shout with joy.

"They all went up to Glasgow," Mrs. Tillotson, the housekeeper at Woodford Court, told her. "They left just yesterday morning. Miz Olivia wrote your mother about their sudden journey. I was to post it when next I got to town."

Sarah chewed the side of her lip. "All of them went, even the children?"

"Yes, miss. Himself had business to tend to—the Glasgow horse fair, it was. Your sister decided a jaunt north would be nice, 'specially now that the weather is warming up."

Sarah made a face. She'd hardly call this warm. But the chilly northern climes were the least of her worries. Olivia and Neville were gone, leaving her alone at Woodford. Once her mother received Olivia's post, she would summon Sarah immediately home again. Then James would probably insist that she be trundled off to a convent or some other equally unpleasant place.

Of course, that was assuming Mother received Olivia's letter.

Sarah grimaced inwardly at such a devious thought. Yet once rooted, the idea would not go away. If her mother was not informed of Olivia's whereabouts, she would assume Sarah was safely in her sister's company. And indeed, for all practical purposes, she was. Under her roof. Under her protection. Just because Olivia and Neville were not physically in residence did not lessen their influence. Besides, the humorless Agnes was here like a dour shadow, dogging her every move.

Though Sarah had not initially wanted to come up to Scotland, the alternative had been far worse. Now that she was here, however, she was content to stay. Besides, now that she thought of it, Olivia's absence was a perfect opportunity. What better way to prove that she was sensible and practical, and had learned to control her impulsive nature?

All she had to do was intercept Olivia's letter.

"Are you all right, miss?" Mrs. Tillotson asked, drawing Sarah back to the present.

Sarah blinked, then turned her brightest, most deliberately sincere smile on the good-natured little woman. "Oh, of course. Of course. Well, I am disappointed, of course. For I so wanted to see them all. When shall they return?"

"Oh, they mean to be gone a good month and more. Perhaps you would like to join them in Glasgow."

For a moment Sarah was sorely tempted to do just that. The city—any city—was sure to be more exciting than the quiet countryside. But if she arrived in Glasgow, Olivia would quiz her on why she'd been sent up from London, then proceed to boss her around as if she were still twelve.

Besides, Sarah decided, the excitement of city life was precisely what she did not need right now. "No. No," she answered the woman. "I believe the best thing will be for me to go on to Byrde Manor."

"Oh, yes. You'll want to spend time with Bertie—I mean, Mrs. Hamilton."

Sarah smiled, and this time without any deception. Her mother's beloved longtime housekeeper and companion had remarried and retired to her native Scotland some years ago. She lived now with her crusty husband in the steward's residence at Byrde Manor, the estate of Sarah's half-sister, Olivia.

While Sarah's own father had left her very well fixed, with numerous investments and income properties, plus an enormous quarterly allowance, Olivia's father had left his one child only that modest estate, with its sheep meadows, home farm, and comfortable but rustic house. Still, Sarah had always enjoyed visiting at Byrde Manor. Staying with the Hamiltons would be like visiting with grandparents.

"Yes," she said. "I believe I would like that. And if you like," she added, "I'll post Olivia's letter to Mama along with my own. For I will want to apprise her of my safe arrival."

Mrs. Tillotson bobbed her head. "Very good, miss. But let me fetch you a cup of tea before you go on to Byrde Manor. My, but Bertie shall be so pleased. Indeed she will."

"So. It is all set," Sarah said out loud when Mrs. Tillotson trundled off to fetch the tea and letter. And if she was being deceitful, she consoled herself that it was not really so terrible a thing she did. She would write to her mother to assure her of her arrival. But Mother needn't know about Olivia's absence. Nor did Olivia need to know just yet the unpleasant circumstances surrounding Sarah's unexpected sojourn to Scotland.

For the next month, at least, she could enjoy a trouble-free existence.

# CHAPTER

# 3

AT Byrde Manor Sarah went to bed early, slept like the dead, and arose just as the sun broke over the eastern horizon. Even then, Agnes was already up, as was Mrs. Hamilton. It was plain that the aging housekeeper and the rigid London maid were not going to get along.

"My Sarah is a good girl," Mrs. Hamilton's voice carried from the dining room as Sarah made her way downstairs. Sarah smiled. Trust Mrs. Hamilton to defend her, no matter what she did. "If she has high spirits, so be it. Her mother was the same and I dare you to name another lady so gracious and well loved as Augusta St. Clare."

"Humph," the reply came, and Sarah's smile faded. She could just picture Agnes's hatchet-faced scowl. "Lady Acton is indeed a gracious lady," the maid retorted. "Gracious and wise enough to know Miss Sarah courts disaster at every turn."

Sarah chose that precise moment to sail serenely into the room. Mrs. Hamilton looked ready to unload a tirade on the outspoken maid. Agnes, however, did not appear in the least perturbed. Nor did she have the good grace to look at all chagrined that her unflattering remarks had been overheard.

Sarah decided to simply ignore the situation. Well, perhaps not entirely ignore it. There were ways to deal with unpleasant servants, even those given special dispensation by an irate brother to take a headstrong sister in hand.

"Agnes," she began. "I noticed my traveling suit is stained on the hem. Also, one of the buttons is loose. Would you be so good as to tend to it before you leave us?

You catch the coach tomorrow, am I right?" She smiled. "And while you're at it, you might examine the rest of my wardrobe and press out any wrinkles from the trunk. And do take special care with my scarlet cloak."

The woman pursed her lips, but with a curt nod she complied. While she had instructions to keep a close eye on Sarah, that did not give her leave to shirk her other duties.

When she stalked from the room, Mrs. Hamilton blew out an exasperated breath. "What a prune of a woman. Whyever did your mother send her with you?"

"Don't worry, she's not staying. Mother has given her leave to spend a month with her family in Carlisle—probably so that she would not have to deal with her," she added with a chuckle. "Agnes is one of my stepfather's longtime retainers and so cannot be sacked."

Mrs. Hamilton poured a cup of tea for Sarah and indicated the table. "He's too softhearted, he is. But come, now. Sit and eat and tell me all the news."

"Only if you sit too," Sarah said.

So it was that they were well immersed in a good gossip, with no reference yet to Sarah's recent imbroglio, when another of the servants approached Mrs. Hamilton.

"There's a gentleman at the door. Come to inquire about fishing in the river."

"A gentleman?" Mrs. Hamilton asked.

"Yes'm. A fine-looking gentleman. Mr. Marshall MacDougal, he gives his name."

Sarah tensed in sudden awareness. Marshall MacDougal, of the broad shoulders and insolent gaze. A satisfied smile curled the corners of her mouth. Had the bold fellow followed her?

Fortunately Mrs. Hamilton's attention remained focused on the maid. "What sort of fellow is he?"

The maid gave a saucy grin, then, spying Sarah, squelched it. "A sporting fellow, by the look of him. Well mannered, well dressed, and riding a horse Mr. Hamilton would approve of."

"Very well, then," the housekeeper said. "Let him fish in our stretch of the river, and good luck to him. I'm certain Mr. Hamilton would not mind. So," she went on, turning back to Sarah. "You'd rather stay here with the old folks than follow your sister up to Glasgow. Lud, child. You must be taken with the fever. I've never known you to choose the countryside over the city—at least not since your come out."

Reining in her curiosity about Mr. MacDougal, Sarah picked up her cup and swirled the tea in a slow circle. "Everyone needs a change of scenery now and again. I swear, all those parties and routs and balls. All the tittering girls and posturing mamas. All the same men making all the same small talk."

"From your mother's letters I would never have thought it, but you're beginning to sound like your sister did, way back when. And you know what happened to her." Mrs. Hamilton cocked her head knowingly. "When she quit lookin' for a man, she found one. And an exceedingly good one, I might add."

Sarah laughed. "If I could find a man half so marvelous as Neville Hawke, I would snatch him up at once."

"Well. You're in Scotland now, and we're a land of brawny men. Not so refined as to be boring, mind you. But not so coarse as to be crude."

"Like your Donnie-boy?" Sarah laughed again when Mrs. Hamilton's face pinkened. "Perhaps I should wait, like you did, until my hair is gray to marry."

"Get on with you, girl. Don't you dare make the same mistake I made. I could have married Donnie Hamilton when I was three-and-twenty. But I was too proud and too headstrong. 'Tis a blessing that God allowed me a second chance with him. And speaking of my Donnie-boy, he'll be wanting his tea—and also to see you. Whyn't you come out to the stables with me and tell him hello?"

"Yes. That would be nice. And perhaps he will saddle me one of the horses, for I'm in the mood for a long ramble. Does he still keep that pretty sorrel mare?"

Less than an hour later, Sarah was mounted and trotting down the curving drive that led up to the river road. The stone fences were in good repair, she noticed. The apple trees were green and healthy, and a border of Nodding Marys danced in the breeze like lavender-clad ladies as she rode by.

Though Olivia lived with Neville at Woodford Court, across the River Tweed, she kept Byrde Manor up, for it had been her childhood home and was all she owned from her father, Cameron Byrde. She primarily used it for overflow guests during the grouse season, for it was a simple manor house, and considerably smaller than Woodford Court. But Sarah had fond memories of it from her own childhood. Its expanse of fields and forests was especially picturesque.

Now, as Sarah guided the mare across the road and through the wooded stand alongside the river, she sucked in a deep breath of the crisp morning air, very glad to be here. The whole world smelled green and verdant today. The alder and birch and sycamore trees, filled with birds, twittered and swayed with the burgeoning season.

She paused in a long, angling field of fescue already nearly knee-high, then breathed deeply, and gazed about her. It was so beautiful here. So wild and exhilarating—and so unlike London. Why on earth had she dreaded this journey? At the moment she would rather be no other place on earth.

Her peaceful meditations, however, were broken by a high-pitched cry and the thunder of hooves. Up came her mare's head, and Sarah twisted about. There, back on the roadway, a horse shot along at a full gallop. A young man hunched over the animal's neck, urging it on with a crop. In his wake two other fellows raced their mounts, shouting curses and exhorting their laboring horses to greater speed.

In a moment they were gone, leaving only a plume of dust and their echoing cries as evidence of their passing. Boys—yet they would soon grow into the brawny Scotsmen of whom Mrs. Hamilton was so proud.

Sarah turned away, envious of the boys' complete freedom, yet also vaguely disapproving. She hoped they walked their animals after such a rousing run. But though the thought of just such a heady gallop tempted her, she had another mission in mind.

Who was this Marshall MacDougal, this American who looked like a gentleman but carried about him the air of a brigand? And why was he here in Lowland Scotland, in Kelso, of all places—fishing in the River Tweed practically just outside her door?

A sudden suspicion occurred to her. Could he be some friend of her brother's, hired to follow her and spy on her? Perhaps even to test her, then report everything to James?

Her mouth turned down in a frown and she chewed her lip. As outdone as he'd been with her, surely James would not stoop that low. Besides, James wasn't likely to know any Americans, and Mr. MacDougal had said he'd only been briefly in London. There could be no connection between the two men. Could there?

There was only one way to find out.

She urged the mare down the path that led to the river's edge. She would confront this Marshall MacDougal and determine the truth, for one thing she prided herself on was her understanding of men.

Well. Perhaps Lord Penley had taken her in.

But that was a first. Besides, she was wiser now than she'd been then—though it was but five days ago. Still and all, she was convinced this American would not be able to deceive her, no matter what his nefarious purpose.

Standing on a mossy bank, Marsh cast his line out to a still portion of the river. The fly fell into a small pool framed by a fallen log and a newly emergent stand of reeds. At once he began to play the fly along the surface. But his mind was occupied by far more than thoughts of game fish.

He'd learned little enough when he'd approached Byrde Manor on the pretext of fishing. He'd left Duff in Kelso with instructions to circulate about town—primarily to the local pub—and take the lay of the land. Who was who.

Where the power lay. Who was complacent; who were the malcontents. Marsh well knew that servants gossiped among themselves, and he wanted to know all the gossip about Byrde Manor, although he wasn't ready to confide that fact in Duff.

Suddenly there was a strike on his line. Caught off guard, he did not react fast enough. When he jerked his rod to set the hook, it was too late. His hook flew high, absent any fish. To make matters worse, merry laughter broke out just behind him.

"You'll never catch any of these wily fellows that way."

Startled, Marsh swung around to find a young woman staring at him from her seat upon a horse at the edge of the trees. She was in shadow and her features were difficult to make out, but he would have known that confident, cultured voice anywhere. Though she wore a plain green riding habit this morning, with no scarlet or sable in sight, it was nonetheless the girl from the traveling carriage.

To hell with the fish; he'd rather catch a pretty green woods nymph any day.

With studied nonchalance he began pulling in his line. "Has no one ever warned you not to startle a fisherman at his work? Had you not made so untimely an entrance, I would easily have landed the fish."

Again she laughed, which was his intention, and she urged her mount nearer, which was his hope.

"You may blame me, if it eases your offended pride, Mr. MacDougal. I don't mind."

The sun caught on her dark hair, glinting chestnut highlights on the long plait which trailed beneath her narrow brimmed straw hat. Despite her well-cut riding habit of some rich spruce-colored cloth decorated with a double march of gold buttons, that casual coiffure gave her an altogether different look from yesterday. She no longer appeared a proper London lady, or even like one of the society chits he was used to in Boston. Instead she looked more like an ordinary woman—an American woman—especially sitting astride as she did.

He propped the fishing rod in front of him, never taking his gaze from her. "So, Miss No-Name. You speak to me now, when no one is here to make note of your social *faux pas.*"

She did not rise to his teasing, but turned her eager mare in a neat circle. She rode well, he noted, with a light touch of her knees and an easy grip on the reins.

Encouraged, he went on. "Are you going to reveal your name, or must I continue to think of you as Red Riding Hood?"

At that her deliberately haughty expression collapsed in a wry grin. "Red Riding Hood. I like that. But tell me, are you the Big Bad Wolf whom I must fear?"

*Oh, yes,* he thought. *You'd better fear me, for you are a delectable morsel and I'd like nothing better than to eat you up.*

"Oh, no," he said. "You've nothing to fear from me. I'm here mainly to fish and enjoy a holiday—and do a little business, perhaps."

She studied him with mock severity. "And what sort of business would that be?"

He smiled. "I'm sure I could answer your question better, did I know to whom I am speaking."

Sarah did not know what to think. Actually, she knew what she did think: that he was impossibly handsome, in a brutish sort of way, and that he was impossibly bold, in what must be an American sort of way.

But she didn't know what she *should* think, nor how she ought to answer him. Whether he was her brother's spy or simply a stranger, it would behoove her to play it very cautious.

"Answer my question, Mr. MacDougal, and perhaps I shall be moved to answer yours."

For a moment he only stared at her with the intent gaze of a very big, very bad wolf. Then with a slight nod he conceded. "I construct things. Buildings. Bridges. Or perhaps I should say that the company I own constructs them."

*Interesting.* "I see. Is that why you are here, to build something?"

He shrugged, a wholly masculine gesture. "As I said, I'm primarily here on holiday. I'm not opposed, however, to viewing some of the finer examples of Scottish architecture. Perhaps you would be good enough to act as my guide?"

She tilted her head, still smiling. "I don't believe that's very likely."

"No?" He shifted his stance. He even moved like a predator, she noticed. Confidently and with more grace than she would expect in such a big man. The silence between them began to grow awkward before he added, "I answered your questions. It's your turn to answer mine."

Beneath Sarah's tight grip on the reins, the mare responded, pawing the ground with one nervous hoof. Sarah blew out her own nervous breath. "I . . . I am Miss Sarah Palmer, though I ought not to reveal even that much to you. Should we ever finally be properly introduced, I trust you will be good enough to pretend we have not previously conversed."

He shook his head, and the wind brushed the longish locks of his dark auburn hair across his brow. "What complicated games society women play."

"Society women?" She gave him a haughty look. "I assure you that it is society men, more so than women, who attach so many rules to the behavior of their daughters and wives. Were it left to us, we would cut our hair, ride astride, and smoke cigars. In public," she added, then was amazed at such an outlandish declaration. Wherever had that come from?

It made him laugh, however, and the low rumbling sound of it tickled something deep inside her.

"Had I a cigar, I'd light it for you now—and you already ride astride," he added. Then his grin faded and his eyes darkened and roamed over her quite freely. "But I have to agree with your Englishmen. Leave your hair long, Sarah Palmer, and leave me with the hope that I may one day see it unbound and spread across your shoulders and arms."

Sarah sucked in a harsh breath, shocked by his outrageous words. He was deliberately provoking her. Deliberately trying to unsettle her. Yet knowing that did nothing to lessen the impact, for the tickle in her belly had coiled into a knot—a hot, churning knot.

She didn't, however, have to let him know that. "*Tsk, tsk,* Mr. MacDougal. I fear you will be awfully disappointed in your visit to our island kingdom if you continue on in that vein. Were my brother to hear you speak so boldly to me, he would surely call you out."

"Oh, would he?"

"Yes, he would. My brother is James Linden, Viscount Farley, and he would take grave offense—"

"Linden?" he interjected. "But your name is Palmer."

She looked down her nose at him. "Yes. For your information, James is my half-brother. We had different fathers."

"I see. That means your father—"

"My father is many years deceased," she stated curtly. "As is my brother's. But make no doubt, our stepfather would second James in an instant."

"I'm sorry. I did not mean to bring up a sensitive subject."

She lifted her chin. "My father was a wonderful man; the very best of fathers. But that is neither here nor there. I am bound for a ride and you still have a river full of fish to torment. Good day, Mr. MacDougal."

"Wait. Don't go yet." He moved closer, his hand extended out to her. "I'd like to see you again, Miss Sarah Palmer. May I call on you? Where do you live?"

"I'm sure that is not possible," she answered at once. But she was aware of an unseemly rush of feminine satisfaction at this newest of conquests. Though she should not be impressed by this unmannered American, she could not deny that he intrigued her. "Remember," she said, turning her horse to leave. "Should we ever be introduced, you are to pretend not to know me."

"I'm afraid I cannot do that."

"What?" She pulled up the mare, then frowned down at him. "But you agreed."

"No. I did not answer you at all on that score. But I'll give you my answer now. When next we meet, I shall be every bit as friendly toward you as we have been these last few minutes."

"You will not!"

Sarah's heart began to pump in rising panic when he sauntered toward her. She sat well above him on a fleet-footed animal, while he looked up at her from his place on the riverbank. Yet it was she who felt uneasy as he approached her; she who felt like hapless prey being stalked by a dangerous carnivore.

And yet he fascinated her still. Did he have this effect on all females? Even the mare seemed captivated by him, for the fickle creature reached her nose forward to nuzzle his extended hand.

Before Sarah could react, he took firm hold of the animal's bridle. At once Sarah's heart began to hammer with real fear. She was alone with a man she had no reason to trust.

She pulled on the reins and snatched up the quirt, prepared to defend herself. But the mare was skittish and, alarmed, the animal reared. When Mr. MacDougal released the bridle, however, the mare swung abruptly back to him.

It was just enough to unbalance Sarah. Though she grabbed for the small pommel, she felt herself start to slide.

"Damn," she swore, bracing herself for a hard landing.

But instead of the rough ground, Sarah landed in a pair of strong arms.

"I've got you—"

"Let me go!"

In the struggle, they both went down.

For a moment she lay there, sprawled over the man in the most awkward position imaginable. Her skirts were flung high, shrouding his head, she realized with horror. Then he sat up from beneath the froth of petticoats and she found herself sitting in his lap, one of his arms trapped beneath her legs.

He spoke first. "Are you hurt?"

"No, you . . . you idiot!"

"Idiot? I just saved your pretty little bottom from a bruising fall, and I'm the idiot?"

"If you hadn't grabbed my horse's bridle—Oh! Let me up," she exclaimed, trying to regain her feet.

"If you weren't such a rude little bitch—"

"Bitch!" Sarah could not believe he'd said that. She glared at him in utter fury. "You called me a *bitch*?"

Marsh reacted without weighing the consequences. She was already furious. What did he have to lose? Besides, those pouty lips of hers were screwed up as if she meant to lambaste him good. He knew only one way to silence a riled woman and so he took it. He captured her pursed mouth with a hard, aggressive kiss.

It achieved the desired result, for no other words assayed from between those lips. But it had another effect as well, not altogether surprising, but not welcome either.

For the moment he pressed his mouth to hers, desire leaped within him like a hungry beast, demanding more than merely one chaste kiss. Though he knew he should not, Marsh deepened the kiss, conscious of her feminine weight upon his lap, her faint, floral fragrance wafting around his head, and her delectable mouth softening beneath his own.

He wanted more of this.

But when he parted those luscious lips and delved deep within the recesses of that sweet, tart mouth, she stiffened, and he knew the moment was done. Before she could resume her tirade, he set her aside, jumped to his feet, then hauled her rudely upright.

"In the future, I suggest you find a more placid mount, since you obviously cannot manage this one." Whether he referred to himself or the mare, however, he was not entirely certain.

He strode up the bank, snatched the sorrel's reins, and

proceeded to check the animal for injury. But he was vitally aware of every movement Sarah Palmer made. How she shook out her disordered skirts and surreptitiously rubbed her bottom. When she intercepted his bold stare, she wrapped her arms around her waist and frowned.

At least she was not hurt, nor, apparently, was her horse. He, however, was feeling the very real ache of an inappropriate arousal.

"Your horse seems all right to ride," he muttered, and led the animal over to Sarah.

She took one step back from him, but no more. "You should not have taken hold of her bridle." When he did not respond, but only stared steadily into her wide blue eyes, she gritted her teeth and stuck out her jaw. "And you had no business at all kissing me like that."

"No? What way would you *have* me kiss you?"

"No way at all!" Her eyes flashed as she snatched the reins from his hand.

"Can I help you up?"

She gave a rude snort. "I believe you've helped me quite enough already."

So Marsh stood there and watched her mount with a sweep of dirtied skirts and petticoats. He admired the glimpse he had of her stockinged ankle, and the rigid set of her spine as she settled herself on the saddle. She was furious and embarrassed and, if he was lucky, just a little bit intrigued.

He grinned as she sent him a scathing look, then wheeled the horse and rode away. He'd either won her over or condemned himself completely in her eyes. He'd learn soon enough which it was.

# CHAPTER 4

SARAH worked the well-worn pair of grooming brushes over the sorrel mare with an energy that, unfortunately, did nothing to dispel her terrible anxiety.

What had she been about, kissing that man?

It did no good to tell herself that he had started it all. He had taken hold of her horse's bridle. He had caused the startled animal to rear and her to fall.

Every bit of it was true. Yet there was another truth, and it was that which had her in such a state. *He* had kissed her; but *she* had kissed him back.

She pressed her lips together and brushed the mare's withers and side, hand over hand, as she hadn't done in a year or more. Not two days in Scotland and she was already courting disaster. And as usual, there was a man involved.

*But what a man,* the traitorous thought intruded. Big. Dangerous. Fascinating despite his arrogant manner. She'd never been so affected by a kiss before. Never.

Then again, she'd thought the very same thing about Lord Penley's stolen kisses. They'd been swift, but they'd been accompanied by effusive vows of love and eternal devotion. How foolish she'd been. For she could see now that Lord Penley's kisses were nothing when compared to the violent passion that Marshall MacDougal had unleashed on her.

Or was the violent passion generated from within her?

She paused, one hand suspended in the air, and gnawed the side of her mouth. She seemed to be progressing from bad to worse when it came to her dealings with men. And her physical reaction to them was getting stronger and stronger. With every kiss and caress, she grew quicker and quicker to succumb.

She let out a little groan. Was it as her brother had said, that there was a wildness in her, a recklessness that would lead her to disaster and ruin, if she did not learn to curb it?

In that moment she feared it was so.

Frowning, she resumed her ministrations to the placid horse, combing out forelock and mane and long sweeping tail. But as she worked, she turned her mind toward a plan to reform herself, to prevent any further decline and, she hoped, to turn herself in a more positive direction.

She could always keep Agnes with her, she mused. That would solve the problem well enough. Unfortunately, that would be a case of the cure being worse than the affliction. No, Agnes was leaving in the morning, and good riddance to her.

What Sarah finally decided she needed were country hours, wholesome exercise, and industry for both her hands and mind. Something to occupy her time. Surely there were numerous tasks and projects she could undertake at Byrde Manor that would fill her days and also help Mrs. Hamilton. Within the month Olivia and Neville would return with the children. If she applied herself, by that time she could prove her usefulness and strength of character, not just to everyone else, but also to herself.

And if she should again run into that bridge-building American, Marshall MacDougal?

With the back of her wrist Sarah pushed a wayward curl from her brow. She would have to make sure she did *not* run into the man. After what had just passed between them, she knew better than to trust him or herself.

Thank goodness he was only in Scotland temporarily. He'd said he was on holiday. That meant he eventually would leave the neighborhood. Though he presented a problem to her, in truth he was only a symbol of a greater problem she still must address: no matter the venue—country or town—she invariably was drawn to the worst sort of man. No honorable gentlemen for her. Oh, no. She gravitated strictly to troublemakers.

Marshall MacDougal would soon enough be gone from Kelso. But unless she worked on improving her own behavior, the problem he presented would return in the form of the next troublesome fellow who came along with a cheeky grin and a charming manner.

She swept her tongue over her lips, aware of the heightened sensitivity that lingered still, and her face lowered in a frown. Perhaps she should simply avoid the company of all men, at least for a while. Keep strictly to the company of women.

She sighed, depressed by that dreary thought. But she vowed to stick to it.

So it was that she sat in the fragrant kitchen not a half hour later, positioning a footstool under Mrs. Hamilton's feet. "There, now. You don't have to move at all. Just sit here like a queen and order us about at your leisure."

Mrs. Hamilton gave her a shrewd look. "My, aren't you the accommodating one today. But I know you better than that, Sarah girl. You've never been one to hang about the kitchen with a pocket full of embroidery."

Mr. Hamilton shuffled through the open door. "She don't hang about the kitchen 'cause she'd ruther hang about the stables, smart lass."

Relieved by his interruption, Sarah grinned. "Of late I've not done enough of either of those." Pulling up a rope-bottomed chair, she sat down at the wide, scarred table that dominated Byrde Manor's cozy kitchen and smiled fondly at the elderly couple. "It's so lovely to be here with the two of you. If I want, I can pretend that I'm twelve again, with no worries or cares at all."

"The onliest thing you need to worry over, girl, is gettin' married," Mr. Hamilton pronounced. "You ought to be wed." He looked at his wife. "She ought to be wed."

"Oh, hush, old man," Mrs. Hamilton retorted. "Not everyone marries at twenty. You didn't."

"But I should've. I should've married you back then

even if you were a shrew." Then, winking at Sarah, he wisely hobbled out of the kitchen.

"You'd better run, old man!" Mrs. Hamilton called after him. "And I wasn't a shrew." She looked over at Sarah. "I wasn't a shrew." Then she chuckled. "Well, maybe I was. But only because he was such a troublesome young buck."

Sarah played with a bit of thread that had unraveled at the cuff of her sleeve. "Do you think, if you had married one another way back then, that . . . that it would have worked out all the same?"

Mrs. Hamilton poured a thick stream of cream into her tea. "No, I do not. There's a time for everything, child, and a reason. It does no good to speculate on how you might have changed the past, for you'll never get the chance. Let the past go. Work on makin' good choices in the here and now, and wait for the future to unfold. That's what I say."

Sarah grimaced. "It's the middle part that's so hard, isn't it? Making good choices in the here and now."

"I s'pose that's why you're here. Your mum sent you up to us to cool your heels, didn't she?"

Sarah made a face. "I see you haven't changed. Still figuring everything out."

"Who else's to do it, if not me? You've been a handful since the first day you drew breath, Sarah Palmer. A strong-willed baby, an energetic child, and now a headstrong young woman. 'Tisn't hard at all to figure that the last thing you would want is to leave London at the height of the season. And since you usually manage to wrap your mother around your little finger—and your brother—my guess is you've gone and done something a mite too outrageous for them to ignore this time."

Sarah twisted her own empty teacup around and around on its saucer. Was she that transparent? She scowled down at her cup. "I fell in love with the wrong sort of man—only he seemed like the right sort at the time. But he wasn't and if James hadn't stopped me, I would be wed to him this very minute. And miserable, I am now convinced."

"I see. And did you thank James for his interference?"

Sarah gave the clever old woman a wry smile. "Eventually."

"Hmm. And have you learned anything from the experience?"

Not enough, if this morning's adventure was any indication. But to Mrs. Hamilton she said, "Oh, I suppose. Mainly that my taste in men is atrocious."

Mrs. Hamilton chuckled. "Just like your mother, you are. Just like her."

"Oh, Lord. I hope that doesn't mean I'm to have four husbands like she's had."

"Now, now. Don't you be criticizing my sweet Augusta. She was unlucky, bein' widowed three times. But she loved each and every one of her husbands, and she's happy now. At least that's what she says in her letters." The old servant leaned forward, her expression earnest. "Tell me the truth, girl, is she happy?"

"You needn't worry yourself on that score at all, for Mother and Justin are just as happy as can be. You'd think they were still newlyweds sometimes, the way they carry on. Apparently, I'm the only worry she has. Just me." She sighed with exaggerated resignation.

"Go on with you, lass. You can't be all that much trouble."

"I don't think so either. But, well, I suppose I have made some foolish choices. Only I shan't make them again. I mean to turn over a new leaf, Mrs. Hamilton. But tell me," she added, hoping to steer the subject away from herself. "What's new in these parts?"

To Sarah's relief, the old woman settled back into her chair. "Oh, not so much. We're pretty quiet hereabouts. Ah, but there is a new upset. Lord Hawke's nephew, that wild Adrian, has gotten himself kicked out of Eton. Came home just yesterday. He's lucky his uncle is gone up to Glasgow, but there's sure to be a scene when he returns." She clucked her tongue and shook her grizzled head. " 'Tis a shame, for Lord Hawke and Livvie worked very hard to get him back in after that last row he had."

Adrian. Sarah hadn't seen Neville's nephew in years. "How old is he now?"

"Fourteen. Fifteen. A terrible age for boys, if you ask me. 'Course, what do you expect when he's got no father and his mother encourages him to think he's above the other village lads? Even though he is natural born, Lord Hawke does right by the lad, him being his dead brother's only child. And Livvie is as good to him as she is to her own two. But so long as that Estelle continues to undermine their every effort to civilize the boy, well, I don't know what Neville and Livvie are going to say when they find out about this."

Sarah vaguely remembered Estelle Kendrick. "What do you mean, she undermines their efforts?"

"Oh, that one. She encourages him to think he's better than the other lads 'round these parts, yet at the same time, she only laughs when he misbehaves. He's a sweet-natured lad. Always has been. But that Estelle, I'm afraid she'll turn him just as selfish and wild as she is." Again Mrs. Hamilton shook her head in disapproval. "You complain about your mother, Sarah girl, but you should thank your lucky stars you don't have a mother like Adrian's."

Sarah considered that. "I saw some boys about his age racing their horses on the road earlier."

"Humph. And Adrian probably at the head of the pack."

"I suppose I ought to look in on him. Perhaps invite him around."

Mrs. Hamilton sighed. "Aye. I s'pose you should." Then she brightened. "Maybe you can have a civilizing effect on the lad. Lord knows no one else has succeeded with him."

As Sarah refilled Mrs. Hamilton's cup with fresh tea, she mulled over the idea. Civilizing a young lad on the brink of manhood, making him acceptable to the young woman he would soon begin to court. She needed something to occupy herself, some sort of project. Perhaps in Adrian she might have found one. And wouldn't everyone be relieved and impressed if she managed to turn the boy into a proper gentleman?

An aberrant thought sprang into her mind. Too bad she could not perform the same service for Mr. MacDougal.

She set down the teapot with a little slosh of hot liquid, then sucked on her burned finger. Drat the man for rattling her so! Why was she thinking such thoughts about him? It was obvious from his outrageous performance today that he was already too set in his ways to alter them now. Adrian was still a boy, but Marshall MacDougal was a grown man. Definitely a full-grown man. And one far too dangerous for her to venture near.

While Mrs. Hamilton rattled on about the vicar's wife and the brouhaha she'd raised last market day, Sarah's mind flitted between the wild child Adrian, and the dangerous Mr. MacDougal. At what age, she wondered, did the male of the species become irredeemably lost to good society?

Perhaps they were born that way, she speculated with a smirk, and it fell to women to improve them.

Well, she was more than up to the task with Adrian Hawke. But as for Marshall MacDougal, he was off limits, she decided. Definitely off limits, and she'd best remember it.

Marsh managed to land two fine trout and one decent-sized pike. Had he truly been on holiday with nothing to trouble his mind, he might have hooked several more of their wilier brethren. But his mind was preoccupied—and not only with finding the truth about his father and the circumstances of his birth. Sarah Palmer, enticing minx that she was, had left him with the beginnings of an arousal that refused to subside.

That mouth had tasted even better than it looked, and that was saying a lot. He'd only wanted to shut her up—at least that's what he'd told himself at the time. After several hours' reflection, however, he knew it was more. He'd wanted to kiss her from the first moment he'd seen her yesterday, flouncing away from him at the posting inn with her hips swaying and her nose in the air. Haughty little brat.

She wasn't so haughty now, though, for he'd felt her lips open under his, and felt her body go soft and willing—if only for a few moments. But it was long enough to have aroused him even further. It aroused him now to recall the intensity of their encounter.

It was only that he'd been too long without any sort of female companionship, he told himself as he pulled his line of fish out of the water and hung them over the butt end of his pole. Though he'd love to silence that mouth again—and with more than merely kisses—he knew that was unlikely to happen. Women like Sarah Palmer—ladies of her sort—might tease a man with a secret smile or a stolen kiss here and there. But they seldom delivered the goods. Especially the virginal ones, which number he was fairly certain Sarah Palmer still belonged.

If he wanted any relief from the ache in his breeches, he'd have to find it from some doxy.

Meanwhile, he had other matters to attend to, so with an effort he turned his thoughts to his main purpose for his fishing expedition. He had decided to present himself at the kitchen door of Byrde Manor, give his catch to the cook by way of thanks, and see what he might learn from the back door that he had not learned at the front.

He'd been simmering with barely repressed anger when first he'd approached the house this morning. Now, as he rode up the drive, he studied it with a more observant eye. Neat, well maintained. The manor house was not large by English standards, yet it was still substantial. And old. Older than anything in Boston or Washington. The gravel drive crunched beneath his saddle mount's heavy measured tread.

Despite what he'd told Miss Palmer about viewing the architectural treasures of the area, Marsh did not generally care for old buildings. After all, the construction portion of his business was one of his most profitable ventures.

But as he stared at the house slowly revealed beyond the trees, he had to admit that there was something compelling about the place. The nearer he came to it, the harder his heart pounded. But not because of the architecture. His father may have lived here—he might still do so. And then what of other relatives? Grandparents. Uncles and aunts? Cousins? How big was his family?

Did they know about Maureen MacDougal and the child she'd raised in America?

He scanned the house, two stories of gray stone with freshly painted windows and three chimneys with ornamental pots piercing the low, undulating tile roof. Moss tinted the walls green in a few shaded areas. But the place looked well tended and fairly prosperous. Though hardly grand, it was a house anyone might reasonably want to possess.

Did he have a legal claim to it?

His jaw tightened. He would find that out soon enough, and if he did, he would pursue that claim no matter who opposed him. He'd had enough of his heritage stolen from him, and his poor mother had had her whole life ruined. It seemed only fitting that those who had benefited in the past should suffer in the future.

Beyond the kitchen garden a laundress gathered linens from the line, watching as he rode into the service yard. A boy with an armful of wood dropped it beside the door stoop, then dashed inside. "A gentleman's comin'! Cook. Cook! A gentleman's comin', an' to the back door!"

Two women appeared at once in the doorway, the aproned cook and her kerchiefed helper, plus the same lad peering out between them.

Marsh tipped his hat. "I thought, by way of thanks to your master and mistress, that I would make a gift of these fish, which I had the great pleasure of taking from their stretch of the river."

The cook wiped her reddened hands on the skirt of her apron. "Very good, sir. Very good. But the family ain't presently t'home."

Disappointed, Marsh murmured, "I see."

"Shall I call the housekeeper?" the woman added.

"No. There's no need," Marsh replied. In truth, he was

more likely to learn details of the Byrde family through lesser servants than through the housekeeper, who was certain to be smarter and more loyal than this simple trio. "Please relay to Mr. Byrde my thanks, and I hope all of you will enjoy the fruits of my day's sport."

He handed down the fish, which the cook prodded the boy to collect from him.

"Thank you, sir. Thank you. But 'tis Lord and Lady Hawke," the cook said, bobbing her head apologetically as she corrected him.

Lord and Lady Hawke? Marsh considered that surprising bit of information. Was Cameron Byrde a lord of the realm? Marsh frowned. The British class system was an enigma to any true American. Surnames *and* title names. As far as he was concerned, this business of titles was a joke. In his book all men were created equal, and he would let no man lord it over him, least of all a spineless cad who would use and abandon an innocent young woman like his mother.

"Well. Give my regards to Lord and Lady Hawke," he said, trying not to choke on the words. "When do you expect them back?"

The boy started to say something, only to be silenced by one stern look from the cook. She shoved him and her silent assistant behind her before she answered. "I'm sure I do not know the plans milord and lady make. But I can send for Mrs. Hamilton. She's housekeeper here."

"Thank you, but I wouldn't want to interrupt her." With another tip of his hat, Marsh turned his animal, and at the same unhurried pace, he made his way out of the yard and headed back to the river road to Kelso. But though his pace was calm, inside tension held Marsh in a taut grip. Lord Hawke? Was that his father? Cameron Byrde, Lord Hawke—and some frivolous society woman his wife? Some woman he considered suitable in a way simple Maureen MacDougal could never have been?

Marsh stewed and seethed during his short ride to Kelso. If only the cook had been more forthcoming. But she'd been leery of him and though he'd deemed it best not to pump her, he'd had to bite his tongue.

Damn! He was a coarse American to the likes of Sarah Palmer, and a high-and-mighty gentleman to the sort of people who served her and her ilk. Was there no class in Britain that fell in-between the two? No middle-class folks independent of the great landowners, who were at liberty to speak the truth as they saw fit?

His stomach growled, for he'd missed the midday meal. As he approached the Cock and Bow, he was hoping the landlady had something left to tide him over until suppertime. Then he spied a familiar-looking horse, a pretty sorrel mare, and all thoughts of food vanished. The animal stood alongside an expansive cottage with deep eaves and roses climbing up the walls. Was this where Sarah Palmer lived, not a stone's throw from his own temporary quarters?

One side of his mouth curved up in a sardonic grin. Perhaps, after a quick wash-up, he would make it his business to find out.

# CHAPTER

# 5

SARAH felt much better. She'd ridden into town to post a letter to her mother and to call on the vicar and his new wife. She could have taken the curricle, however for her one of the pleasures of the borderlands was the different set of rules that governed young women. Here, if she rode astride, it might be considered unusual, but it was by no means shocking. Well, Agnes had been shocked. But the woman had been wise enough to keep her opinion to herself.

So Sarah had taken the refreshed mare and come into town to do her duty as sister to the predominant landowner in this part of the Tweed River valley.

Now, as their visit was winding down, Mrs. Liston, the vicar's wife, smiled at Sarah. That smile faded a little, however, when they stepped into the yard and she spied not a carriage, but a mare tethered outside the garden. "You must plan to attend the subscription ball tomorrow evening, Miss Palmer. I'm certain Mr. Liston would be pleased to retrieve you in his carriage. Woodford Court is not so very far," she added most solicitously. Beside her Mr. Liston smiled and nodded, but he said nothing.

Sarah gave her a bland smile. "I'm sure I could not think of inconveniencing him so. Besides, I'm staying at Byrde Manor, not Woodford Court."

"Really?" Mrs. Liston looked momentarily nonplussed. "But Woodford Court is so much grander."

"Indeed it is. But I prefer Byrde Manor. Well, then. Good day."

"But what of the ball?" Mrs. Liston went on. "You will need some sort of escort. You cannot mean to arrive alone."

"I'm sure I shall manage," Sarah answered, her smile beginning to strain. She understood now Mrs. Hamilton's remarks about the vicar's new wife. Mrs. Liston was as pretentious as the vicar was simple, and as pushy as he was mild. Sarah started at a determined pace for the horse.

"Perhaps I may call on you?" Mrs. Liston continued, still trailing after Sarah. "I should so like to hear the latest news from London."

"How nice that would be . . ." The rest of Sarah's words petered out at the sight of the man striding purposefully toward her.

Marshall MacDougal.

Dear God! Surely he did not mean to reveal her shameless behavior to the vicar!

To her relief—and chagrin—Mr. MacDougal did not acknowledge her at all, save with a tip of his hat to them all. Instead, he addressed Mr. Liston, as very well he ought.

"Good day, Mr. Liston. May I introduce myself? I am Marshall MacDougal, come lately to Kelso from America for a visit. The innkeeper at the Cock and Bow suggested I present myself to you as a new parishioner."

It took all Sarah's willpower to bite her tongue. A new parishioner indeed! But sweet-natured Mr. Liston was unaware of the dubious nature of his new acquaintance. He beamed up at the scoundrel and in short order introduced both Sarah and his wife to the man.

To Sarah's relief, Mr. MacDougal appeared determined to display only his very best behavior. "How do you do, Mrs. Liston. Miss Palmer."

When he bowed over Mrs. Liston's hand, setting the woman to fluttering, Sarah's eyes narrowed. The wretch! He was equally circumspect toward her. Though he held her gloved hand a little too long, it was not enough for Mrs. Liston to notice. But it was long enough, unfortunately, to cause Sarah's heart to hammer within her chest. She snatched her hand back, then knotted them both behind her back, fuming all the while.

At least they had their "proper" introduction out of the way, she reminded herself. At least she no longer had to worry about him embarrassing her on that score.

But then he spoiled everything when he stared too deeply into her eyes. As before, their gazes did not cling long enough for Mrs. Liston to notice. But the impact on Sarah was nevertheless devastating.

She took an awkward step back, feeling short of breath and disoriented. Her stomach clutched just as it had when he'd kissed her, and she had to swallow a little gasp of dismay. Wretched, wretched man. How could he affect her so?

She made an abbreviated farewell and a hasty exit. But she was well aware of Marshall MacDougal's gaze upon her back, as real as a caress. Again she stifled a groan. Not until she had ridden down the street and around the corner did she remember to breathe. And even then, it was a very shaky breath.

Good Lord! What was it about that man? He was rude and hateful and much too bold to suit her. Yet still he managed to rattle her right down to the toes of her Spanish leather riding boots!

Her fingers tightened around the reins and on impulse she leaned low over the mare's neck. At once the animal responded. As one, they flew down the main street toward the river.

Only when they were almost at the turn in the road that led to Byrde Manor did she remember her intention to call upon Adrian. She shifted her weight and the nimble creature beneath her at once shifted direction. Left and across the old stone bridge they thundered, unfazed by two hounds that gave halfhearted pursuit.

Too quickly they reached the scattering of cottages where Adrian and his mother lived. When Sarah dismounted, she was still flustered. And when Estelle Kendrick came to the door, then frowned, it did nothing to improve her mood.

Was there no one in all of Scotland who was pleasant and uncomplicated?

"Hello, Estelle. It's Sarah. Sarah Palmer."

"I know who you are." Estelle crossed her arms over her rather generous chest and leaned one shoulder against the doorjamb. "What I'm wonderin' is why you're here."

Sarah flicked her left palm with the ends of the reins. "I hoped to call upon Adrian, for I understand he has returned from school. Is he perchance at home?"

"No."

The fine hairs on the back of Sarah's neck raised up in irritation. Just as Mrs. Hamilton had warned, Estelle had a chip on her shoulder that no amount of civility seemed able to pierce. Well, if Neville's financial support had not worked, nor Olivia's many attempts at friendship, Sarah's efforts now were not likely to win her over either.

For Adrian's sake, however, Sarah resolved to remain civil, no matter the other woman's rudeness. "I see. Do you expect him to return home soon?"

Estelle shrugged. "Hard to say. You know how high-spirited young men can be."

*Especially if the young man in question has a mother who encourages him to think solely of himself.* But to Estelle she only said, "Would you be good enough to tell him that I called? And also that I'm staying at Byrde Manor and would welcome a visit."

"I'll tell him. Oh, yes, I'll tell him," the woman said. Then her mouth twisted in an unpleasant sneer. "An' you tell your sister that I don't appreciate the way she's turned Neville away from my boy!"

"Turned him away?" Sarah glared at Estelle, appalled by the woman's narrow view of the situation. "Neville has been nothing but good to Adrian, and with Olivia's full support. From what I hear, 'tis you—" She broke off, remembering almost too late her vow to be civil. It was pointless anyway to argue with such an unpleasant creature as Estelle Kendrick.

" 'Tis I who love the boy," the woman stated, her brown

eyes burning with dislike. "An' he loves me. So there's no use you comin' around here, doin' your duty all proper-like. I said I'd give him your message. So whyn't you go now, Miss Sarah Palmer?"

The woman drawled out that last with such contempt Sarah was tempted to slap her. It took every bit of her self-restraint to turn away, remount her horse, and with a curt nod just ride off.

Once outside the cottage yard, however, she was rewarded for her restraint. For who should come cantering up the road on a sweaty, heavily muscled animal but a lanky, dark-haired youth who bore an unmistakable likeness to his Uncle Neville Hawke?

With a cheeky insolence that made her frown, his clear blue eyes swept over her, head to toe and back again. "Well, hello to you." He doffed his hat, winked, and gave her an appreciative grin.

She straightened in the saddle and gave him a stern look. "Hello, Adrian. I suppose you don't remember me. I'm Sarah Palmer. Olivia's sister."

"Sarah Palmer?" From cocky youth to pleased youngster, in an instant his expression altered. "Sarah! Of course I remember you. How grand you look. But why are you come all the way up here to the hinterlands, and in the middle of the season?"

Not much mollified, she gave him a steady look. "I might ask as much of you. Why aren't you at school impressing the tutors there with your grasp of Latin and French and mathematics?"

He had the good grace to look embarrassed. "Me and Eton, we just don't mix. Too much work." His grip on the reins tightened, causing his horse to back up before he brought it back under control. "Too many snobs."

She studied the boy, taking in the dark, wavy hair falling over his brow, and the straight nose and well-formed lips. He was going to break many a young woman's heart, she decided, many a heart before all was said and done. But if he'd inherited as much of the Hawke family intelligence as he had their striking good looks, the classes at Eton could not possibly have been too difficult for him.

"Is that what you shall tell your Uncle Neville when he returns from Glasgow, that Eton was just too hard? Somehow I don't think that shall go over very well with him. And what of this horse?" she went on, not allowing him time to answer. "I assume Neville and Olivia gave him to you. How will you explain it to them should the animal come up lame from your madcap racing about, or if the poor creature should catch a lung infection from improper care?"

Though resentment sprang into Adrian's eyes, the twin spots of color in his cheeks revealed his chagrin. "I'm planning to tend to him directly," he protested. "I only stopped to speak to you."

Sarah sighed. "I'm sorry, Adrian. Despite how it sounds, I did not come here to scold you. Rather, I wanted to invite you to visit me at Byrde Manor. I'm staying there while Livvie and Neville are away."

When his jaw jutted forward as if he meant to decline, she hurried on. "I promise not to harangue you about Eton. I promise. Perhaps we could go riding tomorrow afternoon and you can show me the countryside. After all, I haven't been here in several years," she added, giving him her prettiest, most sincere smile.

It was almost ludicrous how swiftly his stiff jaw softened into a grin—and a little alarming as well. Though Sarah thought of him as a child still, a boy six years her junior, the glint of masculine appreciation she saw in his eyes now was definitely that of a lad on the verge of manhood.

"I'd be pleased to call on you, Miss Sarah."

She pursed her lips and nodded. "Very well. Tomorrow, then." But as she turned her mare and headed back toward Byrde Manor, Sarah had the sinking sensation that civilizing Adrian Hawke was going to be considerably more difficult than she'd originally imagined.

* * *

Back in Kelso, Marsh gazed around the vicar's little office. Along one wall a tall oak bookcase bulged with the books of parish records dating back several centuries. Births, christenings, marriages, deaths—and every conceivable contract in between. Sales of land and livestock. Barters of produce and products.

"I apologize that I must depart just as you've arrived," Mr. Liston was saying to him. "But one of my parishioners is very ill. Mrs. Liston can help you," he added, glancing at his wife, who stood in the doorway eagerly nodding.

"Thank you," Marsh said, hardly aware when the vicar took his leave. Somewhere in this room might be the answer to all his questions.

"Just what sort of family records are you seeking, Mr. MacDougal?" Mrs. Liston bustled about, wiping down the spines of the leather-bound tomes with her linen handkerchief. "My word, but the dust is terrible in Kelso. Just terrible. Not like York, where I am from."

Marsh chose his words carefully, for he was not yet ready to reveal the true purpose of his search. "My dear mother, God rest her soul, may have been born here. She told me little of her home in Scotland, but she did mention Kelso once or twice. I was hoping to find a birth listing, or a christening which might then lead me to her family."

"I see. What was her name?"

Marsh hesitated. It would not do to tell her his mother was a MacDougal, for that would imply she had never wed. Nor could he call her Byrde. Not yet. He pulled out one of the burgundy and gold-trimmed record books. "Shouldn't I begin with the year, since records are listed chronologically?" He opened the book. "What a neat penmanship. Is it yours?" He gave her an earnest smile.

A faint pink blush crept into her wan cheeks. When she giggled and pressed her handkerchief to her mouth, she left a smudge of book dust on her chin. "My word, no. Mr. Liston tends to these records himself. He's most particular, you know. As well he ought to be. It's really too bad," she added, lowering her voice to a confidential level. "Over at the Catholic church the priest is not nearly so careful or accurate."

"Yes. That is just too bad," he murmured. "I wonder. Might I trouble you for a cup of tea?"

To his relief, she was eager to accommodate him. By the time she returned, he was well immersed in records dating back over fifty years. An hour later when she returned with a refill, he'd discovered nothing about his mother, but plenty about his father. Born in 1771, wed to Augusta Linden in 1797. Marsh's teeth clenched. Cameron Byrde had married this Augusta woman *after* the birth of his son in America. And well after his first marriage to Maureen MacDougal.

If only he could find some proof of that earlier marriage!

Agitated, Marsh's gaze skimmed the faded ink notations, running down the page until his eye caught on another entry:

> Cameron Byrde. Died in London, July 9, 1804. Buried in the Byrde family plot, July 16, 1804. Leaving a wife and one girl child.

The blood rushed from his head and, stunned, Marsh sat back in the high-backed armchair.

He could hardly believe it, and yet the words were clear. His father was dead. There would be no revenge on Cameron Byrde for the cruelty he'd done to Maureen MacDougal because the man was already dead.

He had been for twenty-three years.

Then the second part of the entry struck him, and the blood surged back with a rush. One girl child. That meant Marsh had a sister. A half-sister.

"Could I tempt you with scones and lemon curd, Mr. MacDougal? They're fresh baked this morning."

Only half aware, Marsh looked up to see Mrs. Liston standing in the doorway holding a heaping plate in front of her. His stomach clenched, rebelling at the thought of food, rebelling at the awful truth with which he'd just been confronted. He had a half-sister!

Fortunately, good sense kicked in, squelching any outward reaction to this new and bitter turn of events. His eyes locked on the vicar's wife, who wanted so much to help him. He cleared his throat and forced a smile. "You are too kind. Perhaps you can also assuage my curiosity, Mrs. Liston. I see here a listing for a Cameron Byrde. I applied to the housekeeper at Byrde Manor yesterday to fish along their riverbank. Is this the same family?"

She put down the plate of scones and bent low to squint at the entry. "Cameron Byrde," she mused. She gave him an apologetic smile. "I am not from these parts, you see. I am from York, come here only last year to wed my cousin, Mr. Liston. But Cameron Byrde," she went on. "That sounds familiar. I see here that he died in 1804. Oh, yes. I remember now. Yes. He is the one. Drowned, I believe. A very sad case."

Sadder than she knew. "What of his wife and other family? Are they the ones to whom I owe my thanks for the sport I enjoyed yesterday? They have such a pleasant and prosperous-looking estate," he added, hoping to disguise the intensity of his interest.

"Well, yes. I suppose it is pleasant. And I suppose it is prosperous as well. But Byrde Manor is nothing compared to Woodford Court."

"Does Mrs. Byrde live there still?" he said, before she could meander too far afield with the comparison.

"Lud, no. I've never met her meself. But I'm told she's a grand lady now, livin' in London. She wasn't Scottish, you know. She's English like me; of that I am certain."

Yes, grand indeed, Marsh seethed. Cameron Byrde had married a woman nothing like sweet, simple Maureen MacDougal. But he tamped down his fury. "What of the daughter?" he went on.

"The daughter. Let's see. The daughter. Oh." She lit up. "That was her daughter you just met. When you arrived, she was just leaving."

Marsh stared at her, not certain he'd heard her right. "That was Mrs. Byrde's daughter?"

"Oh, yes. I'm certain of that, for she brought Mr. Liston greetings from her mother. She's a countess now. Lady Augusta Acton."

A buzz had started in Marsh's ears. This could not be right. "But her name was Palmer, not Byrde," he pointed out, trying to refute her words. "Sarah Palmer."

"Well." Again she lowered her voice, as if someone else might overhear her. "It seems Lady Acton has been wed four times. Imagine that! Four times! Widowed three times, of course. Perhaps Miss Palmer took her stepfather's name." She straightened up and thrust the plate at him. "Do you want lemon curd with your scones?"

Marsh took a scone. He ate it, hardly conscious of what he did, and washed it down with tepid tea devoid of milk or lemon. What he needed was a tall glass of whiskey.

He bent back to the books and, after fussing a bit more, Mrs. Liston left. But there were no other entries to be found for any Byrdes except for a land lease agreement with a Neville Hawke in 1818.

Then again, the one entry he'd found had been sufficient enough to tilt his entire world off center.

His father was dead and he had a half-sister.

And though he'd anticipated that there might be several such siblings in the offing, never in his wildest, most depraved imaginings had he considered that he might lust after one of them.

# CHAPTER
# 6

ADRIAN handled the phaeton and two like an expert. When he'd come to call in the early afternoon, he'd insisted on escorting her to the country dance in Kelso that evening. A vast improvement, in Sarah's opinion, over the vicar and his curious long-nose of a wife. Now, as the carriage turned smartly into the town square, which glowed beneath dozens of lanterns, the lad pulled up before the mayor's residence, then leaped down with boyish enthusiasm. He appeared all proper manners and decorum, however, when he assisted her down.

She smiled at him. "Why, thank you, Adrian."

He beamed right back. "You see? And you thought I was a hooligan. Confess it, you did. But as you see, I also can play the gentleman. I can show a leg with the best of them." He paused and grinned before adding, "When I want to."

With his eyes so bright and glinting with mischief, Sarah had no choice but to smile back and shake her head. He was too handsome tonight, dressed in his best midnight-blue waistcoat with his white cravat tied in an elaborate knot, and his tall boots polished until they positively gleamed. He was already as tall as a man, though he still retained the gangliness of youth.

She was not alone in that assessment, for a pair of young girls clad in pretty pastel muslin dresses approached the front door arm in arm, giggling and glancing back at Adrian. When he acted as if he did not notice, Sarah nudged him. "Are you acquainted with those young ladies?"

He spared them a brief look, then gave an offhanded shrug. "Just some girls from over the hill."

Just some girls with eyes for handsome young men, Sarah thought as they joined the queue of people entering Mayor Dinkerson's spacious abode. "Please don't feel you need to shepherd me about, Adrian," she whispered to him. "I've been to many a dance in my day, and I know enough people to occupy myself and gain whatever other introductions I desire."

But would she see the man to whom she'd been both properly and improperly introduced yesterday?

At the thought of Marshall MacDougal, a wicked little hum began to tickle down low in her belly. It was annoying and frustrating and mystifying as well. Really, but the man was nothing but an ill-mannered wretch. She should not respond to him so.

But, unfortunately, she did. And as she greeted Mayor Dinkerson, she couldn't help glancing about for the American.

He was not there. The evening progressed with introductions to the mayor's son and daughter-in-law, then to the wool broker, the solicitor's two daughters and their families, and on and on to every person of any consequence in Kelso. Yet despite the bevy of people more than eager to greet the sister of the wealthiest landowner in the area, Sarah was distracted every time the front door opened.

By ten o'clock she had begun to grow discouraged. He was not coming.

It was all so confusing, she fretted as Mrs. Liston cornered her and embarked on a long, boring story. A part of her dreaded seeing Marshall MacDougal, for to even recall the power of those few stolen kisses terrified her all over again. Yet at the same time she perversely yearned to see him. The very thought of conversing with him again sent a scary thrill shooting up her backbone.

Their brief meeting at the vicar's house had only intensified that feeling. At least they were now properly introduced. He hadn't embarrassed her then, so why should she worry that he might do so now?

Indeed, the more Sarah thought about it, the more she wanted to see him. Forgotten was her vow to avoid him at all costs. Surely in such a public venue she was perfectly safe speaking with him. Or even dancing with him.

"Careful, Sarah," she muttered under her breath. She was treading on dangerous ground—or she would be if he were here. But he was not and she ought to be relieved.

She was relieved, she told herself. She would force herself to be relieved. So she smiled brightly at Mr. Goodson, the portly squire from over Ancrum way, who'd gone to fetch her a glass of wine. "Oh. You are too kind," she gushed. She patted him on the arm as she accepted the glass, a gesture she knew was certain to increase his attentions to her.

A short silence fell between them and she fancied she could almost hear him dredging up his courage. Finally he asked, "Would you like to dance?" his ears turning pink in the process.

"How kind you are to rescue me from becoming a wallflower."

"But you promised the next cotillion to me," Adrian interrupted, appearing from behind them. With the grace a court dandy would have envied, he somehow insinuated himself between her and Mr. Goodson. He held his arm out to her, then grinned at the other man. "You can have the next one, Goody."

Sarah had no choice but to take the lad's arm. But as they lined up for the dance, She gave Adrian a stern look. "That was not well done."

"What?" he protested. "You had promised me the dance. Don't you remember?"

"Yes, I remember it well. But a gentleman does not wait until the music is already warming up to claim his next partner. It is rude to her. Nor should you have instructed Mr. Goodson that he may have my next dance, for you do not know whether I have already granted that dance to someone else." They bowed as the music began. "And lastly, you should not have called him Goody in my presence. By rights you shouldn't call him that ever, for he is your elder and deserving of your respect."

If Adrian was at all chagrined by her criticisms, it was banished at her last remark. "Everybody calls him Goody. So will you, once you get to know him." Then, spying her disapproving expression, he relented. "All right, all right. I'll do better the next time. I promise. Only stop frowning at me as if I'm a naughty lad."

*That's precisely what you are.* But Sarah kept silent, for she understood Adrian's desire to be treated as an adult. She well remembered how rabid she'd been to abandon the schoolroom during those last two years before her coming out. But London society was not nearly so lenient as country society and she'd had no choice but to wait. Here in the countryside, however, children were allowed to join the adults in all sorts of social events that they would be banished from in town. Certainly a fourteen-year-old like Adrian would not be dancing like this among his elders.

He was dancing, though, and he was quite good at it. When she remarked as much, he grinned. "My mum insisted. Says all the girls love dancin'. Do you?"

"Indeed I do. Is your mother not coming to the dance?" she inquired, for she'd not yet spied the unpleasant Estelle.

"She'll be here eventually," he retorted, his smile fading.

Now, what did that somber look signify? Sarah wondered as she did her portion of the movement. Didn't he want his mother here?

A half hour later she had her answer. For Estelle arrived on the arm of a tall, thick-waisted brute of a fellow. He was properly dressed, with his hair slicked down, but he had a rough look about him. As for Estelle, she was outfitted in a brilliant blue satin gown that displayed a vast amount of her overly developed chest.

Sarah couldn't help but stare, for the woman's bosom looked very near to popping free of the straining fabric. Everyone else seemed to anticipate the very same event, for every male eye and most of the female ones too fastened on those remarkable breasts.

For a moment Sarah was annoyed with herself for choosing a rather ordinary gown for her first outing in Kelso society. She hadn't wanted to flaunt herself, neither her wealth nor her knowledge of current town style. It seemed, however, that she'd succeeded a little too well. When compared to Estelle's eye-popping ensemble, her own modestly cut summer-green gown looked so sweet as to be almost sickening.

Her brow creased in a faint frown. Really, but that woman had no shame.

Then Sarah's eyes found Adrian standing near one of the windows, and she recognized at once the larger problem that Estelle's appearance created. Adrian was old enough to understand exactly what all the other men thought when they gawked at his mother that way. He was old enough to understand about lust, and if his scowl was any indication, he didn't like it at all.

Excusing herself from the company of Mrs. Dinkerson and the tiresome Mrs. Liston, she threaded her way through the crowd, angling toward Adrian. Though she did not comprehend all the undercurrents of the situation, she was certain that Adrian needed an ally.

But he frowned when he spied her, and like the moody boy he still was, he slipped out through the open window and disappeared into the lavender night. She stared after him in consternation, but when a silky, malicious voice intruded on her thoughts, Sarah's consternation turned to dislike. Estelle.

"I should think he's a mite young for the likes of you, Miss Palmer. No matter that my boy is a handsome lad, he's still no match for a fast town trick like yourself."

As Sarah turned to face the other woman, outwardly she appeared composed. But inside she was seething. "Nor is he any match for a selfish mother who thinks nothing of embarrassing him in front of everyone he knows." She stared pointedly at Estelle's thrusting bosom. "Couldn't you cover those things, if only for his sake?"

For a moment Estelle appeared to be struck dumb. Clearly she had not expected to get just as good as she gave. But when she recovered, it was equally clear that her dislike for Sarah had jelled into something much colder.

"William likes them," she boasted, clasping the arm of her silent companion. "As does every other male in the room."

"Yes. My point precisely. Every man except the one who should matter the most." And with that Sarah glided away, holding her head as high as if she were the queen. But her aplomb was superficial, for she'd never wanted so much to claw another woman's eyes out!

From that unpleasant confrontation the evening slid steadily downhill. While she was finally partnering Mr. Goodson, she spied Marshall MacDougal standing in the foyer. She nearly tripped and fell, and afterward had to concentrate mightily to follow the steps of the dance. Though she continued to honor her dance obligations, she watched surreptitiously as he was introduced around by Mr. Liston. Even Estelle Kendrick was introduced to him, and Sarah had to bite her tongue when she saw his gaze lower to that monstrous mound of pale flesh the woman practically thrust in his face. Her stomach clenched violently at the unwelcome image of him falling face first into that deep cleavage and never coming up again.

"I . . . I believe I need some air," she murmured to her partner of the moment. "If you will excuse me?"

But a quarter hour in the window of the second-floor ladies' resting room did nothing at all to calm Sarah's nerves. Indeed, when she spied a group of boys in the side yard sneaking drinks, then pushing and shoving and laughing too loud, she felt decidedly worse. Adrian was not there among the fellows of his own age, nor was he mingling with the adults downstairs.

The poor boy. He fit in nowhere, she realized. No father, and a slattern for a mother. No wonder he'd fled Eton. He did not fit there either. He might be educated as a gentleman, but he had not yet learned how to escape his less-than-sterling heritage. More than ever she vowed to befriend him. But first she had to find him.

So, with a resolute sigh, she rose from the window seat, smoothed her skirts, then for good measure tugged the seed-pearl-embroidered neckline of her gown as low as it would go. The fact that the dressmaker's mirror in the corner revealed no cleavage at all—not even a little shadow of one—only depressed her further.

Why should she care that her bosom was perfectly ordinary when compared to that woman's? Adrian was her project, not Marshall MacDougal or any other man here tonight. As far as she cared, they could all smother in Estelle's overabundant flesh. In fact, she hoped they did.

Marsh spied Sarah the moment she descended the stairway. He'd come to the mayor's soiree because of the opportunity it gave him to meet a large number of people. But he'd known he would probably have to face Sarah Palmer, and so he'd procrastinated until he could procrastinate no longer. He'd braced himself for revulsion when he saw her, determined to bury any stray remnant of attraction that might still linger. As much as the idea repulsed him, it seemed she was his sister—his half-sister—sired of the same father as himself. To even recall their kiss sent a sick shiver through him.

Yet for the first few seconds after he saw her, he forgot their unsavory relationship. For the first few seconds he simply stared at her, struck by this third facet of her persona. The arrogant scarlet-caped beauty of the carriage; the earthy equestrian alongside the river; and now this vision of innocent perfection.

Mayor Dinkerson, who'd taken over Mr. Liston's task of introducing Marsh around, nudged him in the side. "I suppose you'll be wanting an introduction to her as well?"

Marsh saw the twinkle in the man's eye just in time to prevent himself from making an unwise reply. He cleared his throat. "We've . . . ah, we've already met. The vicar," he added, when the man seemed to expect more details.

"Aha. You couldn't know this, of course, but Miss Palmer is the very image of her mother, though her hair is darker. But the eyes, the smile, and the bearing . . ." The man gazed up at Sarah, smiling. "Yes, that Augusta was quite a beauty."

Augusta. The mother. The one who'd stolen Cameron Byrde from Marsh's sweet, trusting mother. In that moment Sarah's beauty became distasteful in Marsh's eye, the false beauty of the devil, ugly on the inside, where it counted.

Unfortunately, the mayor had met Sarah at the bottom of the stairs and now was leading her back to join their group.

Marsh reacted without thinking, almost as if in a panic. He spun abruptly on his heel and headed toward the first familiar face he spied, that of Mr. Halbrecht, the innkeeper, as it happened, who gestured to him with one beefy hand.

"Mr. MacDougal. Hello. Hello. Over here." His already florid complexion had deepened to a ruddy glow. It was either too much to drink or else the woman he was presently conversing with, Marsh decided. For she was a glittering bird among the otherwise more sedately clad villagers. A bright blue glittering bird with a chest that would do a ship's figurehead proud.

"Miss Estelle Kendrick," the innkeeper said. "May I present Mr. Marshall MacDougal, come to us all the way from the wilds of America, he has."

"We've already been introduced," she cooed. But she curtsied again as he bowed, providing him with an even better view of her outsized chest. There was no ruching in her bodice like his mother had often sewed for one of her employers. That was all warm, trembling flesh—and available for closer inspection, he surmised, if the sultry look in Miss Kendrick's eyes was any indication.

Though he'd not come here tonight with an idea of seduction, Marsh felt a surge of relief to find another woman—any woman—to distract him from Sarah Palmer. So he grinned at the woman and said a silent thank-you to

Mr. Halbrecht. "What a pleasure to meet you again, Miss Kendrick. Had I known the warm welcome awaiting me in Kelso, I would have come years ago."

She grinned right back at him. "An' I wish you had. There's no making up for the past, but let's not waste the present. Aren't you goin' to invite me to dance?"

"But I was hoping to do that meself," Mr. Halbrecht put in.

"Oh, Henry." She placed a hand on the innkeeper's sleeve and squeezed. "You and I, we've danced a hundred times before. An' I promise to dance with you tonight. Only later." She smiled up at Marsh, an expression that was almost predatory. "Right now I want to dance with Mr. MacDougal."

Marsh had no intention of declining, and when it proved to be a waltz, he was not sorry. At every turn Miss Kendrick's bountiful bosom brushed up against his chest. He fancied he could feel her oversized nipples protruding through her bodice and his waistcoat, and he had to fight the urge to look down into the warm, dark cavern between those breasts.

"Are you staying here permanent-like?" she asked, still smiling. Her teeth were slightly crooked, he noticed, with a dull cast to them.

"No. I'm merely visiting."

"Too bad. Oops!" She giggled, stumbling, then clinging to his arms so that her breasts squashed against his chest. Marsh promptly forgot about her teeth, and yet he was also put off by her blatant display. There was a lot to be said for subtlety in a woman. Certainly Sarah had not needed to resort to such—

He squelched the thought. He would not compare Estelle Kendrick to her. In truth, he didn't want to think of Sarah Palmer as a woman at all. She was his half-sister and even though that was a distasteful thought, it was preferable to his previous thoughts about her.

So he concentrated on enjoying Estelle Kendrick's lusty attentions, and when Sarah swept by in the arms of a brawny fellow, he refused to follow her with his eyes.

But he did not entirely succeed, for even a peripheral view of Sarah Palmer made him forget about the warm armful of woman he held. Working to ignore Sarah Palmer took all his energy.

And when Sarah Palmer's dance partner whirled her around to the far side of the room near the open terrace doors, he was nonetheless vitally aware of it.

But he didn't care, he told himself. He refused to care. It was a relief to have his view of her blocked by other dancers. Out of sight, out of mind.

So he forced himself to smile down at Miss Kendrick, availing himself once more of the view from above. The last few stanzas of the song seemed to last forever, though, and when his buxom partner suggested that she was a little overheated, something perverse in him jumped at the chance.

"Perhaps a little fresh air?" he suggested. "A turn in the garden?"

She grinned. "Ooh, love. I believe you've read my mind."

# CHAPTER 7

SARAH was hardly aware of the music, nor of her steps or her dance partner who so vigorously whirled her about the crowded dance floor. She still could not believe that Marshall MacDougal had snubbed her that way. No use to pretend it had been anything other than a very obvious snub. The cut direct. He'd watched her come down the stairs, seen the mayor approach her, then made a hasty exit before she could be led over to the small group that included him.

She did not understand.

Yesterday he'd been flirtatious. Indeed, with his bold kisses he'd seemed bent upon seduction. She'd been horrified, of course, but also secretly thrilled, especially after their proper introduction by the vicar. Certainly the last thing she would ever have anticipated tonight was his pointed avoidance of her.

How dare he!

She clenched her teeth together until they hurt. How dare he snub her? Ill-mannered boor! Ignorant American! Didn't he know that she was a great heiress, that she had been the toast of London for three seasons now?

*Yes. And what use is your vast fortune and all that social acumen? What use is any of it if you are lonely?*

Just that quickly did Sarah's outrage dissolve into misery. She thought about her mother's happy marriage, and her sister's. Why could she not find a wonderful man like Justin or Neville to fall madly in love with and marry? She wouldn't care if he was rich or poor. He could be a town dandy or somewhat the bumpkin, if only he loved her to distraction, and she loved him equally well.

"It's a little warm in here," her partner murmured as he spun her around.

"Yes," she absently replied. But she did not tend too closely to his words, for she was too busy looking for Mr. MacDougal and his dance partner, Estelle Kendrick. Estelle Kendrick in that dress meant to grace the form of a woman of considerably lesser attributes.

Bad enough he had snubbed her. He added insult to that injury, however, when he had led Estelle out to the dance floor, took her in his arms, and joined the circle of enthusiastic dancers. Sarah had not wanted to stare and she had pointedly turned away. Still, she had nearly choked on her outrage. He went out of his way to the point of rudeness to avoid her. Yet he danced eagerly with that . . . that thoroughly unpleasant creature.

To even recall it made her nostrils flare with distaste.

But she didn't care, she once more told herself. She didn't care at all. The two of them deserved one another. He was a rude cad and she a selfish, loose-moraled cat.

With a determined effort, Sarah ceased her ridiculous search of the crowded dance floor. With any luck they were gone and she wouldn't have to look at either of their spiteful faces. She gave her own partner a brilliant smile, brilliant but distracted. Let Estelle and that American ruffian dance. Let them do whatever it was they wanted to do, even out in the shadows. It didn't matter to her.

She was so intent on convincing herself of that fact that when Mr. Guinea pulled her a little nearer, she did not protest. And when he steered them out onto the dimly lit terrace, with its fragrant roses and flickering torchlight, she didn't give it a second thought.

" 'Tis a lovely night," he said, still holding her in his arms, though they had stopped dancing.

"Yes. Lovely," Sarah agreed. *If you happen to enjoy being snubbed by a man when you're the one who should be doing the snubbing.* She slipped gracefully out of his embrace and moved restlessly toward the balustrade.

Everyone must have seen how he avoided her. What

must they think? And why would he do such a thing anyway? Was it because of that horrible Estelle and her overdeveloped chest?

Sarah had never before doubted her own attractiveness. Any woman of even modest appearance seemed beautiful when she smiled and laughed and paid particular attention to a man. Her mother had drummed that message into her and she'd long ago come to know it was true. Smiling and laughing with a man was a skill she'd mastered before she'd even departed the schoolroom.

But it seemed Estelle had mastered it even better.

"You are very beautiful."

She jerked when Mr. Guinea's voice penetrated her sour thoughts. She gave him an automatic smile. "And you are very kind."

He moved nearer—a little too near—and she sidled away on the pretext of smelling a cluster of tightly furled roses. "These flowers must be lovely by day."

"They're nothing compared to you, Miss Palmer."

She looked up, dismayed by the admiring tenor of his voice. She hoped he did not think she'd come out here for any reason other than to cool off from the dancing.

But it was plain he did. His eyes were bright with the light of pursuit—and perhaps a trifle too much whiskey. And she, unfortunately, had backed into a dim and isolated corner of the terrace.

She stifled a groan. This was when a chaperone or even a disapproving maid would come in handy. Only she didn't have one, for Agnes was already gone to Carlisle, and a moody fourteen-year-old boy did not count. It was up to her to nip Mr. Guinea's ardor in the bud, before this evening progressed from bad to worse.

"You are very kind, Mr. Guinea," she repeated, angling herself toward the open ballroom doors. He shifted his bulk, however, effectively cutting off her path.

But Sarah had experience with men of his ilk. Even earls and dukes could not be entirely trusted—especially after they'd had a few glasses of strong spirits. She lifted her chin to an arrogant degree, narrowed her eyes, and stared up at him. Though her expression remained reasonably friendly, her voice was as stern as any governess's.

"I would like to go back inside, Mr. Guinea. Would you be good enough to escort me?"

"Aw. What's your hurry?" he complained, not moving an inch. "It's nice out here. We can talk. You know," he went on, "you've grown up just as pretty as your sister."

*What a crude, mannerless oaf!* "We can talk just as well inside. I insist we go. Now."

"In a minute."

"Now!" When he hesitated, she shoved at his chest, trying to push past him. But he didn't move and with one hand he caught her by the arm.

She knew at once that the time for social niceties was done. In the split second when he bent nearer to her, she regretted what she must do. She had not wanted to create a scene tonight. But there seemed no hope for it.

He lowered his head to kiss her; she lifted her arm to slap him.

But before she could let fly her hand, he let out a yelp and lurched backward so fast she stumbled against the stone balustrade. Was he that intimidated by her threat of violence?

Another man's low and threatening growl swiftly disavowed her of that foolish thought. "I suggest you go inside."

Marshall MacDougal!

Thank goodness! Sarah spun around. But when she spied Estelle just behind him, her relief fled. Had he actually come out here to rescue her, or was he just showing off for Estelle?

That subtlety became unimportant, however, when Mr. Guinea shoved to his feet and turned furiously on his unexpected foe. He raised his knotted fists at Mr. MacDougal. "I dunno who you are, mister, but you're not one to be ordering Clancy Guinea about." And with that he lashed out with a fearsome blow.

Sarah shrank back against the balustrade. This could not be happening!

But it was. Fortunately, Mr. MacDougal had ducked and shifted so that the other man's fist flew harmlessly past his head. His glance flickered momentarily over Sarah, then back to his enraged opponent. But it was long enough for Sarah to recognize how angry the American was at her. At her! So angry as to leave her stunned. What had she done to deserve such animosity?

Then Mr. Guinea lunged at Mr. MacDougal and she gasped. Beyond them Estelle clapped her hands and laughed. Dear God, they were going to fight!

As before, Marshall avoided the man, dancing aside, then shoving Mr. Guinea off his feet. "Stay down, man, else I will have no choice but to hurt you."

"Aw, hurt him, luv. It's the only thing a big oaf like him understands," Estelle threw in. She smirked at Sarah as if to say, *My man can take your man.* Though Sarah wanted neither of the two men, the woman's smugness still irritated her.

But Estelle's nastiness took a distant second to the physical conflict taking place in front of her. For Mr. Guinea faced Mr. MacDougal, fists at the ready. Two ruffians facing one another, Sarah decided, though it distressed her nonetheless.

She had sneaked out once to a boxing match in Cheapside. But that brutal display now seemed controlled compared to this spontaneous display of male aggression.

She turned away, not wanting to watch. Before she could reach the door, however, Mr. Guinea struck out. She heard the ugly sound of flesh thudding violently against flesh. Then someone dropped like a stone. Mr. Guinea, she saw when she looked back. Marshall MacDougal stood over him, grimacing and shaking his right fist.

"Son of a bitch," Marsh muttered. His knuckles stung like the devil. He scowled down at the inert clod at his feet. He hadn't wanted to fight the man—or any other man. So why had he inserted himself into Sarah Palmer's affairs?

He raised his gaze to find her staring at him, her face pale, her eyes huge. Her shock only deepened his scowl. He had not wanted to follow her out onto the terrace. Nor had he wanted to come to her rescue when her bully boy had tried to steal a kiss. After all, what man wouldn't try to steal a kiss from those tart, delectably pouting lips? He'd done the same thing the first chance he'd had.

No, he hadn't wanted to get involved with her at all tonight. Bad enough he was tied to her by the blood of their amoral father.

But he'd lost all control when he'd watched her dance out onto the terrace. Blinded by emotions he did not want to examine too closely, he'd promptly danced his own partner out another door. Then he'd seen Sarah trapped by that scoundrel and he'd been consumed by the need to beat the man senseless.

It had been five years since he'd retired from his short but profitable stint in the boxing ring. Yet that old urge to completely vanquish his opponent had roused instantly to a fever pitch.

Thank God the man stayed down. For even now it took every bit of his self-control not to hurt the oaf.

Instead, he turned those raging emotions on the woman at the center of it all, the reckless beauty—whose beauty he must force himself not to notice ever again.

"You are a menace," he began in a low, furious voice. "To yourself and anyone who comes near you!"

"Me? Why, you—"

"Hey!" Estelle broke in. "Don't you be worryin' about her, luv. Estelle is here to lick your wounds for you."

The fact that she managed to endow the word *lick* with such emotion—and that he was not in the least interested—made Marsh even angrier. He glared at Sarah. "I suggest you get inside before anyone finds out what trouble you've caused."

"*I've* caused?" She was practically sputtering with rage, and with her cheeks flushed and her eyes flashing, she was the picture of affronted dignity. Though Estelle's warm bosom pressed against his arm, it was Sarah who roused his lust.

But he refused to lust after his own sister!

"Go!" he roared at her.

At the same moment another man leaped over the garden wall and onto the terrace. "Here! Don't you be shouting at her!" He glared at Marsh, then at Estelle. "Ma?" The fellow's expression turned to confusion. "Ma? What's goin' on here?"

It was a boy, Marsh realized. A boy who gaped, first at the fallen Mr. Guinea, who'd begun to stir, then at Marsh, who still stood over the ill-mannered brute.

"What's goin' on here?" he repeated. He scowled at Estelle. "Ma? What have you gone and done now?"

"Me? It's her as has caused all this trouble. Her and her loose London ways."

The boy surged forward. "Don't you be ugly to her!"

"An' don't you talk back to your own ma, Adrian Hawke."

Marsh glared at the boy, but he directed his words to Estelle. "This is your son?"

"I am," the boy answered for her. "Who in blazes are you? And why did you lay out Guinea-hen?"

Marsh could hardly answer the question for himself; he had no intentions of trying to do so for this skinny youth. "Take your mother inside, boy. I've something to say to Miss Palmer."

Estelle clasped Marsh's arm tighter. "What business do you have with her? Send her inside, not me."

Meanwhile, the boy glared at them both. "Let go of my mother. I don't want her carousing with the likes of you."

"Shut up, Adrian," Estelle hissed. "An' mind your own business."

Marsh peeled Estelle off him. "Begone, the both of you!"

"*You* begone!" Sarah piped in, her fists planted on her hips. "You're the problem here, not us. Why don't you go away and leave us alone?"

Marsh could have shaken Sarah. "That's the thanks I get for saving you from him?" He advanced on her, but the boy, Adrian, leaped bravely between them. Though nearly Marsh's height, he couldn't have been half his weight. Still, that did not prevent the lad from challenging Marsh.

"Stay away from Sarah, else I'll give you a thrashing!"

Sarah grabbed the boy's arm. "No, Adrian. I won't have you fighting."

"Get away from her, son!" Estelle hissed the order. "Get away from that bitch!"

At the boy's brave display, Marsh's animosity began to wane. The lad had spunk. You had to give him that. Despite having a wanton for a mother, he possessed an odd sort of nobility that Marsh had to respect. "I assure you, boy, that I have no intention whatsoever of hurting Miss Palmer. Nor of fighting with you."

"What's the matter? D'you think I couldn't hurt you? D'you think I won't fight you? 'Cause I will."

Again Sarah caught the lad's sleeve. "Adrian. Please. No!"

But he shook her off, glaring still at Marsh. "I don't know who you are, but you can't come into our town and grab all our women. I won't let you. And even if you knock me down like you did Guinea-hen, my uncle will take care of you."

This time Sarah rolled her eyes. "Adrian, Neville is not going to fight with this man. Olivia will not allow it."

"That's not so! Your sister will make him defend you."

"Your sister?" The words slipped out of Marsh's mouth of their own volition. "You have a sister?"

Between them Mr. Guinea had begun to stir. From the garden Marsh heard a woman's laughter, and inside, the spirited waltz came to an end. But Marsh's attention focused solely on Sarah Palmer and the answer she would make him.

Her brow creased. "Yes, I have a sister. And a brother, if that's any of your concern."

A vein began to pound in his temple. He knew about

her brother, but not about another sister. Why hadn't he considered that possibility before? "Who is your father?" He did not think of the consequences of his question other than his need to hear the answer. "Who is your father?"

Her chin came up to a haughty angle. "Not that it's any of your business, but my father was Humphrey Palmer, one of the finest gentlemen who ever lived—"

"And your sister's father?" he broke in, sweating now.

"I don't see that my family—especially my sister—is any of your concern."

"Oh, just answer the man, why don't you?" Estelle snapped. "Olivia's father was Cameron Byrde. Everyone knows that," she said to Marsh. "She's one of us, born and bred. 'Tis this one who's a snooty Brit come up from London town to lord over us. . . ."

The rest of Estelle's tirade against Sarah fell on deaf ears, for Marsh fixed on that one important fact. Sarah was not his sister. His father was not her father. Rather, her half-sister was the one sired by his own father. He was no blood relation to Sarah Palmer at all.

Thank God!

But his relief was short-lived. For Sarah's brows had drawn together in confusion.

"What is the purpose of all these questions?" She shook her head and planted her fists on her hips. "What is this all about?"

Fortunately for Marsh, Mr. Guinea let out a loud groan, then lurched up into a sitting position, spewing curses as he did.

"Here, here," Adrian said, cuffing the fellow on the top of the head. "There's ladies present."

"Bugger off," the man spat, rubbing his jaw and clambering to his feet. He scowled at the boy, then at Sarah. He looked ready to curse her as well. But then his gaze landed on Marsh and his mouth snapped shut. Ducking his head, he sidled past Marsh, giving him a wide berth, then disappeared into the garden.

Marsh was relieved to see him go, for he had a far more

complex matter to contemplate. Sarah Palmer was not his sister. Someone named Olivia was, and she was wed to the boy Adrian's Uncle Neville. That simple fact changed everything and he needed to think about what it meant.

But not here. Especially not with Sarah's confusion clearly giving way to suspicion.

Abruptly he bowed. "I'll bid you all a good evening." Then he turned and strode back into the ballroom. He heard Estelle's angry call and her son's curt reply. From Sarah there was nothing, however, and as Marsh sidled past the gaily attired men and women queuing up for the next dance, he was grateful.

Someone jostled him. His host, Mayor Dinkinson. "Leaving us so soon, Mr. MacDougal?"

"Ah . . . yes. But thank you for inviting me. It has been a most . . . a most interesting evening."

"Can I not convince you to stay?" the man entreated. "Perhaps you would like a cigar. I have a box of the finest Cubans in my study."

"Thank you, but no."

"Can I not convince you to stay?" a woman's voice came from just behind him.

Marsh stiffened, then turned to find Sarah standing there. Her face was composed into a pleasant enough expression. But there was fire in her eyes. A beautiful, dangerous fire.

Though he knew she meant to grill him—and that he was not yet prepared to address any of her questions—something reckless in his nature made him unable to resist the opportunity she presented.

He knew he ought to make some excuse—any excuse—and depart. But instead he gave her an abrupt bow. So she wanted a confrontation. Well, he would give it to her. Only it would be on his terms, he decided, as the music started up with a flourish of violins and cellos. He held out his arm to her, the light of challenge rising in his eyes.

"Very well, Miss Palmer. Shall we dance?"

## CHAPTER 8

THIS was a mistake.

Sarah knew it as soon as she agreed. Dancing with Marshall MacDougal had hardly been her intention when she had intercepted his departure. She only wanted her questions answered, for there was something odd about his interest in Olivia—or, more accurately, Olivia's father. Something that made her uneasy.

She hesitated as he held his arm out to her. But when one side of his mouth curved up in an annoyingly smug grin, she shoved aside any doubt. She could handle one dance. She would have to.

Mindful of the mayor's avid observation, she gave her nemesis a sweet though utterly false smile. "Why, how astute of you to read my mind, Mr. MacDougal."

She put her hand on his arm, ignoring the warmth and power that came through the fine worsted summer-weight wool. Drat. The musicians had selected another waltz. Her dismay only deepened when the annoying man swung her confidently into position.

Irritated by his high-handedness, she kept as much distance between them as possible as they began to dance. It was awkward, of course, for the waltz required a certain proximity if it was to be performed well, and she knew how to dance it very well.

So did he, it swiftly became clear. Still, she resisted his every effort to pull her close, an effort that made them the only ungainly pair in a room of smoothly circling dancers. It took all her concentration to resist the pressure of his palm at the small of her back.

"I could swear you were a better dancer than this, Sarah. Am I making you nervous?"

She shot him a lethal glare. "What you make me is angry."

He let out a short bark of laughter. "That doesn't seem to be very hard to do. You're the prickliest woman I ever met. Most women would be relieved, even flattered, if a man rescued her from the unwanted attentions of a boor."

"I could have handled him myself. Besides, a gentleman would not have beat the poor man senseless."

"I hit him only once," he replied. But his grin faded somewhat.

"Well, you didn't have to hit him so hard."

He swung her about, and again they faltered as she fought to resist his powerful embrace. This time, though, they nearly collided with another couple.

"We are going to come to a crashing halt if you don't start cooperating," he murmured.

She hated that he was right. Yet she could see that it was impossible for her to concentrate on their conversation and also fight him. So with a taut smile she relented.

He immediately pulled her closer, then whirled her around with a flourish of her skirts and his coattails. Again he gave her that smug half smile. "Much better."

*You think so? Well, we'll soon see.* She met his gaze without blinking. "Why are you in Kelso? Why are you so interested in me and my sister?" she asked without preamble. "And don't give me that balderdash about business and a holiday."

"But it's true."

"It's a lie and we both know it. Do you think I'm a featherhead? Do you think I didn't notice that you first pursued me as if I were some . . . some eager dairy maid—"

"I got the distinct impression that you were eager and that you liked my pursuit—and the kiss we shared."

"Then you turned right around and snubbed me," she continued, ignoring the truth in his words. "Gave me the cut direct in front of all these people."

He pulled his face into a serious expression, one she suspected was wholly false. "I'm sorry if it appeared I was ignoring you earlier." He drew her nearer still. "I promise not to ignore you again."

Sarah felt his hand move, warm and strong, at the small of her back, and her heart's pace increased beyond the demands of the dancing. But she ruthlessly squelched any emotional response to him. He was just trying to divert her from this line of questioning. But she refused to be diverted.

"Now you are Mr. All-That-Is-Charming," she went on. "But there is more to it than that. What is your interest in my family? Why do you care who my father was? Or my sister's father?"

He stared at her a long moment before he answered. "Surely I am not the first man of your acquaintance who you suspect is looking for a rich heiress to wed."

No. He was not. Yet Sarah sensed something false in his words and expression. She shook her head. "That's not what I suspect. You would not be the first well-to-do American come to England looking for a title to wed—though usually it's the rich daughters who find some impoverished fellow of better bloodlines than bank account. But I don't believe that's what you are about, Mr. MacDougal," she finished in a challenging tone. "Not at all."

"I don't see why not," he murmured, not taking up that challenge, but only whirling her about as well as any man she'd ever partnered at the poshest of town balls.

She studied him closely, taking full advantage of the proximity the waltz provided. He had a small scar beneath his right eye, and a slightly crooked line to his otherwise proud nose. She had to force herself to remember that his looks, no matter how appealing, had nothing to do with anything.

She cleared her throat. "I believe something's going on here, something to do with . . ." She trailed off as her mind searched through all the facts she knew. "Something to do with Olivia's father, it seems. With Cameron Byrde."

Once said, what had been just musings became fixed in Sarah's head. "That must be it. You show up at Byrde Manor on the pretext of fishing. Then you see me there and you assume I am related to Cameron Byrde. You thought I was his daughter, didn't you? Then tonight . . ." She stared up at him, at his shuttered gaze and clenched jaw. "Tonight, when you found out I had a sister . . . you wanted to know who her father was."

Her eyes narrowed, trying to pierce the blank wall of his guarded expression. "What does Cameron Byrde have to do with you? He's been dead over twenty years—"

Then all at once it struck her with a terrible, sickening certainty.

Cameron Byrde, who was her mother's second husband and Olivia's father, had been widely renowned as a ladies' man. Though her mother had loved him to distraction, Sarah had heard enough tales of the man's escapades from Mrs. Hamilton to know he'd been a handsome ne'er-do-well, a selfish cad. Charming, to be sure, but also feckless and amoral.

Now here came a man of just the right age, traveling a very long way to make inquiries about him. They'd all been fools not to have anticipated just such an occurrence someday.

Something in her expression might have hinted at her suspicions, for Marshall MacDougal's features darkened.

"You . . . you . . ." She could not quite force the words out. She did not realize she'd stopped dancing until he abruptly propelled her out of the whirling horde toward the edge of the dance floor.

He bent his head very near hers. "Don't leap to any wild conclusions, Sarah."

"You're his son, aren't you? Aren't you?"

"Keep your voice down," he ordered. Then, with his hand wrapped implacably around her arm, he steered her out onto the terrace.

For one long, hysterical moment Sarah imagined he meant to deal with her as he had dealt with Mr. Guinea, just strike her down to prevent her from carrying on in a manner not to his liking. But as quickly as it came, that fear disappeared. Though he was capable of hurting her, she knew instinctively that he would never do so. At least not physically. Still, Sarah was afraid. And angry. Very, very angry.

With a furious shrug, she shook off his hold. The fact that he had not denied her words was proof enough that they were true. "You're his son. That's why you're here." A chill ran down her spine and she wrapped her arms tightly around herself. "Who's your mother? When were you born—and where?"

For a moment he only stared at her. "That's not important."

"Not to you. But to my mother and my sister—" She broke off and stared at him. "If it's true, then she's your sister too. Have you considered that? That makes you my . . . my . . ."

This was not how Marsh had wanted things to go, especially as he watched a look of horror come across her face. For a split second only, he debated the wisdom of admitting the truth to her, before relenting. "You and I are unrelated by blood." *Thank God.* He gave a mirthless grin. "You need not worry that you have lusted for your own brother, Sarah, for I am not your kin."

Outrage sparked in her eyes. "I have never lusted for you!"

"Ha! You say that now. But we both know it's not true," he countered. For some perverse reason he wanted to make her suffer as he'd suffered. More accurately, he wanted to make her admit to her desire for a man she thought completely wrong for her. Not forbidden, just wrong.

So he caught her by both arms and, holding her captive, he vented the whole of his story. "I am Cameron Byrde's son. His firstborn," he added with a bitter sort of satisfaction. "He married my mother and sired me long before he wed your mother and sired your sister. I may have grown up a fatherless child, far away in America, but I am still Cameron Byrde's rightful heir."

He shook her, as if that might erase the expression of denial on her pale but still beautiful face. When it did not, the anger he'd been nursing these past few months erupted. "I am his son, son of a woman whose life he ruined. He is not here to feel my wrath, the bloody son of a bitch. But I will have my due. I will exact payment for the sorrow and misery he visited upon my poor mother."

He pulled her resisting form close enough that their faces were only inches apart. His eyes burned down into hers, and he was painfully conscious of the fear and revulsion he saw there.

"I thought for a short while that you were she, my half-sister. But you are not, Sarah Palmer. We are free to explore the desire that seethes between us, even though it is fueled of hatred and distrust." She shoved at his chest, but he only tightened his grip. "Do you deny it?"

"Yes! Let go of me, you dreadful cad, you horrible . . . horrible bastard!"

It was the wrong thing to say to him, the red flag that made the mad bull in him need to strike back. Immediately.

He yanked her against him, knees, thighs, belly, and breasts. Then he caught her mouth in a violent kiss meant to silence her and prove his power over her.

It was idiocy, of course. A primal reaction of domination. But then, he had a driving need to dominate this woman.

She fought him—at first.

But when he circled her waist and shoulders and caught her head in his hand, then deepened the kiss, working to seduce her with pleasure instead of force, her struggles ceased. Her stiff resistance subsided and her body seemed to melt against his. Then she rose into the kiss and met his thrusting tongue with her own, and he wanted to shout out loud with victory.

She could not deny her desire for him now!

*Nor can you deny yours for her.*

It was a sobering thought, enough for Marsh to release her just as abruptly as he'd first caught her. She stumbled back, disheveled and dazed—and much more desirable than he wanted her to be. He searched his mind desperately for a way to kill his unwelcome desire for her, this snooty English noblewoman, and found it in her last words to him.

"I am not the bastard here. That dishonorable name belongs to your sister, and to your mother, who was never legally wed to Cameron Byrde. I mean to reveal that truth to everyone. To prove who I am," he swore, reveling in the return of righteous anger. "Then I will claim Byrde Manor as mine, all of it, and anything else my father owned. You'll see. All of you will see."

Then, mindful of a couple advancing from the ballroom out onto the terrace, he made her a short bow, turned on his heel, and stalked away into the night.

*Damn her,* he swore as he strode blindly through the mayor's back garden. Damn her and all the other high-and-mighty Brits whose narrow caste system was at the root of his mother's loneliness and sorrow. But he would make them pay. By damn, he would make them pay.

In the wake of Marshall MacDougal's departure, Sarah stood wide-eyed and trembling, staring at the place where he had been, hearing again the hateful threat in his last words. He intended to ruin her family. He could not have stated it any more clearly. Her beloved sister. Her sweet, well-intentioned mother. He meant to hurt them, just as he'd been hurt.

Startled by a pair of voices behind her, she forced herself on wobbly legs to find a shadowed corner. She leaned back against the wall, pressing her hands to her mouth as a fear unlike any she'd ever known welled up in her. But that only made matters worse, for her lips were tender from his violent kiss, sensitive in a way that was mortifying.

"Oh, my God," she whispered, as the full impact of his perfidy hit her. "Oh, my God."

She had to stop him. She had to prevent him from hurting everyone she loved. But how?

Then a glad shout went up from inside the hall as the musicians tuned up for galop, and somehow it cleared her head. To stop Marshall MacDougal she must first know if his preposterous allegations were true. And while she could easily believe that Cameron Byrde had gotten a child on some other woman, that did not mean he'd ever wed her.

Had Mr. MacDougal said he had proof of a previous marriage?

She didn't think so.

So that was where she would start. She must find out who his mother was and whether a wedding had ever been performed. Unfortunately, however, she would have to approach the horrible Mr. MacDougal in order to do it.

She repressed the quiver of emotions raised by the thought of being anywhere near him ever again. Whether it was caused by fear or a perverse sort of anticipation, she refused to succumb to it. He was the most wretched man she'd ever had the displeasure to know. And she was the most terrible sort of woman to have such a visceral reaction to him.

But this was her family he threatened, and for them she would brave any risk. Even Marshall MacDougal.

# CHAPTER 9

MARSH was too wound up to return to his room at the inn. Two pints of ale in the downstairs room had done nothing to take the edge off his agitation, nor was the bottle of whiskey he'd purchased likely to do so. But it was better than stewing in his bed, he decided as he strode to the stables, the bottle clenched in one fist.

Good God! He could hardly believe tonight's events. And all due to Sarah Palmer's interference.

Damn the bitch for causing him to reveal his plan to her! Damn her for rousing him to such a fever pitch of lust that he'd fight a man over her!

*At least she's not Cameron Byrde's daughter. She's not your sister.*

He grimaced at the thought. Damn him for being a twice-damned fool!

"Duff! Saddle my horse," he barked to the valet who sat with three other men, gambling over cards in the tack room.

The man opened his mouth as if to object. But a single glance at Marsh's thunderous expression must have warned him that one of his flippant rejoinders would not presently be wise.

He threw down his cards, muttering to the other men. "You're bloody lucky, Curly. Bloody lucky, for I would've cleaned you out—"

"Hurry up!" Marsh snapped.

The fact that his annoyance was caused of his own frustrations more than Duffy's reluctance didn't improve his mood at all. He would have to rethink his entire plan now. Completely rethink it. And all because he'd felt the idiotic need to come to the rescue of some high-class tart who neither wanted nor needed rescuing.

As Duff led Marsh's horse out of the stall, he shot a skeptical look at the brown bottle in Marsh's hand.

"I hope you don't mean to run this animal through the dark, guv'nor. It ain't wise for him nor for you."

"I don't make a habit of mistreating my horses."

A glint appeared in the wiry fellow's eye. "No. Only your hired help."

Marsh refused to be baited, and in a moment he mounted, then rode out of the yard with no word of direction, destination, or when he expected to return.

But Duff was only mildly concerned about his master's odd behavior. The American was well able to look after himself. Like lightning, news about the contretemps with that stupid Guinea had reached him almost immediately. One swift blow and the thickheaded fellow had dropped like a sack of grain. It confirmed a suspicion that had been growing in his mind ever since he'd hired on with the American. Marshall MacDougal.

The MacDougal.

As a fan of the great sport of fisticuffs, Duffy had followed the careers of all the fighters of any repute in England, Scotland, Ireland, and Wales. He had also known of several American fighters, The MacDougal among them.

Hoo, boy, wouldn't it be something if this intense young employer of his was that MacDougal? No matter that the man had been retired from the American boxing scene for several years, all of Duffy's cronies at the rings in Shepherd's Fields, the Eel Room, and the private boxing club in Berwick would still be awfully impressed.

So he watched his employer ride away with little real concern. If he was that MacDougal—and Duffy meant to find out for sure—then he could take care of himself. Tonight had proven that.

Duff felt an undeniable curiosity, though. The man had a reason for coming to Scotland, and a reason for being so worked up tonight.

He looked across the yard toward the mayor's brightly lit house to see a woman—a pale beauty who looked ethereal by moonlight—pause at the top of the steps. "I think somebody's wanted to bring a carriage 'round," he called back into the tack room.

A man named Cuthbery poked his head out. "That's Miss Palmer. Where's that boy Adrian what brought her here tonight?"

Duff's eyes narrowed. So that was Miss Sarah Palmer. Of course. He stared harder at her as she paced the landing. She was the woman with the red cape, and she was also the woman Marsh had fought over tonight. Very interesting.

He rubbed his bristling chin and a slow smile crept over his face. He might have guessed a woman was at the center of whatever Marshall MacDougal was up to.

He hurried across the yard. "Can I be of any assistance to you, miss? Is it your coachman you're wantin'?"

She gave him a distracted smile, then continued to peer into the gloom. "Not a coachman, precisely. A young lad by the name of Adrian Hawke escorted me here." She sighed, then focused her attention on him. "I can take myself home without him. It's just that I think he might be upset and so I would hate to abandon him."

At that very moment a skinny young fellow with a shock of coal-black hair darted from around the side of the house. The lad was fashionably dressed in a neat wool frock coat and an embroidered waistcoat. But one knee of his breeches was torn, his cravat had come unknotted and dangled askew, and his shirtfront was streaked with dirt. His lip was cut and still bleeding, Duff noticed.

"Adrian?" Miss Palmer lifted her skirts and hurried down the steps. "What on earth? Are you hurt? Don't tell me you have been fighting."

The boy wiped one sleeve across his mouth, leaving a streak of blood on it. "It's nothing. Are you leaving so soon?"

She pulled her shawl tighter across her bare shoulders.

"I wish I'd left an hour ago. Maybe then—" She broke off. "You do not have to accompany me if you prefer to stay here, for I can certainly handle the phaeton myself. I do it all the time."

"No, miss. You mustn't do that," Duff interrupted. "Not at night."

"I'll take her," the boy said, stepping between her and Duff. He straightened to his full height and squared his shoulders. "I'll take you," he repeated to her. "I brought you and I'll see you safely home. That's what a gentleman does."

"Indeed," Miss Palmer echoed.

"Adrian!"

Everyone's head swiveled around at the sound of another woman's cry. Duffy's eyes nearly popped out at the vision that stomped into view. The woman's voice might be far less ladylike and refined than Sarah Palmer's. But her breasts . . .

"Adrian!" the bellow came again. "You better get yourself back over here. I'll be damned if you'll be squirin' around the likes of her!"

"Don't start, Ma."

"Shut up. And you!" The buxom creature came to a heaving halt in front of Miss Palmer, then planted her fists on her hips and stared balefully at her.

Duff stared hopefully at those quivering mounds of heated flesh. Would they burst out of the too-tight bodice? God, how he prayed they might!

The blue-clad Amazon shot him a quick glance—and a wink, God bless her. Then she scowled at the boy—her son, he realized. "You'll stay well away from her, Adrian. And *you* stay away from *him,* you cradle snatcher," she spat, advancing on Miss Palmer.

Duffy shifted from leg to leg. Dare he hope they might get into a good, no-holds-barred, rolling-around-on-the-ground cat fight?

To her credit Miss Palmer met the other woman glare for glare, the ice queen and the Amazon. "How truly awful it must be for Adrian to suffer such a mother as you, Estelle Kendrick. But far be it from me to countermand your orders to him. I would not dream of heaping more trouble upon his youthful shoulders."

So saying, she lifted her skirts and made her way down the steps and past them, just like a haughty queen. As she strode by, however, it was clear that this particular queen did not put herself above mucking about in the stables and handling her own team.

"Bitch," the woman Estelle muttered. But her epithet seemed to fall on deaf ears. The tirade she directed toward her son, however, did not. "You!" she said, rounding on the scowling lad. "You look a sight! Not fit to be in proper company."

"And you are?" he snarled.

"Don't you take that tone with me!"

The boy's fists knotted at his side. "Living here is worse than Eton!"

"So go back! See if I care!"

He turned and stalked to the corner of the house, then broke into a run. She stamped her foot and spat on the ground. Then, recalling Duff's presence, she shot him a smile, smoothed her hair back, then tugged her bodice up a fraction.

"Well, luv. Looks like you've heard more'n you expected to. And seen more too," she added with a knowing laugh.

Regretfully Duff dragged his eyes up from her mountainous breasts to her smirking face. He whipped off his cap and made her an exaggerated bow. "Duffy Erskine at your service, Miss Kendrick. Anytime and anyplace."

"Ha!" she laughed. "Ain't you the dandy." She gestured in the direction her boy had gone. "Got any kids?"

He shook his head. "Not as I know of."

She cocked her head and studied him a moment. "Got any money?"

Duff grinned and patted his coat pocket. "As a matter

of fact, I just cashed in my cards in a fierce game back there."

Her smile increased. "Good. Good. So whyn't you invite me out for a drink, and we can get to know one another?"

Duff did not have to be asked twice. But even as he calculated how much it was going to cost him to wallow between those luscious breasts tonight, he was mindful of all he'd heard. Estelle Kendrick was mother to a lad who must have been fathered by one of the Hawkes, the wealthiest family in these parts, from what he'd learned. The boy, for all his youth, flirted with Sarah Palmer, who was the same woman his employer had fought someone over. Meanwhile, Marsh had stormed off, the young lady was leaving, and the lad had bolted.

But he was still here, and so was his blue Amazon. He squeezed her hand and winked at her, and she winked back. A fistfight, a scandal brewing, and a willing woman on his arm.

Hoo, boy, could matters get any better?

"You must tell me everything you know." Sarah leaned forward and took Mrs. Hamilton's gnarled hand in hers. "You've known my mother longer than anyone, and you know this man's charges would simply destroy her."

Mrs. Hamilton's face lowered in a ferocious scowl. "That no-good scoundrel. That selfish . . . selfish bastard!" she exclaimed. "I knew the man was no good, for all that he had the charm of ten men. But I never suspected he would stoop so low."

Sarah nodded, gritting her teeth. She could not agree more. Marshall MacDougal was an utter wretch. "I am afraid he is far worse than any of us could have guessed."

Mrs. Hamilton stared at the small fire in the kitchen hearth. "I swear, if he weren't already dead—"

"Dead? I only wish he were."

Mrs. Hamilton shook her head. " 'Tis Cameron Byrde I'm speakin' of, child. He's the true scoundrel here. He's the one at fault."

Sarah flopped back in the wooden chair, pursing her lips. The whole night long she'd tossed and turned, raging at Marshall MacDougal and the threat he presented to her family. Though Cameron Byrde might be the source of the problem, for her his horrible American progeny was the manifestation of it. "Well," she said. "Cameron Byrde's son is just as bad—if indeed he actually is his son."

Again the old woman shook her head. "He obviously believes he is. And he does have that same dark russet hair—just like Olivia's."

Sarah slumped down in her chair and dropped her forehead into her palms. "Oh, my God. Poor Olivia. We have got to find a way to stop that man!"

"Let me think. Let me think." The old servant drummed her fingers on the table. "The pity of it is that he probably is Cameron Byrde's son. The question we need to answer is whether or not his mother married his father—and if he did, did he do it before he wed my sweet Augusta?"

Sarah pondered that a moment. "Can you remember anything from those days? Any particular woman? Do you think her name would be MacDougal?"

"P'rhaps. That's a Highlander name. Being a Highlander meself, I b'lieve I would recall any MacDougals hereabouts. But remember, child, if he met her before your mother, I wouldn't've paid any attention to who he was cavortin' with. Though I was a youngster when I came to Byrde Manor, I didn't come into house service until he wed your mother."

They were silent a moment, then Mrs. Hamilton asked, "D'you think he's told anyone else about this quest of his?"

Sarah sighed. "I don't know. But I don't think so. I only became suspicious because he acted so surprised when he found out I had a sister. He wanted to know who her father was. He *demanded* to know." She clenched her fist. "Ooh, he is so devious. He was all that is charming and flattering—until he thought I was his sister. Then he couldn't avoid me enough! But now that he knows I'm not a blood relation at all, he thinks he can—"

She broke off when she realized how much she'd almost revealed. But it was too late.

"Now that he knows you're not a blood relation, what?" the old housekeeper asked, with brows raised and eyes sharp.

Sarah felt a wash of warm color come up in her face. "He's quite the ladies' man—or so he believes. And he was fool enough to think he could sweet-talk me. That's all."

"But he didn't succeed?"

"No. Not at all. And now he never will, for I know just what sort of selfish, spiteful creature he is."

"Well. I can see why you would believe so. But think, Sarah girl. You can hardly blame a man for lookin' for his absent father. Not everyone is so fortunate as you with your dear father."

"How was I fortunate? My father died when I was ten. I don't call that fortunate at all."

"Yes. That's true. Still, he was a wonderful man and he loved you dearly. For that matter, he was a wonderful husband to Augusta, and a very fine employer as well."

"And a good father to Livvie and James," Sarah added, beginning to catch Mrs. Hamilton's drift. "He was everything that Livvie's father was not."

"Precisely. But Mr. MacDougal couldn't know his father's true nature, so of course he wanted to find the man."

"I think you're mistaken, Mrs. Hamilton. He didn't come all this way to find his father for a friendly reunion. He made it clear that he hates the man. He's come here for revenge. Nothing else. And since Cameron Byrde isn't here, I fear he means to vent that revenge upon us. Upon Olivia and Mother, that is. That's why it's so urgent that we stop him. Not for Cameron Byrde's sake—I hate him. But for Livvie's and Mother's. That's why I need your help."

The older woman's face creased once more in worry. "Did he say he had proof that Cameron Byrde married his mother?"

"No." Sarah shook her head, trying to remember every

word that had passed between them. "He didn't say he had proof, like a marriage certificate or anything."

"All right, then. Let's think. How about I go visitin' today, reminiscing with my oldest friends? Maybe I can learn if there's ever been any MacDougals 'round here."

"That's good. As for me . . ." Sarah trailed off, intimidated by what she knew she must do. "As for me, I believe I will pay a call on Mr. MacDougal."

"Oh, but I don't think that's wise, child."

"How else am I to learn anything? I need to discover whether he has any proof, don't I? He slipped up last night and revealed more to me than he had intended. Perhaps I can get him to reveal something more today." She stood up and spread her arms wide. "What other choice do I have?"

## CHAPTER

# 10

MARSH grimaced as he rubbed his eyes. He'd been up all night sitting by the river, with only an empty bottle of whiskey to show for it. His stomach roiled, his head pounded, and his eyelids felt like sanding grit. Even worse, however, he was no more settled on his next line of action than he had been when he'd stormed away from the mayor's house.

He'd been a fool last night: fighting over a woman he should not care about; revealing information he should have kept private; then getting drunk. As if that had ever once improved a situation.

He hadn't even been smart enough to take advantage of the buxom charms that had been so blatantly offered by that woman Estelle.

He rode slowly toward Kelso, painfully aware of every jarring thud of his animal's hooves upon the hard-packed road. Like echoes of his miseries, they pounded the ugly reality of his life into his mind. His mother was dead. His father was dead. His nearest relative was a woman who would be ruined by his appearance in her life.

But at least that sister wasn't Sarah Palmer.

Not that it mattered, he told himself bitterly. Yet all night that had been the central issue his lunatic mind had returned to time and again. Sarah Palmer was not his sister. He did not lust after his own flesh and blood.

"You're an idiot," he muttered, prodding the horse up to a canter. He grimaced at the rocketing pain it sent shooting through his head. Yet it seemed a fitting punishment. How much bigger a fool did he intend to make of himself?

It didn't matter that she was not his flesh and blood. The

plain truth was that Sarah Palmer was not the sort of woman he was interested in. And he had better remember that. She was a wealthy British snob; he was a hardscrabble American businessman. Besides that, she hated him now that she knew he meant to ruin her sister and mother. Lusting after her was madness. Worse, it was pointless.

He massaged his throbbing temple, wanting that last thought to sink in once and for all. Lusting after her was pointless. Better to seek out the willing Estelle. A good tumble with a clever, knowledgeable woman had never failed to improve his outlook in the past.

No sooner was Marsh resolved on that, however, than his first test presented itself to him. For standing outside the inn was a horse he recognized as Sarah Palmer's, the leggy mare she'd ridden the day he kissed her beside the river.

At once his loins tightened. Bloody hell! She was the last person he wanted to see!

He started to turn his mount, to slink away like a coward. But Duffy called out to him. His nosy manservant lounged in the shade of a chestnut tree and, as usual, chose to assist his employer at the one moment Marsh least required his presence.

"Say, guv'nor. It seems you've got a caller. A lady caller." He waggled his bushy brows. Beside him the ostler smothered a laugh. "It's relieved I am to see you," Duff continued. "Another hour an' I would've assembled a search party to seek you out."

"And I would have fired you for the effort," Marsh growled. "See to the horse," he added as he dismounted. In focusing his ire on Duffy Erskine he managed to banish his initial reaction, which was to flee. Better to face the interfering woman and be done with her once and for all, he told himself. He could lust after her all he wanted, but it wouldn't amount to anything. Not now.

But as he strode into the front room of the inn, he girded himself as if for battle. Sarah Palmer was going to make his life miserable. And unfortunately, there was not one thing he could do about it.

Sarah fixed Mr. Halbrecht with her sternest lady-of-the-manor gaze. Behind him his wife practically cowered. And why not? Sarah had dressed very carefully this morning, every garment selected to convey power and rank. A rich burgundy riding habit with a march of gold buttons up the bodice and a cunningly made cap with a curving ostrich feather. She'd dressed to intimidate Marshall MacDougal, and impress him. The fact that he was not here was both a disappointment and a relief.

But her ploy was working exceedingly well with the eager-to-please innkeeper, a blessing she'd not counted on. So she kept her features haughty. "He's paid up a month in advance?"

"Aye, miss. A gold sovereign, don't ya know." He nodded his head continuously. "A very fine gentleman he is, to pay in advance that way."

"An' a separate room for his man," the wife piped in.

*Damn, damn, double damn!* He was here to stay long enough to wreak utter havoc on her family. But though she wanted to rant and rave, Sarah held her emotions strictly in check.

"A month," she managed to say in a reasonably calm voice. "And yet he is already gone."

Mr. Halbrecht shrugged. "He didn't sleep in his room last night. But that doesn't mean he has left for good."

*We should be so lucky.* But what did his absence mean? Then all at once she knew.

Estelle Kendrick.

Something very like nausea rushed over her. He'd spent the night with that hussy Estelle. She could almost see it. Him wrapped in her arms. Smothered between those monstrous . . . those monstrous . . .

Again came that sickening rush and she had to swallow hard to quell it. When she spoke, her voice sounded choked.

"Well. When he returns, would you please tell him I would like to speak to him?"

"Speak to me? About what?"

Sarah spun about at the hard, accusing voice behind her. Marshall MacDougal stood in the low doorway, his brows drawn together in a thunderous expression. "What is so important, Miss Palmer, that you come here with your imperious manner, questioning Mr. and Mrs. Halbrecht about my private comings and goings?"

He glared daggers at her, and for a moment Sarah was completely nonplussed. Had she truly thought that *she* could intimidate *him*? He was too ruthless for that, and too sure of himself. And unlike her, he had nothing to lose.

Fortunately, pride rushed to her defense and she drew herself up to her full height, and her fullest hauteur. She glanced at the wide-eyed Halbrechts. "You may leave us."

They scurried away at once, leaving her alone with Mr. MacDougal in the empty dining parlor. She cleared her throat before she spoke again. "Well, Mr. MacDougal. I had hoped to discover this morning how sincere you were last night in the matter that brought you to Kelso. I had hoped it was only too much spirits that had you flinging such wild accusations around. I see now, however, that you have not yet recovered from last night's debaucheries."

She wrinkled her nose and folded her arms across the front of her chest. "Did you sleep in those clothes?"

"Last night's debaucheries?" For a long, stretched-out moment he only stared at her. Then he smiled, that faint but annoyingly smug smile that always managed to unsettle her. "You are partially right. I did spend the night in these clothes. But I did not sleep."

A new wave of nausea rushed over her, stronger than before. It was just as she had guessed. He'd spent the night in Estelle's arms. Though Sarah fought to control any outward expression of her horror and dismay, she must have failed, for he chuckled at her silent struggle.

"Come, come, Miss Palmer. You of all people should

understand just how far a woman will go to secure the man she sets her sights upon."

Though she wanted to slap him—indeed, to claw his amused eyes right out of his head—Sarah buried those murderous impulses beneath an expression of cold contempt. "I'm sure I am not interested in what hole you wallowed in last night."

He laughed out loud. "How witty you are today."

"Witty?"

"You made a joke, didn't you? A rather risqué double entendre about what hole I wallowed in."

"What?" She stared at him, baffled, which only increased his laughter.

"Tell me," he finally managed to say. "Why have you sought me out, Sarah?"

"Don't call me that."

"But we are family. Not blood, perhaps, but we do share the same half-sister. Surely you are not formal among your own family."

"You are not my family," she swore. "And you never will be." She cut the air with one hand. "I don't believe one word of your story."

"You'd better. It's true."

"And no one else will believe you either."

"Yes. They will."

"Really?" She tapped her riding quirt against her gloved palm and glared at him. "What proof do you plan to offer?"

He spread his arms wide. "I am the proof. I was born in 1797. When was your sister—our half-sister—born?"

When she only stared coldly at him, unwilling to admit he'd been born before Olivia, he grinned. "So it is as I told you. I am Cameron Byrde's eldest child."

"So you say. Who's to prove when you were born?"

"I have my birth records with me."

*Damn.* "And your parents' wedding license? That is the key to your accusation, not your birth records."

He paused and studied her. "So that's why you're here, to ferret out whatever information you can. It seems I have shaken your faith in your family much more than you want to admit, Sarah."

"I have absolute faith in my family."

"Even Cameron Byrde?" He raised his brows in a taunting manner.

Sarah tugged angrily at the hem of her short riding gloves. How galling, to be forced to defend Olivia's father, a man she knew only by his reputation—his bad reputation. "I don't know how you came up with this fabricated tale you tell. But I assure you, it will not work. You have no proof of anything you say, and if you persist in spreading ugly tales about Livvie's father, then I will . . ." Her mind searched for an adequate threat. "I will have our solicitor sue you for slander."

He shook his head and stepped further into the room, studying her all the while as if she were some tasty bit of prey he meant to consume. A shiver of apprehension—or was it anticipation?—slid down her spine. If he meant to intimidate her he was doing a masterful job of it.

But she refused to back down. She lifted her chin to an arrogant angle. "You have no proof and you never will, because it does not exist."

"Oh, it exists, all right. My mother married Cameron Byrde. On that fact she was always very clear. And since she never told a lie her whole life, I believe the proof exists. And I won't leave here until I've found it. As for your solicitors, bring them on. But be careful, Sarah. The more people you involve, the more who will learn all the ugly secrets your family hides." He grinned. "Are you certain you want to do that?"

Sarah wanted to slap that smug expression off his face and scream her frustration. He had her there. No denying it. The conniving cad meant to ruin her family name and destroy the reputations of two of the finest women who had ever lived. And there was no one to stop him but her. To involve solicitors or anyone else was to court disaster.

She could send for her brother, though.

But as swiftly as that idea came, she banished it. If

James learned about any of this, he would challenge Marshall MacDougal to a fight—as would Livvie's husband Neville. Although both James and Neville were sportsmen, there was something dangerous about Marshall MacDougal. Something hard and ruthless. He was not a gentleman, she feared. Nor would he fight like one.

Bad enough the man was willing to ruin the two women in the world whom she most loved. She would not risk him injuring—or killing—the two men she loved best.

She stared at his smug, expectant face.

She would have to outwit him herself, she decided. He believed her to be without resources in a struggle against him, but she knew better.

The light of battle glittered in her eyes. "What is it you want, Mr. MacDougal? Money? Land? A title?" Her tone turned scathing. "I know you Americans are all fascinated by our English titles. Well, I think you should know that Cameron Byrde held no title, save that of gentleman." *And that was up for debate.* "As for land and money . . ." She paused and let out an unpleasant laugh. "The inheritance he left his daughter was modest. You'd profit better by marrying some society chit with a decent dowry."

His amused expression faded at her glib tone. "You think this is about money? Or worse, a title?" He gave a snort of disgust. "You people are pathetic."

"It's hardly pathetic to love and protect your family."

His brows arched and he crossed his arms. "My point exactly."

Sarah blinked, then narrowed her gaze. "What family do you have to love and protect?" A nasty suspicion struck her. "Are you married? Have you a wife and children tucked away in America?"

For some reason, that made him laugh. "Don't worry, Sarah. Your passionate feelings are not wasted upon a married man. At this point, though, I suspect you wish I were. But alas"—he pressed one of his hands dramatically against his chest—"I am neither your brother nor attached to another woman. You cannot castigate me on any score for the lust I inspire in you. That is entirely of your own doing."

How humiliating to hear her own unhappy thoughts expressed so accurately by him. Unable to come up with a cutting rejoinder, she stared coldly at him. "Enjoy your little joke, Mr. MacDougal. But rest assured that any interest I might have had in you—questionable to begin with—is now long departed, replaced by utter contempt. Not all women are brainless twits. But then, how could you know that, given your most recent company? Now, if you'll excuse me."

She swept past him, as regal and dismissive as any queen could aspire to be. But he caught her by the arm and swung her rudely about.

"I've never once thought of you as a brainless twit, Sarah." His dark, piercing gaze captured her shocked one and would not let it go. "What you are is a high-spirited woman who desperately needs to relieve the passionate humors seething inside her. Isn't that so?" he finished, his face only inches from hers.

"N . . . no. No!" she stammered. But his hand, too big and too warm, tightened about her arm, and her blood seemed to heat within her veins. To heat and race faster and faster.

From anger, she told herself as their gazes held. From anger, nothing else. Certainly not from lust!

The tinkling of the doorbell proved her unlikely salvation. The door opened, the bell jumped and jangled, and he abruptly let her go. Sarah sucked in a breath and unconsciously rubbed her arm where he had held it.

Behind him the baker escorted his ancient mother into the main dining room. The portly fellow nodded to them. His birdlike parent, however, eyed them both with suspicion.

"What are you two about?" she demanded to know. Then she called out to the innkeeper in a surprisingly strong—and candid—voice. "Mr. Halbrecht! Give these young people a room at once. 'Tis plain they need more privacy than a public dining room provides." She smirked, her ancient eyes bright and knowing.

"Mother!" her mortified son exclaimed, shooting Sarah and Marshall an apologetic look.

But the old woman was serenely unrepentant. "There's no place like the bedroom for a man and wife to work out their disagreements. That's good advice, you hear? So take it."

Sarah had been struck dumb at the woman's initial remarks. This last portion, however, made her want to die! She wanted to disappear in a poof of smoke and never be seen again. At least not in Kelso.

But that was not to be. She was here, in the low-ceilinged main room of the town's best inn, accused of lewdness by a venerable old matron who no doubt knew everybody in town—and who had no reservations about making her opinions known, even to complete strangers!

No. She hadn't accused her of lewdness, Sarah consoled herself as she stood as if rooted in place. But pretty close. She stared aghast at the old woman, well aware that her cheeks were burning. "You are mistaken. . . . That is, he's not my husband. . . ." Dear lord, that only made it seem worse! She backed toward the door, desiring only to escape. "I'm sorry."

"You're forgettin' your man." The old woman pointed one bony finger at Mr. MacDougal. "Oh, shush yourself," she scolded her son when he would have silenced her. "I'm eighty years old and I can say whatever it is I've a mind to say."

Sarah shot a wild glance at Mr. MacDougal. But she should have known better than to expect him to be embarrassed. The outrageous cad had the bad manners to actually laugh at the old woman's remarks.

Sarah muffled a most unladylike curse, and unable to say anything civil, she stalked from the room. Actually, she fled. She stood a moment, utterly confused, on the low front stoop. Then, spying her horse, she ran pell-mell toward it.

"Sarah!" Mr. MacDougal's call from the front door only

hastened her flight and increased her ire. Did he mean to humiliate her before the entire village?

Apparently so.

And he appeared to be succeeding, for just as Sarah snatched up her horse's reins, Adrian and three other young fellows popped up from behind a hawthorn hedge beside the yard, clearly alerted to the contretemps by all the shouting.

"Sarah?" Adrian called as she wheeled her animal and took off at a gallop. "Sarah!"

Adrian watched Sarah disappear with a mixture of alarm and intense admiration. Hello, but she had a good seat, clinging to the horse like a burr. Added to that, she had a good *seat.* She looked almost as good from the back as she did from the front.

But what had her upset enough to depart so precipitously? When he looked over the hedge, the answer was plain. The American.

Adrian's fists knotted as he glared at the man who stood there staring after Sarah.

"Is that the one?" Will Carter asked, jabbing Adrian in the ribs. "The one 'at took down Guinea with just one punch?"

"Yeah. That's him," another of Adrian's friends answered. He punched at the air. "I hear poor Guinea didn't have a chance."

Adrian scowled at them. " 'Poor' Guinea shouldn't've been pawin' at Sarah."

"Sarah, is it? Sarah." Will drawled out the name.

"Shut your trap! I can call her Sarah 'cause we're related. But she's Miss Palmer to the likes of you."

Will shrugged, but mischief sparkled in his eyes. He gestured with his thumb toward the American. "Well, *he* ain't her family, and he calls her Sarah. Wonder what that means—"

With one punch, Adrian knocked him down. Then, before he could stop himself, he tore around the end of the hedge and started purposefully toward the inn.

## CHAPTER

# 11

FEELING a mixture of satisfaction and regret, Marsh watched Sarah gallop away. He'd rattled her, which was good. She was not nearly as confident of her position as she pretended to be.

On the other hand, it was clear she meant to oppose him on this issue of his heritage, to fight him tooth and nail, and stop him any way she could. That worried him, for he too was not as confident of his situation as he professed.

He rubbed one palm over his bristly jaw, vaguely aware of the querulous old woman behind him, terrorizing both her son and the hapless Mr. Halbrecht. Across the yard, his own servant, Duff, and a pair of stablemen had witnessed Sarah's furious departure. Damn! If small towns in Britain were anything like small towns in America, by evening speculation about his confrontation with Miss Sarah Palmer would be the main conversation at suppers everywhere. Though he did not think it would damage his purpose for being here, it was nevertheless not the way he had planned things.

Then again, Sarah might possess the wherewithal to locate records he did not know existed. Now that she knew what he was up to, she might search out the proof he needed before he could. And when she found it, she was certain to destroy it.

Damn! He raked one hand through his disheveled hair as he watched the dust kicked up by her mare's hooves settle back onto the dusty yard. Once again he'd revealed more to her than a wiser man would.

Why was he so consistently a dolt when it came to the prickly Sarah Palmer? He should never have jumped so swiftly to the conclusion that she was his half-sister. Nor should he have let his attraction to her dominate his real purpose for coming to this place. Since first meeting her, he'd not done a damn thing right.

He laughed out loud, though without any real mirth. He'd gone about everything wrong, and all on account of one irritating, infuriating female. But he couldn't afford to behave that way any longer.

Unfortunately, matters were not going to improve anytime soon, he realized when he spied the lad stalking his way. Estelle's boy Adrian. The one who'd leaped to Sarah's defense last night. Marsh crossed his arms, waiting for what he assumed would be another unpleasant encounter.

He was not mistaken.

"What did you do to her now?" The boy scowled so fiercely, Marsh was tempted to smile. Apparently he was not the only one to play the fool for the ungrateful woman. Not only was the lad confronting Marsh now, it seemed he was equally willing to oppose his own mother on Sarah's behalf.

But Marsh didn't smile. No use to rile the young hothead any further. "She sought me out, Adrian. Perhaps you ought to direct your question to her."

"But you upset her. I saw how she just rode off, like the devil was after her. What did you do?"

Marsh shook his head. "She doesn't like me. That's all."

"Then why'd she come here, to the very inn where you are staying? And why *doesn't* she like you?"

Marsh uncrossed his arms. Enough of this. He was not about to be interrogated by some unlicked cub carrying a torch for a woman much too old for him. "Like I said before, ask her." When he turned back to the inn, however, the boy grabbed him by the sleeve.

Marsh reacted instinctively. He whirled, shoved, and in an instant stood spraddle-legged over the boy. Flat on his back in the dirt, the lad stared up at him, first in surprise, then in fury.

Marsh stepped back, chagrined by his violent reaction. "A little advice, son. Never grab at a man from behind."

Ignoring Marsh's proffered hand, the boy leaped to his feet and backed out of arm's reach. "We don't go for men like you around here. You dally with one of our women and then another. Go home, American, before somebody makes you sorry you ever came here."

*I'm already sorry,* Marsh thought as he watched the boy lope away. Sorry he'd gone to that dance last night; sorry he'd kissed Sarah Palmer; sorry he'd ever had to find out just what a pitiful excuse for a man his father had been. But he couldn't undo any of it, and he wasn't about to change his plans now.

"Hoo, but that lad is a feisty one," came Duffy's remark from behind him.

"Feisty?" Marsh snorted. "More like foolish."

"Foolish to go tugging at a man twice his weight, p'rhaps. Proves he's got ballocks, is all. But I saw him lay a facer on a bloke more his size. Laid him down with one poke, he did. With a natural talent like that, the boy oughta be considerin' a career in the boxing. You know, in the ring."

Marsh slanted his manservant a look. "The boy can do better than that."

"I dunno, guv'nor. There's money to be made in the ring. And you didn't see the way he swung, not with his fist, but with his whole body behind it. Sorta like you did to that fellow last night." When Marsh did not respond to that, the fellow grinned and spat. "Funny, I could swear both fights was over the same woman."

Marsh was in no mood for any of this speculation, not over his ability as a boxer, nor the reason he and Adrian had both been reduced to fisticuffs because of one Sarah Palmer. "Women are trouble, Duff. You're old enough to have learned that on your own. We'd all do better staying the hell away from them."

The man laughed. "Personally, I like women, 'specially the uncomplicated ones like that boy's mama."

Marsh didn't reply, but only turned back for the inn. An uncomplicated woman. Yes, he could use one of those right now. Work out all this frustration and rage with an energetic tussle between the sheets.

But as he stalked through the inn and up the stairs, he knew he wasn't going to find that sort of relief anytime soon. He and Sarah Palmer would clash, but not in bed, more's the pity.

He threw his hat on a chair and shrugged out of his rumpled coat. God, but he was a stinking mess. After last night's ugly scene and the way he looked today, she had every reason to look down her pretty, aristocratic nose at him. Brawling and drinking like some low-class ruffian. His mother would be just as appalled as Sarah.

Thinking of his mother, however, helped Marsh refocus on his reason for being here. This was not about Sarah Palmer, but rather, Maureen MacDougal Byrde.

His mother had been cheated out of the life she'd deserved. One man had let her down. He was not about to let her down too.

The next morning Sarah sat at the table in her bedchamber making a list. She'd had plenty of time to consider her options and they all led back to the same thing. If she couldn't strangle Marshall MacDougal—and she sincerely wanted to do just that—then she must outwit him. She had to make sure no proof of a wedding between his mother and Cameron Byrde existed.

*And if it does?*

The pen in her hand trembled and a large inkblot promptly spread across the last three entries on her list. St. Mary's of the Meadows was completely obliterated.

"Botheration," she muttered. She tossed the offending pen aside, then crumpled the offending sheet of parchment as well. Chances were that the amoral Cameron Byrde had never wed the woman, and she would find no marriage recorded at St. Mary's of the Meadows, nor at any other church in Scotland.

As for churches in England, she'd ruled them out. Mr. MacDougal had told her at their first meeting that he'd come from London. Probably searching for the proof there—with no success, she suspected. That's why he'd come up to Scotland.

But he wouldn't find proof here either. From everything she'd heard, Cameron Byrde had been a self-centered cad. Surely he'd been far too wily to be trapped in marriage by a woman of limited means. Mr. MacDougal's mother had probably fabricated the entire story to protect herself and her young son from ostracism. That's why he believed it so—it was the only story he'd ever been told.

For a moment Sarah felt a stab of sympathy for Mr. MacDougal. How hard it must have been to grow up fatherless. Like Adrian, he must have felt sorely the absence of any father. Try as he might, even Neville could not entirely fill the void for Adrian. Had anyone ever tried to fill that void for Mr. MacDougal?

Then she stood and, shaking off any vestiges of sympathy for the man, walked to the window. Outside, a dense row of apple trees rimmed the kitchen garden. They would bear a heavy crop this year. And the shepherds' flocks abounded with new lambs. Byrde Manor thrived, thanks to Neville and Olivia, and all of Kelso and the surrounding countryside benefited. If Adrian did not, it was not for want of their efforts. And she meant to continue her efforts with him too.

But this business with that American came first. She would not let him claim the home that rightly belonged to Livvie, and to her children as well. It was her family he threatened. Hers. Perhaps she'd let them down in the past with her reckless, self-serving behavior. But this time she would not fail them.

She squared her shoulders. She had three weeks until Olivia and her family returned from Glasgow. If she could not prove the truth by then and send Mr. MacDougal packing, she supposed she would have to tell Livvie and Neville what was going on. Till then, however, the battle was hers to fight. And hers to win.

She snatched up her crumpled list of churches in the surrounding countryside. If they'd married, the records must exist somewhere, and she would not find them pacing the halls of Byrde Manor.

Downstairs, Mrs. Hamilton sat knitting in a sunny kitchen window. "Well, child." She smiled when Sarah walked in. "I've learnt one bit of information."

"Have you?"

"Yes. There was a MacDougal girl in service at Woodford Court. Mrs. Tillotson remembers her. A sweet girl, but she didn't stay long."

Sarah stood stock-still. "When was that? Did she remember?"

"A good thirty years, she said, for Mrs. Tillotson was still at home and not yet in service."

Sarah's mouth felt suddenly dry. "Does she know what became of her?"

Mrs. Hamilton made a face. "She thinks the lass married a fellow from Maxton. O' course, that means she couldn't be this American's mother. Though she could be related to her. But I didn't think it wise to ask Mrs. Tillotson too many questions about that."

"Maxton." It wasn't much to go on, yet at least it was something. Sarah wasted no time. She would have taken a saddle horse except for Mrs. Hamilton's adamant objection. Nor would the old housekeeper allow Sarah to travel in the lighter phaeton. Instead, within the hour Sarah and a driver set out in the traveling coach with a basket of vittles and strict orders to be back before bedtime.

With the roads dry and the weather promising, Sarah was certain she could reach Maxton by early afternoon, delve through the church records there, and return at an hour acceptable to Mrs. Hamilton. But should circumstances require she stay longer, she was fully prepared to do so, propriety be hanged.

The three-hour journey provided her too much time to think, however. And unfortunately, the topic uppermost in her mind was Marshall MacDougal.

By the time she reached the ancient village of Maxton, she was a bundle of nerves. As a result, she did not react well to the reluctance of the novitiate at St. Patrick's to provide her access to the church's records.

"Wot I want to know is wot is going on here?" the skinny fellow demanded to know. He'd invited her in, but once she made her request, he'd turned unpleasantly belligerent. He stood now in his cassock, his legs spread wide in a protective stance before the doorway of the priest's office. "Why would you care about our church records? You say you're come up from Kelso. But you sound more like a Londoner to me."

Sarah tried to maintain a civil tone with the man, but it was hard. The fellow looked as if a breeze could blow him down, and at the moment she felt like a tornado.

*Violence will not aid your cause,* she reminded herself.

But it certainly had aided Marshall MacDougal's cause at the dance. One punch and he'd sent Mr. Guinea packing.

At the thought of Mr. MacDougal's high-handed behavior, a truly awful suspicion lodged in her head. She stared intently at the sallow-faced fellow before her. "I'm not the first one to come to you with this request, am I?" When he hesitated, she pressed on. "I know all about it, so you might as well stop lying. It ill suits your profession."

This time he averted his gaze and his sallow complexion grew pink. She was right! Sarah's elation on that score turned to fury at being upstaged. That wretched Marshall MacDougal had beaten her here.

She fixed him with a narrow glare. "I suppose he threatened to thrash you if you told anyone—especially me—about his visit. But don't worry, I'll protect you."

"You? Protect me?" The man tugged at his robes in an aggrieved manner. "Female minds understand nothing but drama. For your information, Mr. MacDougal made a very generous contribution. To the parish," he hastened to add when her brows raised skeptically.

Though Sarah severely doubted that money had gone anywhere near the poor box, she was not about to be bested by Marshall MacDougal. She opened her reticule with dramatic flair. "I can be every bit as generous as can he. Now show me what you showed him."

Sure enough, a Miss Magda MacDougal had wed in October of 1797. Not to Cameron Byrde, though, but to a Horace MacNeil.

Sarah rubbed her finger back and forth across the thirty-year-old entry. The paper was thin, the ink beginning to fade. But the name was clear. Horace MacNeil.

She looked up at the self-righteous novitiate. "Do they still live here, Magda MacDougal and Horace MacNeil?"

His head wobbled on his skinny neck. "He does. She died last winter and is buried in the churchyard."

Sarah was silent on the short drive out to the MacNeil abode. Magda MacDougal McNeil could not be Mr. MacDougal's mother, she realized, not unless this whole tale was an elaborate sham. She didn't think that was the case, however. Mr. MacDougal really believed his mother had married Cameron Byrde. That meant this woman was, at best, related to Marshall MacDougal. Perhaps she was an aunt? The important thing was, did her family know anything about Marshall MacDougal's mother and her relationship with one Cameron Byrde?

Then also, what if the American had already been out to question the MacNeils? Would they receive her now? And if they were as reluctant as that novitiate had been, did she have enough money left to coerce them?

She rummaged through her reticule. Why hadn't she thought to carry more money with her? There was nothing like a shiny sovereign to tempt a person whose pockets more usually held pennies.

In short order the coach pulled up at the MacNeils' cottage. It was a low, rambling affair, stuccoed and with two chimneys, marking them as a more prosperous family than their neighbors. But the yard was a disordered mess, and behind the cottage the laundry flapped perilously near to the ground, hanging from carelessly propped-up poles.

Two dogs rushed out, fur up and legs stiff, to announce her. On their heels came five little children, two women, and finally one bowlegged old man. She stared at him, with his braces stretched across his bulging belly. Perhaps he was Mr. MacNeil, husband of Magda.

He stomped across the yard, scowling with every step. As if they sensed his mood, the dogs grew bolder. Sarah's driver had to keep a firm hold on the nervous pair of horses.

"Get on wit' you!" the old man shouted, gesticulating with his fists at the carriage, not the dogs.

With his whip the driver deftly flicked one of the curs that came too near, then scowled at the old fellow. "Here, now. Call off yer dogs. There ain't no cause to be ugly-like."

The man only shook his knotted fists harder. "If she's come around here for the same purpose as that other one, well, she can just be on her way now. We don't talk about them that has sinned and been sent out of the family. I tol' him that, an' I tell you the same. That Maureen weren't worth the dirt under my Magda's shoes. Now go on. Go back to America with that bastard son of hers!"

Stiff with outrage, Sarah called out before the driver could argue, "Drive on." Marshall had been here already—and no doubt had been just as rudely rebuffed. Still and all, she'd learned enough from that rude old man to guess the rest. Marsh's mother must have been this Maureen, sister to Magda MacDougal MacNeil.

And her sin?

Sarah stared blindly at the vacant squabs opposite her. There was only one sin she knew of that would cause a young woman to be ostracized by her family that way. Maureen MacDougal must have been pregnant without benefit of marriage.

A cold shiver ran down her back. With no husband, Maureen MacDougal had been sent away—all the way to

America, it seemed. Cameron Byrde might have been the woman's lover, but just as Sarah had suspected, he'd never been her husband.

Mr. MacDougal had no proof of a marriage and he would not find one here. She was now certain of that.

And then, the man had referred to Marsh as a bastard.

But as the coach made a circle on the rutted road and started back for the road to Kelso, Sarah did not feel nearly the satisfaction she'd expected. Instead, an image of a frightened young woman, alone and with child, kept rising in her mind's eye.

How would she feel in just such circumstances? Not that she would ever allow herself to get into such circumstances. Nevertheless, to be abandoned by everyone: lover, sister, family. To be sent all the way across an ocean to make your own way in the world. To be the sole support of yourself and your helpless little child.

It was a terrible thought, and despite her distrust and dislike of Marshall MacDougal, she felt a real pang of sympathy for his unknown mother—and for the fatherless boy he must have been. Neither of them had deserved the fate handed down to them. Most especially he did not deserve the lingering censure of that thoroughly unpleasant Mr. MacNeil.

She pulled off her gloves and untied and removed her bonnet. Was that the sort of treatment that had driven Adrian from Eton, that mean-spirited sort of contempt?

No doubt it was.

Sarah sighed. She would have to redouble her efforts on the boy's behalf, she decided as she settled in for the long return journey. And perhaps once Mr. MacDougal returned to America—for surely he must be disheartened by today's revelation—she might confide all this in Neville and caution him not to be put off by Adrian's brave show of nonchalance. The boy needed a father, else he was bound to grow up as difficult and unhappy as the troublesome Mr. MacDougal.

* * *

Sitting in the shade of a chestnut tree outside the squat posting house in Rutherford and nursing his third glass of whiskey, Marsh clenched his jaw in unconscious rhythm. That sorry son of a bitch! Thirty years gone by and with his own wife dead and buried, yet still Horace MacNeil had shunned Maureen MacDougal—and also her son. If that was the way her family had treated her, no wonder his mother had denied having any family left in Scotland.

Marsh tossed back the hard Scotch whiskey, reveling in its burning heat. Anything to keep his mind turned away from the doubt that had grown so quickly to life in his mind. Could it be true? Could his mother have been sent away heavy with child and without a husband? Could Cameron Byrde have refused to wed her? Could she have lied in order to ease a little boy's desperate longing for a father he could never have?

His hand trembled and he set the heavy tumbler down.

Of all his setbacks—the long, wearying sea journey, the dead ends in London, the leads and misleads since he'd arrived in Scotland—today's confrontation with his mother's family had hit Marsh the hardest.

The man had called him a bastard, not a remark that generally bothered him. But this time . . . this time he'd begun to believe it might actually be true.

He closed his eyes, picturing his mother as he'd last seen her. So pretty and frail, and always smiling at him with love shining in her eyes. He'd been the center of her world. He understood that now. And he'd taken that exalted position entirely for granted. Only now, when she was gone, did he finally understand how important her love and faith had been to him.

Would he ever be that important to anyone again?

So he sat there as the late afternoon shadows drew purple across the yard. It was not his way to wallow in self-pity. Yet this day he allowed himself that dubious luxury.

Across the yard Duff waited, unconcerned as always about where they might spend the night. The man was curious about what Marsh was up to—and about his quick fists. Though Marsh was not ashamed of his early career as a boxer, it was not something he bragged about. He should have expected that a sporting man like Duffy Erskine might recognize the name MacDougal. But that was immaterial, a part of his past. What concerned him now was an even earlier part of his past.

Marsh watched as a plump maid came out of the kitchen for the third time to flirt with Duff, then heaved a great sigh. He wished his life were once again that simple and uncomplicated.

A carriage creaked and rumbled into the yard, and Marsh idly followed its progress. Something about it looked familiar. Then he spied a woman in profile within its dim interior and suddenly his every sense came into heightened focus.

Sarah Palmer. She must have followed him.

His heart began to beat at a heavier, faster pace. So she was here. That meant life was about to get even more complicated now. He should not be surprised, for she was nothing if not determined. And intelligent. He had to give her that.

But was she smart enough to have discovered the MacNeils and their connection to the MacDougals?

He watched the carriage halt near the stables and the driver leap down; then he stood and raked his hands though his hair. Every aspect of his brief bout of self-pity disappeared as he contemplated the opportunity her presence here provided him.

He'd been rebuffed by Horace MacNeil as a bastard.

It would interesting to see how Sarah Palmer felt about bastards.

# CHAPTER 12

SARAH reached for the carriage door, then abruptly fell back against the leather squabs. No! He could not be here!

But, of course, he was. Marshall MacDougal, striding across the yard, making straight for her carriage. Oh, why of all places must they stop here to water the horses? A little over an hour and she would have been home. Even a half hour later and they could have stopped in Trows instead.

But no, she was caught here, without a maid and with nightfall fast approaching—and Marshall MacDougal clearly intent on confronting her.

Distracted, she pushed a damp curl back from her brow. All right. So he wanted to confront her. Let him. She had nothing to be ashamed of for being here. She was only protecting her family interests, a commendable goal by anyone's standards. And anyway, she was in a stronger position now than she'd been before—assuming that the unpleasant Mr. MacNeil's remarks were true.

So she made herself smile, the lofty, assured smile that she'd long ago learned was a necessity for anyone intent on sailing the rough waters of social discourse, especially when dealing with difficult persons like Marshall MacDougal. And she completely ignored the fact that her heart was racing from any emotion other than irritation.

He halted outside the door, his head on a level with her window. "Why, hello, Miss Palmer," he said in a suspiciously hearty tone. "Fancy running into you here. The gods must be smiling on me today, to provide me with such welcome company."

Welcome company? Her eyes narrowed. If it was a game of mock and taunt he wanted, she would show him that she could thrust and parry with the best of them.

"My, my. How you do go on, Mr. MacDougal. I'm afraid, however, that our delay here shall be brief. We stop only to refresh the horses before continuing on to Kelso."

"As do I. I'd be pleased to accompany you."

"I'm sure that will not be necessary."

"But I insist. I'm sure your mother would not want you traveling these country roads alone—"

"Ha!" she interrupted him. "As we both know, you are the last person to concern yourself over my mother's wishes. Besides, I have my driver."

"As I said," he continued as if she hadn't broken in, "you should not be traveling these country roads alone, especially after dark. I've been warned that highwaymen are rampant in these parts."

Though Sarah had been warned of the very same thing, she was not about to agree with him. "I'm sure that's pure exaggeration."

"I don't think so." He was grinning now, a cheeky, triumphant grin that made it very hard for her to maintain any semblance of serenity.

Thrusting out her jaw, she decided to be forthright. "Let us drop this ridiculous farce, Mr. MacDougal. You do not care for my safety, and given your bad feelings toward my mother, you cannot seriously cast yourself as someone considerate of her feelings. Besides, as you well know, we have not met here by accident. Like me, you are recently come from Maxton, apparently arriving there before I did. I suspect, however, that we have both come away with the same interesting bit of information. Of course, I suspect I enjoy it a little better than do you."

It was like watching a curtain fall across his eyes. The taunting light went out, replaced by wariness. "The same bit of information?" He enunciated the words carefully.

Sarah hesitated before speaking. "I've been to see Mr. MacNeil."

The wariness turned at once to ice. "Mr. MacNeil is eager to make his ugly opinions known. Whether that opinion is supported by fact, however, remains to be seen. But I'm glad to know you are content with his pronouncements, Sarah. Perhaps you will no longer feel the need to follow me about the countryside."

With that he made her a short bow and departed. Not at all what she'd expected. He hadn't even allowed her time to berate him for using her given name without permission.

Though Sarah had kept her distance from the open window, now she leaned her head all the way out, watching as he strode stiffly away.

A part of her felt sorry for him. He'd come so far—halfway around the world—only to learn that he was the casual by-blow of a man who had lived his life without any regard for the people he hurt. How painful that must be.

Surely he would return to America now.

The next quarter hour, Sarah remained seated in the carriage, mulling matters over as the horses were tended. With each passing minute, unfortunately, she grew more convinced that Mr. MacDougal did not mean to give up this easily. No, not him. Was she, therefore, wise to assume victory on the strength of one rather nasty and vindictive fellow's remarks?

But even as she worried about whether or not Mr. MacNeil's cruel words were the whole truth, a small part of her also worried about how those words might have wounded Mr. MacDougal.

Why she should give even passing thought to his feelings, she could not fathom. Perhaps it was due to Adrian's similar circumstances. After all, she would not like to see the boy belittled for the circumstances of his birth. So how could she enjoy seeing Mr. MacDougal treated in the same cruel manner?

Then there was the fact that despite everything, he was very likely Olivia's half-brother. That meant he was also an extended part of her own family.

She shifted uncomfortably on the bench seat. If only he

would behave like family instead of their enemy. Knowing her sister, Sarah was certain that Livvie would accept him as her natural-born brother. In time she supposed even their mother might grow accustomed to the idea of her second husband having had an outside son. He certainly wouldn't be the first man to have done so.

But none of them could ever accept Marshall MacDougal so long as he insisted that he was Cameron Byrde's rightful son and heir, and that his mother was Cameron Byrde's true wife.

Sarah grimaced and massaged her temples, which had begun to throb. Everything was in such a muddle!

By the time they started off again, it was dark enough that the driver lit the front lantern. A crescent moon provided some illumination of a pale and erratic sort. But within a couple of miles a thick layer of clouds rolled in, and darkness settled over them like a heavy, smothering hand.

Sarah perched anxiously beside the window, staring out into the gloom. She could hardly make out anything beyond the lumpy mass of the occasional hedgerows and stone fences, and the infrequent light from a distant house or cottage. Added to that, her curt discussion of highwaymen with Mr. MacDougal had left her jumpy in the extreme.

She should have taken a room in Rutherford. Though her driver had not voiced his opinion, she'd known by his expectant stare that he'd hoped for just that. But she had promised Mrs. Hamilton that she'd be back tonight. Plus, Marshall MacDougal had been there, with his arrogant attitude and his unsettling appeal. As a result, instead of making a logical decision, she'd let emotions rule her thinking.

Why was it he always managed to rattle her so? Why was it she got her back up whenever he was around?

Somewhere in the distance the dull flash of summer lightning provided momentary relief to the stifling dark. After a few seconds, thunder rolled low and threatening over them.

*Please don't let it rain,* she prayed. That was all she

needed. Already they'd slowed to little more than a walk. A storm would bring them to a complete halt.

Then she heard another sound. Horses' hooves and a man's voice. At once she recalled Marshall MacDougal's words: *Highwaymen are rampant in these parts.*

*Dear God, please do not let that be true!*

Oh, why had she been so unwise as to chance returning home after dark?

"Miss?" came the driver's voice. He sounded nervous. "Best you hold on tight. It might be rough going."

Rough going?

That proved to be an understatement of the grossest nature. For with a snap of his whip, the carriage surged forward and though Sarah kept a death grip on the window stile and her feet planted firmly on the floor, she was still buffeted side to side and jounced violently up and down.

Dear lord, how could the driver keep his seat? And how did the team see their way down the pitch dark roadway?

Yet those concerns were nothing to her bigger fear. Were the highwaymen gaining ground?

"Hold up!" She heard the cry behind them.

"Go faster!" Sarah shouted through her chattering teeth.

"Sarah! Slow down, damn it!"

He knew her name? Sarah thrust her head out of the window. Did she know that voice?

"Sarah! Make your driver slow down!"

Though the darkness surrounded them, it did not disguise that voice, nor the broad American accent.

"Stop! Stop!" she cried out to the driver. That was no highwayman at all, but rather, Mr. MacDougal. Thank God.

As quickly as the driver pulled the laboring team in, however, Sarah's relief turned to outrage. How dare that man spook them that way!

She was out of the carriage almost before it swayed to a stop. Mr. MacDougal had to pull his snorting animal up short to avoid colliding with her.

"You had better be a highwayman," she bit out. "For you have absolutely no other reason for terrifying me so!"

The man who rode up behind Mr. MacDougal let out a bark of laughter. "I b'lieve the chit wants tying up and ravishing, guv'nor. More'n one lady is peculiar that way."

"Shut up," Mr. MacDougal muttered. To Sarah he said, "I did not begin to chase you until you began to run. Up to then I was content to keep my distance."

Sarah planted her fists on her hips. "Why are you following me at all? You could have stayed in Rutherford."

"Believe me, I would have," he threw right back at her. "Only I was uneasy about you traveling alone after dark."

Behind them her driver cleared his throat. "Excuse me, miss."

But Sarah kept her glare upon Marshall MacDougal. In the dark he loomed big and threatening, and she didn't trust him any more than she'd trust some highwayman. "I do not need you to look out for me."

He dismounted, though that didn't lessen at all his threatening aura. Indeed, when he stopped just in front of her, she felt more threatened than ever. Did highwaymen ravish the women they stopped? Was he considering ravishing her?

A rush of heat went through her at the very thought, and she let out a little groan of dismay. How could she react to him that way? Him, of all people?

"Excuse me, miss," her driver again said from beside the still excited and blowing horses. "Excuse me, but this here horse, he looks like he's done for."

Done for? Sarah whirled around and stared at the man. She wanted to cry. She wanted to stamp her foot and pitch a fit—not that it would do any good, of course. But it would provide an outlet for the confusion of emotions roiling inside her—chief among them, frustration. Instead she summoned every ounce of her self-control and addressed the coachman. "What do you mean, 'done for'?"

Even in the dark she recognized his nervousness. "Well, he's pulled up lame. Must've stepped wrong or somethin' in that madcap race."

Thunder echoed across the sky, nearer now, and Sarah

felt an impending sense of doom. "Can he continue on?"

"Well, he'll have to walk home hisself, back to Byrde Manor. But I dinna think he can pull any sort of weight. Not on this leg."

"But he will recover?" Sarah asked, concerned now about the poor animal's injury.

"Oh, I believe so, miss. I believe a week or two of rest will see him all right again."

Relieved of that worry, Sarah faced her own dilemma. What was she to do now?

Something awfully near to a snicker came from the vicinity of Mr. MacDougal's outspoken manservant.

"Can the other horse manage the carriage alone?" she asked her driver.

"If he weren't already weary, if we didn't have Gannet Hill to climb, well, maybe. But considerin' all that . . ."

"We can put one of our horses in the traces," Mr. MacDougal offered, much to Sarah's surprise.

"I don't think so," she began.

"I insist. I cannot leave you here, and I feel responsible for your predicament."

"Well, I'm glad you at least admit that. Nonetheless, I do not believe your horse is up to the task. A fine saddle animal is not used to being in traces."

"My man's animal is temperate enough for the job," he insisted. "He can then ride my horse while I accompany you in the carriage. But if you dislike that alternative," he went on, "you can ride with me." He patted his animal's neck. "Dukie is more than capable of carrying the two of us."

He paused just long enough for her to imagine how disastrous that possibility would be. Her sitting before him, nestled in the circle of his arms, pressed against his chest.

Sarah's frustration dissolved into something akin to panic. Good Lord! That would never do!

"Either option is acceptable to me," he continued. "The only thing I will not allow is for you to spend the night here in this carriage. One way or the other, you must be delivered home."

Behind him his man dismounted and went over to the carriage team to confer with her driver. That left Sarah relatively alone with Marshall MacDougal, alone to answer him, though she liked neither of the answers open to her. She crossed her arms, angry, upset, and agitated. Was there no other way?

"You can't stand it, can you?" he whispered in a voice that did not carry to the two servants.

"If you refer to being stranded in the middle of the night with a storm bearing down on me, then no, I cannot."

"I mean you cannot stand me being right." He was closer now.

Her chin came up. "What is it you want, Mr. MacDougal? Does it please you to put me in such a predicament? I concede that I find both options unpleasant." She paused. "Repugnant."

He chuckled. "If it were the good vicar, or even Mr. Halbrecht, you would not be so upset. Admit it. You would ride before Mr. Liston, and you would happily suffer Mr. Halbrecht's presence within your carriage. But with me . . ." He let his words trail off.

"Do you blame me?" she retorted in a sharp whisper. "Neither Mr. Liston nor Mr. Halbrecht harbors any intentions of harming my family."

He shrugged. "I think it's more than that."

She drew herself up, uncomfortably aware of his implication. Unfortunately, there was only one way to deny it. She tugged at the waist of her bodice. "I'm sure you will think whatever evil thoughts you like regardless of anything I say, so I shall not squander my breath debating the matter. I accept your offer, Mr. MacDougal. Harness your animal to the carriage. But be quick about it, if you please. The heavens sound ready to open up."

And open up they did.

No sooner were the animals switched than the storm pitched a fit over them. The driver, wrapped in an oilcloth slicker, walked at the two animals' heads, leading them through the tempest, while Mr. MacDougal's man mounted and led the lame horse behind them.

To Sarah's chagrin, Mr. MacDougal wasted no time in joining her inside the curtained carriage.

He removed his beaver hat, shaking the raindrops from it, then fastened down the canvas window covers. Finally he faced her. "What a story we shall have to tell about this night."

Sarah did not respond, but only watched warily as he settled himself across from her. The rain beat furiously upon the carriage as he laid his hat aside, then removed his riding gloves, and stretched his long legs out before him.

She shifted her legs and swept her skirts aside so they would not brush his boots or breeches. Then she arranged a satin tufted pillow behind her head and closed her eyes.

"Planning to sleep? Or just pretending?"

Despite his amused tone, Sarah kept her eyes closed. "I am feigning sleep, Mr. MacDougal, because I did not wish to hurt your feelings by not conversing with you. If you were a gentleman, you would understand, and you would cooperate."

When she heard his snort of derision, she continued. "But alas, as I should know by now, you are not a gentleman."

"No, I suppose I'm not. Not by your exalted standards. But I'm glad of that," he added. "From what I've seen, most of your so-called gentlemen are men of leisure who've never once lifted a hand in honest labor."

Her eyes popped open with a snap. "That's absurd. My brother is a perfect gentleman; he also manages his estates and my mother's. My brother-in-law—also a gentleman—breeds the finest horseflesh, besides keeping at least a hundred people gainfully employed." She gave him a superior smile. "Can you say as much for yourself?"

He crossed his arms. "As a matter of fact, yes."

Despite her best effort not to, she gaped at him. "You can?"

"I can. But I'm curious. Did your brother and brother-in-law inherit their properties from their fathers?"

When she pursed her lips without answering, he continued. "Of course they did. That's how it works over here. But it's different in America. Where I'm from, anyone with the intelligence, the willingness to work hard, and the drive to succeed can do so. Everything I have—property, business, reputation—I earned with the sweat of my own brow. No one gave me anything. And yes, I keep a crew of anywhere from fifty to two hundred men working on my various projects."

Though she did not want to be, Sarah was nevertheless impressed. Assuming, of course, that what he said was true. Yet somehow she knew it was. He might not be a gentleman by her society's stringent standards, but he was a man of some talent and honor. Like James and Neville, it seemed he worked hard for his family and the other people who depended on him. Added to that, he had embarked on this lengthy quest to find his father for the most loyal of reasons: to prove his mother an honest woman.

Despite all her reasons to hate and fear the man, Sarah found herself hard-pressed to do so, even though in the low light of the inside lantern, with that one-sided smirk curving his lips, he looked less the gentleman than ever. He'd loosened his cravat, and his casual dishabille, coupled with his relaxed sprawl, proved him nothing like the gentlemen of her acquaintance.

Yet that very difference seemed also to draw her to him. There was something about the man, something physical. Even relaxed, he exuded power, and something in her—something coarse and primitive—reacted in the most perverse manner.

He scared her, he infuriated her, and she had every reason in the world to despise him. Yet he managed all the same to excite her. She knew enough of that wicked emotion to recognize it, especially when it was so terrifyingly powerful.

That his eyes were so steady upon her only exacerbated

her reckless response to him, but she was hard-pressed to look away.

Then it occurred to her that she'd planned to elope with Lord Penley based on feelings not nearly so strong as this, and she jerked her gaze away from his. Good Lord, what a dreadful thought!

For a while they rode in silence, with only the slackening drum of the rain to fill the void. Sarah struggled to tamp down her inappropriate feelings for this man—this enemy of her family, she brutally reminded herself.

As his silent presence moved in on her, however, as his aura of barely checked masculine power made her stomach jump, her skin burn, and her fingers twitch, she knew she must do everything in her power to resist his allure. She'd set out to prove to her family that she was not the silly social butterfly they all thought her to be. Succumbing to this man's virile appeal would only prove them right.

And then there was the matter of her sister's birthright. It didn't matter that she could understand the position he took. She could not allow him to hurt anyone in her family. That was the only reason she had for dealing with him at all, her sister's birthright and her mother's happiness.

So she straightened against the heavily padded squabs, cleared her throat, and assumed her haughtiest tone. "I assume you've had time to think on your discovery today."

"My discovery?" His brows arched as if in question, but his eyes grew wary.

"Yes. Mr. MacNeil's revelation." She hesitated a moment, disliking the cruelty she must resort to. "I know . . . I know it must have been unpleasant to hear. He seems a very ugly sort of person. Nevertheless, you cannot still hope to prove your allegation."

He crossed his arms. "I do not discount the possibility that my parents only wed after they learned my mother was breeding. The way I see it, once the truth came out, MacNeil and his wife—my aunt—abandoned my mother. She then turned to her lover, who married her but then probably got cold feet at the thought of introducing such a simple lass to his grandiose family. So he sent her—trusting soul that she was—on to America, promising to follow. Of course, the lying bastard never did."

"That's pure conjecture," she protested. Though privately she agreed with his coarse assessment of Cameron Byrde's character.

He leaned forward, elbows on his knees, and addressed her earnestly. "I found his letters to her, Sarah. He knew where she was because she'd written to him. And he knew about me."

"I do not doubt you are his son," she said. "But just because he wrote to your mother does not mean he married her."

"He sent her a hundred pounds," he bit out. "He sent her a hundred pounds, then washed his hands of us both!"

His voice, though low, had grown angry. Yet Sarah also detected an edge of pain in it and it was that which most affected her. He was so completely sincere in his quest. Everything he said *could* have happened, she supposed. Obviously he believed it had.

But there was still no proof, she reminded herself. No proof. Certainly there was no reason to throw her sister's and mother's lives into total disarray over the tragic scenario he painted. So she brutally beat back any feelings of sympathy for him.

"Have you never considered, Mr. MacDougal, that you are precisely what Mr. MacNeil said?" She cringed inside at her hurtful words, though she knew she must say them.

In the ensuing silence the interior of the carriage seemed actually to grow cold.

"If I am a bastard," he said, enunciating the word with icy precision, "it is not by birthright, but rather by conscious choice. Just as you were born a lady," he went on, "but have chosen to become a coldhearted bitch."

Sarah flinched. She deserved that, and more. But she had finally realized what she must do if she was to resist this man's dangerous appeal. She must make him hate her, so that she could then hate him in return. She thrust her nose in the air and regarded him through slitted eyes.

"I believe you had better ride outside, Mr. MacDougal."

"Why? Afraid the heat between us might melt the frost you keep wrapped about you like a cape?"

"Get out!" she cried, shaken to the core by his perceptiveness. "Now!"

"No."

The finality of that single word was so unexpected she gaped at him in shock. "What?"

With one swift movement he lunged forward, leaning over her, trapping her between his powerful arms. "I said no, Sarah. No. You will not order me about like some lackey. You will not turn up your nose at me, not when we both know it's all a farce. Call me a bastard if you want. I don't care. Before this night is done, I vow, you'll be calling me your darling bastard."

Then he kissed her, hard and fierce, forcing her head back against the high leather seat.

Caught utterly off guard, Sarah shoved at his chest, though a part of her knew it was useless. He was strong, both his body and his will—and his masculine appeal. He meant to teach her a lesson, about him and about herself.

And she, foolish girl that she was, reckless woman that she'd grown into, she wanted to learn everything.

# CHAPTER 13

MARSH knew his behavior was reprehensible. He knew he was taking advantage of the situation. But there was something in him that would not stop. She wanted to deny everything—that Cameron Byrde could have been such a callous lout; that Maureen MacDougal could have been his first wife; that he himself could be the man's true heir.

But it was not those denials that drove him to such violent passion. Even as he took possession of Sarah's lips and held her trapped in his embrace, he knew that much. It was her denial of the attraction between them that struck the most incendiary sparks in him. It was that denial that fed this insatiable need of his to make her admit to the truth.

Beneath them the carriage swayed gingerly down the wet, rutted road. Above them the rain eased to an erratic, pattering drumbeat. But between them lightning struck, igniting a firestorm of feelings that flared swiftly out of control.

Marsh was not certain what he'd meant to prove, how far he meant to press her. But when Sarah's fingers curled around his coat front, when her lips softened and her mouth parted beneath his, he forgot everything except the need to delve deeper into this font of pure pleasure.

His tongue tasted, tested, and probed, and found greater acceptance with every thrust. Then she let out a little moan, her tongue met with his, and had he the wherewithal to have realized it, he was immediately and irrevocably lost.

No longer was it merely his own pleasure he sought. No longer was revenge the fuel that urged him on. What he wanted, what he needed—what he must have—was that little moan again. He wanted to make her moan and whimper and cry out with the pleasure he brought to her.

In that mad moment inside the lumbering coach, with the driver and his own manservant only a call away, he wanted to make Sarah Palmer soar with pleasure until she was limp with it.

That it would bring him physical satisfaction too was undeniable. But it was not his primary aim. For all her sophistication, this difficult, arrogant snob of a woman was a novice in the art of pleasure. He had no doubt of that. And he was something of an expert.

So he would give her an introduction, and then . . . and then he would just see where it would end.

He pressed his suit and drank deeply of the sweetness she offered. Delicious mouth that tasted of minted tea; flawless skin that looked like pearl and smelled like lilies. He shifted to the seat alongside her, drawing her against him, reveling in the firm, feminine weight of her. Beneath all the trappings of civility and the strictures of society that she clung to, Sarah Palmer was a passionate woman, one long past being ready for a taste of sexual desire.

He slid an arm around her waist and drew her forcefully to him. Yes, she was ready, and so was he.

Sarah slid onto Marshall MacDougal's lap—sprawled over him, actually. How had this happened, this sudden shift of their positions, this unbelievable shift in her attitude toward him? For heaven's sake, she was kissing him as if she wanted him to continue.

But then the truth was, she did.

She let out a little groan of dismay, or perhaps it was a moan of surrender. At once his tongue delved deeper, possessing her mouth in a manner she ought to find obscene. But she did not. To her dismay his tongue, sliding between her lips then out again, filled not only her mouth, but somehow her whole body as well. He heated her with that simple, primitive act so that she felt full, almost to bursting.

And when his arm clasped her fully against him, the feelings only increased.

Then she realized that one of her thighs was trapped between his, and that her skirts were bunched up nearly to her knees. Alarmed, the first bit of good sense finally intruded into her utterly besotted brain.

"Oh, no," she breathed when he moved his boldly seeking lips to the side of her neck, then down to the exposed curve of her shoulder. "This will . . . this will never do. . . ."

"Don't resist me, Sarah. I promise you will be glad if you just do not resist."

"But . . . but I must," she murmured, even as she arched her neck to let his lips move in a series of devastating nibbles along her excruciatingly sensitive flesh. "You will . . . you will have to get out of the carriage."

By then, however, he'd pulled her around to face him so that she actually straddled one of his hard, muscular thighs. No skirt protected her own thighs from his. No petticoat or even chemise. Only the finely twilled wool of his riding breeches separated that most private of her feminine parts from his solid male flesh.

She thought she would melt all over him.

He clasped both of his hands around her waist and pushed her slightly away from him. Then he pulled her back.

She heard herself moan out loud. Good heavens, she *was* melting! Like butter put to the flame, she was heating and dissolving, and it all centered down there right between her legs.

She was horrified by her reaction and embarrassed, yet completely unable to resist him when he performed that excruciatingly exciting movement once more.

"Damn, but you taste so sweet." He whispered the words, hot and thrilling in her ear. "I want to lap you up."

*Lap you up.* Yes, she would like him to do just that. Run those lips all over her. Taste her. Lick her. Suck her.

She squirmed in agitation, wanting things she did not

entirely understand, feeling her body in ways she'd never felt it before. She felt wild and reckless—

*Reckless.*

The word ricocheted in Sarah's head. Reckless, in her mother's voice and her brother's.

Hadn't her reckless behavior been the cause of all the other disasters in her past? Hadn't she vowed to keep those reckless impulses under control?

But before she could summon the will to react as she knew she ought to that cautionary voice, he slid her along his thigh once more, and lifted one of her knees to open her legs even wider.

She nearly swooned. Indeed, she would have toppled over had his arm not held her fast before him. Once more he caught her mouth with his, taking liberties no man had ever taken. The thrusting of his tongue mirrored the movement of her hips upon his thigh. He slid his tongue in and out and she shifted herself forward and back. His teeth and lips and tongue abraded hers, and his hard wool-clad thighs abraded the precious center of her.

Even his breathing, harder now and faster, seemed a part of a conspiracy, rousing her to unnamable heights. Her faint moans of dismay had long become cries of excitement, and she found herself panting and kissing him back, burning up with the feelings he roused in her, the lust. When would it stop? When would it end? She would die soon, for she could take no more.

Then one of his hands slid past her stockings and garter, and farther, up along her bare thigh. He was under her skirt, stroking her burning flesh with his broad, callused palm.

Sarah's head was spinning. She was short of breath and light-headed, and she knew she should make him stop. But she couldn't. Not for the life of her could she make him stop, for he stroked her now where she was burning, where she was melting.

Then he pushed his hand higher still and his finger slid within her.

That was when she exploded. That was when she arched

up and cried out, an eruption as emotional as it was physical. She erupted and erupted again, feeling as if the last of her had melted all over him.

Afterward she lay limp and utterly spent, too stunned and bewildered to summon her wits about her. Only as she struggled for her very breath did she slowly become aware of the man beneath her, struggling to control his own breathing. Reality returned with a horrifying jolt.

Good God! What had she done?

Sitting on his thigh as she was, with her skirts hiked up around her hips, gave her an immediate and humiliating answer.

"Oh, no," she gasped. With trembling arms she pushed herself awkwardly upright. Skirts up, legs apart, and wrapped in the arms of a scoundrel who would stop at nothing, it seemed, to hurt her family. And like the reckless—oh, so reckless—fool that she was, she'd cooperated fully with him.

This time she lurched backward, landing awkwardly on the opposite seat with her skirts up in her lap and her knees and thighs exposed to his view. Frantically she beat down the tangled layers of fabric, sheltering her legs from the air and from his watching eyes. But that still left her sitting opposite Marshall MacDougal in the aftermath of the most torrid interlude of her life. It did no good trying to restore her clothing to order, when they both knew how willingly she'd participated in what had just happened.

But what exactly *had* just happened?

She twisted her fingers together in her lap, and her downcast eyes stared blankly at the short space between his knees and hers.

Her heart was still racing; she could hear his breaths, harsh but beginning to slow. Outside, the rain beat steadily upon the carriage roof, isolating the vehicle from the rest of the world and making it a small island of light and heat all unto itself. And only she and Marshall MacDougal in it.

Rallying the remnants of her tattered pride, she managed

to lift her gaze to his. What she saw on his face, however, made her choke on the words she was trying to form. Words of denial. Words of accusation. But the look in his eyes drove them all from her mind.

He still desired her.

Though she had no experience with the secret relations between man and woman, she knew a little bit about lust. She'd been the target of many a man's seductive gaze, gazes that often became lustful as the evening drew on and the drinking grew heavy. But those other men's lustful looks had meant nothing more to her than a distasteful sort of victory. Let them look and lust after her. They had better not presume, however, to touch.

But this man had touched. She'd let him. And worse, she liked it. She'd loved every torrid, shameful caress.

She averted her eyes again, only to have them focus on a suspicious dark spot upon the leg of his breeches. A damp spot right where she'd straddled his thigh.

*Oh, God!* Not just straddling, but pressing and rubbing and grinding herself against him! That melting sensation had not been her imagination at all. *She* had made that damp spot on his breeches!

As if he sensed the turn of her thoughts, Mr. MacDougal moved one of his hands to his thigh, then smoothed his thumb back and forth over that awful, incriminating spot. "It's no use denying your full participation this time, Sarah. It seems I have the proof."

She refused to look at him. It was cowardly and it gained her nothing at all. But Sarah was completely unable to face him. Even her dread of that terrible interview with her mother, brother, and stepfather when they'd decided to send her north to Scotland had been nothing compared to this.

They rode on in an oppressive silence that seemed to amplify her guilt. Sarah struggled to focus her scattered senses upon the ordinary humdrum sounds around them. The rhythmic squeal of the left rear wheel. The steady drumming of the rain. The lantern swayed, setting weak shadows to dancing. All ordinary, everyday occurrences.

But they seemed strange now, surreal, given the unimaginable circumstances she found herself in, and her extraordinary, unforgivable behavior.

"I gather that was a new experience for you."

Sarah felt his low voice like a physical stroke along her overstimulated nerves. How was she possibly to respond to that?

"Yes," he went on. "Totally new. Do you . . . ah . . . understand what just occurred here, Sarah?"

She swallowed hard. "You took advantage of me," she said. But her voice possessed little force and even less conviction.

He leaned forward, causing her to jump, and at last their eyes met. "Had I taken advantage of you, we would not yet be finished. Nor would I still remain in this painfully aroused and unrelieved state."

When his meaning sank in, Sarah's eyes widened and he gave her a wry smile. "I see you understand. I take it, then, that you also understand that you have not actually lost your virginity."

Sarah's lips trembled. "Perhaps . . . perhaps not. But I have certainly lost some part of my innocence."

At that admission, as much to herself as to him, tears began to burn in the backs of her eyes. But she vowed not to cry—at least not in his presence. And so she fought them down.

He reached out and caught her hand in his, then held it firm when she would have pulled it free. "Do you understand what happened, what you felt?" he asked once more.

"No!" she snapped. "No. Nor do I wish to. I only want for you to be gone. Out of this carriage. Out of Scotland. Out of my life—all our lives!"

He released her hand and sat back.

She scooted to the corner farthest from him.

Not that the additional foot or so of distance was any particular help to her. He was still there, too close, too overwhelming, too masculine and virile and appealing for her to bear. But she could not take her eyes off him, nor let her guard down. There was no telling what he might do, now that he knew how susceptible she was to him. He had only to look at that awful damp place she'd made on his thigh to know the power he wielded over her.

He settled into his corner and studied her back with dark, impassive eyes. "You have just felt what the French call *le petit morte*. The little death. It's the result of sexual arousal. The goal of it."

*Le petit morte*. She'd heard of it in one of the books her mother would have been horrified to know she'd read.

And what would her mother think of her actually experiencing it?

Sarah simply could not cope with that right now. She'd behaved in the most reprehensible manner; there remained nothing but for her to brazen it out. She stared balefully at him. "So. Are you happy now? You achieved your goal."

One side of his mouth curved up in a half grin. "You achieved it. Unfortunately, I did not quite attain the little death."

Too upset to be cautious, Sarah blurted out, "And why not?"

"I'm asking myself the same question." His grin faded and something glittered, hot and dangerous, in his eyes. His hand tightened into a fist upon his thigh. "Would you be willing to help me get there?"

*No!* Sarah didn't say the word out loud; she couldn't have, for her bravado had fled, leaving her mouth as dry as a desert. Her expression of horror must have given her away, however, for Marsh let out an inelegant snort.

"No. I didn't think you would—at least not tonight. But maybe someday." He shifted on his seat. "Someday very soon," he added in a lower tone. Then he crossed his arms, leaned his head back, and shut his eyes.

Did he sleep? It hardly mattered as they rolled along the pitch-black highway, for his last words echoed in Sarah's mind with increasing force. *Someday very soon.*

*Not ever,* she told herself, repeating the vow silently, over and over, for the next hour. *Not ever. Not ever. Never,*

*never, never.* It turned into a chant that mirrored the coach's slow, lumbering progress. By the time they turned into the drive at Byrde Manor, it had become an anxious, desperate prayer. *Never let me succumb to him again. Never let me see him again. Never let me think about this again.*

But Sarah knew that last portion, at least, was not meant to be. This was one night she would never forget, and in truth, she was not completely sure she wanted to forget. A part of her wanted to go over every portion of those brief but intense moments. She wanted to understand them, dissect them, and examine every aspect of them.

She descended from the carriage, deliberately using the door opposite the one he'd used, then hurried across the muddy yard to the kitchen door. As she fled, however, she feared that understanding the violent reaction she'd had to him would never be enough. Only an hour had gone by, yet she already recognized the wicked, wanton truth.

She wanted to feel that way again.

She wanted to feel that eruption inside her, that faintness, that terrifying surrender. She wanted it and all the rest—whatever it was—that went with it.

A faint moan of utter dismay slipped past her lips. Oh, but she was the vilest sort of person, the lowest sort of woman.

Yet still the truth was a huge monster confronting her, no matter how she wished to avoid it. She desired Marshall MacDougal, the man who would not hesitate to destroy her beloved sister's and mother's lives.

It did not matter that his purpose was honorable, that he defended his mother with his quest. She still must not desire this man, this man above all men.

And yet she did. She desired him in the worst sort of way.

Though she hurried away from him without looking back to where he waited for his man's horse to be unharnessed from the carriage, his image haunted her still.

And as Marsh rode away through the damp darkness, back to his empty room at the Cock and Bow, Sarah Palmer's image haunted him as well. Her face, flushed and beautiful, as she'd found her release; her helpless cries, like some erotic music in his ears. Her womanly scent and maidenly sensibilities.

Damnation. He'd started something today that he feared now he would come to regret. He groaned as his damnably insistent arousal pressed painfully against the unforgiving rigidity of his saddle.

Hell, he regretted it already.

# CHAPTER

# 14

"ARE you sick?" Adrian eyed Sarah skeptically. Behind him Mrs. Hamilton's face creased in a worried frown. Due to Adrian's early morning visit, they'd not yet had the opportunity to discuss the results of her journey the previous day. "It's a glorious day for a ride," the boy went on, his tone cajoling. "What else have you to do?"

Sarah grimaced, for her head was throbbing already and Adrian's presence only made it worse. She'd hardly slept at all last night; now she was met with Adrian's petulance and the old housekeeper's alarm. Had Mrs. Hamilton spoken yet to the coachman about Mr. MacDougal's presence in the carriage with her last night? Good Lord, she hoped not, for she was not sure she could successfully deceive Mrs. Hamilton, should the older woman ply her with too many questions.

The fat kitchen cat jumped down from Sarah's lap and sauntered toward the boy. Sarah sighed. "Perhaps I am a little under the weather," she said in a deliberately faint voice.

"I knew it," Mrs. Hamilton said. "You got wet last night, didn't you? And now you've taken ill." She shook her head. "I hope you do not come down with the ague."

"It's not the ague, only a headache."

"That's how it starts. Come. You'd better drink some tea and get yourself back into bed. I should've known better than to let you go traipsin' about the countryside—"

She broke off, but it was too late. Adrian looked up from the cat he'd been petting. "Traipsing about where?"

"Nowhere," Sarah said, this time too brightly. "I took

an evening ride and . . . and I got caught in the rain."

But that only sharpened the boy's interest. "It didn't rain till awful late. Too late for an evening ride."

Mrs. Hamilton glanced briefly at Sarah before rounding on Adrian. "Whyever she's feelin' poorly is none of your concern, young Master Hawke. Go on with you, now. Leave my Sarah in peace so's she can recover. Go find Mr. Hamilton if it's company you're wantin'. He'll put you to work straightaway."

Only after Adrian had reluctantly departed did Mrs. Hamilton turn on Sarah. "Now, how about you telling me what's goin' on, child? I'm agreed to helping you, 'cause it's for the family. But I'll not be hoodwinked by your pretty ways. Out with it now, else I'll write your mum this very afternoon. And your sister. *And* your brother."

So Sarah told her everything—everything, that is, except the one thing she could not tell anyone, ever.

"Well." Mrs. Hamilton fussed with her tea a long moment. "Well, though I cannot like that he rode with you in the closed carriage, under the circumstances I s'pose you had no choice but to let him. And perhaps it is all for the best. After all, we know now that he is not Cameron Byrde's heir." She shook her head. "I cannot tell you, child, how relieved I am for that. I hate to think how that would have affected your mother." She drank the rest of her tea. "D'you think he will leave us in peace now?"

*No.*

"I hope so," Sarah said, ignoring her real fear that Marshall MacDougal was not done with them. Not by a long shot.

She spent the remainder of the morning in an aimless sort of idleness. She did not wish to ride or walk, nor sit and sew. Reading required too much concentration for her restless mood, and there was no one she wished to visit. No one, that is, except the one person she should hope never to see again.

She tossed down an old copy of *The Ladies' Gazetteer and Pattern Book* that she'd picked up in the morning room, then made another aimless circuit of the parlor. If only her sister were here. Olivia would understand about the unlikely flare of passion between Sarah and the troublesome Marshall MacDougal. Not that Olivia would approve of her younger sister's behavior. But Sarah remembered enough of Olivia and Neville's tumultuous courtship to know that Olivia would at least understand.

Only she could not tell Olivia anything about Marshall MacDougal and his presence in Scotland. At least not until he was gone.

She pushed aside a lace panel in one of the parlor windows and stared out at the placid scene beyond. Green meadows, fully budded trees. Life at Byrde Manor had a stolid sort of rhythm to it, centered on the seasons and the tasks that must be accomplished during each season. Nothing like in town where life revolved around an altogether different sort of season. Politics, parties, people. That sort of season had been her downfall and so she'd been sent packing to a place where she could find no trouble.

Yet find it she nonetheless had.

She let the lace curtain fall. What was wrong with her? Did trouble follow her, or was she the one to create trouble wherever she went? Was her whole life to be a series of crises? Was she to create chaos no matter the place or the people she circulated among?

Sarah rubbed her aching temples with her fingertips. Everything had changed last night. No matter that she had not technically lost her virginity, she had shared something more than she'd ever imagined, with a man she would never see again. Just as bad, however, the man whom she knew she must banish from her life had suddenly become the central figure in it. Though he no longer seemed so great a threat to Olivia's happy existence, overnight he had become a huge threat to hers.

How could she possibly go the rest of her life without ever seeing him again?

* * *

Marsh had spent the entire night replaying those few incredible minutes with Sarah over and over in his mind. Neither the painful ride from Byrde Manor to Kelso nor the cold bath he'd taken had chilled the fire that now burned in him. Even seeking relief in the solitude of his own bed had done little to ease the need that clawed at his insides. He wanted her—Sarah Palmer—naked beside him. Until he had that, his suffering was not likely to abate.

But he was not likely ever to have that chance again. Not now. After that debacle with Horace MacNeil, followed by that incredible scene between them in the carriage, she must be convinced that he was only some profligate Lothario. And a fortune hunter as well.

He would not be able to count on a lame horse and a thunderstorm to throw them together again.

He sat now in the public room of the Cock and Bow, finishing a meal he had hardly tasted, while Duffy sat opposite him, shoveling in every morsel on his plate with great gusto

"So. Where to today?" the man said, wiping his mouth on his sleeve after downing a tankard of ale. "Or have you had enough gaddin' about the Scottish countryside?"

Marsh scowled down into his own tankard. Where to indeed?

"P'rhaps you're thinkin' about goin' out to visit your lady love?" Duffy persisted. There was a knowing glint in his eyes.

"No," Marsh muttered through gritted teeth. Despite his denial, however, that was precisely what he wanted to do. But it was too soon to seek her out.

He should never have taken advantage of her that way, and he suspected she would be a long time getting over it. By the same token, however, he would be a long while getting over it himself. And he would not take those few moments back, even if he could. He still wanted to know how she was and how she felt about what had happened between them. But not yet.

He looked up at his grinning servant. "You can wipe

that cheeky look off your face. Get the carriage ready. I'm thinking of taking a lengthy journey."

"A lengthy journey? Where to?" the man asked, his grin fading to consternation. "An' here I just found the love of my life in Kelso."

The love of his life? It must be Estelle, the boy's mother. "Don't worry, we'll be back," Marsh muttered.

"Good. 'Cause I don't want her eye wanderin' around while we're gone. So. Where to, guv'nor?"

"I have a sudden desire to see the Atlantic coast of Scotland," Marsh answered slowly as the idea evolved in his head. His mother had mentioned once or twice that she had sailed to America from the port city of Dumfries. Cameron Byrde might not have wed her anyplace around Kelso that MacNeil would have heard about. But he might well have done so in one of the Atlantic port towns and villages where no one would have known them. Marsh had found no proof of a marriage around here, but perhaps there he might.

Besides, it would get him away from Sarah for a few days. Maybe by then his blood might have cooled down a little. Maybe then he'd be able to think straight about what was going on between him and Sarah Palmer, something that had nothing to do with Cameron Byrde or Olivia Byrde Hawke.

He saddled his own horse, his mood considerably lightened. Sarah Palmer might think the subject of his true heritage settled, but he knew better. He had not given up his quest, not by a long shot. He'd only broadened it. He still wanted his birthright. But now he wanted Sarah Palmer too.

If last night had proven anything, it was that the two were not mutually exclusive.

Mrs. Hamilton's hovering eventually drove Sarah outdoors. The air was clean and sharp, and the sun had burned away most of the puddles. Dressed in an everyday gown with a pair of garden clogs on her feet, Sarah had set herself to puttering about in the garden. The roses needed retying along the garden fence and the rosemary shrubs ought to have their tips pinched so that the plants wouldn't grow too leggy. Plus, some wild creature had tunneled beneath the fence that separated the sheep meadows from the garden plot, and played havoc with the newly emerging pansies.

Unfortunately, the mindless labor of gardening left a big, empty space for uneasy memories to cavort in. And cavort Sarah's memories did. By early afternoon she had worked herself into quite a state. Bad enough her hands were filthy, her manicure ruined, and her hem stained with mud. Far worse, however, was the shame upon her soul. She'd behaved like a wanton last night, yet still she thrilled to the memory. Her body reacted with longing every time she recalled what she'd done with him.

Her mind fought it, but her body won.

This must be why parents guarded their daughters so carefully and tried to marry them off so quickly, she decided. To avoid this terrible limbo of shame and desire. At least within a marriage this physical yearning could be slaked.

Nonetheless, ignoring the situation was doing her no good at all. Perhaps she should simply go into Kelso and find out whether he had left. For if he was gone, then she had nothing to worry about—except, perhaps, the latest wickedness he had loosed within her.

She took the chaise to town, determined to appear the proper lady despite her improper behavior of late. She drove first to the bakery to purchase sugared rolls for Mrs. Hamilton. Unfortunately, the baker's outspoken mother sat in the window, watching Sarah's every movement without the least show of subtlety. Recalling their previous encounter, Sarah only nodded to her, then gave the baker her order.

*Hurry up. Hurry up.* Her foot began nervously to tap.

But the baker was too slow and his mother too nosy.

"Have you driven him off so fast, then? A strapping fellow like him needs a woman to match." Those quick, birdlike eyes swept over Sarah. "Give her an extra loaf, son. I'm thinking she needs more flesh on her bones if she's to keep the next bonny lad that comes along."

"Mother!" the poor fellow moaned, sending Sarah an apologetic glance. But he duly added a loaf as his mother had ordered.

Sarah steeled herself to ignore the old woman's candid remarks—all except for one. Feigning disinterest, she turned toward the woman. "So he's left, has he? What a relief."

"Sure, an' he's left. But don't you go pretending you don't care, lassie. I know better. I can tell."

The baker shoved Sarah's purchase at her. "I'll add it to your bill," he said, gesturing toward the door with a pleading expression on his round face. He couldn't get her out of there fast enough.

Sarah was also eager to leave. But she wanted to know more about Mr. MacDougal's departure, every detail, and she was willing to endure the old busybody's uncomfortable observations to do so.

She cleared her throat and stared at the other woman, who waited in her tall armchair, an expectant expression on her wrinkled face. "You're right. I do care that he's gone. But not for the reason you think. Mr. MacDougal is not the sort of man my mother would approve of. I did not wish to hurt his feelings with an outright rebuff, so you see, his absence removes the necessity for me to do so."

The woman readjusted her gray knitted shawl across her thin shoulders. "Rather see you get him than that Estelle," she grunted. "But what will be, will be. And what won't, won't. Fetch me a fresh cup of tea," she called over to her son.

Sarah stood there a moment, aware she'd been dismissed. But the mention of Estelle's name raised up the hairs on the back of her neck. Surely he had not run from her to Estelle. Surely he would not do such a thing to her!

Yet why should he not?

She forced her legs to move and, with a nod to the embarrassed baker, left his fragrant little shop. Marshall MacDougal was gone, she told herself. *Be glad of that and do not worry about the details.*

But it was awfully hard. So mired was she in her jealous fit that when Mrs. Liston called out to her, she did not at first hear.

"Miss Palmer. Oh, Miss Palmer!"

Sarah drew up, not even aware of her destination, and glanced around. Another busybody to deal with. Yet Sarah was not entirely sorry to see the vicar's wife. Perhaps she had better information than the baker's mother.

"My dear, how are you? How are you?" Mrs. Liston gushed. "I have been meaning to call on you. But with all of Mr. Liston's duties and then my own as his wife, well, as you can only imagine, I have been exceedingly busy."

"I'm sure you have," Sarah concurred. "But I am glad to see you now. How are you? And Mr. Liston?"

Sarah suffered through a quarter hour of various complaints, cautions, and dull bits of gossip. She was struggling for a way to escape, sorry she'd ever encouraged the conversation, when the discourse at last turned to the topic she desired yet did not dare bring up herself.

". . . and I bade good-bye to that American. You know the one. That handsome Mr. MacDougal."

"Oh, yes." Sarah nodded. She shifted her package from one arm to the next. "He has left Kelso?"

"Well. He has come and gone quite a bit. Most curious, those comings and goings of his. He rode into town very late last night, then departed again just after noon."

"Has he? Well, who's to say he won't return later this evening? Or perhaps tomorrow?"

Mrs. Liston shook her head so hard the fat curls on either side of her thin cheeks quivered. "This time he took all his luggage, and though I hear he is paid up through the month, he said there's a chance he mayn't be back. I had it from Mrs. Halbrecht herself. Gone to Dumfries, she said. That's a goodly journey. P'rhaps he means to set sail back to America from there."

Dumfries. Sarah had to think a moment to place the town. It was all the way to the east, along the Atlantic coast.

Sarah escaped Mrs. Liston as quickly as she could, mulling over that odd bit of information. She refused to think about how relieved she was that Marshall MacDougal was not with Estelle Kendrick. She refused also to examine too closely the hollow feeling in her chest at the idea of him actually being gone forever.

It was what she'd been hoping for, and now it had come to pass. After hearing Mr. MacNeil's ugly remarks, Mr. MacDougal must have given up his foolish quest to prove himself Cameron Byrde's rightful heir and gone back to America. What other reason to head to Dumfries? After all, it was a port city. Ships must arrive and depart to America on a regular basis.

Had they done so thirty years ago?

Thirty years ago. The thought brought Sarah to a sudden halt outside the leather goods store. Had his mother sailed from Dumfries to America all those years ago? She had to have sailed from somewhere, and most likely it had been Cameron Byrde who'd paid for her passage.

Could he also have wed her while they were there?

Sarah's heart sank.

It was more than possible. The terrible truth was that it would be just like the Cameron Byrde she'd always heard about to do just such a devious thing. Marry his pregnant lover in secret, then ship her halfway around the world with the promise to join her later.

She clenched the paper package in her arms, unmindful of the damage she did to its contents. Though the scenario she imagined was not likely, it nevertheless was possible. And that meant she must follow Mr. MacDougal to Dumfries. She simply could not afford to take the chance that he might find a record of a marriage she prayed had never taken place.

# CHAPTER 15

Mr. Hamilton threatened not to provide either the horses or the vehicle for such an outrageous purpose.

"What's to see in Dumfries?" the old fellow demanded to know. "If it's ocean scenery you're wanting, farther south at Maryport's the place, not Dumfries. And what's wrong with the North Sea, anyway?"

"I've seen the North Sea," Sarah muttered, shooting Mrs. Hamilton a beseeching look.

Mrs. Hamilton struggled with conflicting emotions. Sarah did not want anyone else to know her true reason for this sudden journey west. But the housekeeper was worried. Something was afoot between Sarah and that man. Something beyond this battle over his claim to Olivia's properties. That alone was reason enough for her to forbid Sarah to go after him to Dumfries.

But perhaps there was a stronger reason to let her go. Sarah needed to be married. She was a good-hearted girl, but she was impulsive and reckless and headed for trouble, if the past was any indication. What if she got herself into a compromising situation with this American gent? Apparently she'd already come close with some other fellow. Why James had prevented their marriage, she didn't know. Better Sarah wed than not.

But James wasn't here now. And from the looks of things, Sarah was not about to take no for an answer.

Mrs. Hamilton lowered herself into a chair. "Perhaps a jaunt to Dumfries would be good for you, child."

"Are you daft?" Mr. Hamilton interrupted. "She don't need to go there."

"Hush, old man. She'll do just fine. I'll send a maid with her, and an extra footman. What do you say to that, Sarah, girl?"

"Yes. Thank you," Sarah replied, smiling her gratitude. "Thank you." She ran off to begin packing. Mr. Hamilton trudged off, grumbling, but in reluctant agreement.

Mrs. Hamilton remained seated in her favorite kitchen chair, however, drumming her gnarled fingers upon the scarred oak tabletop and thinking.

If Sarah was to be compromised, as it seemed she was destined to be, better that it happen here than in London. Mr. MacDougal was not leaving for America just yet; somehow she was sure of it. Let him compromise her—if he hadn't already done so in the carriage last night. Once found out, they would be forced to wed, and once wed, his threat to Olivia and Augusta would be considerably lessened.

Mrs. Hamilton smiled to herself, then bent down to rub her aching knee. Sarah could pursue one plan to protect her family, while she would pursue another. Oh, but this was more excitement than she'd had in many a day.

So it was that the next morning Sarah and an entourage of three rocked briskly down the highway, heading west with a team of four horses. Sarah was taking no chances this time should one of the animals go lame. From Kelso to Dumfries would normally have been a two-day journey. But Sarah felt compelled to stop at every church whose spire showed on the horizon. This time she'd brought a small chest of money with her, adequate to make a significant enough donation to ensure cooperation at every church she approached.

The answer at each one was, thankfully, always the same. No entry in the parish records for a Cameron Byrde, nor for a Maureen MacDougal.

But though relieved, Sarah was not reassured. Her sister's birthright would not be safe until Marshall MacDougal was on board a ship headed back to America. Until that happenstance, she could not let down her guard, nor relax her vigilance.

As for Marshall MacDougal himself, though she was alarmed that he too had stopped in each of those churches, she was relieved not to have run into him. She meant to avoid the man at all costs. Confronting him would do no good, and it might do much harm—if her unsettling dreams of the past few nights were any indication.

Sarah shuddered to remember the wicked bent her dreams had begun to take of late. To recall his kisses made her skin heat. And to remember how he'd touched her and roused her . . .

To relive those unbelievable few minutes was enough to make her tremble and grow damp all over again. No matter how she tried to put it out of her head, something inside her yearned for him. It was a terrible thing to admit, even to herself. But it was true. And to her great chagrin, it seemed to be getting worse.

Across from her, Mary, the maid Mrs. Hamilton had insisted she bring along, yawned and shifted in her sleep.

So far the young woman had not asked too many questions. It helped considerably that Sarah had suggested the pretty, unattached Mary, and also a handsome, unattached groom named Fleming. The two had quickly progressed from curious glances to appreciative stares to blatant flirtation. Just as Sarah had hoped, the two of them kept one another occupied while she went about her secretive business at each of the churches along the way.

But now, as they approached the outskirts of the busy port town of Dumfries, Sarah was not nearly so confident of her hastily contrived plan. What if she should run into Mr. MacDougal? After all, Dumfries was not that large and he would be asking the same questions in the same places as she.

"Oh," Mary groaned, and again yawned, then straightened up and stuck her head out the window. "Are we there yet?"

"Yes," Sarah answered. "But we shan't be staying very

long. A day or two and we should begin back."

When the girl looked outside again, craning her neck and obviously searching for a glimpse of Fleming up beside the driver, Sarah felt a stab of guilt. Though she had deliberately promoted this little romance between them for her own convenience, she did not want Mary to do anything she ought not do. She'd learned firsthand the perils of that sort of reckless behavior, and after all, the girl was in her employ and therefore under her care.

"Mary. I think you ought to exercise a little caution when it comes to Fleming. Do not be too quick to fall under his spell."

The girl sat back in the seat, her pose as demure as any lady's maid's should be. But her brown eyes sparkled with mischief. "Don't you worry. I can take care of myself with the likes of him, Miss Sarah. Better you warn him not to break his heart over Mary Douglass."

Sarah suppressed a grin. "That confident, are you?"

Mary crossed her arms and stared frankly at Sarah. "I know you're well above me, miss. But some things don't change, no matter if you're in society or in service. A man's a man. They all want the same thing, an' I don't think I have to tell you what that is. At the same time, a woman's a woman. What we most want is something we can only purchase if we spend our fortune well—if you catch my drift."

Sarah caught her drift. As the girl rattled on and the carriage rolled on, she caught Mary's drift very well indeed. And as they settled into a comfortable inn, and Sarah sat down to a warm meal, she had to wonder if she'd already squandered too much of her fortune on the wrong man—and whether, if he reappeared, she would throw the rest of her sorely diminished fortune into his hands.

Marsh was in a foul mood. He had been ever since he'd left Kelso in such a state of frustration. On the long journey to the coast, his failure to find any proof of his mother's claim to have wed Cameron Byrde had hammered at him, one blow at a time, until he found himself mired in both frustration and depression. Unfortunately, neither of those emotions seemed to have decreased his need for some physical release.

He stood now on the main street of Dumfries, outside a coffeehouse very like the ones that lined the streets of London, and looked about. A pair of women glided by, trailed by their maids. They were a young and comely pair, probably well-to-do young matrons, dressed in the fashions of London and Paris, but with rust-colored hair and bright brown eyes that proclaimed their Scottish heritage.

One of them glanced at him, then away, then back again, smiling this time at his frank stare. He followed their progress as they swept by, appreciating the full bosoms and swaying hips revealed by their close-fitting walking gowns.

Why could he not lust after a winsome Scottish lass like one of them, instead of a difficult English priss like Sarah Palmer?

He dragged his gaze reluctantly from the two women and slapped his riding gloves against his open palm. The fact was, Sarah Palmer might be difficult, but he had to admit that she was no priss, at least not once you scratched beneath that polished veneer she wore so well.

Again he slapped his gloves, then, frowning, started across the street. He'd been to three churches today, with as many left to approach. Though he fought it, he was fast growing discouraged. Could his mother have made up the story of a marriage, just as she'd made up the story of his father's death during the Atlantic crossing?

And could he really blame her for doing so? Could any decent person with any amount of feelings blame her for anything she might have done to ensure her survival and that of her little child?

Bedeviled, he turned the door ringer of the handsome residence attached to the grandiose St. Andrew's. Marsh didn't think a devious bastard like Cameron Byrde would have brought his serving girl/lover to so grand a church as this. Then again, thirty years ago it might not have been so grand.

An hour later he trudged out, depressed anew. Only two churches left. Of course, there were other port towns he could try. But a feeling of defeat dogged his steps as he retrieved his horse and started up the granite-paved street.

A half hour later he decided that St. Jerome's was as far a cry from St. Andrew's as he could have found. A small, beaten-down church, its stone walls were blackened with moss, its sagging roof jagged with loosened slates.

Marsh tried to picture it thirty years ago, how it might have looked to a simple country lass, her view of the world colored by the love she felt for the man at her side. Damn Cameron Byrde! He had not deserved her love, nor that of his second wife and subsequent child.

He was weary and frustrated, so when the graying priest answered the door to the rectory himself, Marsh was less cordial than he should be. "I would like to examine your parish records of marriage," he said without preamble. "I'm willing to pay for the privilege."

The old priest blinked in surprise. "I . . . ah . . . I was just sitting down with a cup of tea. But . . . ah . . . come in. Come in." He stepped back and gestured Marsh into a neat but rather shabby little parlor. "Will you join me, Mr. . . . Mr. . . . ?"

Marsh whipped off his hat, immediately chagrined at his poor manners. "MacDougal. Marshall MacDougal. And thank you for the offer," he added, glancing around as he entered. No fire in the grate. One cup on the small tray, with only a single biscuit beside it. "Thank you, but I've already intruded enough on your tea. I wouldn't think of disturbing you any more than I must."

At least his donation here would be more useful than in those other, more prosperous parishes.

"Ah, but it's not intrusion, my son. Indeed, I welcome the company. I am Father Paterson," he added. "And I've been at St. Jerome's for many a year. Now, whose marriage records do you seek to find?"

The small, low-ceilinged office was as crammed with books and artifacts as the parlor was clean of them. Father Paterson lit a lamp and, after dusting off first this shelf, then that, he finally tugged out an old volume bound in well-worn burlap. The letters on the spine, barely legible, read, *1754 to 1805.*

Marsh stared at the ledger wobbling before him in the old priest's trembling hands, and for a long moment he could not reach for it. A sudden fear of the truth gripped him, and though he knew there were other churches in other ports still to search, he was nonetheless afraid of what he would learn in this book. It made no sense at all, and after a moment he shook his head, chasing that cold feeling away. He took the book, then rested it on the cluttered table beside the lamp.

The entries were carefully made, long rows with names, ages, places of birth and current residences. Marsh looked up at the silently hovering old man. "How long have you been here?"

The skinny fellow smiled and pointed to the page in front of Marsh, where a crisp upright penmanship gave way to a slanted flourishing one. "Right here. April 1793. Almost thirty-five years now, though we've not nearly so many marriages these days as we used to. My flock is mostly past marryin' age, you see, and . . ."

Marsh didn't hear the rest of the priest's words. He couldn't, for the sudden thudding of his heart and subsequent roaring of blood in his ears precluded any other sound. He stared at the carefully inscribed names, third line down from the top.

> Cameron Byrde, age 22, of Kelso, and Maureen MacDougal, age 20, born in Eyemouth, now residing in Kelso. September 15, 1796.

The date blurred and Marsh had to blink to clear his eyes.

September 15, 1796. Six months before he was born.

He looked up, conscious of the very real feeling that something in his chest was constricting. His mother had stood here, probably in this very room, just as he now did. She'd stood here beside Cameron Byrde, both of them aware of the child they'd conceived within her. She'd stood here and pledged herself to a man she loved, a man who'd said his vows with no intentions of keeping them.

How long until he'd sent her off alone on that ship bound for America?

How many lies had he said to her to convince her to go on to America without him?

Marsh looked up at the priest, who gazed at him now with a faint smile on his lined face.

"Have you found what you were searching for?"

Marsh nodded. "Did you . . . did you marry them?"

The priest bent and, squinting, read the line pointed to. "I must have, for that's my entry."

"Do you remember them?"

The priest continued to stare at the entry as if some image from the past might rise up from the page to remind him. But when his faded eyes lifted to meet Marsh's, the answer was clear.

" 'Twas a long time ago, laddie. I'm sorry. Did you say you were a MacDougal like her?"

Marsh couldn't answer right away, not aloud. *Yes, I am related to her. I am a MacDougal, just like her. And I always will be.* In that moment, with the proof of his legitimacy staring up at him, confirming his right to claim Byrde as his true name, Marsh vowed never to use that name again. Never.

He'd used his mother's surname during his boxing days. Mac MacDougal. God, but that seemed a lifetime ago. Now he would become a MacDougal again, as a tribute to his mother. He would use her name, even if he had to go to court in America to make the change legal.

So he only nodded to the little priest, then forced himself to become practical once more. "I would like to write down this record of their marriage, and have you witness and sign the document as a true representation of your parish records."

It took such a very little amount of time to do it. After months of travel and search, once he'd found the records it was only a matter of minutes before Marsh had the proof he'd wanted folded up, safe within his inside coat pocket. He patted his chest as Father Paterson showed him out. It was there. He had it now.

"I want to thank you, Father, and make a donation to your church." He pulled out the leather pouch he kept for these donations, then added several coins from his own purse. "Thank you," he repeated. Then on impulse he asked, "Might I have a few minutes alone in the church itself?"

"Why, of course, my son." The priest stared from Marsh to the weighty pouch in his hand, then back to Marsh. Though puzzled, he was plainly pleased. "Take as long as you like."

Alone in the little church, Marsh stared about—at the one stained-glass window, patched with a clear fragment where a portion of St. Jerome's foot had at some point been smashed. The altar cloths were yellowed and patched as well, and only one brace of candles stood unlit upon the altar.

A fitting church in which to pray for his mother, he decided as he dropped to his knees on the uneven floor. She'd never aspired to riches or titles, or even the grand home he gladly would have built for her. Simple Maureen MacDougal Byrde had remained the same sweet and unassuming woman all her life, unchanged by the adversity Cameron Byrde's betrayal had visited upon her.

Though he knew revenge had no place in a church, Marsh was not ready to forgive his father. So he prayed instead for his mother.

*Thank you for making her my mother,* was all he could say. *Thank you for letting me have her for all those years.*

Only when he was calmer—and emotionally drained—did he finally depart the church. He stood on the little stoop, put his hat on, and stared out into the sunny street.

He'd accomplished exactly what he'd set out to do, found the proof of his mother's claim and his own.

Now it was time to put that proof to work, and that meant returning to Kelso and Byrde Manor.

And to Sarah Palmer.

# CHAPTER 16

SARAH spied Marshall MacDougal on the other side of the street, standing head and shoulders above a heavily loaded coal cart lumbering past. At once she shrank back against a bayfront window displaying the knitted sweaters and fine men's wear of a tailor's shop, hoping to avoid detection.

But it was for naught. As if he felt the weight of her startled stare, he looked up and fixed his gaze upon hers. He halted midstride, and hesitated only for a moment before altering his direction toward her. She had but a few seconds to catch her breath—and to send Mary to wait at the carriage with Fleming—before Mr. MacDougal stopped before her.

She knew at once that something had changed. The expression on his face was belligerent and his dark eyes glittered with a righteous sort of anger. Nothing surprising in that. But something about his mouth looked raw and perhaps even a little vulnerable.

She had no time to contemplate that odd possibility, for he spoke directly to her without any play at social chitchat. "I'm glad you're here, Sarah. It saves me having to seek you out."

She averted her eyes from his intense stare and looked beyond him at the shabby little church he seemed to have just left. The very church she'd been heading for.

Could he have found the proof he sought? Her heart began to race, and with a sinking certainty, she knew he had. If only she had arrived an hour earlier!

Yet what could she have done? Destroy that proof? She

wasn't sure she could do such a despicable thing, not even for her mother and her beloved older sister.

So she raised her face back up to him and waited with dread for what was to come.

To her surprise, he took her arm in one hand and steered her down the street. "I need a drink, if you don't mind."

"A drink? At a public house?"

"At a public house. Don't worry, Sarah. It's unlikely any of your society friends will ever learn of it. Dumfries is too far off the beaten track for them." He laughed, a harsh, mirthless sound. "My father was right in that. His first wedding at a tiny little church in faraway Dumfries probably never would have been found out if his eldest son had not set out to avenge his wronged mother."

Though she'd feared as much, Sarah gasped at his revelation. She stumbled, but his hand tightened around her arm. In a moment he steered her through the low doorway of a public house and into a dimly lit room only partially occupied by a few men. He guided her to a corner table, then with one large hand on her shoulder forced her to sit. He signaled to the barman and gave his order before pulling out a chair and straddling it.

"Yes," he confirmed, facing her with that same belligerent expression. "I have the proof. My parents wed here at St. Jerome's Church in Dumfries, September 15, 1796. A year before his second wedding to your mother." He paused, but the impact of his words seemed to echo like hammer blows in Sarah's ears.

"I assume you understand the import of that single, unassailable fact," he went on, adding one last final blow. It very nearly took the last bit of wind out of her sails.

But Sarah was not one to let anyone revel for long in her defeat. Gathering her courage, she lifted her chin and met his dark, watchful gaze. "Oh, yes. I understand what it means. You have your proof, whatever it is, and you intend to use it to humiliate my family. To ruin us. Do I have the right of it?"

A muscle ticked in his jaw. "I can see why you would

view it thus. I wonder, though, if you have it in you to understand my perspective. My mother was denied her rights as Cameron Byrde's true wife. I was denied my rights as his true heir. Can you honestly fault me for wanting to collect what has always been my due?" He leaned forward, and his eyes fairly burned into hers. "It's not your sister I wish to shame. I only want what is rightly mine."

He sat back when their glasses and a bottle of amber liquid arrived. Though Sarah had never been in a public house before and was now sitting unchaperoned and drinking with a man she hardly knew, she did not flinch when he poured her a glass of what smelled like brandy.

She picked up the squat tumbler, holding it tight, for her hand shook so, then drank down the contents in one quick gulp. Her throat burned and her eyes watered profusely, but again she did not flinch. She'd failed her family, and now this man—whom she'd also behaved abominably with—was going to undermine every facet of their lives.

Though her own personal fortune was not affected, nor her brother's, they were nonetheless all in this together. Mother, brother, sisters. When her mother and Olivia hurt, she too hurt. That was what being a family was all about.

So when he tossed his own drink down and refilled his glass, she knew she must do whatever it took to fight off this attack on the people she most loved, even if she did understand why Mr. MacDougal felt the need to attack them.

He held the bottle toward her, and she picked up her glass, wanting whatever courage the fiery liquid might impart. *Focus on Olivia, not him,* she told herself. Marshall MacDougal could take care of himself, as he'd already more than proven. But then she put her glass down and slid it aside. Drinking strong spirits would only give her a false sense of courage. It would not help her solve her dilemma.

Instead she took a deep, slow breath, then faced him squarely. "All right, Mr. MacDougal. Let us assume you do have some sort of proof to support your claim—sufficient proof to cast serious doubt on my mother's marriage to that . . . that damnable man." She pressed her lips together, then took another calming breath. "Assuming that, and assuming you are not lying when you say you do not wish to shame my sister, tell me, then: Just what is it you *do* wish?"

She watched as he shifted on the chair. He fingered his empty glass, rotating it in a slow circle on the pitted tabletop. "I want what any first son would be legally entitled to—"

"There is no title," she interrupted him. "I told you that before."

He slammed his glass down on the table. "And I told you I don't give a damn about titles!" He leaned forward, glaring at her from beneath lowered brows. "I don't give a damn about any English title. I want Byrde Manor. That's all. The house, the lands, the livestock. The right to proclaim it as mine."

She considered that. "Are you saying you're going to move in there?"

"Maybe." Then after a moment he added, "I don't know. I haven't decided."

Sarah shook her head. "You have no idea what a responsibility an estate like Byrde Manor is. It's not just land. It's not just fields and flocks of sheep. It's families who work there and have done so for generations. It's tenant farmers and house servants and field workers." It was her turn to lean forward. "It's a history of one family's responsibility to many others, and it is beyond valuation."

His eyes burned into hers. "I am as much a part of that history and family as anyone!"

It was an angry, passionate declaration, and for a moment Sarah was taken aback. "That may be true," she conceded. "But . . . but the attachment you have to Byrde Manor is based solely on revenge. In contrast, the attachment Olivia has is love. It's love," she repeated. "It will break her heart to lose Byrde Manor, whereas for you it is merely the spoils of some war you are waging with the horrible man who sired you both."

Despite her emotion-laden words, he appeared unmoved. He filled his tumbler anew and slowly sipped at the contents. "Your loyalty to your sister—"

"*Our* sister!"

"—is admirable. I've told you that before, Sarah, and I mean it. But that changes nothing. We are plainly arrived at an impasse, for I will not leave Scotland without collecting my due."

*Without collecting my due.*

Those last few words echoed in Sarah's head. He wanted his due, his inheritance. He'd come to Great Britain to take Olivia's modest fortune from her. Once he achieved that, he would probably depart, leaving some agent to handle the property. After all, he'd expressed his disdain for her country's social class system often enough. All he really wanted was the income Byrde Manor would provide. The income, and the revenge it stood for.

Her hand clenched around her glass. In the end this was all about money. Nothing else.

Then it occurred to her, the solution to everything. She would buy him off.

She'd known ever since she was a child that her father had left her much better provided for than Olivia's father had. In truth, she did not even know the full extent of her own inheritance: profitable tenant holdings; extensive investments in the three-percents; and a quarterly allowance that had always been bigger than her sister's annual one.

Surely it was enough to purchase Marshall MacDougal's silence. Even if she dipped into the investments themselves in order to pay him the full value of Byrde Manor, she would still never want for anything. And it would be worth it if that meant he would leave them in peace forever. Though the rest of her family might object, she had no compunction about spending her money that way. Certainly her dear departed father, who had adored Livvie, would approve of her plan.

Taking a slow, steadying breath, she smiled, sure of herself once more, then raised the glass to her mouth—only for a sip. "Yes, it might seem we have reached an impasse. However, I would like to put forth another solution."

He settled back in his chair, his arms crossed and an expression of skepticism on his face. "Another solution? This I have to hear."

She took a deep breath, too nervous about how he would respond to her offer to be angry at his unpleasant attitude. James would be furious when he found out about this, but she didn't care.

"I am very rich, Mr. MacDougal. Much more so than Olivia. And as you have surely ascertained, I love my sister and my mother dearly. Much as you love your own mother," she added. "If you are not lying when you say you do not wish to hurt my family, to punish us for the misdeeds of your father—which misdeeds we played absolutely no role in—then I believe I have a solution to all this unpleasantness."

Marsh kept his arms crossed and his features composed. But he knew at once what she was going to say. He knew. But he didn't want to hear it, because he didn't know how to respond.

Her eyes were as steady as a card sharp's upon him. "I am willing to pay you the full value of Byrde Manor, in coin or note or any other venue you wish. The full value, Mr. MacDougal, if you agree to return to America at once and promise never to pose a threat to my family again."

She sat there opposite him, looking just as poised and remote as she had the very first time he'd laid eyes on her, swathed in a red sable-trimmed cape and all the arrogance of her class and wealth. Now, as then, Marsh could only stare at her. She meant to buy him off. He was surprised, now that her offer was made, that she hadn't tried this tactic sooner.

"This has been an expensive undertaking," he said, more to buy time than for any other purpose. How was he supposed to respond to her?

Her expression grew more brittle, the blue of her eyes colder. Her full lips compressed into a taut line. "I can add your traveling expenses to the cost."

*Of buying you off.* The unsaid words resounded in the silence between them.

As that silence lengthened, however, he saw her swallow. It was just a faint movement, the creamy skin of her throat undulating beneath the velvet ribbon tied there.

Two thoughts occurred to him in quick succession. The first was that she was not so sure of herself as she pretended to be. The second was that he wanted to kiss that throat, to tug that ribbon off with his teeth, and all the rest of her garments as well.

Blood rushed to his loins at the very idea. That soft, pale skin would be even softer and paler in places presently hidden from his view—and pinker in others.

He stifled a curse as his manhood stiffened almost to the point of pain.

Misreading his continuing silence, she leaned forward, her expression earnest. "You said you did not mean to hurt them. Well, this is your chance to prove it. You will have your inheritance—every penny of it—and they need never know about what your father did to all of you. But you must agree never to come near them again."

*Or near me.*

It was that implication which drove Marsh to make his answer, an answer he had not planned, but which he knew immediately he would not swerve from.

"I will consider your offer, Sarah."

"You will?"

She swallowed again and took a deep breath, and had he needed further resolve, the press of her lovely breasts against her muslin bodice would have done the trick.

"I will," he said, dragging his gaze up to her face. "But we have other unfinished business between us. Business I would see brought to completion."

He stared intently at her and knew, when blood rushed hot color to her cheeks, that she understood. Yet she fought the idea. "You . . . you cannot mean—No. You cannot."

"But I do." He reached for her hand, trapping those warm, slender fingers within his own. "I will take your money in lieu of Byrde Manor. I will return to America without confronting your sister or your mother. The secret of my father's first marriage will sail with me and they need never know the truth—unless you choose to tell them. But I want one night with you."

He took a harsh breath and his nostrils flared. He was so hard beneath the table that he could not have stood upright if he wanted to.

He turned her stiff, gloved hand in his so that they were palm to palm, their fingers entwined. Likewise, her shocked gaze clung to his. But no matter her shock, he was resolved on this matter. "Spend the night with me, Sarah, and we will finish what we only started in your carriage that night on the road.

"Surrender yourself to me, for that's the only way you will ever be rid of me."

# CHAPTER

# 17

STUNNED by his ultimatum, Sarah just sat there—like an idiot, she feared.

At a table behind her two men chortled at someone's jest. A heavy tankard thunked down on one of the other plank tables, and the low entry door slammed behind a customer just leaving. She heard the myriad comings and goings around her, yet she remained oblivious to them all.

Marshall MacDougal had uttered the unthinkable. He had just confronted her with the most unbelievable proposition.

A hysterical giggle threatened to rise from her chest and burst forth. *Proposition.* What an appropriate word. Was it a business arrangement or a lewd suggestion? Both, it seemed. He'd just made her a lewd business proposition, much as he might to any other woman foolish enough to sit unchaperoned with him in a public house.

But Sarah did not laugh, for there was no humor in the awful circumstances in which she now found herself mired. She stared at him, as horrified by his suggestion as she was by her shameful physical reaction to it. Something very near to that incredible melting sensation had begun to form in her belly and she forced it back by only the most stringent effort.

"I refuse to dignify such a crass suggestion with an answer," she muttered, practically choking on the words.

"I see. I suppose, then, that I must take that for a no." He paused one long, tense moment. "Are you certain about this, Sarah?"

"Quite certain!" She rose to stand upon legs that trembled. How could he be so crude—and so calm? She took a shaky breath. "I will have my solicitor draw up the papers."

"For what?"

"For the draft of money. What else?"

"But we have no deal."

"We have a deal," she countered. "All except for that last . . . that last part."

He shook his head slowly, deliberately, then sprawled back in his chair with a maddening air of ease. Sarah felt a dreadful foreboding. "Then we have no deal."

She stared at him, unable to make any response. Her legs threatened to give out, so she sat back down with a thump. "You cannot be serious."

One of his dark brows hitched up in the taunting manner she had become far too familiar with. "I am entirely serious, Sarah. You are asking me to abandon the truth of my parentage, and while your monetary offer is tempting, money could never recompense me for the loss of my personal history."

"Your personal history!" she exclaimed, finally finding her voice. "You came to Scotland to find your father and punish him. Don't pretend otherwise. Personal history? Hah! You ought to be glad for the wealth you will leave here with."

"I don't need your money!"

She sat back, stunned by the sudden fury in his voice.

"This has never been about money," he went on, in a low but passionate tone. "But you can't understand that, can you? You're nothing but a self-indulgent child inside a woman's body. You talk about loyalty, but you don't begin to know what it means. Loyalty or sacrifice. All you know is wealth and status. Position in society. That's all any of you mercenary, class-obsessed British care about. My mother understood, though. She was loyal to her husband all her life, and she sacrificed everything for me. But she still wasn't good enough for my father. Oh, no. He didn't mind fucking her, but he wasn't about to bring her home to meet his family, let alone become a part of it.

"Well, this is no different. I don't want to meet your family, Miss high-and-mighty Sarah Palmer. I just want to fuck you."

Sarah was too taken aback by his coarse revelation to react. In the terrible silence, he stood and threw a coin down on the table for the bottle. "That's the deal. Take it or leave it. I'll give you one week to make up your mind." Then he made her a curt bow, put his hat on, and said, "See you in Kelso."

Marsh was shaking when he stalked out of the half-timbered public house. His hands had knotted into fists, and had anyone looked crosswise at him, he would have knocked the bastard down. But the cobbled road was clear, save for a pair of clerks conversing on the opposite side, and a rag picker pushing his cart.

He slapped his gloves viciously against his thigh. Damn her!

He wanted to howl his rage and frustration at a cold dark moon. Instead he had to cross this street with the occasional puddle glinting bright sunshine back at him, and behave as if nothing were wrong.

*But nothing is,* a small, rational voice pointed out. *You've won. No matter what decision she makes, you've won.*

So why didn't he feel like he'd won?

Why did he feel like a piece of garbage not even good enough for her to step over?

Because that was how she'd reacted to him, as if he weren't good enough for the likes of her.

But he *was* good enough. Good enough. Smart enough. Clever enough to have bested her. He'd won, and she knew it.

*Then why that parting jab, that nasty demand that she forsake her virginity to you?*

When he realized he was passing the nondescript inn he'd taken a room at, he changed direction. Disgusted, elated. Depressed, jubilant. So many conflicting emotions beset him, he felt ready to explode. On impulse he fetched his saddle horse from the stable, left word for Duffy that they were returning to Kelso, then started out of town at an abrupt gallop. He had to do something strenuous or burst with frustration.

But even a headlong race into the open countryside couldn't erase the accusations that circled in his head. Why that parting jab? Why torment her that way?

He'd reached Lockerbie before he could face the ugly truth. He'd put that coarse caveat on their agreement because he wanted her. And he knew he couldn't get her any other way.

Sarah reached Byrde Manor after two very hard and long days on the road. She'd slept little and eaten less, and when she alighted well after dark, Mrs. Hamilton fussed around her like a hen with a sickly chick. But Sarah had rebuffed all the worried woman's ministrations and made straight for her bed.

That Mrs. Hamilton turned immediately to grill poor Mary on what had happened didn't concern Sarah. The maid knew nothing. And as far as Sarah was concerned, neither Mary nor anyone else would ever learn the truth. Not even Mrs. Hamilton. Because if Mrs. Hamilton learned the truth about Mr. MacDougal being Cameron Byrde's true heir, then she would want to know why the man hadn't revealed that fact to everyone. Sarah would then be forced to explain about her offer to buy him off.

It would eventually come out anyway, for James was bound to find out about the financial transactions. But she didn't want anyone to learn anything until Marshall MacDougal was long departed for America. If Mrs. Hamilton learned the truth now, she might even go so far as to approach Mr. MacDougal. And if she did that, he might reveal his counteroffer.

The very thought of that outrageous counteroffer made her stomach knot. If anyone ever learned what he was demanding of her, then they would swiftly determine also what her answer was. What it *must* be. For Sarah had come to the awful conclusion that there was only one answer she *could* make. She would not let him ruin her mother and sister. Therefore she must let him ruin her.

From the knot in her stomach an uncontrollable trembling radiated out through her arms and legs, all the way to her fingertips and toes. In desperation she pressed her leather-shod feet against the floor, clenched her hands into fists, and made herself focus on the practical aspects of her predicament. Namely: Was a woman ruined if no one ever learned of it?

She lay on her bed still fully clothed and stared up at the ceiling. No one expected a man to be a virgin when he wed. No one considered him ruined. Indeed, there was an unspoken understanding that he ought to be experienced enough to teach his new bride the intimate secrets of the marriage bed.

But that was neither here nor there. The question was, on her wedding night, would her eventual husband be able to tell that she'd once been touched by some other man?

She groaned and sat up, then began to unlace her half boots. She'd already been touched by a man in ways no one but a husband should touch her. Would taking that final leap be so very much worse?

*He said it would be even better.*

To even consider that possibility sent a wonderful, terrible thrill shuddering through her. She concentrated instead on his hard expression and cruel words as he'd left her in that public house in Dumfries.

*I just want to fuck you.*

What a horrible man! What a hateful, coarse . . . hateful American. He was no better than Penley, who'd tried to extort money from his married lover. Of course, Mr. MacDougal did not want money from her. She'd already offered him that. It was her innocence he wanted, the crude act of copulation without any emotion attached to it.

And yet *her* emotions were involved!

Sarah wanted to cry with frustration. Yet tears would

not come. So she lay back again, listening to her own breaths in the silent night and wishing her mother was there, or her sister. Even her brother's presence would be a great comfort to her.

But they were not here, and she knew that was for the best. She alone had to fight this battle with Marshall MacDougal, for to tell her family was to chance everything being made public. At least this way the dreadful truth could all be kept secret.

And then, perhaps she still might change his mind.

Perhaps.

She had only one thought left when exhaustion finally claimed her. When would she hear from him again? After all, there were only five days left.

Adrian straddled an upturned bucket and watched as Sarah's driver washed mud from the undercarriage of Byrde Manor's old traveling coach. Something odd was afoot and he wanted to know what. But grilling a longtime family retainer who prided himself on loyalty was not the way to find out anything. So he squinted at the man and said in an offhand manner, "D'you want any help with that? I can wipe the road dirt from the seats and shake out the curtains."

"Thanks, lad, but I can manage."

Adrian considered. "How old's this carriage anyway? You keep it all painted and polished, but I know it's not new."

The man grinned proudly. "She's older'n you. But you're right. She don't look it."

Adrian shrugged. "Course it ought to look new. Hardly anybody uses it anymore."

"Hunh. So you say. D'you think all this mud got on it from sittin' in the carriage house?"

Adrian shrugged. "I don't know."

"Well, just you race to the ocean and back and see how clean your carriage would be."

"To the ocean? You mean the Atlantic Ocean?"

"You know any others?" the man quipped, intent on his work.

"I've never seen the ocean," Adrian said.

"Hmph. Hardly saw it meself, what with two days to Dumfries, two days back, and hardly time to turn around in between."

Dumfries. Adrian pushed aside his yearning to travel all the way to the Atlantic someday. Sarah had gone racing madcap to Dumfries, forgetting all about her plans to go fishing with him. Then she had raced back. And for what?

He stood, then kicked over the stool, earning himself a frown from the coachman. But he didn't care. Sarah had left Byrde Manor the day after Marshall MacDougal had. She'd returned last night—and Mr. MacDougal had returned this morning. He knew that because at lunchtime he'd heard his mother talking to one of her friends about the man's hireling being back in town. If the man's servant was back, so was the master. That's what had sent him charging straightaway to Byrde Manor and this unhappy confrontation with the truth.

Sarah Palmer—his Sarah—was chasing after a man she shouldn't bother even to look twice at. At the same time, she behaved as if she hated the fellow. So what did that mean? What was going on between the two of them?

Adrian lingered at Byrde Manor a long while. But as the afternoon wore on and Sarah never left the house, the boy's resolve hardened. He would ferret out the truth, one way or another.

Sarah wasted two more days waiting to hear from Marshall MacDougal. Or were they two days spent hiding from him?

When Mrs. Hamilton confronted her, she had no choice but to lie. "He's found nothing yet. We have but to wait him out."

Though the other woman had not liked that answer, she had accepted it. But with no one to confide the truth in, and with Mr. MacDougal awaiting her reply in Kelso, Sarah remained on pins and needles.

Sunday morning she decided on impulse to attend services in town with Mrs. Hamilton. That would be safe, yet might also provide her with some insight as to his comings and goings of late.

As they were driving up to town in the open chaise, however, who should they spy riding his tall bay animal but Marshall MacDougal himself. Sarah felt her heart begin to hammer. "Oh, no. Not him," she muttered, then glanced nervously at Mrs. Hamilton.

"So that's him," the loyal servant commented, staring unabashedly at the American.

It was the first time the old woman had actually laid eyes on the man, Sarah realized. "Try to be civil," she muttered as they drew closer. "Don't let on you know anything about what's going on."

When Mr. MacDougal slowed, then stopped, so did their driver.

"Good morning, Miss Palmer," he said, in so pleasant and affable a manner no one would ever guess at the complexity of their tangled relationship. "Lovely day for a drive, isn't it?"

Sarah forced a smile, amazed at her ability to appear so calm when her insides were shaking. "We are on our way to church. This is Mrs. Hamilton, a longtime family retainer and loyal friend."

Something in his eyes glinted, as if she amused him. But mercifully he turned the brilliance of his gaze on Mrs. Hamilton.

As they traded pleasantries, Sarah took a deep breath, only then realizing she'd been holding it. Mrs. Hamilton was acting just as pleasant to the man as if he were a suitor come to call.

Despite her better judgment, Sarah's gaze slipped over him. From the bright glints in his dark hair, past the perfectly tied stock, across the well-fitted shoulders and chest of his superfine coat of dove gray, then down to the powerful thighs in their wool twill, and the Spanish leather of his tall riding boots, he exceeded anyone's image of the perfect gentleman.

She searched for a flaw—any flaw—and decided in desperation that he was a little too finely honed for a proper gentleman. He carried about him an aura that did not quite fit with a gentleman of leisure, for he was too watchful, too intense. Too dangerous.

It took Mrs. Hamilton's hand on her arm to alert Sarah that one of them had addressed her.

"Excuse me?" She turned to face Mrs. Hamilton.

"Mr. MacDougal has kindly offered to accompany us to church."

A light sparkled in the older woman's faded eyes. Knowing Mrs. Hamilton's fierce loyalty to Augusta and Olivia, Sarah suspected it was probably the light of battle. Taking advantage of the fact that her own face was turned away from Mr. MacDougal, she silently mouthed the reminder, "Remember, say nothing. Nothing."

Only when Mrs. Hamilton gave a faint nod did Sarah turn to face him. "If you like. I'm sure we can all benefit from some time spent in prayer."

An hour later she was not so certain. Any number of heads had turned when the three of them entered the small church together. The baker's outspoken mother nodded and clucked. Mrs. Liston's brows raised almost to her hairline and she pursed her lips in a knowing smile. In an aisle seat Estelle Kendrick stared, then turned her face pointedly away. But the man sitting beside her watched them with a grin, and Mr. MacDougal nodded to him as they passed.

Sarah wanted to turn right around and leave. Of course, she did no such thing. She slid into the family pew with Mrs. Hamilton on one side and Marshall MacDougal on the other and tried very hard to concentrate on Mr. Liston's sermon. But it was nearly impossible.

It had been five days since their fateful confrontation in the rough public house in Dumfries. Yet her awareness of him here in the silence of these hallowed halls was even more acute than there. His leg lay but inches from hers, the fine dark fabric of his breeches in marked contrast to the sprigged muslin that covered her own limbs. His hands rested on his knees and she stared at first one, then the other. They were tan and strong. Square palms, shapely fingers, and neat nails. Sprinkles of dark hair gave them a strange, masculine appeal, an appeal she did not want to notice.

But as Mr. Liston droned on, as feet shuffled restlessly, and coughs were discreetly muffled by raised palms, Sarah stared at his hands, remembering how they'd felt running up and down her thighs.

She nearly choked, then started coughing, and only stopped when Mrs. Hamilton pounded her on the back.

"Sorry," she muttered, keeping her eyes downcast onto her own knotted hands. "Sorry." Fortunately, the service ended, Mrs. Liston struck up "Holy, Holy, Holy" on the organ, and everyone stood to sing.

The first people they encountered afterward were Estelle and her escort, a man Sarah realized was Mr. MacDougal's manservant.

"Well, well. If it isn't the hot-tempered Mr. MacDougal," Estelle said. She smiled archly at Sarah, all the while pressing her breast against her escort's arm. "Has he pummeled anyone else on your behalf?"

Sarah gave her a tight smile. "I certainly hope not. Is Adrian here?" she added, changing the subject.

Estelle smirked. "I don't see him."

How Sarah wanted to slap the woman. But she couldn't, especially here in a church. So she gave the couple a curt nod, then pushed past them out into the open square.

"I haven't pummeled anyone on your behalf lately," Mr. MacDougal's quiet voice came from right beside her. He matched her stride for stride. "But I would."

"So," Mrs. Hamilton called, hurrying up behind them and preventing any further private conversation. "I've been meaning to thank you, Mr. MacDougal, for the fine trout you provided us. Have you done any further fishing since then?"

Sarah was relieved when he focused his attention back on Mrs. Hamilton. "Sadly, I have not had the time."

"Then you must make the time. Mr. Hamilton took a monstrous fish out of the river just two days past. Quite a spirited battle the creature provided him."

Sarah wanted to groan. Though she'd instructed Mrs. Hamilton to act friendly toward him, she didn't mean for her to act *that* friendly.

"Actually, that sounds a very pleasant way to pass the afternoon," he said when they reached the carriage. "Might I presume on your generosity once more?"

"By all means," Mrs. Hamilton agreed, ignoring Sarah's pointed stare. "I'm certain Sarah's sister Olivia would not mind," she added. " 'Tis her estate, you know."

Despite her own frustration, Sarah could have kissed Mrs. Hamilton for that last loyal remark, and for the subtle jab it carried.

"So I've been told," Mr. MacDougal responded. He helped Mrs. Hamilton into the carriage. When he came around to assist Sarah up, he whispered, "At least she thinks it's hers." Before she could respond, he raised his voice to a more carrying tone. "Would you care to join me in a fishing expedition, Miss Palmer?"

# CHAPTER 18

ADRIAN watched from a stand of elms just upriver as Sarah and that blasted American approached the bank. The man carried two poles and a basket of gear. Sarah carried a smaller basket and a blanket.

A twig of newly budded leaves snapped off in his clenched fingers, silencing the squirrels scolding him from above. His eyes darted to Mr. MacDougal. Bloody ballocks, they would see him!

But the tripping water and the rustling leaves must have muffled the sound. Unfortunately, they also made it hard for him to make out all their words.

He watched as the man knelt and began to assemble his fishing gear. Sarah stood back, the blanket still clutched in her arms. She had changed into a peach-colored dress, and a wide-brimmed straw bonnet sheltered her face from the sun. Had he not known better, Adrian could have believed her a simple country lass, not much older than himself.

How he wished she were! His only consolation was that she didn't look very pleased to be alone with Mr. MacDougal.

So why had she accompanied him?

The man looked up and said something to her, and even from his hidden bower Adrian could see her face pinken.

Another twig snapped in his hands. The cheeky bastard! What had he said to her? Something lewd, he'd wager.

Sarah threw the blanket down, then dropped her basket beside it. She waggled one of her fingers at the man. ". . . hateful proposal . . ." Adrian heard that much of her response and he blinked in astonishment. Had the man gone so far as to propose marriage to her?

Surely not, he decided. Sarah was too well bred to term a marriage proposal as hateful. Could the American have proposed something else?

Adrian sucked in a harsh breath. Bloody right he could!

He glared at the lowly bastard, watching while the man cast his line upon the river, as if Sarah's vehemently expressed words were of no account.

It made no sense. Why would Sarah willingly suffer this bounder's presence and whatever unsavory proposal the man had made to her? If she wanted to freeze him out, she could easily do so. So why didn't she? Could it be that she feared the man? Had he bullied her in some way?

Adrian's thoughts tumbled around and around. Could the lowdown cad be blackmailing her over something she'd done? After all, her arrival in Kelso was unexpected and Mr. MacDougal had shown up at the very same time.

Had he followed her here?

Adrian leaned back against the elm trunk behind him and considered that possibility. He understood about blackmail. Even though his mother hadn't sunk quite that low, she still subsidized the already generous allowance his Uncle Neville gave her with gifts from the men who sometimes came around to their cottage late at night—gifts meant to keep her quiet about their secret visits. Just last month the mayor had paid off her milliner's bill, and the butcher kept them well supplied with pork, beef, and mutton.

A muscle ticked in his jaw. It was only one short step from his mother expecting gifts for her silence, to this American demanding it for his. Yes, all the signs pointed to the man blackmailing Sarah. Otherwise she would not suffer his presence. But what hold could the man have over a well-bred young woman like Sarah Palmer?

Adrian grimaced, for the answer was as bitter as it was obvious. Most likely the American had the same hold over Sarah that his mother held over the mayor and the butcher.

He closed his eyes at the thought. Not sweet, beautiful Sarah. Yet what else could it be? They must have become lovers, perhaps back in London. That's why the man had pounded poor Guinea to a pulp the night of the dance. Jealousy.

Now the cad meant to capitalize on their affair, to hold her reputation hostage to her misguided behavior. Was it money the villain wanted from her? Or maybe he was going to force her to marry him and thereby gain access to her entire fortune.

Stubble it all! Could the lout really be that low?

Of course he could.

A vein throbbed in Adrian's temple. Love of money was the root of all evil. In the past he'd scoffed when Mr. Liston had preached that particular sermon. But not now. Now he understood exactly what the vicar meant.

But that scurvy American had underestimated the situation if he thought he could bully a sweet woman like Sarah Palmer and get away with it. For she had friends and admirers who would go to great lengths on her behalf.

Adrian glared at the American as the man fought a fish that had been hooked, and his hands tightened into fists. Yes, Sarah had friends who would go to *any* lengths on her behalf.

Sarah stared at the poor fish, thrashing back and forth as Mr. MacDougal removed the hook from its mouth. When he placed it in the submerged willow basket to keep it alive while he cast his line to hook another, she felt the strongest urge to release the hapless creature from its unfortunate dilemma.

She enjoyed dining on trout and salmon and every other sort of fish. Today, however, she did not see the trout as a fine meal but rather as a fellow hostage, caught in a trap with only one way out: to be consumed. Mr. MacDougal had thrown out lures to each of them and despite their caution and their certainty that he posed a terrible danger to them, they'd each of them taken their respective lures. And now they must pay the price.

That's why she'd come with him to the river on the pretext of a friendly fishing expedition: to agree once and for all to his price.

"This is a fine piece of river," he remarked as he played his line across a still part of the water. "Are both banks a part of Byrde Manor?"

Sarah glared at him through slitted eyes. "I'm sure you already know that they are."

He shot her a grin over his shoulder. " 'Tis truly a paradise," he said, rolling his *r*'s in an exaggerated parody of a Scottish accent. "A man could happily live out his days fishing this river, riding these hills, and counting up his rents."

"Some men," she bit out. "But not you."

Holding her gaze captive with just the force of his eyes, he turned and lay down his fishing pole. "Maybe me. It all depends on you. So." He took several steps toward her, then halted, his arms spread wide. He looked so perfectly at his ease, while she was agitated enough to jump right out of her skin. "Have you an answer for me, Sarah?"

*Yes.*

"No." Sarah choked out the word. She'd come here to agree. But shame at how easy it would be to say yes forced her now to deny the inevitable. Oh, but she was a pitiful creature, more pitiful than the poor, hapless fish. All she could do was stare at the man who'd caught her so neatly in his trap. Stare at him with fear and awe and the most frightening sort of anticipation.

He looked more handsome today than any time she'd ever seen him. It was utterly absurd for her even to notice such a thing. But notice it she did. Casually dressed, with his hair windblown, his coat tossed aside, and his sleeves rolled up to expose his forearms, he somehow seemed a more accurate image of himself. Though he wore the trappings of the gentleman well enough, this picture of an outdoorsman, smiling and content, rang so much truer. And much more appealing.

*But he's still dangerous. He's still the same man—Cameron Byrde's son, who is just as heartless and merciless as was his sire.*

"You have two days left, Sarah. But I warn you, if you've come fishing with me today hoping to change my mind, you have wasted your time."

He moved up the bank, his boots crunching on the gravel beach, and stopped an arm's length from her. "Or have you come here to be convinced? Do you need to be seduced so that you can console yourself later that you had no choice but to give in to my dastardly demands?"

Was that the reason she was unable to make the answer she knew she must? Did she want him to seduce her again?

Sarah recoiled at the idea, yet it was disturbingly close to the truth. "You delude yourself if you believe I wish you to seduce me," she said with what she hoped was a credible amount of disdain.

"I'm glad to hear it, for I will not be the one doing the seducing this time, Sarah. If you wish to strike this deal with me—a deal *you* initiated—then you must come to me of your own free will."

"My own free will?" She laughed at the very notion. "You hold my family's fate in your hands. You make this shameful offer to me. Then you say I must come to you of my own free will? Ha!"

His face darkened a little. "You know what I mean."

"Oh, yes. I'm afraid I do. Like your father before you, you take pleasure in ruining innocent women, in corrupting everything you touch." Fear lent her voice an even harsher tone than she'd intended. But despite that, her words bounced off him like grapeshot off a granite boulder.

"This is hardly the same thing," he countered. "You offered me a deal—money in exchange for my departure. I merely countered with terms of my own. The ball is in your court, Sarah. If you do not like my terms, then decline them."

"And then what? Stand by and watch you destroy Livvie and Mother?"

"Destroy them? Don't be so dramatic. What will happen to them? Will they be put out on the street, destitute and starving? Forced to work as servants in the homes of their former friends?" His jaw clenched and his eyes glittered with rising anger. "They both have husbands and other family to assist them. If you're rich enough to buy me off, then surely you're rich enough to help them out should their husbands elect to abandon them." Angrily he cut the air with his fist. "But there was no one to help my mother. No one! She was destroyed by her husband's perfidy. By contrast, your mother and sister will merely be inconvenienced."

He stood there, shaking with rage. From easy confidence to uncontrolled fury, he'd made the transition so fast Sarah took a step back from him. She wanted to be glad that she could affect his composure so easily. Unfortunately, his words seemed to have affected her composure just as much, for everything he said was true. No matter what happened, Livvie and Augusta would never want for physical comforts. They would keep their homes, their children, and their husbands. They were both married to men who adored them. Cameron Byrde's behavior thirty years ago did not have the power to affect that.

But others would not be so kind. And putting aside their reputations, there was still the matter of the personal hurt they would feel. Despite his faults, Augusta had dearly loved Cameron Byrde, and he had doted on his little daughter.

So she faced Mr. MacDougal, determined not to give ground, no matter how persuasive his argument.

"I am not going to enter into a debate with you about whom Cameron Byrde has harmed more. The question now is, who you are harming? And why?"

"No one—if you will simply accept my terms."

"Oh!" She stamped her foot. "You do your father very proud with those terms. I'm sure he would applaud you, were he here. But I wonder," she added in biting tones, "whether your mother would admire this behavior in her beloved son."

He stiffened, almost as if she'd struck him full in the face. "Leave her out of this."

But Sarah was not about to abandon the one weapon that seemed to pierce the armor of his righteous anger, and so she pressed on. "Was she that embittered by the life forced on her that she would have you punish other women for it? Women like her, susceptible to a ruthless man's whims—"

"You're nothing like her!" He caught Sarah by both arms and gave her a hard shake. "Don't *you* talk to *me* about her. She has nothing to do with this."

"She has everything to do with it—"

He cut her off with a violent kiss, as brutal as it was anguished. He silenced her in a fierce embrace that crushed her against his powerful, masculine form. The breath rushed out of Sarah's lungs, and in its wake her opposition disappeared as well.

She should fight him. She should hate him. She should fear him. Instead she clung to him, drenched in a flood of desire, letting him vent thirty years of fury upon her.

She swayed in that storm of emotions; she would have fallen had he not gripped her so tightly. But as the seconds passed in the thunder of their heartbeats, she did not fall.

There was something so intense about the way he took absolute possession of her mouth, the way he wrapped his steely arm around her waist. Somehow he turned every emotion she felt for him into desire.

Anger. Fear. Even sympathy for the pain he felt became desire. It became lust. He pushed her to extremes no man ever had and no man ever should.

His other hand cupped her head, tangling in her hair. His lips moved, slanting and fitting their mouths even closer. His tongue probed, demanded, tempted. And she was tempted. She kissed him back with a shamelessness she did not want to acknowledge. Something in him made her feel so wild, so reckless.

*So reckless.*

She turned her head to the side, gasping for breath. But she did not pull away from him. She knew she should, but she did not want to. Oh, but she was doomed. For she seemed completely unable to resist the physical urges he roused in her. Even recognizing how reckless her behavior was, she could not resist him.

It was he who shoved out of their embrace. He who glared at her as if she'd done something unforgivable.

"You know my terms," he bit out in a hoarse voice. "You have two days left to make your answer, Sarah. Two days." Then he turned around, snatched up the fishing pole and stalked toward the river.

Once more Sarah swayed, one hand pressed to her chest, the other to her lips. She knew her answer now, but she could not manage the words, not when he had again become so angry with her. As ludicrous as it was, the two of them seemed to find common ground only when they gave in to the intense physical attraction that flared so out of control between them.

They could not talk without fighting for their respective positions, but locked in an embrace . . .

Sarah stared at his back, at the rigid set of his shoulders as he tried to cast the fly across the river. She needed to compose herself, to catch her breath.

So she turned away from him and on awkward legs clambered up the sloping bank, heading for the shade of an ancient willow tree. She did not see Marsh close his eyes and shake his head at the perversity of his behavior. Nor did she see dislike harden to hatred in the young man who shrank back among the elm saplings not a stone's throw from where she passed.

The former doubted for the first time the rightness of his demands.

The latter made a solemn vow to do whatever he must to protect Sarah from the American who tormented her.

* * *

Marsh let the only fish he'd caught go free. Instead of delivering the fishing gear back to Byrde Manor, he tied it to his saddle, for he did not want to see Sarah. Not yet.

He had to tell her, of course. He'd time to mull over his despicable behavior, and he'd come to the only conclusion he could. He had to tell Sarah that she was right. He was no better than his father. And like Cameron Byrde, he had let Maureen MacDougal Byrde down. His sweet-natured mother would be appalled at what he had proposed to do in her name.

He was appalled himself. And disgusted. He wasn't sure anymore that he should even accept Sarah's original offer to purchase Byrde Manor from him. Though it legally belonged to him, morally he was no longer so certain of his position.

Leading his horse, he walked along the irregular shoreline of the river, seeing everything, yet not really seeing a thing.

What a fiasco this had turned out to be. A simple quest for justice, except that the target of his vengeance had been dead for twenty-odd years. Then he'd fallen under the spell of a woman he'd feared was his own sister, only to learn they shared no blood relationship.

But what difference did that make? There was a spark between them—hell, it was an inferno!—and he knew he could make her succumb to him. But they were on opposite sides of an issue that would never go away. In her eyes he would always be a threat to her mother and sister. That she was probably loyal enough to buy their security with her virginity only made it worse.

It made *him* worse.

At least he could relieve her on that score. She probably would not believe him if he just left. She wouldn't trust him to keep his word. So he would let her buy him off if she still wanted to, he decided. But with money only. He would not force her to his bed. Then he would leave. There seemed no other choice.

He paused in the shade of a swaying willow and rubbed the back of his neck. He stared out at the river just beyond his boot tips, watching the trailing ends of the willow tease the surface of the water. He needed to make arrangements for his return trip to America. It would be good to be home, he told himself.

Only it would not really be home, not with his mother gone. She had always been his only family—except for the half-sister he had never known existed.

Something in his chest felt empty and hollow. He hadn't wanted Cameron Byrde to have another child, and once he'd found out about her, he certainly hadn't wanted to meet her. He wasn't sure he wanted to now. Once he left, however, he'd be giving up the last bit of family he had.

He'd also be giving up Sarah.

Though that should not bother him, it did. He'd already lost his past—the father he'd never known, the mother he hadn't appreciated nearly enough. Now it felt as if he were losing his future too.

Something rustled behind him. A twig snapped as if someone had stepped on it.

"Sarah?" He turned, overwhelmed with a hope he had no right to feel. He was met, however, not by her beautiful, somber face, but by a blast of light and smoke that spun him backward. Backward. Throwing him off balance and crashing him into the icy river.

He cried out in pain and gulped a mouthful of choking water. Vaguely he heard his horse whinny with fright, then thunder away. Some part of him felt the cold and the pain, and knew he had been shot. But why? And by whom?

As everything closed in, numbing him—killing him—only one answer formed in his head. One face. One name.

Only one person hated him this much.

Sarah.

## CHAPTER

# 19

SARAH jerked when she heard the gunshot, then frowned. What careless fool was hunting so near Byrde Manor? And along the river, where anyone might be fishing?

Then an awful fear grabbed hold of her. The shot was too near Byrde Manor for a hunter—and it was too near where she'd left Mr. MacDougal. She started running before the fear could paralyze her. She just knew she must get back to the river. To Marshall MacDougal.

Down the same path she'd just trudged, she now flew, straight for where she'd left him on the riverbank.

Behind her she heard calls from Byrde Manor, Mrs. Hamilton's worried cry and Mr. Hamilton's alarmed reply. Someone would come to investigate, she knew, for Mr. Hamilton was steward to these lands, and no one hunted here without his express approval. But they were so very far away, and no matter how fast she tried to run, she seemed to be moving too slow.

Bursting out of the leafy undergrowth, she skidded to a halt. Where was he? For he was not where she'd last seen him.

Her foreboding increased. "Marsh? Marsh!" Desperately she scanned up and down the riverbank.

On impulse she turned downstream toward Kelso, calling out to him again and again. But there was no reply, and with every step her panic grew stronger. Something was not right!

Then she spied something in the river, something lodged up against a fallen alder tree. "Marsh!"

Dear God! Had someone shot him?

Without pausing to think, she plunged into the river, wading through the shallows, driven forward by the worst fear of her life. But like before, she could not move fast enough, slowed even more by the drag of her sodden skirts. Just as he was about to drift into the center current of the river, she lunged forward and caught him by the foot. Somehow she fought her way to his head, then muscled him over onto his back.

Was he breathing?

She stood in the hip-deep water at the very spot where Olivia had taught her to swim, and cradled his shoulders and head in her arms. "Marsh? Mr. MacDougal?" Her heart slammed in her chest. Was he dead? *Please, God. No.*

She had to get him to the shore.

Slowly, scrabbling for a firm foothold, Sarah inched backward toward the bank, floating him on the water, trying to keep his head above the surface, yet also tipped to the side. She slipped and fell—but the water was shallower here.

When Mr. Hamilton and one of the stableboys found her, she was sitting in the water still, cradling him in her arms.

"I think somebody shot him." She was sobbing and hadn't even realized it. "He fell in the river and was drowning. I think someone shot him," she repeated, like a trained parrot that could only repeat one phrase over and over again. "I think someone shot him."

"Who would do such a thing?" Mr. Hamilton cried, wading into the water. "Help me, boy. Help me!"

"Is he dead?" The boy's voice quavered and he hung back.

Sarah glared at him. "No!"

Together they dragged the inert Mr. MacDougal onto the shore; then, when Mr. Hamilton collapsed, breathing hard, the boy tore back to the house for more help.

"Marsh? Mr. MacDougal?" Sarah rolled him to the side, hoping any water he'd sucked in would drain from his slack mouth. Though she searched for a bullet wound, she knew the most important thing was to get him breathing. So kneeling behind him, she began to pound his back with her open hand.

"Breathe," she chanted between blows to his upper back. "Breathe!"

Then he groaned and began to cough, and water gushed out of his mouth.

"Breathe!" she kept on demanding, bending over him, her own breaths coming in great heaves. Only then did she see the ugly stain of blood on his sleeve.

He *had* been shot!

She tried to be gentle as she probed for the wound. But he still winced and groaned, then let out a muttered oath. "Damnation! That hurts!"

He was awake! Sarah was so relieved she could not begrudge him the curse. She bent over him. "Marshall MacDougal. Can you hear me?"

He coughed again, then turned partially onto his back, putting his face only inches from hers. "I can hear you. What in the damn hell happened?" His good hand reached for his injured arm. "Son of a bitch!"

"We heard a gunshot. I . . . I think you were shot."

His eyes locked with hers. From a distance she heard more people coming to help, calling out to them. And she heard Mr. Hamilton's shout, guiding them closer. But the words that stayed with her—the words that chilled her to the bone—were the words Mr. MacDougal muttered next, his head resting on her knee.

"Yes. I've been shot." He coughed then groaned. "And there's only one person I can think of who would be happy if I were dead."

Only then did he look away. He shoved up on his good arm, wincing at the pain as he struggled still to breathe. Behind her Mr. Hamilton was still huffing, but he knelt down beside them. "Don't try to get up, lad. I've got help comin'."

Sarah sat back, relieved that Mr. Hamilton had not heard that awful accusation. Yet still her gaze sought out Mr.

MacDougal's. Did he really believe that? The suspicion she saw in his dark eyes confirmed it. It also cut her to the quick.

Then all at once the riverbank was alive with people. The gardener, two of the fieldworkers, Fleming the footman, Cook, and even Mrs. Hamilton had all come running.

"Good Lord! What happened?"

"Did he drown?"

"Someone shot him!"

"Where are you hurt?" That was Mrs. Hamilton, breathing hard from the unaccustomed activity, yet still as calm and levelheaded as ever. "Push aside, Cook. Let me see. Where is the wound?"

It was a relief for Sarah to let Mrs. Hamilton take charge. In truth, she was trembling too hard herself to be much help to anyone else. But it was not the cold that had her shaking. Rather, it was the drama of the last few minutes. She'd been yanked from fury to panic to utter shock, and it was almost too much to take in.

Mrs. Hamilton removed Mr. MacDougal's coat and tore his sleeve to probe his wounded arm. "Appears to be a flesh wound, thank God. The bullet's gone clean through." Then she bound his arm with the sleeve of his own coat. Despite Mr. MacDougal's protests, the gardener and Fleming helped him upright. Then, with him supported between them, they all headed for the road and the cart that one of the lads had hied off to fetch.

Only then did Sarah rise from her knees. Her legs shook so violently, however, that she wavered. Had not Mrs. Hamilton turned to her, then grabbed her arm, Sarah feared she might have fallen.

"Dear girl! Here, sit. Sit another moment. You've had a terrible fright."

"No. I'm all right. I . . . I'm just a little shaken."

"And so you should be." The old woman slipped an arm around her waist, and Sarah leaned gratefully on her. "Oh, and you're soaked to the skin, child." Mrs. Hamilton squeezed her tighter still. "You saved him, Sarah. Had you not leaped into the river, who knows whether Mr. MacDougal would have drowned? But who could have shot him, then left him that way to die?"

It was a question Marsh pondered as well while he lay in a big bed in one of the upstairs rooms at Byrde Manor. Under the efficient supervision of the stern housekeeper, he'd been stripped of his wet clothes, washed, dried, swabbed, bandaged, and dressed in a clean nightshirt of ancient origins.

And through it all the same question circled in his head. Who had shot him?

He was no longer so certain it was Sarah. She had been the one to come racing to his rescue and pull him from the river's clutches, then keep his head up until help came. Mrs. Hamilton had been sure to let him know all the details.

Of course, Mrs. Hamilton could be lying. Or exaggerating. She was nothing if not a loyal retainer.

He needed to learn the truth, and he needed to learn it from Sarah.

"I'd like to speak to Miss Palmer," he said, pushing upright and swinging his legs around to dangle over the side of the bed.

"I'll tell her." Mrs. Hamilton held out a spoonful of some new evil-smelling concoction. "Here. Take this. And get yourself back under those covers."

"I need to see her now."

"And I said I'd tell her."

"Yes, but—"

"If you must know, she's takin' a bath. She's had quite a shock, she has. But she did what she had to do." The woman stared sternly at him. "She saved your life. You know that, don't you?"

He frowned. "I know."

She stared at him a moment longer, then nodded. "I'll let her know you're askin' for her. Meanwhile, take this."

"What is it?"

"It's a special medicine. I make it myself. It promotes healin'," she added when he hesitated.

Finally he took it, then nearly choked. "God Almighty! The cure is worse than the injury."

"What kind of talk is that from a strapping bucko like yourself, I'd like to know? Just shush yourself and lie down. I'll go see if Miss Sarah's fit to come visit with you."

Marsh lay back, only partially mollified. But he could hardly go prowling the place clad only in a nightshirt. "Where are my clothes?" he asked before she could shut the door.

"Your coat and shirt were ruined. The rest is being washed. I've sent word to the Cock and Bow for your man to bring some things up here for you. The sheriff has been summoned as well."

"The sheriff?"

"Somebody shot you, lad. We canna let such a one wander the countryside, now, can we?"

By the time the sheriff and Duffy Erskine arrived, Marsh could hardly keep his eyes open.

No, he hadn't seen his attacker.

No, he had no idea who would want to hurt him. *Aside from Sarah Palmer and everyone else in her family.*

"He's lost a goodly bit of blood," he heard Mrs. Hamilton say. "Plus, I gave the poor lad something to help him rest. He'll feel better tomorrow. You can talk to him then."

They all filed out. Only then did he voice his overriding concern. "Where is Sarah?" he asked once more, though his tongue felt thick and his voice slurred.

Mrs. Hamilton's gray brows arched in interest. "Sarah, is it? Humph. I expect she'll be along soon enough, lad. Meanwhile, you do as I say and rest yourself."

Once he had subsided against the pillows, Mrs. Hamilton shook her head, then made her weary way down the hall toward Sarah's bedchamber. This was a troubling business. Very troubling, indeed. The entire household was in a dither, with not a jot of work done since that gunshot had sounded. Mr. Hamilton had uncorked a fresh jug of whiskey to calm his nerves and had handed it around to calm everyone else's as well. Supper would be a haphazard affair at best. As for herself, she was shaken up enough not to really care.

But it was Sarah's silence and her refusal to see Mr. MacDougal that had the housekeeper most worried. She had delivered the man's message to her, but Sarah had only turned away.

Mrs. Hamilton paused outside her door and rubbed an aching spot at the small of her back. The question remained. What was going on between those two? She'd thought she knew, but now she wasn't so sure. And who had shot Mr. MacDougal?

She knocked on Sarah's door, then entered without waiting for a response. Sarah sat before a small fire, combing her hair to dry it. With her hair down and dressed in a pale pink wrapper with eyelet lace at the collar and cuffs, she looked almost as young as she'd been the very first time she'd come to Byrde Manor. Just twelve, sweet, yet full of high spirits, she'd had a real talent for getting into one scrape after another.

A precursor of things to come, Mrs. Hamilton now realized. But this business with Mr. MacDougal was more than merely a scrape.

And now this shooting . . .

She planted her fists on her hips. "This is getting too dangerous, Sarah, girl. Too dangerous. It's past time for you to write Livvie and Neville and inform them exactly what's going on around here."

Sarah had been lost in her own dark thoughts, but at the older woman's pronouncement she whirled around. "No. Not yet."

"This has gotten out of hand, child. Can't you see that?"

"No." Sarah stood. "Involving Livvie and Neville will not help. Please, Mrs. Hamilton." She took the woman's hands in hers. "I don't know who shot Mr. MacDougal, but I do know that he and I had finally reached an agreement."

"An agreement? Are you saying he's given up his search to prove his rights to Byrde Manor?"

Sarah averted her gaze from the other woman's watchful

stare. She would have to take the chance on telling Mrs. Hamilton the truth about Cameron Byrde's first marriage to Marshall MacDougal's mother. And about her offer to buy Mr. MacDougal's silence.

But not about his counteroffer. That was strictly between him and her.

She looked up at her mother's oldest, most loyal retainer. "I was not entirely honest when I told you he'd learned nothing in Dumfries."

Mrs. Hamilton listened without interruption to the whole of it, only going a little paler. "And so," Sarah concluded, "he has agreed to accept payment from me for the value of Byrde Manor."

The woman shook her head. "That Cameron Byrde. What a scoundrel! I suppose we owe Mr. MacDougal a great debt that he has agreed not to shame Livvie and Augusta. But Sarah, such a large amount of money!"

"It is. But what better use for my money than to protect my sister? And my mother," she added, for she knew Mrs. Hamilton was as close to Augusta as a person could be. "I have more than enough money. But I only have one family."

Mrs. Hamilton sighed. "Well put, child. Well put. And you say he has agreed?"

"Yes. We were . . . we were working out the details of our agreement there by the river. You know, how to transfer the funds and all. I had started back for the house, and he had gone back to fishing when I heard the gunshot."

Mrs. Hamilton shivered, then tugged Sarah into a smothering embrace. "Thank God you weren't still there. You might've just as easily been shot as him."

"Yes," Sarah murmured. But she didn't think so. She was very afraid that someone had deliberately shot Mr. MacDougal, that whoever it was had waited until she'd left to do the deed. But who would want to do such a thing? No one in Kelso had reason to hurt him.

Except maybe Mr. Guinea, whom Mr. MacDougal had pummeled on her behalf. But somehow she did not think it was him. Could Mr. MacDougal have been followed here by someone else? Someone from his past who held a grudge against him?

It would have to be a considerable grudge, to justify murder.

"He's been askin' for you," Mrs. Hamilton said when she finally released Sarah. "Probably wants to thank you for plucking him out of the river."

*If only that were true.* Sarah knew she had to face him, but the thought of his horrible accusation overwhelmed her. If it were any other man she would be indignant, indeed furious, at such an unreasonable suspicion. But Marshall MacDougal was not just any other man. To think that he believed her to be that awful was crushing. Though she knew she must convince him otherwise, she wasn't certain she was quite ready to do so.

"I'll go and see him later."

"Better you wait till tomorrow. That arm of his is going to throb all night. So I gave him a dose of laudanum and minted honey to help him sleep. Sleeping promotes healing, don't you know. Come, now," she added, guiding Sarah toward the door. "Let's go on down to the kitchen and find you something to eat."

Sarah ate because it was the only way to appease Mrs. Hamilton. But after a half bowl of mutton stew and a portion of bread and butter, she made her excuses and returned to her bedchamber. Pulling a chair up to the window, she sat there with a lamp at her shoulder and a book in her lap, watching the sun go down. The dusk stretched out a long, lingering time, as was typical of spring in the northern climes. Azure to deep blue to lavender streaked with coral. Then slowly, slowly deepening to the dark purple blue of a clear spring night. The stars appeared one by one, spreading silently across the heavens, and at some point she dozed off.

That was how Marsh found her.

He'd awakened groggy and disoriented in a bed he did not recognize. With one shift of position, however, and the piercing pain that resulted, he recalled everything. His confrontation with Sarah at the river; her departure; the gun blast.

Looking at her now, he was hard-pressed to believe she'd had anything to do with the attack on him. He stood in the open doorway to her dimly lit chamber and simply stared at her. She sat slumped down in a chair beside the window. The lamp had begun to burn low, but the meager light was still enough to illuminate her.

Her hair cascaded loose over her shoulders and chest, a thick curtain of lustrous silk that fell nearly to her waist. Though a dark rich brown, the golden light lent it a burnished color, like sunlight shining through amber.

Her thick lashes made innocent crescent-shaped shadows on her pale cheeks. Her lips, by contrast, enticed him with every pink, pouting curve.

Despite the ache in his arm, the doubts in his mind, and the lingering effects of the laudanum, he felt the distinct rise of desire. If ever a woman had drawn him to her, Sarah did. She, who was the one woman he should turn away from, was perversely the only one he wanted to cleave himself to. Even now, when he could not be certain whether she was friend or foe, she remained the one woman for whom he seemed willing to alter all his plans in order to possess.

Only he could not have her, especially not the way he'd so cruelly propositioned her.

God, but he was a hateful bastard! He could hardly blame her if she *were* his attacker. Any man who'd propose so vile a deal as he had, deserved to be shot.

All he could do now was agree to her original offer. To allow her to buy her family's freedom from the threat he made to them. For his mother's sake—but mostly for Sarah's sake—he knew now that he must give her that freedom.

And to do that, he must leave Scotland forever.

He knelt on one knee before her and rested his good hand on her knee. "Sarah. Sarah?"

She stirred, shifting sideways in the chair, and a small frown marred her previously serene features. "Go 'way. Just go . . ." Her mumbling trailed off.

"I'm going. Just as soon as we finalize our agreement." He jiggled her knee, excruciatingly aware of her warmth and the firm flesh of her thigh. He reluctantly pulled his hand away. "Sarah, wake up. We need to talk."

Though her eyes remained closed, she smiled, a soft, slight curving of her lips that made the blood pool in his loins. Such a beautiful, guileless smile. Then she opened her eyes and for a moment she simply gazed up at him. "Mr. MacDougal."

"Marsh," he said. "I want you to call me Marsh."

"Marsh," she repeated, still smiling.

He shifted, leaning nearer, then grimaced at the pain in his arm. At once her smile began to fade. Her eyes cleared, and he realized with a stab of disappointment that she'd been dreaming. When she'd smiled and used his first name, she'd not been fully awake

But she was awake now. She scooted upright in the chair, blinking at him. "I did not shoot you."

How he wanted to believe that.

"Nor did I hire someone else to do it."

He sat back on his heels and forced himself not to notice her sleep-tousled hair or her thin, clinging wrapper that gaped open in the vicinity of her bosom. "Do you have any idea who did it?"

She shook her head. "No." Then, "Why are you here in my room? It's the middle of the night?"

He rose to his feet. "You would not come to me."

"With good reason," she shot right back at him.

He tilted his head in acknowledgment. "My accusation was probably hasty."

She lifted her chin to a haughty angle. "If I wanted you dead, I would not have plunged into the river to save you."

"Unless your conscience overcame your fury," he snapped, goaded by her arrogant attitude. As casually as she was garbed, curled up like a child in that chair, she still managed to make him feel like a gauche boy.

"You have your nerve, talking to me about conscience!"

"I did not come here to argue with you." He leaned over her, bracing his good hand on one arm of the chair, effectively trapping her there.

"Then why did you come?"

They were but inches apart, her face turned up to him, her wary eyes clashing with his. He'd come to find out if she'd been the one to shoot him. And to find out why she'd saved him. But mostly he'd come to find out if she could ever forgive him for the hateful demands he'd made of her. He'd come to get answers to all of those questions—and none of them, he realized with sudden clarity.

The truth was, he'd come for no other reason than that he had to. Everything that drew them together was wrong. He knew that. Yet it was too strong to resist.

So he leaned down lower, lower, until one of her hands came up to press against his chest. His heart thundered so violently he was certain she must hear it, for never in his life had he been so aroused by a woman.

"I came for this," he said, lowering his face to hers. "I came for you."

# CHAPTER

# 20

SARAH stared wide-eyed at Mr. MacDougal. Only he wasn't Mr. MacDougal to her anymore. Somewhere along the way he'd become Marshall. He'd become Marsh.

She felt his warm breath upon her cheek and felt his heart drumming beneath her hand. Her own heart drummed as fiercely as if she'd run all the way from Kelso.

He meant to kiss her.

She closed her eyes as any thoughts of resisting fled. He meant to kiss her, and she knew she had to kiss him back. There was no way she could not. Just his nearness, just the anticipation, just the touch of her palm to his thinly clad chest, were enough to dissolve any last remnants of logic and self-preservation she still possessed.

She could have averted her face, or turned away—or even cried out in alarm.

But of course she did not. For she was reckless enough to want to kiss Marshall MacDougal, consequences be damned. Besides, given the trauma they'd just gone through, was kissing him really so awful?

So her lips clung to his when his mouth finally touched upon hers. And her breath mingled with his. Even their heartbeats, so fast and frantic, seemed to find a tandem rhythm. Mad, but tandem.

When he pulled a scant inch back from her, Sarah let out a faint, telling moan, and her fingers tightened in the ancient silk of the dressing gown he wore.

He murmured something. It sounded like "Yes" against her lips. If there was more, the words disappeared when she pressed up to kiss him. And he accepted her kiss.

Any tentativeness on his part disappeared too. For this time he forced her down into the chair, and her head back against the rest. Like a long-festering wound finally lanced, emotion erupted between them. One of his hands tangled in her hair. His lips parted; his tongue probed; and she opened fully to him.

Could a person be devoured body and soul, and yet revel in the devouring? Could a person submit her will, her sanity, and every modicum of good sense, and yet rejoice in that surrender?

Oh, yes, she thought as he somehow reversed their positions and drew her down onto his lap. Oh, yes, a person could be devoured, could surrender everything, and never care for the consequences which surely must follow. For she was doing so now.

Her arms wound around his neck; her legs draped over the arm of the chair; and her bottom nestled wantonly against his hard thighs and harder arousal.

She knew what that was and how things worked. Yet instead of fear, she knew a terrible yearning to learn more. And she squirmed in anticipation.

He growled in his throat and thrust up against her bottom. Then she felt his hand slide up her side, from her waist to just below her left breast.

She dragged in a greedy gulp of air. But as if he feared that she meant to voice some objection, he swiftly recaptured her mouth, delving deeper this time, thrusting his tongue in and out of her mouth, stroking her sensitive inner lips, and driving her mad in the process. Then he cupped her breast, lifting the unbound weight of it, and dragged his thumb back and forth across the taut nub of her nipple.

She thought she would expire of pleasure!

He must have known how intensely that simple little movement affected her, for he continued the wonderful, terrible caress until she was writhing in mindless passion. He used his lips and tongue to pleasure her mouth, and his hand to pleasure her breast.

Yet it was much lower, in the nether regions of her belly

and the warm vee of her legs, that the greatest portion of her pleasure was centered. Everything he did made her hotter and wetter down there. Every touch, every movement—every breath he shared with her—ignited an inferno in her belly. And she remembered from before just what an explosion he could coax from her down there.

She shivered in anticipation—in fear and longing. But there was no stopping. Not now. And anyway, hadn't she already decided to accept the terms of his agreement?

In truth, agreement or no, she wanted this as much as he did. Maybe more.

So she rose up against his hand, almost fainting at the feel of his warm palm making an erotic circle, flattening her breast and making her press harder still against him.

The cool night air fairly boiled between them. She felt too hot for her own skin. Again his thumb flicked her aroused nipple, and she gasped at the exquisite agony. Mindless with the intense pleasure of it, she arched her head back.

"Marsh . . ."

"I'm here," he murmured as he moved his mouth down the column of her throat, kissing, biting, eating her alive. His hand loosened the already gaping neck of her wrapper and she felt his callused palm move over first one bare breast, then the other. No pliable muslin to protect her skin from his. No slippery fabric to soften the rough scrape of his thumbnail across her taut, aching nipple.

Skin to skin, as man and woman were designed to be.

"I'm here," he repeated. Then he bent her farther over the chair arm, and his mouth fastened upon her breasts.

Her arms fell away from his neck and clutched instead at his arms.

"Marsh!"

The cry was a plea, not a protest, and he seemed to understand that. For he parted the wrapper wider and cupped both her breasts with his hands. He turned the attention of his lips, from one to the other, sucking, biting, squeezing, and kneading until she was quivering beneath him, melting over him, given up wholly to him. She was his, and he knew it.

He knew also all the secret uses of her secret body parts, the parts that she might swipe with a washcloth, but never lingered over. But he lingered over them. Her breasts, her earlobes. The hollow of her throat. The indentation along her collarbone. And her breasts. Again. His mouth and fingers lingered over every one of those secret places.

He did not acknowledge, however, the one place that pleaded most for his attention. Though she squirmed and rubbed her bottom shamelessly against his rigid manhood, his hands never strayed down to the melting heat between her legs.

Didn't he know what he was doing to her? Couldn't he tell how she yearned for him to stroke her as he'd done before? In desperation her fingers stole down past her belly to that aching place between her legs.

But he caught her hand in his. "Sarah." He breathed the word hot and moist against her palm.

She opened her eyes and met his dark, searching gaze. Though she was draped over his lap like a pagan offering, her wrapper open to reveal every part of her body to him, it was not her nudity which most unsettled her. Rather, it was the intensity of his stare, the total awareness in it. His hand cupped hers, their fingers intertwined, opening her palm to his lips, and as she watched—as their eyes held in the most intimate of connections—he kissed the center of her palm.

Why that should push her over the edge, Sarah did not know. Nor could she reason it out. He pressed the kiss to her open hand, his tongue made a slow, hot circle there, and she erupted just as she had that night in the carriage.

It was terrifying and wonderful, and was made even more intense because he watched her every response. Though she wanted to close her eyes and somehow hide from him, she was unable to. Her body stiffened as the tremors rushed through her; her skin seemed to quiver over the length and breadth of her entire body; and he watched and saw it all.

Only when the tremors ended and her body went limp did he release her hand—and release her captive gaze.

But he was not done with her, that was plain, for both of his hands began to move over her, knees to thighs, across her belly, up her sides, then stroking up from her arms, raising them to her neck once more.

"You have tortured me too long," he murmured. "Too long." Then, with one hand beneath her knees and the other cradling her back, he rose and carried her to her bed.

She clung to him, only remembering his wounded arm when he grunted as he lowered her to the bed. "Your arm! Oh, Marsh, I forgot. Are you hurt?"

He came down on the satin coverlet, stretching out beside her. "I'm in agony."

"Oh, no!" Despite the lethargy lingering from that most personal explosion, she pushed up to her knees. "What can I do to help?"

"Open my robe."

She fumbled with the tie of his robe, then opened it and pushed it gently down from his shoulder until she saw his bandaged arm. At least the wound had not bled through. "Just try to relax," she murmured.

"I can't."

Sarah bit her lip. "What can I do?"

"Open the bottom of my robe."

Her gaze jerked back to his face, only to be scorched by the potent heat in his eyes.

"Open it," he repeated.

"But . . . but your arm."

"That's not what hurts me, Sarah. Open it." His chest rose and fell with every harsh breath he took. "Open it and soothe my pain."

Soothe his pain. *That* pain. Sarah blushed a hot red when she finally understood. She knelt over him, her own gown gaping open, her body still thrumming from the pleasure he'd given her. Could she do anything but what he asked?

Slowly, with shaking hands, she parted his dressing gown. Then she just stared at the mighty arousal that awaited her ministrations.

Tentatively she reached out and stroked it with the backs of her fingertips. At once it lifted, as if wanting more. She glanced up at his face. His eyes had closed and he looked as if he were caught somewhere between absolute pleasure and excruciating pain.

On impulse she said, "Look at me."

When he did, she stroked him again—and again. She progressed from fingertips to thumb to a full hand caress. And the entire time she stared into his midnight-dark eyes.

Though she'd never done such a thing, nor ever imagined such intimacy with a man, Sarah somehow sensed when he was near to his own breaking point. She felt very near there again herself.

She gripped the hard, hot, incredibly silky shaft of his manhood, wanting to see the rest, to watch him erupt as he'd watched her.

But he had other plans. He caught her wrist with his one good hand and swiftly rolled her back onto her bed. "Not this time," he murmured, as he lowered himself over her. He swallowed her protest with an urgent kiss.

Though disappointed at being thwarted, Sarah did not long regret his high-handedness. For one of his thighs parted hers and she felt the rigid heat of him press demandingly against her belly. At once she was as aroused as before, wet and yearning for that one intimate act they'd so far danced around. She wanted to feel him inside her. She wanted to feel it all. Everything.

She circled his neck with her arms and arched insistently beneath him. In a moment his other thigh forced her legs wider apart, and she felt him shift lower. The proud tip of his arousal slid down past the aching nub of her desire to a place below it that throbbed with need.

He levered himself upon one elbow, breaking their kiss. "This may hurt a little," he warned, staring down at her.

"I'm not afraid," she whispered, meeting his gaze.

He took her at her word. With their gazes locked, he pushed into her, each thrust going a little deeper. Each thrust stoking the fire that already burned out of control. He thrust, stroking her harder, filling her deeper, until with one powerful move he pushed past the barrier of her maidenhead.

It did hurt—but only for a moment. And she regretted it for an even briefer moment.

She sucked in a short breath, then exhaled when he flexed his maleness within her.

"Oh, my."

He smiled, then began to withdraw.

"No. Wait—"

He thrust back in.

Her eyes widened farther. "Oh, my."

"Oh, my," he echoed with a grin. Then he began a rhythm of thrust and withdraw which she quickly joined in. It was like dancing, some fragment of her mind decided. He led and she followed, but as in a waltz, it took their efforts together to make the movements beautiful.

And beautiful it was, like nothing she'd ever known. They moved in a perfect tandem. One rose and the other met. One pulled back just far enough to prompt some answering motions, and the other responded to the unspoken command. They dipped and swayed and whirled higher and faster. Like some unearthly music, the melody called to them and they responded. They danced their midnight waltz across the sheets in the shadows of her room until the rhythm grew too frantic, too violent, until Sarah could do nothing but hold on to him and urge him on.

Thrust. Withdraw.

Hold on tight.

And breathe. Breathe.

Then came the explosion, the crescendo where the physical met the ethereal.

She cried out and he swallowed it up with a kiss of such fierce possession it left her deaf to all but him and his own shout of physical release. She erupted; he erupted; and the eruption went on and on, a single, interminable moment of capitulation and triumph.

Afterward they collapsed, their bodies melded together—forever, it seemed. For Sarah was certain she could never move again. Never. Nor did she want to. A huge wave of lethargy washed over her, weariness, completion, and an unprecedented sense of contentment. And all on account of this man, so warm and heavy in her arms.

She smiled into the dark, absurdly pleased with herself, then sighed when he rolled to his side, keeping her wrapped in his arms. Though some part of her knew she should regret this—indeed, that someday she *would* regret it—for now she refused to acknowledge it. How could she ever regret such soaring, powerful feelings? At that perfect moment in time, she was certain she never would.

# CHAPTER

# 21

He hurt all over. And he'd never felt so good.

Marsh shifted, wincing at the shooting pain in his upper arm. Beside him the soft, fragrant form of a woman also shifted, their bare skin sticking a little in the warm cocoon of the bed linens.

For a moment longer he reveled in the intimate slide of naked skin on naked skin, and he sighed as his intense sense of well-being soared. There was nothing like a willing woman to mend a man's aches and chase his troubles away.

His troubles?

Like a rude slap across the face, the reality of his situation hit him and Marsh's contentment abruptly fled. He twisted his head to the side and stared down into Sarah Palmer's sleeping face, and in a rush every detail of yesterday—and last night—returned.

His arm hurt because he'd been shot.

The rest of him hurt because he'd made such ferocious, overdue love to Sarah. She was his nemesis; she was his enemy; and she was the most delicious, responsive lover he'd ever had.

But was she also the one who'd shot him, or had him shot?

He levered himself away from her, stifling a grunt of pain. Funny, he'd not felt any pain during their lovemaking. But his arm hurt like hell now.

So did the unhappy fact that he'd gotten exactly what he'd demanded, that last sticking point in their perverse agreement. He'd rightly decided not to hold her to that demand. Yet at the first opportunity he'd still taken complete advantage of her.

God, but he was the lowest sort of heel. He'd fucked her, as he'd so crudely termed it. Now it remained only for him to have the legal papers prepared, and for her to transfer the funds to his account.

Frowning, he shoved down the coverlet. He was naked and in her bed, not his. He swung his feet onto the floor, gritting his teeth. He'd gotten what he wanted all along, despite his belated attack of conscience. So why did he have this nagging sense of dissatisfaction? Why did he feel like punching someone—anyone—in the nose?

Spying his discarded dressing gown, he snatched it up and put it on, intending to retreat to the bedchamber he'd been given. Then it occurred to him that he was inside Byrde Manor. He was inside his father's home, the home that should have been his all these years.

And the woman still asleep in her bed, with her glorious hair strewn in a tangle, had just purchased it from him with her sweet virgin's body.

His nostrils flared in revulsion even as his body reacted with lust. He'd given up his heritage to her, something he'd sworn he would have back, if only for his mother's sake. He'd given in to Sarah Palmer, though. But why? She was a self-indulgent English aristocrat who believed her money could buy anyone off. When it could not buy him off, however, she'd willingly thrown herself into the pot. Anything to protect her family's reputation among the rest of their loathsome peers.

He clenched his jaw again. Though he knew he must share the blame for what they'd done together—after all, he'd been the one to add that caveat to the agreement she'd offered—that only made it worse. Why must he react so violently to her? So urgently? Why did he lust after her when there were so many other less complicated women to be had? Why her?

As if to taunt him, she sighed and rolled onto her back, revealing even in the feeble light of the guttering candle the pearly skin of her shoulder and the upper swells of her breasts. Like a goad, his perverse desire sharpened almost to pain.

But it was done between them, he told himself. It was done.

He clung to that simple but excruciatingly hard thought as he backed from the room. It was done now between them. He'd won a handsome sum of money and an energetic night in her bed.

But his eyes clung to the womanly figure sprawled on the shadowy bed. His gaze remained fixed upon her until the door closed between them. Even then, when he turned down the quiet hall that led to his bedchamber, victory did not taste particularly sweet.

Sarah awakened early, at least by her standards. The sun was up and she heard voices in the yard. But no maid had yet entered her room.

She rolled over, stretching her drowsy body—then realized with a gasp that she was naked.

Naked.

Then a far worse realization struck her like a cruel blow. She was also no longer an innocent maiden.

Wide awake now, and trembling, she yanked the counterpane up to her chin and peered cautiously about. Where was he? Where was Marshall MacDougal, the man who had come to her last night? Marshall MacDougal, whom she'd welcomed into her bed without even a pretense of objection?

Wherever he was, however, it was not in her room. Piercing disappointment left a hollow feeling in her chest. Though she should have felt relief, her first and truest reaction to his absence was keen disappointment.

But it was the wrong reaction, and she buried those inappropriate feelings with a quick burst of activity. The maid must not find her naked.

She fished her wrapper from its puddle on the floor near the foot of the bed. Her hair she twisted into a messy rope and secured with a ribbon, and for good measure she donned her slippers.

But there was something wrong. Something . . .

She checked the sheets and saw a half-dried stain and a faint smear of blood. Her virgin's blood.

Her heart, which had already been racing, thundered now with the heavy rhythm of guilt. She grabbed a washcloth and, using water from the pitcher on the washstand, soaked and scrubbed until the blood was gone. Then she blotted it with her towel and flung the top sheets and counterpane over the telltale patch.

There. She was safe.

But she remained uneasy. There was something else. She couldn't determine what, but she knew anyone entering this room would immediately guess what had happened here. She took a deep breath, trying to calm herself, and at once she knew.

Her bedchamber smelled different, of seething emotions and physical intercourse. Of a man and a woman coming together in that most intimate of acts.

"Oh, no!" She sniffed again, feeling for all the world like a harried fox done in by her own scent lingering on the air, with the hounds, meanwhile, quick behind her.

In an instant she yanked the gold damask curtains open, then flung the narrow window sashes wide. Was there anything else she could do—besides die of humiliation?

With her head bowed, she leaned on the windowsill and tried to think, to calm herself. But any chance of calm was shattered when she raised her head and spied Marshall MacDougal standing just outside the stables.

She sucked in a sharp breath, for the very sight of him seemed to tighten every muscle in her body. This was the man she'd shared every intimate secret with. The man who'd made her moan and sigh and cry out with pleasure. Though she ought to look away from him, she could not. Her eyes fairly drank in the sight of him, so straight and tall in his buff-colored breeches, white shirt, and dark blue frock coat. He might have been some well-heeled country squire, or even a titled lord, for he had that air of command about him. He looked so right, so perfect standing there.

But then, he was a country squire, she reminded herself. He was by birth Cameron Byrde's legal heir, and therefore a Scottish country squire. And now, thanks to the deal she'd made with him, he would be quite wealthy. Even wealthier than he already was.

She started to back away, trying hard to tear her gaze away from him. But as if he sensed her eyes upon him, he turned and looked up at the house, straight at her window. She could not move. She saw his arm, in its sling. But that did not lessen the virile impact he had upon her. She quivered, legs, belly, and every square inch of her skin. She quivered and swallowed hard despite her suddenly dry mouth.

She would have to face him eventually. Perhaps she should just get dressed, go down there, and be done with it now. Be done with *him.*

One of his companions spoke to him, he glanced away from her, and Sarah noisily exhaled. Her fingers tightened on the windowsill, for she felt almost dizzy from the impact of Marsh's stare. How could one man affect her so profoundly?

The answer was as disheartening as it was obvious. She had a history of responding to the wrong sort of man, of being attracted to charming troublemakers. No settled, good-hearted fellows for her. Oh, no.

She turned away from the window and slumped with her back against the wall. The good-hearted fellows were all too dull for foolish, reckless Sarah Palmer. She must pick those mysterious fellows with ulterior motives. She must court disaster at every turn. And now disaster had overtaken her.

But at least she'd spared her mother and sister the pain and humiliation of having Marshall MacDougal's true identity made known. She'd accomplished what she'd set out to do. Surely there was some sort of honor in that.

She pressed one palm to her chest and willed her pulse

to slow. Then she lifted her chin, pushed off from the wall, and started with a determined stride for her armoire to dress. After everything she'd been through in the last few weeks, the fear, the racing about—

The sex.

She halted with a simple day dress in her hand, grimacing at that crude term for such wondrous intimacies. Yet wasn't that how he thought about it? He'd said he wanted to "fuck" her. Well, last night he had. She would be a fool to think it was anything more to him than that.

*But I am a fool,* some anguished part of her cried out.

*Not today. Not anymore,* her practical side insisted. *You cannot be a fool anymore.*

So she squared her shoulders and braced herself for the coming ordeal. She would see him; she would converse with him; and she would conclude her dealings with him once and for all. After everything else she'd gone through, facing him this one last time could not be that hard.

Only when Sarah crossed the yard a few minutes later, heading for the small knot of men, did she notice the mayor and sheriff among them. Mr. Hamilton held Marsh's horse, while the valet, Mr. Erskine, saddled the animal. The sheriff doffed his hat when he spied Sarah, and the others all did the same.

She smiled in reply but kept her gaze fixed upon the stout sheriff. It was stupid, of course, but she was afraid to look at Marshall MacDougal, afraid that if she did, somehow everyone would know. Something in her face would give her away and reveal what she'd done with him—and how much she wanted to do it again—

"No!" She nearly choked on the word.

"No?" The sheriff's forehead creased as he stared at her.

"No. I mean *know,*" she amended, floundering around for some solid ground in the quagmire of her traitorous, deviant thoughts. "Do you know who . . . who shot Mr. MacDougal?" she finally managed to say.

The mayor and sheriff both shook their shining, balding heads. "That's why we're here, to see if Mr. MacDougal has any ideas, any reason someone 'round here might wish him ill."

Sarah could not prevent her gaze from darting toward Marsh. They both knew she was the only one who had reason to wish him ill. But she would never—*never*—go so far as to shoot him.

But did he know that?

Their eyes met and held for one long, troubling moment. Then he turned his attention back to the two village officials. "As I told you, I can think of no one who has reason to fear me."

"It mightn't be fear," the sheriff replied, holding on to his lapels and rocking back on his heels. "How's about robbery?"

Marsh shrugged his uninjured shoulder. "Robbery? Perhaps. But shooting a man in broad daylight for a few coins seems unlikely. Although I have been told there are highwaymen in these parts."

Again his glance flickered to Sarah, then away. But it was enough for her to feel the weight of his accusation. Did he still think she'd masterminded the attack on him? More to the point, did he feel that she was stealing his heritage, his family history? His entire past?

For the first time Sarah considered their agreement from his perspective, what he was giving up. But with the sheriff there to ask questions, there was no time to dwell on that subject. The sheriff quizzed her on what she'd heard and seen, and also commended her on her cool head and swift action in fishing Mr. MacDougal from the river.

She accepted his praise with as much good grace as she could muster. If he only knew what her true nature was, the sheriff would be aghast. As would the mayor also, and anyone else who found out how devious and wanton a creature she actually was. By the time the two men left, her neck and shoulders ached with tension, and a headache had begun to throb in her temples.

"Could we speak a moment?" Marsh asked her once they were alone. At her nod, he took her arm and steered her away from the watchful Mr. Hamilton and Mr. Erskine. She tried not to read too much into it when he released her arm as soon as they were out of earshot of the two servants.

"So," he said in a cool tone. "It seems the sticking point to our agreement is now moot."

"Yes. So it is." Sarah stared straight ahead. To anyone watching, they probably appeared a gentleman and a lady taking a leisurely stroll to while away time on a pleasant spring morning. How she wished that was all it was. "I suppose all that remains now is to make arrangements for the transfer of funds from my account into yours."

He cleared his throat. "I'll have my agent contact you with the details."

She nodded but did not speak. A bee circled them once, then flew away. They had nearly reached the low stone wall that separated the east field from the house grounds. The silence became almost painful. "How am I to be certain you will hold to your end of our agreement?" she finally asked.

He looked down at her, and she felt the heat of his anger. "You have my word. That will have to suffice."

Inside she was trembling. Outside, however, she held herself so stiffly she betrayed nothing. "You will be returning to America soon?"

"Immediately. Today."

The trembling escaped to her hands. She knotted them together in one big fist. "Today. That is probably for the best."

"The only thing that holds me back is the identity of my attacker."

"I would like to know his identity as well." She looked up at him. "I had nothing to do with that cowardly attack on you, Marsh—I mean, Mr. MacDougal." She swallowed hard. "I hope you know that."

"Marsh." His voice was low and husky. "I think after all that's passed between us that you can at least call me Marsh." His eyes were dark and intense. Too intense.

She shook her head and bit her lip. "I had nothing to do

with it," she went on. "Nor do I wish such a violent person roaming the countryside, for he poses a threat to us all. Should his identity be discovered in your absence, I assure you that I will press to have him punished to the full limits of the law."

He did not respond, and for a long time they stood there, side by side, staring up the long, sloping hillside pasture, dotted here and there with skinny, recently shorn sheep.

"What will you tell them?" he finally asked.

"Who?" But she knew to whom he referred. "You mean my sister and mother." She chewed on her lip. "I don't know. Perhaps nothing. Especially my mother."

"How will you explain withdrawing so large a sum of money from your accounts?"

She glanced sidelong at him. Why should he care? "I'll think of something."

"I know enough of legal matters in Britain to know a single woman—even an heiress—has little access to her own wealth."

"You will get your money!" she snapped, suddenly furious at his fixation on the money when so much more had passed between them. But what she thought should be important obviously was not as important to him.

She glared at him. "You will have what you most value—a fat bank account—while I will retain what I most value—a happy family. You have taught me a hard lesson, Mr. MacDougal," she said, drawing out his name until it was almost an insult. "I will never take my family for granted. Never. They are more important to me than anything. Money. Property—"

"And you think that's all that's important to me? Son of a bitch!" he swore, raking the fingers of his good hand through his hair.

She found herself suddenly on the brink of tears. "Well, isn't it?"

He shook his head slowly, as if it were heavy and he was very tired. "No. No, Sarah. I came to you last night . . ."

She stiffened, pressing her lips together.

He went on. "I came to you to tell you . . . to apologize for the deal I tried to make with you. About making love to you," he added.

They were the last words she expected to hear from him, and for a moment she was too shocked to respond. "That's not what you called it before."

"What?"

"You said . . ." She was trembling, even her jaw, for her teeth were chattering. "You said you want to . . . to fuck me."

He let out a harsh breath. "I'm sorry for that. Sorrier than you can know."

"You say that now."

Again he shook his head. "What happened last night, it wasn't what I planned. I had decided to release you from that abominable deal I forced on you. I was going to tell you. But then when I saw you asleep in that chair . . ." Again he exhaled. "I can't undo what has happened between us, Sarah. God knows I wish I could. But I can't."

For a long moment their gazes held, hers still doubting, his filled with remorse. He *was* sorry, she realized. Yet that knowledge gave her little relief. He was sorry for the wonderful thrilling, terrifying things he had done to her. He wished he could take it back. Whereas she . . . she didn't know what she wanted anymore.

The silence stretched out between them, long, tumultuous, but silent all the same. Then he shifted his weight from one leg to the other. "I, ah, I'm not exactly sure of the customs here, but in America if you . . . well, when you ruin a woman—not that I think you are ruined," he added. "But, well, if you think we should marry . . ."

If he said anything further, Sarah didn't hear it. She stared at him in utter shock. "Marry? You and I?"

He frowned and his jaw worked back and forth. "I thought it only right to make the offer."

Like a dagger, those words tore a hole in her heart. Of course he was offering to marry her. Any man who would cross an ocean to make an honest woman of his mother would also feel an obligation to do right by a woman he had ruined. *Any* woman he had ruined.

But Sarah didn't want to be just any woman to him. So she shook her head. "I . . . I don't think that would be wise."

He let out a short bark of laughter. "I suppose I should not be surprised, considering everything. Well." He took a breath and made her a curt bow. "Since it seems our business is done, perhaps I'd better take my leave of you now."

Without further word, he turned his back and strode away. Sarah stared after him, watching him go, yet unable to utter even one word to make him stay. He was leaving. Forever. Going back to America, where he belonged. Instead of feeling a happy relief, however, what she felt was devastation. He would have married her. He would have done the right thing by her, just as she now saw he always tried to do the right thing by everyone. His mother. Adrian.

Her.

But he was leaving now, and all she could do was follow him with her eyes.

"Good-bye!" she whispered to his retreating figure. Good-bye to the man who'd taken her innocence—and not just the innocence of her body. She pressed her clasped palms against the center of her aching chest.

He'd taken also the innocence of her heart.

# CHAPTER

# 22

ADRIAN had not slept at home last night. Not that his mother would care. No doubt she'd had enough company to keep her otherwise occupied. Of late she'd taken up with that bandy-legged fellow who worked for the American.

His agitation increased at the thought. How could she?

But he knew how. Because she didn't care about him. Nor did anyone else. No one would notice if he disappeared and never came back again.

He shivered despite the warmth of the morning. Ever since that disaster on the riverbank yesterday, he'd kept himself well hidden. He'd also kept watch on all the comings and goings around Byrde Manor. He'd seen Sarah drag the American out of the river, and then watched as everybody else had come to his aid.

The whole night he'd huddled in a holly thicket near the road, watching and listening, and he'd breathed an enormous sigh of relief to learn that the man lived.

Now the mayor and sheriff had come out to investigate and Adrian's heart pounded a new panic-driven rhythm. Had the American seen him? Did he know who had wielded that ancient fowling piece? Would everyone be looking for him now?

The boy clenched his jaws to stop their trembling. Clenched them until they ached. He'd never meant to kill the American. Not really. He'd only wanted him gone far away from Sarah. Far away. For it was plain the man had some nefarious hold on her that was making her miserable. But Adrian hadn't meant to shoot him.

*Yes, you did.*

Adrian squeezed his eyes shut against the accusing voice that would not leave him alone. All yesterday evening, all night, and now again this morning the voice persisted. *You stole the gun from Mr. Hamilton's collection of sporting pieces stored in the tack room. You hunted the American down. You raised the gun, you aimed, and you shot him.*

A shudder racked his body and he hugged himself close in the shadow of the well house. For the first time in his life he was glad he did not have a father, for a father would have taken him hunting and taught him how to shoot better, and maybe there would not be a hole in the American's arm, but rather in his chest.

His stomach heaved and the bitter taste of bile rose into his mouth.

*But it's all right,* he told himself. *It's all right.* The American would survive.

But as Adrian watched the man stalk away from Sarah now, a new fear rose in his chest. Sarah had saved him, yet the man was obviously furious with her. Why? Could he think that *she* had told Adrian to do him in? Had he made an accusation like that to the sheriff?

Adrian lurked behind the elder bushes until the American mounted his horse and rode away, his servant trailing behind. Then Adrian cut his gaze back to Sarah.

She stood stiff and unmoving where the man had left her, staring away from the manor house, away from the long drive. Away from the road Mr. MacDougal had taken.

Though he knew the chance he took—though he knew he ought to run away and never come back to this area—Adrian nevertheless started toward her. She looked so slight and frail in contrast to the vast open fields beyond her. So vulnerable. He had to be certain no one was blaming her for what he had done.

He tugged at his wrinkled coat as he made his way to her, and swiped at the leaves and twigs still clinging to his breeches. Then he spit on his hand and tried to smooth down his hopelessly rumpled hair. But all the while he kept his eyes fixed upon Sarah.

He had the awful, sinking suspicion that she and the American had become lovers. He didn't like the idea—he hated it, just as he hated his mother's numerous dalliances. But he'd learned long ago that there was nothing he could do about his mother, and Sarah was no different. Still, the American had left, and Sarah might need him. He was not about to let her down.

Standing beside the ancient dry-stack wall, Sarah clutched her hands against the flat top stone. She pressed hard, feeling every crevice beneath her palms, aware beneath her fingers of where last year's dried and crumbling mosses gave way to the moist green of spring's velvety new growth.

The hoofbeats had long since faded away. No dust cloud hung above the drive; no voices reverberated up from the road. He'd left silently, disappearing from her life with no mark anywhere to record his passing.

No mark except the invisible one he'd left in her. And though it too seemed a silent mark, inside where only she could hear, she was shrieking.

What was the point of all this? Why had he come here? Why did he have to leave?

*You could have made him stay. You could have accepted his offer and married him.*

And married a man who didn't really want to be married to her? A man who had every reason in the world to hate her family? A man who could wreak such havoc on the lives of the two women she loved most in the whole world?

She began to tremble and, stiff as an old woman, she wrapped her arms across her chest. When she heard a step in the stubby grass behind her, she jerked.

Had he returned?

She spun around, then could not disguise the disappointment in her expression when she saw Adrian.

At once she looked away.

"Don't be sorry that he's gone, Sarah." The boy's voice was low and imploring, rough and cracking. "All he does is make you unhappy. I hope he never comes back."

His earnestness forced a sad smile to her lips.

"I believe you have nothing to fear on that score, Adrian. He is leaving for America. And I am glad," she added, trying hard to sound convincing. "He really doesn't fit in here."

"Why did he come, then? Ever since he's shown up, he's made trouble for everyone. Scaring you. Beating up poor Guinea. Will says he used to be a boxer in America. That's what the men in the livery all say." The boy's face lowered in a truculent frown. "Just a common, brawling ruffian, he is. He never had any business pesterin' a lady like you."

"He's not a boxer," Sarah retorted, even as she considered that he might very well once have been. That would explain his athlete's body and graceful way of moving. "He constructs bridges and buildings. He has his own company with lots of other men working for him. But it doesn't matter what he does," she added with a vague wave of her hand. "It doesn't matter why he came here. He's gone now."

She took a breath and let it out, then pasted a pleasant expression firmly on her face. "Dear me, but the day is nearly half gone and I've accomplished nothing at all. So tell me, what brings you here?" Then her eyes narrowed as she noticed his disheveled state. "My goodness, Adrian, where did you sleep last night? The barn?"

His eyes flashed, then looked away. Was that guilt she saw in their dark blue depths?

"Does your mother know where you are?"

He snorted. "No. Nor is she likely to care."

"Come now. Don't say that."

"Well, she doesn't. Except for the money my Uncle Neville gives her for me, she doesn't care what I do."

She reached out and squeezed his arm. "Neville and Livvie love you very much, Adrian. And so do I."

His Adam's apple bobbed as he swallowed, and his eyes

shone with the intensity of his emotions. "I love you too, Sarah. I really do."

He reached out to embrace her, but she backed away. There was a long awkward moment as they both recovered.

She'd not meant her words as he'd obviously taken them. Good heavens, could she do nothing right?

"Adrian, I . . . I'm sorry."

"No. Um . . ." He shook his head, looking bewildered. Again she saw the struggle between the little boy he'd been and the young man he was becoming. He shoved his fists into his pockets. "I have to go," he muttered. Then, just like Marsh had done, he turned and stalked away.

Sarah watched him go with a heavy heart. If only she were young enough—and innocent enough—to deserve the admiration of a lad like Adrian. She'd trade everything she had to go back three years, to have her coming out again and do everything right this time.

But what could she have done differently and still protect her mother and sister from the unexpected threat Marshall MacDougal had brought into their lives?

Nothing, she morosely decided. Nothing. And if that was the case, then she had nothing to regret—and no cause for this hollow feeling in her chest. Best that she focus on the details of her agreement with Marshall MacDougal.

So she squared her shoulders and started for the house. She had a letter to write to her man of business, one that would probably give him an attack of apoplexy and send him screaming to her brother.

She blew out a weary breath. She had better write a letter to James as well.

Adrian had never missed having a father as much as he did this horrible, wretched day. If his uncle had been here, he would know what to do.

Then again, when Uncle Neville found out he'd left Eton in the middle of the term, he might be too furious to listen to anything else Adrian had to say.

With one booted toe the boy lashed out at a stone lying

innocently in the middle of the road. Then, with head down and shoulders slumped, he trudged on toward home. He'd hated Eton. From the very first day he'd dreamed of nothing but returning home to Kelso. But nothing had gone right since his return. Nothing.

His mother had only become more brazen during his absence. Or was it that when compared to his classmates' families she only seemed worse?

He'd thought he was too smart for those spoiled rich boys with their valets and riding masters. But all of a sudden he did not feel very smart at all. He was a rich man's bastard—a dead rich man's bastard—and while his uncle had been good to him, how long could Uncle Neville be expected to continue on in that vein? Especially when the results were so spectacularly bad.

He was an idiot. A fool. He was so stupid he'd even convinced himself that a fine lady like Sarah Palmer might develop an attachment for him.

He grimaced to even remember his idiotic declaration of love just now. How stupid he must look to her. How childish. And then there was the shooting.

His chest heaved, yet no matter the great gulps of air he sucked in, he still felt as if he could not breathe. So far no one seemed to suspect him—at least the sheriff and mayor had not said anything to Sarah. Still, guilt weighed heavily upon his shoulders, nearly crushing him when he thought how close he'd come to killing a man.

*Killing* him.

Had he truly believed Sarah would be glad if the American were dead? Today she'd looked utterly devastated by the man's departure.

He reached Kelso and stared past the bridge that arched over the River Tweed toward the cluster of stone cottages were he and his mother lived.

He didn't want to go home.

He twisted his head to stare toward town. Did he dare go into Kelso? What if Marshall MacDougal were still there? It seemed that the man had not identified him as his attacker. Maybe he'd forgotten. But what if he saw him and then began to remember everything?

Even though Adrian was terrified of being found out, he could not turn away from town. Something drew him there, something twisted and perverse. Maybe it was guilt, he speculated as he forced himself to walk into town, his head high this time, his hands stuffed nonchalantly in the pockets of his breeches. Maybe he would feel better if he was caught and accused and hauled off to the gaol.

His chin trembled and came down a notch. That's what he deserved, being thrown in the small village gaol.

A gusty wind ruffled his hair as he looked around at the town, and his skin prickled. It looked just like it did on any other day. Shoppers made their way from butcher to baker to greengrocer. The milliner's simple-minded daughter washed their square shop window. The wheelwright worked in his open stable doorway, and stout Mayor Dinkerson burst frowning from the sheriff's office, banging the door, then striding purposefully toward his own house.

Adrian shrank back into the shadow cast by a pair of stacked kegs, then jerked around when someone shoved into him.

"Where ya been?" a boyish voice chirruped.

It was all Adrian could do not to punch his sometime cohort Will. "None of your business," he muttered, pushing Will back. Though his heart thudded with alarm, he covered it with a threatening scowl. "Next time you sneak up on me I won't be so easy on you."

"Bet I know somethin' you don't know," the smaller boy taunted, dancing out of Adrian's reach.

"So what?" But once again alarm speeded up Adrian's pulse. Did Will know what he'd done?

"So a lot. Somebody shot that American fighting bloke. Shot 'im and almost killed 'im."

"Really?" Adrian struggled to look interested. But not too interested. "How'd it happen?"

By the time Will finished spinning out the tale, complete with his own theory about gypsies and highwaymen and other sorts of dastardly troublemakers, Adrian was reassured that at least *he* was not a suspect. But it didn't make him feel a whole lot better.

"Look!" Will elbowed him in the side and pointed. "There he is."

"Who?"

The American. And like the mayor, he was coming out of the sheriff's office.

Adrian stared at him, at the arm cradled in a sling, and the dark scowling expression. The man's servant followed on his heels, then swiftly departed toward the public stable. But the American just stood there, staring around as if he were studying the town—or else looking for someone. When his head swung around and his hard gaze alighted upon Adrian, the boy lurched back.

"Holy weezus," Will muttered, then tore off in the opposite direction. Adrian wanted to run also, but his boots might as well have been rooted to the ground. He could not move an inch.

For a long, terrible moment the man's stare kept him pinned there. For an hour, a whole day, it seemed. But then the American nodded, a curt jerk of his head, before striding down the swept stone walkway.

Adrian watched him until he turned into the vicar's front yard, and all the time his heart pounded like a herd of Clydesdales in full gallop. Sarah was wrong. The American wasn't leaving at all. He was looking for the person who'd tried to murder him. He had the sheriff, the mayor, and now the vicar helping him. He might not yet know who the culprit was, but eventually he would figure it out.

Adrian lurched awkwardly in a full circle, trying to decide. He would go back to Eton.

No. He would run away to Edinburgh.

No. No, he would ship out on a North Sea whaling ship.

Again the crushing weight on his chest made it hard to breathe. Then his gaze fastened upon the faded sign of the Cock and Bow, swinging on its chains in the brisk morning breeze. Without pausing to think or reason out his purpose, he started across the street, half walking, half running, before he could change his mind.

He had to confess.

It was the only thing he could think of to do. He had to wait for the man in his room, where no one else could hear them. He would confess his crime, and if Mr. MacDougal wanted to march him straight over to the sheriff and the gaol, then . . . then march over there he would. He would shoulder his responsibilities like a man. He would own up to his mistakes like his Uncle Neville always said a man should do.

And he would be a man.

Only a few patrons sat in the inn's public room, and Adrian easily slipped up the stairs without notice. There were four rooms on the second floor. Since three were open and empty, he made his way to the fourth and slumped against the closed door. His knees quaked and he felt limp with fear. His heart banged against his ribs hard enough to jump right out through his chest.

When he heard a woman's voice, followed by the tramp of footsteps rising from the stairwell, he jumped to his feet. Without considering the consequences, he barged through the door and into the room, and when the steps drew closer still, he dove under the bed.

The maid stayed but a few minutes, refilling the ewer, replacing the candles, and making up the bed. Her toes in their worn leather slippers came within inches of Adrian's face. Her skirt hem was frayed, and her stockings did not match. He held his breath, sure he would be found out.

What new trouble had he gotten himself into? But eventually she left, and eventually he could breathe again. He crawled out from his hiding place, then sat a few minutes just looking around. A leather satchel sat beside a square wooden desk under the window. At the foot of the bed a small trunk was partially packed.

Perhaps the American was leaving.

A stack of papers lay on the desk, and as the minutes

ticked past and Adrian's nervousness increased, he crossed to the desk and stared down at them.

A list of churches. St. Matthias of the Sea. St. Leonid's. St. Anne the Poor. His gaze sharpened. Nearly half of the churches had a line drawn through them.

Curious, he lifted the corner of that page to peek at the one below. That one listed cities. Port cities, he quickly discerned. And again, some were crossed out.

He frowned. What was all this? Did the man mean to visit all those places? He did say he was on holiday. But who visited churches on holiday? And who wanted to go to Badensea? He'd been there once and it was a nasty hole of a town that stank of rotten fish.

Adrian shook his head. Perhaps the man was searching for someone in those places. Someone or something at those churches and towns. But what could it be?

He sifted through the rest of the papers. A letter of introduction from a Boston bank. A hand-drawn map of the area around Kelso, down toward Byrde Manor. He studied that a long while before lifting it to find a letter addressed to Mr. MacDougal. Another name leaped out from the body of that letter, however. Maureen MacDougal.

Was Marshall MacDougal married to some other woman while he pursued Sarah? Was that why she was so unhappy, because she'd found out he had a family in America?

But Maureen MacDougal was not the American's wife, Adrian swiftly discovered. She was his mother and the letter was from someone in London who had been searching for information about her and about Cameron Byrde.

Adrian sat back in the chair, his brow furrowed in thought. Cameron Byrde. That was his Aunt Livvie's father. But he'd been dead a long, long time. What would some American have to do with him?

Then all at once it struck him, struck him with all the clarity and pain that only a bastard child could understand.

Marshall MacDougal, given his mother's name, but very likely the son of Cameron Byrde.

Adrian dropped the letter back on the desk. Hadn't he

gone by the name Adrian Kendrick, his mother's name, until his uncle had insisted he be called by his father's name? He was Adrian Hawke now.

And Marshall MacDougal must be Marshall Byrde.

But what did it all mean? And did Sarah know?

"What in the hell are you doing in my room?"

Adrian spun around so fast the papers went flying.

In the door stood the American, blocking his flight and demanding the truth.

Adrian's eyes grew round with fear and his heels dug into the floor, scraping the chair backward until it collided with the desk. "I . . . I . . ."

"Spit it out boy, before I box your ears." He stalked nearer until he loomed over Adrian. "What are you doing in my private room? Going through my private papers?"

"I . . . I came here to . . . to confess." His voice sounded like a dry croaking frog's.

"Confess? What are you, a thief? A spy?"

Adrian couldn't answer. His wide eyes lowered to stare at the man's wounded arm in its sling, then slowly raised up again to meet the man's suspicious glare. *That,* he wanted to say. *I did that.*

But he didn't have to say it. He saw when the man understood, when his eyes narrowed and his nostrils flared.

"You son of a bitch!" The man grabbed him by the shoulder, pinning him in place with a grip like a hawk's fierce talons. "You little bastard!"

Guilty, terrified, afraid for his life, Adrian latched on to the only weapon available to him. "I may be a bastard," he finally gasped out. "But so are you. *Mr. Byrde!*"

# CHAPTER 23

THANK God his other arm was injured and trapped within the sling the doctor had insisted on. Otherwise Marsh was afraid he might have struck the insolent brat he'd pinned in the chair.

He was the one, the one who'd shot him. Yet at that moment, it was not that crime which goaded Marsh to such fury. Rather, it was the accusation of bastardy.

When he'd called the boy a bastard, it had been an oath, nothing more. An expression of rage. But when the brat flung the ugly epithet right back at him, it had meant more. Much more.

"I'm nobody's bastard," he swore from between gritted teeth. His good hand tightened on the skinny youth's shoulder and he bent forward until their faces were on a level and only inches apart. "Nobody's!"

But as if he sensed Marsh's one vulnerability, the boy's eyes sparked now with a temper of his own. "You're Cameron Byrde's bastard. Don't deny it. You're one of his byblows come here to try and get some money from his family. That's why Sarah's so scared of you!"

"Close, but—" Marsh caught himself just in time. Though he wanted to proclaim the truth—though it burned for release on his tongue—he couldn't do it. He'd just finalized his bargain with Sarah, her money and her innocence for his silence. Though he didn't want her damned money anymore, he couldn't renege on their deal. Bad enough that he already felt like a heel for holding her to the agreement they'd struck in anger. Now he tasted the bitterness of the other side of that agreement. For he had to deny his own legitimacy to this boy.

He had made the deal. Now he had to live with it.

But what if Sarah had sent this boy to sift through his papers? If she were that underhanded, all deals would be off. And if she'd sent the brat to shoot him . . .

"Why are you here? Why the confession now?"

He took some satisfaction when Adrian's chin trembled. He released the boy's shoulder and stood back, staring sternly down at the lad. "Why did you try to kill me?"

The boy took a few deep breaths and a few hard swallows. "I thought you had hurt Sarah. She was afraid of you. I could tell." Again anger sparked in the boy's blue eyes. "And then down by the river I saw you kiss her."

"You spied on us?" Marsh shook his head. As furious as he was, he had to give the lad credit, for he'd not missed a trick. He'd suspected something was going on and his suspicions were right on the mark. And how could he remain angry with the boy when he was so loyal to Sarah—especially considering Marsh's own part in this whole mess? Added to that was the pointlessness of it all.

"You shot me because you thought she was afraid of me, or because I kissed her?" He snorted when the boy's expression turned mutinous. "Aren't you a little young for jealous rages?"

"I'm not too young to know she's scared to death of you," Adrian muttered. "And that she hates you."

Marsh groaned and turned away. Yes. She hated him. But she also desired him. And he could probably make her desire him again. Only he couldn't do that to her, because of their agreement.

She'd met her part of the bargain. He had no choice but to meet his.

Meanwhile, he had to deal with this new wrinkle. So he paced the room, rubbing the back of his neck and trying to reason out some solution to the problem this boy's prying presented.

He turned and fixed Adrian with a stern stare. "You shot

me. You intended to kill me. What do you think I should do with that sort of information?"

The boy paled and squirmed in his chair. But his sullen expression did not alter. "I don't know."

"I think you do. I should drag you down to the sheriff's office by the scruff of your skinny neck, and I should tell him to lock you in his jail. I should stand in the front row and watch as they hang you. Hang you!" he furiously repeated. "Attempted murder is a hanging offense, Adrian. Do you realize that? Did you ever once stop to think about the consequences of such a reckless action?"

With every word the boy sank lower in his chair. He hung his head and said nothing.

Marsh clenched his jaw. "I ought to drag you down there right this minute." He breathed deeply and his nostrils flared. "I ought to turn you over to the sheriff, and to hell with you. But I'm not. I'm not going to do that."

The boy's head snapped up. "You're not?"

"No. Not if you answer a few questions honestly. Honestly. Remember, I know where you live. I can find you again and turn you over to the sheriff if I ever find out you lied to me."

"I don't lie. Not to anyone. That's why I'm here now. I didn't *have* to come."

Marsh conceded that point with a nod. "All right. Why did you shoot me?"

"I told you. I wanted to help Sarah. It was the wrong way to help her," he grudgingly added. "I know that now."

"Did she put you up to it?"

"No!"

"What about this?" He gestured to the disordered desktop. "You rifling through my papers. Did she put you up to that?"

"No! Sarah doesn't know about any of it. And anyway, that's not why I came here."

"Then why *did* you go through my papers?"

Adrian sighed. "I was waiting for you to come back. To tell you I was the one who shot you. I . . . I was nervous.

So when I heard the maid coming, I hid in your room. Under the bed."

"My papers are on the desk."

Again the boy sighed and averted his eyes. "I just sort of looked at them. You shouldn't've left them out where anyone could read them."

"The maid here doesn't *know* how to read."

When there was no answer to that, Marsh ran his hand through his hair. Though it galled him, he knew he had to walk away from Adrian and Kelso—and Sarah. It didn't matter if Adrian thought he was Cameron Byrde's bastard. It didn't matter anymore.

Still, Sarah ought to know what the boy had learned. If word got out that Marsh was Cameron Byrde's son, who knew what else might eventually be found out? And if it *should* come out, he did not want Sarah to think he'd been the source of that leak.

It made no sense, of course. She already hated him. So what if she should someday hate him even more?

But it did matter. Marsh turned and stared at the gangly young boy slouched in the desk chair, trying desperately to affect the appearance of nonchalance. Would he keep secret what he knew about Cameron Byrde and the son he'd sired? Maybe for Sarah he would.

"Let's go," he ordered. He snatched up the papers, folded them, and stuffed them inside his coat.

The boy's eyes widened, then narrowed in suspicion. His fingers tightened on the chair arms, but he did not rise. "Go where?"

"To Byrde Manor. To see Sarah."

Clearly surprised, the boy cocked his head to one side. "Why?"

"I'm leaving Kelso. Today, if possible. Your wild speculations can't hurt me. But they can hurt her."

"I would never hurt Sarah." Adrian lunged up from the chair, glowering. "Never!"

"Tell *her* that," Marsh muttered. *Maybe she'll believe your good intentions; she'll never believe mine.*

* * *

"You have two callers, miss."

Sarah looked up from the blank sheet of ivory-colored parchment that lay on the desk in her quiet bedchamber. She'd been staring at it for over an hour, staring at the only four words she'd yet written: *My dearest brother James.* That was it. She hadn't yet figured a way to explain the mad tangle she'd become embroiled in.

Perhaps she should just take herself off to London and tell him face-to-face. But then she'd have to face her mother as well. With Livvie and Neville due back from Glasgow shortly, she knew she ought not leave Kelso. But she had to do something to explain the huge withdrawal she would shortly make from her investment accounts. A letter seemed her best choice. Only she could not think how to begin.

So it was that she looked up at the maid with great relief. Not that she was up to visitors. Still . . . "Two callers?"

"Yes'm. Young Master Adrian and that Mr. MacDougal."

Sarah lurched to her feet, her heart in her throat. "Mr. MacDougal?"

"Yes'm." One corner of the girl's mouth curved up in a faint, knowing smile. "Mrs. Hamilton put 'em in the parlor. Shall I tell them you'll be a minute, so's you can freshen up?"

Sarah's inner turmoil was too great to notice the girl's mistaken assumption, let alone correct it. There was no need for her to primp for Marshall MacDougal. There could be nothing between them.

But her heart nonetheless raced and she was hard-pressed to catch her breath. Why had he come? They'd made their deal. Surely he did not mean to go back on it now?

Most certainly he could not have come to renew his duty-bound offer to marry her.

Trying to regain her composure, Sarah pressed her lips together, then smoothed out her rumpled skirts. "No need to delay. I'll see them directly. Have Cook send a tea tray, will you?"

Schooling her features, the girl curtsied, then disappeared. But Sarah took a few moments before following. He'd come back, but with Adrian in tow. What could that mean?

She learned quickly enough.

Adrian's confession shocked her. He'd been the one to shoot Marsh? "But why? Why, Adrian?"

The boy hung his head and stared morosely at his feet.

"He thought he was protecting you. From me," Marsh said. Sarah's startled gaze swung back to his and held.

Such power there was in that long, breathless lingering of their eyes. Such an intimate connection. It was almost too intimate, beyond even the physical intimacies they'd shared. She almost fancied she could see all the way into his heart, past his anger and his need for revenge and deeper, to the part of him that had once been a fatherless boy. She clenched her fingers together, then, when he spoke, had to blink back the unreasonable burn of tears.

"I cannot entirely fault him for defending you, Sarah. It was a foolish act. That of a boy, not a man." He fixed a stern gaze on Adrian. "But in coming to me, in confessing his crime, he has proven himself more a man than a boy."

His gaze returned to her. "I don't plan to report any of this to the sheriff, or to anyone else."

Sarah could hardly believe that Marsh did not mean to seek revenge on the misguided boy. Yet there was another part of her that was not in the least surprised. This was so like him, she realized. "Thank you," she choked out as gratitude swelled in her chest. She could see from Adrian's relieved expression how thankful he was also. "This means so much to me," she managed to add. "And to Adrian."

"Unfortunately, there is more," Marsh said, his face still somber.

"More?" Sarah looked from Marsh to Adrian, then back again.

"He has found out my secret."

"Your secret?" Sarah shook her head in bewilderment, then gasped when she understood. "Your secret! You mean that you—"

"That Cameron Byrde was my father," he interrupted her. "That he sired me before he wed your mother."

His gaze was intent upon her, as if he meant to imbue his words with more weight than merely their spoken meaning. Sarah hesitated. "He knows . . . everything?"

"Just about."

Still unsure of the complete extent of Adrian's knowledge, she addressed the boy, choosing her words carefully. "How did you find out?"

Adrian shrugged. "I waited in his room to tell him I was the one that shot him. And then I saw some papers and a letter and, well, it wasn't so hard to figure out. He's a bastard, just like me. And he's Aunt Livvie's half-brother."

Sarah's gaze darted to Marsh's face. But he wasn't looking at her. Instead he was staring at the boy, his face wiped clean of any expression. Adrian's words seemed to hover over them all. "He's a bastard, just like me." Marsh wasn't really a bastard, though. But it seemed she and he were the only ones who would ever know the complete truth.

When Marsh's eyes shifted to meet hers, Sarah knew with absolute certainty that he could be trusted to keep his side of the bargain. If he could suffer that aspersion without dissent, it proved to her that his word was reliable.

Feeling as if a monstrous load finally had been lifted from her shoulders, she took a deep breath. Livvie's secret was safe; her birthright and good name would never be threatened by this man.

But at the same time an inexplicable sense of sorrow washed over her. He'd come so far, all the way across an ocean, for revenge. For justice. That he would depart a far richer man than before seemed to mean very little to him. Indeed, in some ways he departed with far less than he'd arrived with. For he knew that he had another family, but he would never be able to acknowledge it. Though she'd been surrounded by family all her life, Sarah had only begun in recent weeks to understand how precious—how priceless—that family truly was.

She wrapped her arms around her waist, holding in a multitude of emotions she would never be free to express to him. How she understood that it was love more than hate that had brought him to Scotland to confront his father. How she understood now that he would not deliberately hurt her or her family. How she respected him for earning his success through hard work, not family connections.

How she wished the two of them could meet afresh and begin all over again. She swallowed hard. Oh, how she wished they could.

But they couldn't. She knew that, as did he. He'd done the honorable thing in offering to marry her. She'd done the honorable thing by not accepting.

So she said nothing, and after a moment his jaw flexed and he cleared his throat. "I'll leave it to you to deal with the boy," he said. "I just wanted you to know that I did not break our agreement."

"I know that." She heard the tremor in her voice. Why was this so hard? "I know."

He nodded once, then turned and left the room. Just left. And in the hollow that remained after his leaving, Sarah heard the echoes of the past few tumultuous weeks. Echoes she wanted to remember and savor and hold on to in the empty weeks to come. For she knew with painful certainty that they would be empty.

When Adrian stood, however, she realized that such a luxury was not to be hers. She had still to deal with him and the knowledge he had about Livvie's connection to Marshall MacDougal.

As if he read her mind, Adrian said, "You're not going to tell her about him, are you? That she has a brother."

Grimacing, Sarah faced him. "Not just yet. But . . . but eventually, yes. I think she ought to know."

Adrian frowned. "I don't know why you want to wait.

He's leaving for America. If you wait, she'll miss seeing him."

"I . . . I think that's what he wants."

"You mean he doesn't want to meet his own sister?" The boy crossed to the window and peered out, but Marshall MacDougal was gone. He swiveled his head and stared back at Sarah. "If I had a sister, I'd want to meet her. It doesn't make sense."

"Well. Mr. MacDougal is a man of unpredictable behavior. It doesn't make sense either that he has elected not to tell the sheriff what you did."

When Adrian's expression turned sheepish, she pressed on. "I expect you to keep Mr. MacDougal's secret, Adrian. That means not telling one soul. Ever. I'll keep your secret from the sheriff and all the good law-abiding people of Kelso, and you'll keep Mr. MacDougal's—and Olivia's—secret. Are we agreed?"

Of course he agreed. Later, however, once Adrian had left for home and Sarah was alone with her morose thoughts, it occurred to her, unpleasantly, that though Adrian had one secret to keep, she had three.

It was not a hardship to hide the identity of the person who'd shot Marsh. It would be harder to keep silent on the subject of who the American really was. But it would be nearly impossible to suppress the truth about what had passed between her and Marsh. The battle of wills, the eruption of passion, and now, at his leaving, the immense depth of her emotions.

She'd given her innocence to him—an enormous enough event on its own. But in that moment, as she sat alone in the empty parlor, her biggest secret was the sure knowledge that she had also given him her heart.

CHAPTER

# 24

"DAMNATION, boy. What the hell are you doing here?"

Bad enough Marsh had a throbbing headache, an aching shoulder, and a tongue thick with the aftereffects of far too much liquor. Did he also have to be pestered all over again by the skinny little thug who had put a bullet through his arm?

He glared at the sweaty figure that stood in the doorway of the room he'd taken in St. Boswell's. He'd left Kelso two days ago. By rights he should be in Dumfries by now, arranging for passage on some western-bound ship. But something held him back. He'd stopped the first afternoon here, and he'd never gone any farther.

Once he caught a ship, within a matter of weeks he would be home in America. But that knowledge only made him shake his head. He would not be home. He had no home. Home was a place where someone loved you, and no one loved him. Not anymore. He had a business and a house; a few friends that were more business acquaintances than anything else. That was all.

And so he stewed in this shabby posting house, drinking too much, spoiling for a fight, and thinking far too much about Sarah.

Irritated with himself, he focused his ire on the boy he'd not expected ever to see again. "I said, what are you doing here? Why did you follow me? You don't have a gun, do you?" he growled. "Or have you come to finish me off once and for all?"

The lad at first did not answer. Instead he swatted his dusty breeches with his dusty hat as if searching for the right words. "I . . . uh . . . I wanted to talk to you."

"No." Marsh started to close the door, but the boy darted past him and into the room. "Damn it! Get out of here!"

"I just want to ask you something!"

"What?"

The boy swallowed hard. He was nervous, and Marsh felt a twinge of sympathy. Softening his tone, he repeated, "What?"

"I . . . I know you don't owe me anything," the boy began. "I mean, I shot you and all. I owe you. So . . . so I came here because I thought perhaps . . . perhaps I could go with you. To America."

It was hardly what Marsh had expected to hear. He stared at Adrian, baffled.

"I could work for you," the boy hurried on, his ears growing red. "I could do anything you want—"

"First you want to kill me. Now you want to work for me?" Again Marsh shook his head. "I don't understand you. Why would you want to go with me? You have a home here. A family."

"I don't fit in!"

"What about your mother? Your aunt and uncle? And what about Sarah?"

"They don't understand."

"Understand what?"

"About being a bastard!"

With his good hand, Marsh rubbed the back of his neck. Bloody hell. How was he to answer that? Like Adrian, he'd never had a father. But he'd always *believed* he had a father. Even now, knowing the truth about Cameron Byrde's defection and second marriage, he could still take some comfort in knowing he was no man's bastard.

But that was only paper and ink, a legal technicality.

The truth was, Adrian and he did share a bond. They were boys whose fathers had never assumed their responsibilities; boys whose careless fathers had died young, never bothering to impart any knowledge of manhood to their sons.

He stared down into the hopeful eyes of the long-legged colt of a boy before him, and as the seconds ticked by, he watched as that hopefulness faded to dejection.

He sighed. "Sit down, Adrian. Let's think about this a little more." He gestured to a ewer of ale. "Help yourself. Are you hungry?" He called for a plate of food and watched the boy wolf it down. Easy to slake a boy's physical hunger and thirst. It was harder, however, to address the hunger and thirst of his soul.

He pulled a chair opposite Adrian and sat, his elbows braced on his knees. "You think because our situations are similar—namely, that neither of us has fathers—that you and I are alike. But we're not, Adrian. My life is in America. Yours is here."

"But it's not. I've tried. I hate that school my uncle sent me to. And at home—" He broke off, scowling down at his hands. "You saw my mother," he muttered in barely audible tones.

"That doesn't mean you can just abandon her."

"She won't care. Anyway, she's got your man to keep her happy."

Marsh shook his head. "Did you tell her you were leaving?"

When there was no response save a deepening of the boy's frown, Marsh continued. "You have to go back to Kelso, Adrian. Talk to your uncle. If he's willing to finance your education, you'd be a fool to turn down his aid. An idiot. Talk to the man. Find a different school. In a few years you'll be ready to make your own way in the world. But you're not ready yet, son."

"I *am* ready!" The boy lurched out of his chair and began to pace.

"You think so?" Marsh rose also. "What kind of job do you think an uneducated boy can get? What kind of living can he earn? Not much. And in a few years when you're ready to marry—or worse, when you get some girl in the family way—what sort of future will you be able to provide for them? What you do with your life now will determine what sort of father you'll be then. God willing, you'll be better at it than your father was. Or mine."

They weren't the words Adrian wanted to hear. But Marsh could tell they'd made an impact. The boy's fists clenched and his jaw worked. But he had no ready reply. When he finally spoke, however, it was not in his own defense.

"I hope you mean what you say. And I hope whatever education you got will make you a good father someday. But I don't guess we'll ever know that, will we?"

Marsh frowned back at him. "What does that have to do with anything?"

"What about Sarah?"

Marsh tensed. He knew exactly where Adrian was going with this, because he'd been brooding about the very same subject. Sarah had turned down his offer of marriage, but that didn't mean she might not change her mind. Especially if anything were to result from that incredible night they'd spent together.

When he was too slow to respond, Adrian's jaw jutted out. "Did you get a child upon her?"

"No." As an answer it was not very convincing, and the boy's eyes narrowed.

"So you say. But you can't be certain."

Marsh swallowed hard. The last thing he wanted was to ruin Sarah's reputation. Yet another part of him wanted to proclaim to the entire world what they'd done together, and then to claim her as his own. It was the whole reason he'd parked himself in this crossroads of a town and not continued on to the coast, he realized.

At his hesitation, Adrian smiled triumphantly. "You don't know, do you? You might have got a child on her, but you just don't know. And if you leave, you'll never know. But then," the boy added, sneering, "maybe you don't really *want* to know."

Marsh stiffened. "Mind your own business," he growled at the boy. The truth was, he didn't know what he wanted anymore.

"Do you *want* to get a bastard on her?" Adrian went on. "Was that your plan once you learned your own father was dead, to wreak your revenge upon the rest of your father's family by ruining *her*?"

"That's ridiculous!" Marsh glared at the boy. "What reason do I have to seek revenge upon Sarah? She's not even related to my father."

Adrian snorted. "I saw how you looked at her. You wanted her. And it seems like you must have gotten her. But maybe even after that she still didn't want you because . . . because you're not *good* enough for her," he said, pouncing on that reason with a nasty grin. "You being a bastard and all."

Marsh could hardly restrain the urge to shout the truth at his youthful tormentor. *I'm nobody's bastard! I'm the rightful heir to Byrde Manor!* But he couldn't. He'd made a deal with Sarah.

In the end, he made a deal with Adrian as well.

The boy would return to Kelso and when his uncle returned, Adrian would have a long talk with him about his future. In return, Marsh would remain in Scotland long enough to learn whether or not Sarah had conceived a child from their union.

It was no more than he'd intended to do anyway, Marsh realized. That's why he was stewing in this rat hole of a place. He simply couldn't depart for America until he knew that Sarah's situation would be all right.

They traveled back toward Kelso that afternoon, Marsh and Adrian riding side by side while Duffy handled the carriage. The boy made no bones about his animosity toward Duff.

"But me intentions are honorable," Duff protested when Marsh explained the problem in private.

"Honorable?"

Duff scowled at Marsh's skepticism. "Estelle mayn't've lived the most sterling life, but she's got a good heart." Then his trademark grin burst through. "A good heart hidden beneath a goodly pair of bosoms."

"She's the lad's mother."

"I know. I know."

"Then guard your tongue around him."

"All right. But y'know, guv'nor," Duff said, squinting at him, "seems to me I'm doin' better with my ladylove than you're doin' with yours."

Marsh stiffened. "If I want advice, I'll ask for it."

Duff shook his head. "If I was a famous boxer, I'd tell her. Ladies like that sorta stuff—even fine ladies who act like they don't."

Marsh wanted to snap at the man, to tell him to mind his own business. But instead he rubbed the back of his neck. "I only wish it were that simple," he muttered.

Duff grinned. "I knew it. I knew you was that MacDougal," he exulted. "Mac MacDougal."

"That's in the past," Marsh said, cutting the man off. "It doesn't matter, especially not to Sarah."

"Ah, but you can never tell," Duff said. "Maybe if you clear the air between you, you know, spill all your secrets, you might find out it's a lot simpler than you think."

But Marsh knew better. He might be as wellborn as Sarah, but he'd lived a hardscrabble life so removed from hers as to be unbelievable. And even if that didn't matter to her, there was still the issue of her half-sister—*his* half-sister too.

So they made their awkward way back. Marsh did not take a room in Kelso, however. Instead he settled in Rutherford, an hour and a half away, at the inn where he'd run into Sarah the fateful night of the storm.

Adrian promised to inform Marsh if he heard anything one way or another about Sarah's situation. As the days passed, however, Marsh found the enforced idleness maddening. He did the mathematics a hundred times. Two weeks until she should have her monthly. Ten days. A week.

The weather grew hotter. The farmers prayed for rain. He rode through the hills and fields every day. But never in the direction of Kelso and Byrde Manor.

Duff did, however. Each night he rode out to see Estelle, and the knowledge of their happy liaison tormented Marsh. Each night he lay awake remembering everything about Sarah. Her energy and determination, the fire in her eyes. He remembered also the softness of her skin and the strength in her young body. The feminine power. The passion.

It drove him mad to remember her response to him, her incredible passion—and his.

But those were dangerous thoughts. Insane thoughts. To drive them out, he forced himself to imagine how his life might have been as the heir to Byrde Manor. Learning to ride and hunt at his father's side. Dining at the same table with both of his parents. Watching his mother smile at the man she loved.

Those thoughts were almost as dangerous as the others, however. And pointless. What was done was done. The past could not be changed.

But the nights were so long. If his parents had remained wed, there would have been no second wife for Cameron Byrde, he reminded himself. No Olivia and no chance for him ever to have met Sarah Palmer. He would not have been an American but a British subject.

Somehow that held no appeal. Perhaps his mother would have been happier, but as for himself . . .

One night he could not bear all those difficult thoughts. Enough time had passed. Every day he expected some news from Adrian. And every night he castigated himself for his cowardice.

Marsh rubbed his neck in agitation. Why couldn't he just confront Sarah himself? Just ride up the drive, request an audience with her, and then ask the question.

*Have we made a child together?*

And what answer did he want to hear?

He didn't know. That was the crux of his problem. Of his hesitation. Of his cowardice.

He wanted to know that she was not breeding and thereby absolve himself of some portion of the guilt he felt toward her. But if that were in fact the case, then he would have no reason at all not to leave this accursed island. And that terrified him.

But if she were breeding . . .

That terrified him too.

He didn't know what answer he wanted to have from her. He didn't know, and the not knowing was driving him mad. So he leaped up from his restless bed, threw on breeches and a shirt, and drew on his boots. Then he strode out to the four-stall stable, saddled his horse, and set out for Kelso. He had to see her, to confront her, and ask her outright.

A part of him realized that she might not yet know one way or the other. But he didn't care. He needed to move, to see Byrde Manor. To see her.

It was insane. He ought to wait another week at least. But he couldn't. He had to go now because he didn't know what else to do.

He didn't know himself at all anymore.

Sarah lay awake in her darkened bedchamber. By day she could ignore the evidence that with each dawn grew more damning. At night, however, with no distractions, her fears had free rein to torture her.

It had been six weeks since her last monthly flow. She remembered, because it had occurred just before her short-lived elopement with Lord Penley. At the time she'd put him off, delaying their elopement until the pesky problem of her monthlies was over.

It seemed as if a year had gone by since then, not merely a month and a half. So much had happened during that time. So much had changed. Especially her.

What she feared, however, was a far greater change than anything else she'd ever been through. One of her hands crept down to rest lightly upon her belly. Could she be breeding?

Could Marshall MacDougal's child have taken root inside her and even now be growing?

She counted the weeks backward once more; then counted the months forward. March. By next March she could very well be a mother. It was a terrifying thought. If she'd ever courted disaster before, those times were absolutely nothing compared to this.

And yet in the midst of all her terrible trembling fear, the tiniest glimmer of joy glowed. A baby. Growing in her. Marshall MacDougal's baby. All the loneliness of these past few weeks, all the regrets, all her unhappy yearning to see him again—all of it seemed so much easier to bear if she indeed had his child growing inside her.

"Oh, God. You are going completely mad," she muttered, turning face down in her disheveled bed. "Completely out of your mind."

*Forget joy. Think about the reality. Becoming pregnant without benefit of a husband is the ultimate ruination.*

As if in confirmation, an image of Estelle Kendrick forced its unwelcome way into her mind and she shuddered. Was it the birth of her fatherless child that had turned Estelle into such a bitter and unhappy woman, one who desperately sought the attention of every man she laid her eyes upon?

Yet even with his unfortunate mother and the unfortunate circumstances of his birth, Adrian was still a wonderful boy. Despite his struggles and the mistakes he'd made, with Neville and Livvie's help Adrian was certain to grow into an honorable man.

She rolled over again and faced the darkened ceiling. If she should be with child, she would have to go away. She could not stay here, nor return to London. She would have to go away when Neville & Livvie returned from Glasgow and raise her child alone. For she could not allow the stain on her reputation to taint her blameless family, especially her innocent niece and nephew.

But her problems in the future were less important than her problem right now. Should she try to send word to Marsh?

She sat up, feeling as if she were going to jump right

out of her skin. How she wanted to follow him, to reveal her suspicions to him. She wanted to say, *I love you. Please come back from America and marry me.*

But she could never do any of that. Marsh's true name was Byrde. If he were to come back to Kelso, it would create an impossible situation for her family. A disastrous situation.

And anyway, he was gone. He was probably somewhere in the middle of the Atlantic, eager to return to his old life without all the problems he'd left behind in Scotland.

Besides, she didn't know for sure if she was breeding. Perhaps her monthly courses were simply late. Perhaps.

Too restless to remain in her bed, she rose and slipped on her wrapper, then made her way downstairs, running her fingers along the wall to guide herself through the dark and silent house. It was cool outside, but that didn't deter her. Nor did the rough gravel beneath her bare feet. At that moment even her clothes felt too confining. Something in her felt a driving need to break free, to burst out of the confinements of her life.

She stood in the open court before the manor house and stared around at the lumpy shadows that were house and stables and fences and shrubs. Behind her a dog came up barking. But once it recognized a familiar scent, the animal sniffed her ankles, whined, then, when it was plain she had no food to offer, ambled back around the side of the house, leaving her alone once more.

But then, she *was* all alone, she acknowledged. Alone with the same problem Maureen MacDougal and Estelle Kendrick and innumerable other women through the ages had faced. She laughed out loud. At least she had the wherewithal to live without prostituting herself or going into service. At least she could make a modest home for herself and her child. A modest, decent sort of life.

That knowledge was small comfort, however. Suddenly the darkness that surrounded her seemed terribly intimidating. Hunching her shoulders, she turned back for the house.

Marsh watched her go. He couldn't make out her features or any other aspect of the slender figure in the front court, but he knew it was Sarah. Who else but his passionate, imprudent Sarah would wander the grounds by moonlight, charming old dogs and bedeviling sleepless men like him?

He watched her disappear into the dark mouth of the house, and clenched his lips against any impulse to call out to her. He'd come here to see her; he'd been given this unexpected opportunity to do just that. Yet he found himself unaccountably petrified with fear.

Beneath him his horse pawed at the dusty ground. From beyond the house the dog came out again, barking at this new disturbance in the night.

Slowly Marsh wheeled his animal around. The dog's barking grew louder, like an accusation, and it echoed long after Marsh had left Byrde Manor behind.

*Bastard, bastard,* the baying seemed to say. *Bastard.*

Though he might not be a bastard in fact, the truth was, in his heart where it counted, he *was* a bastard—and a coward. No better than his father, who'd used a woman for his own selfish needs, then left her alone to deal with the consequences. That's what he'd done to Sarah.

He would never be able to give her back her innocence. But he could return her money to her. And he could also wait a little longer until she *had* to know the truth about a child.

And then?

And then, if she bore a child of his, he could marry her. No matter the consequences and the ties that would then forever bind him to his bastard of a father's family, he would marry Sarah Palmer.

That was the least he could do.

# CHAPTER 25

"SARAH!" Olivia burst into Sarah's room and, without letting her rise from the chair where she dozed, enveloped her in a fierce hug. "Oh, Sarah. When Mrs. Tillotson told me you'd been here in the Borders for over a month now, I could hardly credit it! The letter you sent me in Glasgow must have gone astray." She pulled away, then cocked her head to one side and studied her younger sister with a narrowed gaze. "That's assuming you actually did write to me."

Sarah was much too happy to see her older half-sister to withhold the truth. "I'm sorry, I'm sorry," she repeated, holding tight to Olivia's hands. She drew her to sit in the adjacent chair. "I should have written to you, and I feel terrible for deceiving poor Mrs. Tillotson. The truth is, Mother sent me here in disgrace for plotting to run away with some fellow who turned out to be truly awful. I needed to prove to her—and to James—that I could manage my life better than I had heretofore been doing."

She smiled sheepishly at Livvie's wry expression. "I know. I know. You're thinking I'm just as reckless as I ever was. But I'm learning, Livvie. I really am. And I've changed. I'm not a silly little London miss any longer. I've outgrown all that." She squeezed her beloved sister's hands. "And I'm so very happy to see you."

They stared at each other a long, telling moment. "Finding you here is such a treat for me," Olivia said. "Though I shan't be surprised if there's quite a bit more to your story than you've yet revealed, we'll have plenty of time to talk about that later. Come. I want you to pack up right away and move over to Woodford Court with us. Neville's at home, huddling with his steward. But the children are downstairs with Mrs. Hamilton, and they're both eager to see you."

She paused and once again cocked her head. "Are you well?"

Sarah forced a wide smile. "Of course I am. Oh, I didn't sleep so well last night, so perhaps I look tired. Do I? But come," she hurried on. "I'm simply dying to see the children."

"Meanwhile, the maid can pack you up."

It was swiftly planned and swiftly executed, and within an hour they were on the road to Woodford Court.

Really, it was all to the good, Sarah told herself as they crossed the River Tweed and made the turn toward Olivia and Neville's impressive country estate. As much as she loved Byrde Manor's rustic charm, that house held too many memories now. Especially in her upstairs corner bedroom, the one where Marsh had come to her the night after he'd been shot. The night they'd made love.

An unwelcome frisson of erotic memory shivered down her spine to settle like a hot little knot deep in her belly. She clenched her jaws against those wicked urgings that threatened to overwhelm her and instead stared out the window of Olivia's well-appointed carriage. How long would she feel this way? How long would memories of Marshall MacDougal torment her?

Her hand stole down to her belly. *For the rest of your life,* the answer came. *If you are indeed with child, you will never escape from memories of Marsh.*

Thankfully, once arrived at Woodford, Sarah was swiftly absorbed into the boisterous home life of a family with two energetic and noisy children. Mrs. Tillotson suggested a picnic beside the river and Catherine and Philip announced their delight with whoops of joy. Olivia consented, calling it a welcome lunch for Sarah, and Neville joined them too.

"And you don't miss all those balls and parties and folderol of the season?" Neville asked, reclining on a blanket with his sturdy four-year-old son straddling his stomach.

"I think I outgrew them. After all, I've had two previous seasons," Sarah responded, twisting a curving bit of grass back and forth between her fingers. The marvel of it was that her answer was true. She didn't miss it at all.

"Here. Have some chicken," Olivia offered. "You've hardly eaten a thing."

Sarah waved it away. "Thank you, but I'm not really that hungry." She hadn't wanted breakfast either, and she blanched at the implication. Though she was hungry, the thought and especially the smell of food were just too unappealing. "Too much hubbub," she added with another bright, utterly false smile. She avoided her sister's eyes.

"Are you going to live with us now?" Catherine asked. She was nearly seven years old, with her father's dark eyes and her mother's sweet smile.

Sarah smiled back. "For a little while I am."

Olivia chuckled. "Even if you wish to give up London—and I can wholeheartedly understand why you would—Mother shall not long let you stay away. She is dying to marry you off, with a huge wedding in town. My own quiet nuptials here in Scotland could not have satisfied her, and that's been nine years now. Since James seems immune to the lure of marriage, it appears all her hopes ride on you, Sarah. I'd wager a very large sum that she sends for you before summer is done. Certainly before everyone packs off for the hunting season."

*You'd lose that wager,* Sarah thought. For by summer's end, if she was breeding, the truth would be obvious. Then she would be kept as far from London and town society—from *any* society—as was humanly possible.

But she would not think about that just now. It was pointless to worry about a future she could not alter. Today the sun was shining; a lark trilled enthusiastically from a nearby elm tree; and her niece and nephew were laughing at a little frog their father had caught for them. For now she would simply enjoy Olivia and her delightful family.

Maybe later, when she was absolutely certain about her situation, she would confide in her sister.

A warm breeze played with a curl at her temple. It also carried a whiff of roasted chicken, and without warning, her stomach lurched in revulsion.

She pressed her lips together and swallowed. Perhaps she did not have to wait to be certain. She swallowed again and turned her face away from the breeze and breathed deeply. Perhaps she already knew the difficult truth.

She just prayed Olivia would help her. For she knew she could never ask for help from Marshall MacDougal.

Adrian arrived at the main house just as the picnickers meandered up from the riverbank. The children both clamored over him, especially little Philip, who clearly adored his older cousin. But after greeting them with great cheer and shooting Sarah a wary look, he turned to address his uncle, whose demeanor had changed from one of initial surprise and welcome, to one of suspicion.

Neville's first words to Adrian's made clear his position. "What are you doing in Kelso so soon? By my calculation, the school session does not end for a few more weeks."

Adrian's brow creased in resentment, and Sarah feared an unpleasant scene in the forecourt in front of everyone. To his credit, however, he only said, "That's what I came to discuss with you."

Neville's face darkened, but Olivia laid a cautionary hand on his arm, and after a moment he gave a curt nod. "Very well. If you'll excuse us," he said to the rest of them. "Adrian and I will be in my study."

The children dispersed to other activities as well, leaving Sarah and Olivia alone in the gravel front court.

"Oh, but he looks so much like Neville, doesn't he?" Olivia remarked, watching the two men walk away. "How long has he been back?"

"I think he arrived just a day or so before I did," Sarah answered, then added, "I've had occasion to speak with his mother."

"Ah, yes. Estelle." Olivia sighed, then hooked her arm in Sarah's, and together they strolled toward the house. "She has never forgiven Neville's brother for not marrying her before he died. Nor Neville for not doing so in his brother's stead. She thinks to strike out at us through Adrian. But really, it is her own child she most wounds."

Sarah was silent a moment. Yes, that sounded exactly like Estelle. And yet Sarah could not dismiss the woman so easily now as she might have before. "It must have been difficult for her, raising a child without benefit of a husband."

"I'm sure it was, and still is. But is it any easier for the child to grow up without benefit of a father?"

"We managed," Sarah replied. "We each lost our fathers—you, me, and James. Yet we grew up all right."

"True. However, our mother loved us dearly, and besides, we did not suffer the stigma that Adrian bears. Plus, Mother's subsequent husbands were always good fathers to all her children. Your father especially was so good to me and James. Then later Justin provided that same sort of constancy in your life."

"That he did. But doesn't Adrian have Neville?"

"He does, and Neville has never once shirked his duty to the boy. But it's not the same. He's not in our household every day. And then, sometimes Estelle makes matters more difficult than they have to be."

Sarah grimaced. "Sometimes I think she enjoys other people's discomfort."

Olivia chuckled. "Should I assume that the two of you have had a run-in or two?"

Fortunately, Mrs. Tillotson came up to Olivia at that moment, allowing Sarah to escape into the morning room to compose her thoughts—and her answer. Eventually Olivia would hear everything about Marshall MacDougal's brief but memorable visit to Kelso. About his fight with Guinea as well as the shooting, and all the other odd comings and goings of the past few weeks—hers included. She might as well be the first one to tell Olivia.

But not about Marshall MacDougal's parentage. Not yet.

And not about her own situation either. That could wait a little longer too.

"Livvie," she began when her sister came into the room. "Sit with me, will you, and I'll fill you in on the latest goings-on in these parts."

In the study Adrian was doing the same with his Uncle Neville.

"So you shot him!" Neville's eyes fairly bulged from his head. "You shot this man? This American?"

"Yes. But Sarah saved him from drowning and . . . and the wound was not so very terrible—"

"Does the sheriff know about this?"

"No. I mean, yes. I mean, he knows Mr. MacDougal was shot. But not who did it." The boy's head sank lower between his shoulders. "Mr. MacDougal decided not to tell him."

"Why? Why would he withhold that sort of information and let you get off without any punishment at all?"

"I don't know. I . . . I think he likes me."

"Likes you?" In frustration, Neville threw his hands up in the air. "You try to kill him and he *likes* you?"

Adrian shook his head. It was hard to tell the truth and yet hide parts of it too. "I faced him like a man and admitted my guilt and he . . . he respected that."

Neville massaged his temples. "Where is he now?"

"Gone." Adrian blurted out the lie. "Why do you want to know?"

"Why? Because I'm your guardian and it's my responsibility to make matters right."

"But . . . but I already did that."

Neville snorted. "Where has he gone to?"

Adrian thought fast. "He told Mr. Halbrecht he was going home to America." That wasn't a lie, for he had said exactly that to the innkeeper.

"America? Why did he come all this way just to turn around after a month and go back to America?"

"How should I know?" Adrian answered with a shrug. "Are you going to send me back to that school?" he added, so desperate to divert the subject away from him shooting Mr. MacDougal that he'd even discuss Eton.

To his great relief, it worked, for after another long moment Neville shook his head. In a skeptical tone he asked, "If I sent you, would you stay?"

Later that night, in the privacy of the master bedroom, Neville revealed to Olivia the gist of his discussion with Adrian. "I swear, that boy is going to end up in jail one day on charges too serious for me to circumvent."

Olivia sat at her vanity removing the pins from her hair, then took up her brush and began slowly to work out the tangles. "This Marshall MacDougal certainly seems to have had a great impact during his short residency in Kelso. I'm awfully sorry we missed meeting him. Do you know, every time Sarah spoke of him she either ducked her head or averted her eyes from mine."

Her brow furrowed and the brush stilled in her hands. "What do you think that signifies?"

Neville tossed his dressing gown aside and sat on the bed. "What are you implying—that she has had some sort of dalliance with the man? Good God, do you think that's why Adrian shot him? The hooligan seemed awfully vague on that subject."

"Perhaps. But didn't you just say that Adrian believes the man likes him now? That would hardly make sense."

"Nothing that boy does or says makes sense," Neville grumbled. "You know, he agreed today to return to Eton. But I hold out little hope of him completing his studies there. I need to explore other options for him. Something that will engage his interest and challenge his mind." Then his eyes focused on her, and he smiled and patted the bed beside him. "Come over here, Livvie. You can forget brushing your hair, for I intend to muss it up."

She smiled, then rose and approached the bed. "You know, when I first met you, I behaved precisely as Sarah is behaving now."

One of his brows went up. "Are you saying Sarah is smitten with this MacDougal fellow, just as you were smitten with me?"

"Smitten?" Olivia's smile slowly turned sultry. "As I recall, my first reaction to you was outrage, closely followed by fear and then fury."

"Which were quickly replaced by curiosity, infatuation, and lust." He caught her about the waist and dragged her down on top of him.

Though she let out a little shriek of surprise, she went down willingly. "What about love? Aren't you forgetting about that?"

"No. Not hardly."

"I wonder what phase Sarah is in," Olivia mused as her husband rolled her onto her back. "Not outrage or fear. Or even fury, I think."

"Can we forget about Sarah for now? Besides, this MacDougal fellow is gone. But I'm here," he added, kissing the words along her throat.

Despite the warm shiver of desire that snaked through her, Olivia's thoughts were not quite ready to abandon her little sister. "She could be curious. Or maybe even infatuated."

"Sounds to me like she lusts after the man. After all, it's not like she's just out of the schoolroom. What is she, twenty or so? And you said she's already tried once to run away with a man. Mmm," he added, licking along her collarbone. "Want to run away with me, little girl?"

Olivia laughed and shoved him back, but her face swiftly turned serious. "Good Lord, you don't think they've *done* anything, do you?"

"Please, Olivia, can we postpone this discussion of your sister until tomorrow?" He moved over her, then pressed his hard arousal against her belly.

"Good Lord," Olivia repeated, but with a whole new meaning attached to it.

Afterward, however, as they lay together in the warm, sex-scented cocoon of the marriage bed, Olivia once more considered her younger sister's odd behavior. Sarah had been extremely forthcoming with the details of her aborted elopement with Lord Penley. She'd explained her reason for concealing her presence in Kelso from Olivia and Neville, and also her intention to help civilize the rebellious Adrian. She'd even expressed an awfully mature opinion of Estelle Kendrick and that woman's often impossible behavior.

But whenever the subject of the absent Mr. MacDougal had come up, she'd become positively closemouthed. Olivia had a strong feeling that something was going on between them, some secret Sarah was keeping.

Could she have fallen in love with the man?

Olivia snuggled her backside against Neville and smiled into the pillow when his arm came around her. Even in his sleep he loved her. How fortunate she was.

But it seemed Sarah was not so fortunate, for this Mr. MacDougal whom she was so pained to speak of apparently did not feel the same way toward her. Otherwise he would not have departed for America.

As her sister, Olivia felt responsible to help Sarah get over her broken heart. Assuming it was broken.

She sighed and relaxed in Neville's arms. Whatever the truth, in time she would wheedle it out of Sarah. They'd never kept secrets from one another in the past; she wasn't about to let Sarah start doing so now.

# CHAPTER 26

MARSH rode through Kelso without stopping. He spied the baker and his ever-vigilant mother. He saw the vicar arm-in-arm with his nosy wife, and Mr. Halbrecht sweeping the front stoop of the Cock and Bow. But except for a nod or a tip of the hat, he did not pause.

To pause was to allow himself to reconsider what he meant to do, and he did not want to do that.

When he reached Byrde Manor, however, and learned that Sarah had gone with her sister to live at Woodford Court, he almost did turn back. Olivia Byrde Hawke had returned. To see Sarah, he would almost certainly have to see his half-sister, and he didn't think he was ready for that. He wasn't sure he ever would be.

But in the end he forged on. Reversing direction, he returned to Kelso, crossed the river, and passed the cluster of cottages where Adrian lived. Adrian, who'd pricked his conscience and who had a deep streak of loyalty and moral responsibility despite that one notable lapse into violence.

Laundry waved from a line strung between two of the stone cottages. A dog barked but did not rise from his spot in the sunshine. Someone called out his name—probably Adrian. But Marsh did not look around. He was bound for Woodford Court to see Sarah and somehow ferret out the truth.

That was a terrifying enough task, for what if she was with child? No less terrifying, however, was the prospect of finally encountering his sister.

Only his half-sister, he told himself. Still, Olivia Byrde Hawke was his nearest living kin.

He rode steadily on, with a sprightly breeze playing at his back. Through an apple orchard he spied the ancient stone facade of Woodford Court. As if sensing Marsh's hesitation, the horse slowed. Marsh had to consciously ease his taut grip on the reins and nudge the animal forward with his heels.

He refused to turn back now, for he could not go on in this limbo of not knowing. Not knowing if Sarah was pregnant. Not knowing if she had told his half-sister about him. Not knowing if he could go back to his old life as if none of this had ever happened.

So he turned in at the dry-laid stone gate posts with their Celtic carvings half concealed by centuries-old mosses. He rode slowly through the towering shade of a stand of beech trees, then out across the sunlit lawn that the long drive bisected. The house was impressive, more fortress than residence. He felt like an interloper, some shabby knight-errant from an earlier age, come to try and claim his ladylove.

This time the horse stopped completely.

Marsh stared blindly up at the fortified house. Was that what he was doing here?

His heart banged the painful rhythm of denial in the hollow place that was his chest. Sarah was not his ladylove. Just because she was beautiful enough to incite any man's lust . . . just because she was smart and loyal and determined . . . just because she loved her family with a ferocity he had reluctantly grown to admire . . . none of that meant anything more than what it was: She did not deserve to be left pregnant and unwed.

His mother had endured that life, rejected by her entire family. He would not provide Sarah's family the chance to do that to her. Even if he had to break his vow to Sarah, he would confront Olivia with the ugly truth of her own heritage before he would let Sarah be hurt as his own mother had been hurt.

He urged the horse forward again. An old man leaning upon a stone fence called over his shoulder as Marsh rode by. At once a young groom popped out of the distant stables, then headed Marsh's way at a fast trot.

"Just water him," Marsh told the lad as he dismounted. "I won't be very long."

"Yessir. Very good, sir."

When the boy squinted at the horse, Marsh asked, "Is there something else?"

"Oh, no, sir. That is . . . I b'lieve this here animal is one of our own. Sold a few years ago at a horse auction in Berwick."

"You raise horses here?"

"Oh, yessir. The very best horses in all of the Borders. And beyond," he added, his young face reflecting his pride. "My father runs the breeding stables here. And his father before him."

And no doubt the boy would inherit the job one day, Marsh thought as the young fellow led his horse away. More family longevity. Everywhere he looked there were families. Except for him—and to a lesser degree, Adrian—everyone here had mothers and fathers, brothers and sisters. Aunts and uncles. And those people were happy—happier, at least, than he and Adrian were. He and Adrian were both miserable and unhappy. But mostly they were lonely.

How ironic that in the midst of that loneliness, they were the ones most willing to abandon what few remnants of family they still possessed.

He stared at the house again, paralyzed by that new and depressing knowledge. He had to go through with this. He had to find out if Sarah was pregnant. But beyond that he could do nothing, even if he wanted to. If she was not breeding he would have to leave; he had to honor their agreement.

But there was one thing he could do. Afterward he could find Adrian and impress upon the boy the absolute importance of this extended family of his. Marsh might never be able to become a part of the Byrde/Hawke/Palmer clan. But he'd make certain Adrian stayed sheltered in its midst.

When Sarah spied the rider, her heart came to a stuttering halt. Disbelievingly, she stared from her second-floor window. He had already left for his home in America. He could not still be in Scotland, and certainly not here. Certainly *not* here.

Yet there was no mistaking those wide shoulders and that upright carriage. No misplacing the dark russet of his hair and the determination of his approach.

Marshall MacDougal had come for her. That was the first foolish thought that took hold in her pathetically addled brain. He had come for her because he could not live without her, just as she was coming to believe she could not live without him. She clung to that hope as he rode over the dry moat. She clung to that hope as she craned her head to watch him dismount and hand his horse over to one of the stableboys.

Only when he disappeared into the ancient gatehouse did her foolish yearnings collide with a far less pleasant reality. If he was here, it was more likely because he'd decided against the deal they had struck. He must have decided that his father's name—and his own place as the man's rightful heir—was more important to him than the money she'd offered to him.

Sarah remained frozen in the window, her breath coming fast and hard as terror swept through her. No. After all her efforts to prevent it, he could not do that to her now—or to Livvie.

Forgetting decorum, she hiked up her skirts and dashed from the room. Down the hall past a gallery of Hawke portraits, then down the stone stairwell, so old its treads were worn from all the people who'd passed down them. Five centuries of people. Five centuries of their joys and woes. But had any of those long-ago men and women been so completely betrayed as she, or so heartbroken? Though her head knew there must be many, at the moment her heart said no. No one could ever have felt this crushed. No one.

And yet she must somehow hide it.

Through a narrow bank of windows she spied Olivia in the old pleasure garden, a straw hat sheltering her face as she worked among her spice plants and herbs. Mrs. Tillotson crossed the downstairs hall near the foot of the stairs, probably heading out to announce their caller.

She caught the housekeeper by the sleeve. "Is that Mr. MacDougal I saw riding up?" She tried to appear calm, but feared she failed.

"Why, yes, it is. Come to call on you, as it happens. I thought you might be out-of-doors with Lady Hawke and Catherine, and so—"

"There's no need to disturb them," Sarah broke in. She tried to smile but knew it was feeble at best. "I'll see him privately, if you don't mind."

Mrs. Tillotson nodded agreeably, but on her round face her curiosity showed. Sarah knew she would not have much time. "Very well, Miss Sarah. I left him in the drawing room."

Sarah was breathless when she arrived at the drawing room door. Breathless and without one idea as to how she should deal with Marshall MacDougal. There was no time, however, to contemplate or prepare. She stepped into the drawing room, which was once the fortified house's great hall, and watched as Marsh turned to face her.

It was so much harder than she had imagined. Just seeing him again wreaked a violence upon her heart that she could never have prepared for. She did love him, she realized. She must, for no other emotion could possibly evoke such extreme reactions from her.

She took a sharp breath. It hurt even to breathe in his presence. How absurd was that?

But despite that pain, she took another breath and lifted her chin as if she were no more affected by him than she had been the very first time they'd met. "You are the last person I thought to see here," she began. "I hope you have not come to renege on our agreement."

His eyes were intense and turbulent, yet she could read no specific emotion in them. She closed the door behind her but did not advance farther into the room. "So, why have you come?"

* * *

Olivia looked up at Mrs. Tillotson. "You mean he's here? The mysterious Mr. MacDougal?"

"In the drawing room right now." Mrs. Tillotson grimaced and wiped her hands nervously on her ever-present apron. "She closed the door. They're alone in there. I wasn't rightly sure you would approve."

Olivia looked over at the narrow drawing room windows with raised brows. "Well, well. Normally I might be a bit more cautious. But I think I'll give them a little time—just a little—before I join them. Where is my husband?" she added.

"Over to the breeding stables. I understand that the Barbary mare is about to foal."

"Good. And Philip?"

"He's napping."

Olivia smiled to herself and glanced over at her daughter, who was weaving clover blossoms into a crown for her head. "Stay here with Catherine, will you?" she asked Mrs. Tillotson. Then her smile broadened. "I think I shall go wash up, then wander around a bit."

She had just entered the house from the back entrance when the front door opened and Adrian burst in. He gasped for breath when he spied her and wasted no time on pleasantries. "Is Sarah here? Is Mr. MacDougal?"

Olivia held a finger up to her lips. "Shhh. Yes to both." She pointed at the closed drawing room door, then signaled for him to follow her up the stairwell. "Now," she said when there were nearly to the second level, "what has been going on around here in my absence?"

"Nothing," he replied too quickly.

"Really. So you've come racing over here for nothing? No 'Hello Aunt Olivia. So nice to see you, Aunt Olivia. How are you doing today, Aunt Olivia?' "

He had the good grace to look sheepish.

"Well?" She crossed her arms expectantly. "It's plain you know what this is all about. After all, I'm told you shot the man, she saved him, and he forgave you."

Despite his frown, hot color crept onto the boy's cheeks.

"It's . . . it's complicated," he finally muttered.

"So I gather. Go on."

"What else did Sarah tell you?" he hedged.

"Not much else, other than that the mysterious Mr. MacDougal had returned to America. Only it's obvious he hasn't. Do you perchance know why he is here?"

He worked his jaw back and forth. "I think so. But I can't tell you," he added in a plaintive tone. "You have to ask Sarah, not me."

She cocked her head. "All right, then. I will."

"No!" He caught her arm when she would have started down the stairs again. "No. Don't go in there yet."

She fixed him with an expectant stare. "Only if you give me some reason not to. And you can leave off scowling at me, Adrian Hawke. She's my only sister and I love her too much to ignore all the undercurrents going on around here."

He muttered something under his breath. All Olivia caught was something about women and the word *troublesome.* She wanted to laugh but dared not do so.

"All right," the boy finally said in an aggrieved tone. "He's here—at least I think he's here—because he has formed an attachment to her."

"And she has formed an *attachment* to him," Olivia said, exaggerating the word.

"Who can tell? You women are too mixed up for a bloke ever to know what you're thinking."

This time Olivia did smile. Fourteen and already sounding like every other man alive. "I beg to differ, Adrian. I know exactly what I'm thinking: if my sister's morose mood of late is any indication, she must like this American very much." She hooked her arm in his and started down the stairs and back toward the garden. "And I also think that you must approve of the match. Am I right?"

"Perhaps," he allowed. But as he accompanied her, Adrian's spirits began to lift. Perhaps this was all going to work out, he mused. If Sarah did care for the man—and he was fairly certain Mr. MacDougal cared for her—then perhaps they could work out their differences and get married. Especially if Sarah was bearing their child.

But what if she wasn't?

He was prevented pursuing that worrisome vein of thought when Olivia squeezed his arm. "It seems to me, Adrian, that you have lately been dabbling in the art of matchmaking, an area of meddling I've long been interested in. I confess, however, that I never would have thought that shooting a man might be the best way to convince him to settle down. Tell me, do you think I ought to try out the same scheme on your mother?"

# CHAPTER 27

"WHY are you here?" Sarah repeated.

Marsh considered his answer. But mostly he just stared at Sarah. She was dressed casually, for a morning at home. But still the blue-striped muslin dress with its round neckline and short sleeves managed to emphasize her youth and vitality. Her hair was loosely tied back with a short length of ribbon and tumbled down her back in a way he'd seen only once before. In her bedchamber.

He felt the rush of blood to his loins. God, but he wanted to hold her. To kiss her.

She wore no jewelry, nor adornment of any sort, an altogether simple and unpretentious garb. Yet in that moment she appeared more beautiful to him than she ever had before. More desirable.

*Let her be with child.*

It was a mad thought but a sincere one. *If she is with child, then she cannot send me away. We will have to be wed.*

He cleared his throat and tried to suppress the intense yearning he felt for her. He knew how to stroke her and please her and give her physical pleasure. But a simple conversation, the words he wanted to say to her—those he could not seem to dredge up.

If only he could hold her.

But he tightened his hands into fists and kept his arms rigidly at his side. "I came here," he began, "because there is unfinished business between us."

"You will get your money," she retorted with tightly

held composure. "You did not have to come here to harangue me."

"That's not why I came!"

"Then why? To alarm me? To renege on our agreement? To make more trouble than you already have?" She crossed to the window and glanced warily out, then turned back to face him. "You want Olivia to find out who you are, don't you? Even though we've agreed, you still need to strike out at your father. And since you can't do that, you mean to hurt her—"

"No! No, Sarah, that's not it at all."

"Keep your voice down," she hissed. Back to the door she scurried and looked out before she closed it and spun around once more. "What do you want? Tell me, then be on your way."

"Damnation, Sarah. What do you think I want?" he burst out. "I want to know if you're pregnant!"

It wasn't how he'd meant to say it, so loud and angry. When she went pale and fell back a step, he grimaced. "It's a possibility," he went on in a more reasonable tone. "Surely you considered it too."

Mutely she shook her head.

"No? No, you hadn't considered it? Or no, you're not . . . ah . . . in the family way?"

She opened her mouth, closed it, then wrapped her arms around her waist and looked away. "No. I'm not . . . in the family way."

Disappointment washed over him, illogical, deep-seated disappointment. "Are you certain?"

*Quite the opposite.* But Sarah nodded vigorously as if that could somehow make it true. She was not at all certain. But she did not want him to marry her merely out of a sense of duty. "I'm certain."

In truth, all she felt certain of was that Marshall MacDougal was nothing like his father. Marsh would not abandon his child. That's why he wasn't halfway across the Atlantic Ocean. The loyalty to his mother that had brought him all this way would extend also to any child he made.

If she hadn't already been in love with him, this new knowledge would have pushed her over that edge. He was such a good and loving son—and father. But that did not mean those familial bonds would extend to her. He might do right by her, but that did not mean he loved her.

She took a painful breath, shaken by the overwhelming power of her own love for him and the devastating realization that he did not return it. "You came here for nothing, Mr. MacDougal. Your purpose is commendable, but . . . but you are free to return to America now. Really free."

They stared at one another for what felt like forever. Sarah was afraid to move, afraid even to breathe, for fear she might break down and beg him to stay. The spacious drawing room felt like a monstrous tomb, an enormous well that echoed back every least sound. Beyond the door, two maids passed by, their muted conversation something about fresh water and airing out the burgundy room.

With a nod, Marsh finally released them both from that state of awful suspension. His eyes were shuttered and his mouth set in a grim line. "Very well, then." He scooped up his hat from one of the chairs. Sarah sidled away from the door. He paused there with his hand upon the knob. "Good-bye, Sarah."

"Good . . . good-bye," she choked out.

Olivia was waiting when the American descended from the front door of her house. She'd positioned herself strategically on a bench halfway between the front door and the shaded watering trough where Mr. MacDougal's horse had been tied. Adrian had wanted to stay with her, but she'd sent him off to the stables. She wanted to take this Mr. MacDougal's measure without any other distractions.

She looked up when he strode in her direction. He did not notice her at first. In fact, she wondered if he meant to march right past her, he was that mired in his own thoughts. Dark thoughts, if his furrowed brow and downturned mouth were any indication. When she stood, however, his eyes jerked up from the path. His frown turned into a look of surprise. Then, most confusing of all, his sun-browned face seemed to pale. When he came to an abrupt stop, just staring at her, almost as if in fear, her brow creased in puzzlement.

Wasn't he the odd fellow? Good-looking, in a rugged sort of way. Tall, fit, and handsomely attired. But exceedingly odd of manner.

Still and all, she *was* the lady of the house and she knew her role well. So she smiled and extended one hand to him. "I am guessing that you are Mr. MacDougal. I am Olivia Hawke, Sarah's sister, and I'm so happy to finally meet you."

Marsh stared at the attractive woman standing before him, the woman he'd known he might run into. He'd tried to prepare himself, yet all the preparation in the world could not have equipped him for his thunderstruck reaction to her. She was pretty and smiling, only a year or so younger than he. With her open demeanor and extended hand, she was exactly the sort of woman he would ordinarily be pleased to know. A young matron easy to converse and dance with, without the pressure of any further expectations.

But Olivia Byrde Hawke was not just any other pretty wife and mother. She was his father's other child, and his closest living relative.

"You *are* Mr. MacDougal, aren't you?" she asked when he did not immediately respond.

"Ah. Yes. Yes, I am Marshall MacDougal." *Marshall MacDougal Byrde.* But he did not add his true name. He'd made a promise and he would stand by his word. But he wanted to tell her. As he took his half-sister's proffered hand and made a very correct bow over it, he wanted to tell her everything.

But not if it would hurt her.

To his own amazement, he realized that his plans for revenge had at some point fallen by the wayside. Not grudgingly, but completely. There was nothing left of his need for revenge against the Scottish side of his family. Now, as he stared into his half-sister's curious blue eyes,

eyes very like Sarah's, he could hardly believe he'd ever considered striking out at any of them.

He released her hand and they stood there, awkwardly facing one another. He couldn't think of anything to say. First Sarah, leaving him as tongue-tied as a green lad. Now this woman—this stranger who was his sister—paralyzing him with emotions he did not understand.

"Well, Mr. MacDougal, as I said, I'm very pleased to meet you. I've heard much about you since I've returned from Glasgow." She paused and her eyes made a swift inspection of his person. "I was very sorry to hear that you had departed before we could meet. So of course I am elated to see that you are not gone at all, but rather are here at Woodford Court calling upon my sister. Where is Sarah, anyway?"

"I . . . uh . . . I left her in the drawing room."

She cocked her head slightly and toyed with the delicate rose she held. "Does that mean she did not invite you to join us for luncheon?"

Marsh shifted from one foot to the other. "I don't believe she would appreciate my company right now."

"And why is that?"

He should have bristled at her nosy question. He should have brushed her off and been on his way. But her nosiness was tempered with such obvious love for Sarah that he could not. He cast about for some answer that might satisfy her.

"Sarah does not enjoy my company." That was true enough.

"How curious. I'm told she saved you from drowning— Oh, I am remiss not to have already thanked you for not pressing charges against Adrian. There are not many men who could be so generous. In case you had not noticed, he seems belatedly to have developed quite a case of hero worship for you."

"He should not."

"Really?" Though she smiled, her gaze grew sharper. "I'm afraid it's too late to change that. It's plain to us all that Adrian worships you. And equally plain, at least to me, that Sarah mopes around here all because of you."

"She does?"

"Oh, yes. That's why I cannot understand her sending you so brusquely away. Or is it you who are so eager to depart?"

"No—" He broke off when her smile became a grin. Then slowly he grinned at her in return. "Am I that obvious?"

She chuckled. "You're here, aren't you? I can't think of any reason save because you and she have formed some sort of attachment."

Her happy assumption unfortunately chilled Marsh's soul. For a moment he'd begun to relax with her, to respond to her as the pleasant, astute woman she seemed to be. But he could not discuss Sarah with her, not if he was to keep his true identity hidden. "I'm afraid you mistake the situation. Your sister feels no such attachment to me."

"And I'm quite convinced you're wrong."

How he wished he were. His voice altered from determined pleasantry to morose frustration. "You must be awfully eager to foist her off on anyone if you think that. She has sent me away. How much clearer can a woman be?"

Olivia crossed her arms and gave him an impatient look. "Mr. MacDougal. I realize we have only just met. Nonetheless, I feel I must speak frankly with you. There is something going on here, something between you and my sister. That you say 'she has sent me away' only proves it, so there is no need to deny it." She paused, studying him. "Perhaps I should tell you that I am something of a matchmaker and have always been attuned to such things. That's why I would like you to join us today for luncheon."

"Sarah will not appreciate your meddling."

"I'm sure she will recover. After all, I'm her sister—her only sister. It goes without saying that I have her best interest at heart."

Marsh heaved a sigh. "Perhaps I ought to tell you, then, that your sister despises me."

"Really?" Her gaze was searching. "Why?"

Too late he realized he'd gotten into water over his head. He clamped down on any display of emotion. "Again, that's a subject best addressed to Sarah."

Olivia shook her head. "I confess, you leave me bewildered, Mr. MacDougal. Adrian thinks the world of you. He says you are honorable and generous and brave, and I have no reason to doubt him, save on one point. I could swear that you are terrified of Sarah."

They were challenging words. Insulting, by some standards. But there was such compassion shining in Olivia's eyes that he could not take offense. By the same token, however, he was not about to admit anything.

"I would not use so strong a word as *terrified*," he countered. "I will admit, however, that I do not understand her. Certainly we do not get along."

"Ha! If she terrifies you, it's probably because you love her!"

Coming on the heels of his lie, her confident statement took Marsh by surprise. So much so that he could come up with no reply, he was that paralyzed. She took immediate advantage and hooked her arm in his, then started for the house, tugging him until he reluctantly accompanied her. "Come along."

"This will not work."

"It will. My sister has always been the troublemaker of the family. But I've always been the matchmaker."

The matchmaker. Was that what he wanted, for this stranger who was his half-sister to make a match for him with a woman who saw him only as a threat to her family—and to herself? It made a reasonable sort of sense if Sarah was pregnant with his child. Under those circumstances he had a mandate to pursue her, a rope to hang on to. But she wasn't pregnant, and she wanted him gone.

Most certainly, seeing him in the company of her sister would rouse her animosity to a fever pitch.

Halfway back to the house, he came to an abrupt halt. "I'm sorry, Lady Hawke, but I cannot do this."

"Of course you can. Oh, look. There's Neville."

Marsh had the distinct feeling of being sucked into a whirlwind, that wind increasing exponentially with every person dragged into the storm. He watched Lord Hawke stride toward them, a man who would likely call him out before he'd allow Marsh to tamper with his wife's reputation. It didn't help that Adrian trotted on his heels, or that a little girl came charging out of the house straight for them.

He stiffened when he spied Sarah fast upon the child's heels. She skidded to a halt when she saw him with Olivia. He could almost see her tense with outrage and accusation. And disappointment.

*Ah, Sarah,* he wanted to say. *Can't you trust me, just a little? Can't you see that the last thing I want—the very last—is to hurt you or anyone that you love?*

At the sight of Marsh with Olivia, Sarah's breath caught in her throat. Oh, no. What was he doing here still, and with Olivia? She stifled a groan, but like a painful knot of pent-up emotion, it remained there in her chest, churning and growing, the culmination of the last month's desperate struggle against him.

Only she was losing. After everything that had happened, the very thing she'd most feared had finally come to pass.

The oddest part was that she couldn't blame him. Nor could she hate him. She pressed a hand to stomach, where buried deep down within her there beat the tiny heart of their unborn child. She should tell him.

She *had* to tell him. It struck her then with such certainty that she could not believe she'd actually considered any other course of action.

No matter the repercussion, to hide the truth was to create a monstrosity of lies that would one day haunt their child, just as Cameron Byrde's deceit now haunted Marsh and Olivia.

She watched young Catherine run into Neville's arms. She smiled at the child's squeals when her father tossed her high and, as he had a thousand times, caught her safely in his strong, secure hold. Their simple joy in one another brought a painful lump to her throat. All children needed to know their fathers. Sons, daughters, toddlers, youths. Even grown men and women needed to understand their heritage.

What would be, would be, she told herself as she started forward again. Neville and Olivia stood close together, with little Catherine's arms wrapped tight around each of their necks. Marsh stood nearby, as did Adrian.

Sarah's gaze played over the boy for a moment. Ever since Marsh had forgiven him for that shooting disaster, Adrian's attitude toward Marsh had done a complete about-face. Probably a part of the boy's need for a father of his own. His hair was combed straight back like Marsh's; his stock sported the same simple knot that wasn't at all pretentious.

She shook her head. Adrian did not hide his admiration for the man. Olivia seemed to like him, if her behavior was any indication, and Sarah suspected that Neville could grow to like him as well, were there not so much threat attached to his presence here. They didn't know about all that, though.

But Adrian did.

She dragged her eyes away from Marsh and once more stared searchingly at the boy. He wanted Marsh to stay. Couldn't he see that was impossible?

"Oh, Sarah. Look who's here," Olivia called, smiling as if she were not on fire with curiosity. "It's your Mr. MacDougal." She ignored Sarah's scowl at referring to him thus. "I've asked him to join us for luncheon."

All eyes turned to her, waiting for her reaction.

In the end she did the only thing she could: She capitulated. Perhaps it was for the best. Perhaps all these secrets were the problem. If only she had time to think it all through. "How . . . how pleasant. I . . . I ought to have thought to issue the invitation myself," she managed to say.

"Indeed you should have," Olivia chastened her, though with an even bigger smile than before. "You must have known how eager Neville and I were to meet him."

Sarah let that go with only an aggrieved glance at her sister. As they all started for the house, Adrian fell into step with Sarah, while Marsh strolled alongside Olivia and Neville.

"How're you feeling?" the boy asked in a voice that did not carry to the others.

"Fine," she replied, only half listening to him. Her attention remained fixed upon Marsh, whom she must somehow maneuver aside and arrange a private meeting with.

A frisson of excitement shivered through her, but she fought it down. It was not to be *that* sort of meeting. Anything but.

Still, it was hard not to think about it. She had admitted, at least to herself, that she loved him. He would no doubt be as good a father as he was a son. And heaven knew—*she* knew—that he was a wonderful lover.

Again excitement coursed through her veins. She could be very happy married to this man. But what should have been the most satisfying realization of her life only depressed her. He'd come here today out of a sense of duty. If she'd admitted she was pregnant, he would have offered to marry her at once. She was sure of that now. But she did not want him to marry her only out of duty.

She watched as Neville moved his hand from around Olivia's waist to pluck a tiny leaf from where it had caught in her thick auburn hair. Such an innocuous movement, and yet it summed up everything Sarah felt about love and marriage. She wanted that sort of relationship with her eventual husband, created from a solid love and an ever-increasing history together.

"Are you sure?" came Adrian's insistent voice.

She cut her eyes over to him. "Sure of what?"

"That you're feeling fine," he answered, with curiosity that was just a little too intent.

He knew!

Sarah sucked in a sharp breath. Somehow Adrian knew—or thought he knew—what had passed between her and Marsh. How mortifying! Yet it explained so much. Had Adrian assumed that she and Marsh were intimate when he shot Marsh? Probably.

The boy's eyes flickered momentarily to her stomach and she felt the rise of guilty color in her cheeks. Now he wanted to know if she was pregnant.

Upset and confused, Sarah frowned. "You two are in this together, aren't you? You and him. Well, let me tell you, Adrian Hawke. You will only find out how I am *feeling* when everyone else does. All you need know at the moment is that I am *feeling* just fine."

But she wasn't. Not emotionally, not physically. Every time she looked at Marsh or heard him speak, her chest hurt. Longing, regret, fear. All of those combined to torture her. Avoiding Olivia's probing stares only increased her pain. Why couldn't Marsh be just a man that she liked—that she loved—without all these terrible entanglements between them?

They sat down in the dining room to a casual spread of cold meats, warm breads, fresh-baked fish, and spicy apples and cream. They were a genial group on the surface, spread out around the broad table.

Sarah braced herself for an hour of waiting, of dodging innuendo, and trying to speak privately with Marsh. But a new form of torture caught her in its unexpected grip. Not in her chest but lower down, though just as incapacitating as her heartache. The wonderful aromas of yeasty bread and spiced apples combined in the most revolting way.

Her stomach revolted. Her throat revolted. Her entire body reacted so swiftly she thought she might embarrass herself right there on the dining room table in front of everyone.

As it was, she embarrassed herself by lurching up from her chair, spilling it over backward, then rushing from the room with a napkin clapped over her mouth.

Outside on the terrace, away from those normally delectable fragrances, she took one shaky breath, then another, fighting back the violent nausea. On trembling arms she slumped over the balustrade, slowly regaining control of herself.

Unfortunately, Olivia had followed her, and after shutting the door behind her, she leaned back on it, staring hard at her younger sister.

"All right, Sarah. I've left you alone long enough with your secrets. It's time for you to tell me about this very strange behavior of yours. Either you tell me, or I'll have to ask Mr. MacDougal about it."

# CHAPTER 28

"MR. MacDougal?" Sarah blanched and avoided her sister's probing stare. The last thing she wanted was for Olivia to confront Marsh before she could talk to him. "Could we perhaps speak of this later? After all, you have company."

"He's your company, Sarah. Not mine. He came to see you. Except that you sent him away when we both know you've been pining over him for days. Thank goodness I caught him before he left. And now this business of you rushing out of the dining room so rudely—"

Olivia broke off. "Rushing out of the dining room," she repeated in a more thoughtful tone. Her eyes grew bright with curiosity. "You're awfully pale. I'd swear your face appears almost greenish in cast. Have you simply lost your appetite—or is it something else?" she added, anticipation rising in her voice.

This time Sarah's gaze remained steady. This was not how she'd planned to speak to Olivia about this, but it seemed inevitable. "Before you begin weaving tales in that matchmaking mind of yours, Livvie, I wish you would do something for me."

"Has he forced you? Just answer me that," Olivia demanded, her fists planted on her hips.

"Olivia!"

"Why else would you send him away? If you loved him enough to . . . to be intimate with him—"

"Olivia!"

"—you wouldn't send him away. But you did send him away, and so I must assume he has treated you cruelly."

"Olivia!" Sarah stamped her foot. "It is nothing so simple as that!"

There was a moment of silence, but only one, before Olivia let out a shocked gasp. "Oh, my goodness. Do not say it was . . . it was that other man. That . . . that Penley you meant to elope with."

"What? Good grief no!" Sarah practically shouted. "Please, Livvie, will you just let me be?"

"No. I will not let you be." Bewilderment softened the anger on Olivia's countenance. "What is it, Sarah? Something is going on, something that involves Marshall MacDougal and you. I'm your older sister and I love you. If you cannot confide the truth in me, then who on earth can you confide in?"

Indeed, there was no one on earth with whom Sarah would rather share this heavy load. But not just yet. She gave her sister a wry smile. "I suppose you have a point. But . . . but I think there is something Mr. MacDougal needs to tell you first, Livvie. First you must talk to him."

Olivia crossed her arms. "I already tried that. He wouldn't tell me anything."

"He wouldn't?" Sarah smiled to herself. Wasn't that just like him? He meant to keep his word to her, no matter what. She heaved a sigh. "To tell you the truth, I'm not terribly surprised. But I think he will talk to you now. If I ask him to."

Marsh stared down at the food he'd served himself. He sat in his father's house, at a table his father and grandparents and their parents before them had probably dined at every day of their lives. His closest living family was gathered around him now. His brother-in-law, a niece, and a young nephew as well. Even Adrian was there, a nephew of sorts, though strictly through marriage.

This should be a meal to enjoy like no other, to savor and linger over, not for the food, but for the people. These pleasant, genial people were not at all what he'd expected.

Then again, nothing about this sojourn to Great Britain was at all as he'd expected.

"Where's Mama?" young Catherine inquired.

"Mama's outside," Philip piped up, kneeling backward on his chair and pointing past the tall windows to the terrace beyond. "Mama 'n' Aunt Sawah."

"Turn around, son. Sarah and Mama will be back soon," Neville said. He glanced meaningfully at Marsh. "It seems they have something important to discuss. Any inkling what that might be?"

Indeed he did. Sarah had looked positively green, as if she were about to be sick. He'd felt that way once or twice on the ship over from America. She could not blame this on seasickness, however.

That left one obvious reason: She must be pregnant with his child. Their child.

Marsh excused himself from the table without comment. When Adrian rose also, Neville stopped him, for which Marsh was grateful. The next few minutes might be the most momentous of his life. From no family at all to a large and nosy one, he seemed to have made the transition awfully fast.

Still, they could only be his family if they accepted him—if they all accepted him—and there were still two impediments to that happening.

His entire being thrummed with both anticipation and fear. It was time, he knew, as he let himself out of the dining room. He had to get Sarah's permission to tell Olivia the truth, so that he could then try to get Olivia's approval to marry Sarah.

He thrust his hands through his hair and stepped out onto the sunny terrace, trembling as if he were cold. It wasn't cold, however, but rather a fear like nothing he'd ever known before. The fear of rejection; the fear of loneliness; the fear of losing that most valuable commodity of all: the love of a woman. And the love of a family.

He found the two sisters sitting on a bench surrounded by heavily budded rosebushes. Some flowers were open to the bright sunshine, while others were only partially unfurled. Still others were tight buds, green with the promise of their great beauty hidden from view for another day. Another week.

But to him the most beautiful flower of them all was Sarah.

He paused, just to look at her. Her hair shone in the midday sun, glinting chestnut highlights. When she glanced up at him with her beautiful, vulnerable eyes, she appeared incredibly young, too young for the lustful thoughts she always inspired in him. It was only that there was no artifice in her expression. No wariness or deception either. She was so beautiful, it almost hurt to look at her.

For a fanciful moment he wished he might have met her when they were children, when they might have become friends first, with neither suspicion nor lust to cloud their budding romance.

But they were not children. There was suspicion and there was lust. Though he meant once and for all to banish the former, he doubted a lifetime would be long enough to banish the latter.

She stood when he started forward. "Marsh—I mean, Mr. MacDougal. I . . . ah . . ."

"I have something to discuss with you," he broke in. He nodded to Olivia, who remained seated on the bench. "I beg your pardon, madam, but this cannot wait."

"No, Mr. MacDougal," Sarah countered, gently shaking her head. "I think it is Olivia with whom you need to speak. Not me."

Marsh hesitated. He'd not expected that response from her. He stared at her, unsure of her purpose. "You *want* me to talk with your sister?"

Her eyes remained locked with his. Beautiful. Shining with compassion. Shining with . . . He blinked and swallowed hard. It could not be. Surely that was not love shining in her eyes.

She ducked her head, then turned and made her exit without allowing him the opportunity to determine just what he'd seen in her eyes. He stared after her, hopeful and yet afraid to be too hopeful. Did she love him? Did she want him to tell Olivia who he really was, and his real purpose for coming here?

Behind him, Olivia cleared her throat, and he was reminded of the main reason he should not become too hopeful about Sarah. Slowly he turned on his heel and looked down upon the lovely woman sitting there, waiting for some explanation of just what was going on. She did not look angry, only expectant, and more than a little curious.

But then, she probably thought he meant to ask her permission to marry Sarah. And she probably meant to approve. He could see that plain enough.

Whether she would feel the same way five minutes from now, however . . .

He took a fortifying breath and locked his hands together behind his back. "I . . . uh . . . I know you have guessed at the attachment formed between your sister and me."

She folded her hands in her lap and smiled. "Yes."

"And . . . uh . . . you probably wonder what the difficulty is between us."

"I have wondered."

"Well, the difficulty is . . . it is you."

"Me?"

"No. I put that badly. The problem is me. And you."

Olivia shook her head, a bewildered expression on her face. But still she was smiling. "You needn't be afraid to speak to me about this matter, Mr. MacDougal. I've already deduced the truth. And while I cannot approve of some, shall we say, *aspects* of your behavior with Sarah, I suppose I do understand. Especially if you now mean to put things right."

"It's not that simple."

"Of course it is." Then her smile fled. "Wait a minute. You're not . . . not married, are you?"

"No!" Marsh thrust his hands through his hair. First Sarah wondering about that, and now Olivia. This was not going to get any easier. "I'm not married," he blurted out. "I'm your brother."

She sat motionless in the wake of that admission, as if waiting for the reverberations of his shocking revelation to cease. When she did speak, her voice had become considerably fainter. "My brother?" she echoed. "I'm afraid I don't follow you, Mr. MacDougal."

Beset by a sudden need to reassure her, he sat beside her on the bench and took her folded hands in his. "I was born Marshall MacDougal Byrde. Like you, I am Cameron Byrde's child."

She followed him now, for the shock was plain upon her face. The center of her eyes grew darker, as if she were trying to take in all the ramifications of his words at once. "My . . . brother."

"Half-brother. My mother was a MacDougal."

"I see. But . . . but you and Sarah, you two are not related by blood." Despite his unexpected announcement, she homed in on that fact, much to his amazement. "There is no impediment on that score."

"No. But there is more."

"It's all right," she said, though her smile wobbled a bit, revealing a different emotion than he'd expected. Wasn't she at all horrified by any of this? "Just give me a moment to take it all in," she went on, staring up at him, studying his face. "My brother. We have the same hair." She smiled. "It's a wonder I never noticed. And the same square chin."

She touched his chin and her smile increased. "Another brother. Oh, my. You do know that, like Sarah and me, James is also a half-sibling. But we love one another as much as any full siblings could. It's all right," she repeated when he did not return her smile. "It will be all right. I know what sort of man my father was—our father."

Marsh steeled himself. *Just tell her. Tell her the rest of it and get it over with.* "No, Olivia. You don't know what he was like." He released her hands, bracing himself. "Nobody knew the whole truth about him."

She frowned. "I know he was charming and selfish, and

that he broke my mother's heart more than once—and mine as well. No doubt he did the same to your mother and you. Tell me, did he acknowledge you at all? Did he at least provide for you and your mother?"

Marsh gritted his teeth. "Passage to America and a hundred pounds."

She sighed. "I suppose that's why you've come back here. To confront him."

He nodded.

"Only he was dead." She turned her hands to grasp his and squeezed. "How you must have hated all of us when you found out."

Marsh was momentarily nonplussed. "Yes," he admitted. "At first I did. Only . . . only I don't hate you anymore. I couldn't. Not once I met Sarah."

She smiled at that, a sweet, sincere smile that floored him. She was more concerned with Sarah's happiness than with the repercussions of her father's perfidy. Like a brilliant light, that smile lit all the darkest places in Marsh's soul, and he suddenly realized the truth, the unexpected, satisfying truth.

He was not going to tell her that their father was a bigamist. He could not do that to her. This woman was his sister, his closest living relative. She loved Sarah just as much as he did, and so he must love her in return. Not that he expected it to be a difficult task. But loving her meant protecting her as he would have protected his mother—or his wife. She was his sister and he would protect her from anyone, even himself.

He rose, his heart lightened and his purpose fixed. "Come, Livvie—may I call you that?"

"Of course you may. You're my brother. Marsh."

She rose and took his proffered arm, and together they headed for the house. It was so easy to walk beside her, to adjust his longer stride to match her eager one. But she halted in front of the French doors. "Wait a minute. Aren't you going to ask me if you can marry Sarah?" She stared at him with her brows expectantly arched.

He grinned. He couldn't seem to stop grinning. He was going to learn to love this sister very much. "I am. If the stubborn witch will agree."

Olivia laughed. "Oh, I'm certain you'll find a way to convince her." She patted his arm. "However, the last thing you need right now is an audience. Wait here. Let me make sure she's alone before I send you in to her."

Sarah paced the main hall in agitation. From towering fireplace, to window ell, to the ancient stone dais, she made the circuit. Once. Twice. A dozen times.

It would be all right.

She shook her head. It would never be right again.

But the truth was always better than a lie.

Hah! Only for those who benefited from the truth.

But wouldn't she be the one to most benefit?

After her sudden departure from the dining room, he must suspect that she was pregnant. And if he didn't, Olivia had probably already told him. She knew Marsh well enough to believe that no matter what else passed between him and Olivia, he would still do right by his child.

He would insist upon marrying her. He would save her from social ruin and protect their baby as well. And he would protect her family from the shame—and the disappointment—of her recklessness.

She wrapped her arms around her stomach. She knew what she must tell him, and she knew how he would respond. She ought to be so happy, but still she was afraid.

Because she loved him. And because she knew he would still do right by her, even if he didn't love her.

It was enough to break a body's heart.

Then he was there. She had only an instant of warning. The determined tread of his leather heels on the hard slate floor; the solid thud of ancient door meeting ancient doorframe as he closed it behind him.

She turned and they faced one another across the vast old hall. Dust motes danced in a stray beam of sunlight. He wasn't smiling.

"How is Olivia?" Her voice was shaking. "You did tell her who you are?"

"I told her I was Cameron Byrde's son and her half-brother."

She compressed her lips and nodded. "And?"

"And . . . she seems very happy to have me for a brother." He seemed a little amazed by it all. But she could see also the vulnerability he fought to hide. He'd been prepared for rejection, but Livvie—generous, fair-minded Livvie, who was kind enough to love her husband's bastard nephew and any other stray, whether four-legged or two-legged—had accepted him.

She smiled, genuinely happy for him. "So you have a sister now? Despite the change in her own fortunes, she accepts you?"

"She accepts me. But . . ."

"But?"

"But there will be no change in her fortunes."

Their eyes held a long, telling moment. "But you said you told her you were Cameron Byrde's son—"

"But not about his previous marriage."

Sarah's heart began to pound. "Why? Why didn't you tell her that part?"

He spread his arms wide, then let them fall, all the time shaking his head. "There's no point in telling her that now."

"But . . . but . . ."

"I don't want to hurt her, Sarah. I'll never hurt her. And I'll never hurt you."

The sincere emotion in those few words sailed like a loving arrow straight into Sarah's heart. And they evoked an equally emotional response. "I love you." The words came out of her mouth of their own volition. Though softly said, they seemed to echo across the hall as profoundly as if she'd shouted them.

*I love you.*

He looked just as stunned as if she had shouted them at the top of her voice. "You do?"

Sarah could hardly catch her breath. *Of course I do. How*

could I not? But she could do no more than nod.

He walked toward her, slow steady steps that seemed to take forever.

"You love me? After everything I have put you through?"

Again she nodded. He started to smile. "You love me." He chuckled. Then he threw back his head and laughed out loud. "She loves me!" he shouted up to the rafters.

From somewhere behind her Sarah heard a giggle that was quickly shushed. But her attention remained focused on Marsh.

He stopped before her, just an arm's length away. "If you love me as much as I love you, there can be no impediment to us marrying."

"No," she whispered through a throat gone suddenly tight with emotion. He loved her too?

Then he caught her knotted hands in his own and pulled her close. As if he knew it was not the proposal that had affected her, but rather those few words which had preceded, he repeated them. "I love you, Sarah. As much as I have fought it, as much as I wanted to hate your entire family, I find I cannot. I love you."

They were the most glorious words she'd ever heard. Yet she was beset by doubt. "Do you . . . do *you* feel this way because of, you know, the baby?"

"The baby?" Again he laughed, then gathered her in a smothering embrace. "No. I wanted to marry you because of the baby—or so I told myself. But I love you, baby or no. I love *you*."

Sarah pressed the side of her face against his chest, conscious of the steady pounding of his heart and the dampness on her cheeks and now on his shirtfront. A smile began to form on her mouth. "And it's not because of Livvie? Because you discovered you wanted to be a part of her lovely family?"

He tilted her chin up so that they were face to face, eye to eye. Lip nearly to lip. "I am already a part of her family, willing or no—though I confess to being very willing.

What I want now, more than anything, is to be a part of *your* family. To make a family with you. You first, Sarah. Then all the other little MacDougals to come."

"But you're really a Byrde," she said, gazing up into his smiling eyes.

"I think I'm going to like being a MacDougal much better. Do you think you'll like being a MacDougal?" He finished the question with a kiss, soft and questing. Intimate as no other kiss between them ever had been.

Sarah rose into the kiss, answering him, loving him so much it hurt.

"Yes," she said, breathless, when they finally broke apart. "I think I shall love being a MacDougal."

# EPILOGUE

**BOSTON, MASSACHUSETTS**
**SEPTEMBER 1828**

SARAH waved her handkerchief up at the tall ship as it eased from its moorings and farther out into Boston Harbor. Through eyes blurred by tears she saw Olivia's answering wave, and that of Neville, Catherine, and Philip. They looked so small on the departing ship, she could hardly make out their features. But still she would not look away. Not until they were completely out of sight.

How she wished they could stay!

As if he understood the silent wish in her heart, Marsh slid one arm around her waist and pulled her close against his side. "We'll see them again. Perhaps we can go next year, when Patrick is old enough to travel."

She nodded, blinking back tears and sniffling despite her best effort not to. "I shall miss them so much."

He handed her his handkerchief. "As will I."

Sarah turned to look up at her husband. It was still a wonder to her that they were wed. Even more so that they had a wonderful baby boy already six months old. But the most surprising aspect about her husband was his deep and abiding love for his sister. No one would think, to see them together, that they had not shared their entire lives with each other.

She leaned her head against his shoulder, comforted by his strong, unwavering presence in her life, and by the knowledge that he loved Livvie and her family just as much as she did. "I had thought you might tell Olivia the truth about your father's first marriage before they left. Why didn't you?"

He rubbed one hand up and down her arm. "I almost

did. But then I decided I didn't want to cast even one cloud over their visit. And what does it matter, anyway?" He smiled down into her eyes. "For all that I should hate the man, I find now that I cannot. In his own way, Cameron Byrde gave me everything I could ever want. My wife. My sister. My child. I have a family now. I don't need anything more."

He bent to kiss her, right there on the public docks where anyone might see them. A low whistle informed her that someone indeed had noticed.

"Hey, hey," Adrian chided them. "Is that how gentlemen behave here in America? They just kiss whomever they want right in front of everyone?"

Sarah laughed, then turned in Marsh's arms to face Adrian. He'd grown half a head taller in the year since they'd left Scotland. To see the lanky young fellow holding baby Patrick still amazed and delighted her. "Married men are allowed a little leeway in America. But not too much," she informed him. "So don't you be getting any troublesome ideas, Adrian Hawke."

He shrugged and laughed. For a while longer they watched the ship's departure, but then it was time to go. The house would seem empty without Livvie's noisy crowd there. But at least they would have Adrian.

"Did you send a letter to your mother with Livvie?" she asked the boy as he helped her up into their carriage.

"Yes. Plus a silk scarf for her and a box of cigars for Duffy."

Sarah chuckled as Adrian handed the baby up to her. "I can scarcely believe those two have married. But I'm very pleased," she added.

Again Adrian shrugged, a wholly masculine gesture that Sarah suspected was going to garner him entirely too much feminine attention. "They seem to be well suited. I don't think I could have left her if he was not there to keep her in line."

"Yes," Marsh said. "These women all seem to require a steady hand to keep them out of trouble."

Though Sarah cuddled the sleeping Patrick to her chest, that did not prevent her from shooting Marsh a disbelieving look as he settled beside her. "That's up for debate. You've always been far more troublesome than I."

He laughed. "From what I hear from Olivia, you were born a troublemaker. Certainly you were not in your mother's good graces when first we met."

"Yes, but at least I wasn't *looking* for trouble, like you were. In my case, trouble just seemed always to find me."

Marsh gazed down at his beautiful wife.

There was no arguing the point that he had indeed been looking for trouble when he had found her. Looking for his father and for vengeance. Instead he'd collided with Sarah, opinionated, loyal, headstrong. As Marsh's heart swelled with love he tightened his embrace around his wife and their slumbering child.

His Sarah was indeed a handful of trouble. But he wouldn't have it any other way.

Shy Eliza Thoroughgood is traveling to Madeira with her frail young cousin Aubrey when they find themselves held captive on the ship of Cyprian Dare. Desperate to save herself and her innocent ward, Eliza will do anything.

Full of bitterness, Cyprian intends to wreak revenge on Aubrey's father—the man who years before abandoned his mother and made him a bastard. And Cyprian is confident he can tame the lovely Eliza in the dark, seaswept night . . . until her heart challenges him to a choice he could never have foreseen.

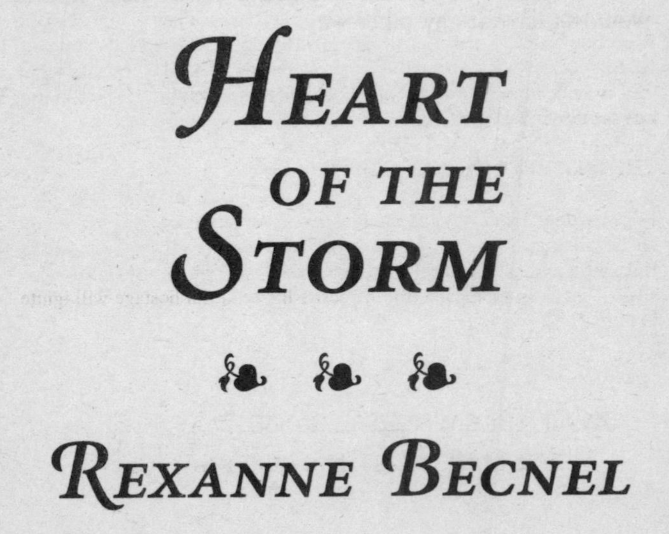


HS 3/97

A SCINTILLATING NEW SERIES OF MEDIEVAL WALES FROM AWARD-WINNING AUTHOR

# REXANNE BECNEL

## THE BRIDE OF ROSECLIFFE

Randulf (Rand) Fitz Hugh, a loyal warrior and favorite of Henry I, is sent to Wales to colonize for his King. When he meets an English-speaking Welsh beauty, Josselyn ap Carreg Du, he hires her to teach him Welsh. The attraction between them is undeniable. But can love overcome the bitter enmity between their two worlds?

## THE KNIGHT OF ROSECLIFFE

Young Jasper Fitz Hugh is to guard his brother Rand's family in the half-built Rosecliffe Castle. Attempting to keep rebels at bay, Jasper doesn't expect his fiercest enemy to be a beautiful woman—or one who saved his life when they were children. Now the two are torn between their growing desire for one another and the many forces that could keep them apart forever.

## THE MISTRESS OF ROSECLIFFE

Rogue Welsh knight Rhys ap Owain arrives at Rosecliffe Castle to reclaim his birthright and take vengeance on his hated enemy. Rhys plans to seize Rosecliffe and his enemy's daughter. He has everything planned for his siege—yet he is unprepared for the desire his beautiful hostage will ignite in him...

AVAILABLE WHEREVER BOOKS ARE SOLD FROM ST. MARTIN'S PAPERBACKS

ROSECLIFFE 3/00